I0647371

Recoveries

A Clio Project Time Travel Story

Mark S. Roberts

Green Bay, Wisconsin (USA)

Recoveries
A Clio Project Time Travel Story

ISBN: 978-1-7356511-4-9

Green Bay, Wisconsin (USA)

Dedication

This book is dedicated to all who have served in the United States military, past present and for those in the future.

"America without her soldiers would be like God without His angels."
— **Claudia Pemberton**

Air Force Officers by Rank

Insignia											
Air Force Service Dress Uniform Insignia											
Title	Second Lieutenant	First Lieutenant	Captain	Major	Lieutenant Colonel	Colonel	Brigadier General	Major General	Lieutenant General	General	General of the Air Force
Abbreviation	2d Lt	1st Lt	Capt.	Maj	Lt Col	Col	Brig Gen	Maj Gen	Lt Gen	Gen	GAF

Air Force Enlisted by Rank

Insignia	*No Insignia*										
Title	Airman Basic	Airman	Airman First Class	Senior Airman	Staff Sergeant	Technical Sergeant	Master Sergeant[1]	Senior Master Sergeant[1]	Chief Master Sergeant[1]	Command Chief Master Sergeant	Chief Master Sergeant of the Air Force
Abbreviation	AB	Amn	A1C	SrA	SSgt	TSgt	MSgt	SMSgt	CMSgt	CCM	CMSAF

Contents

Foreword

When *The Clio Project* was first published in 2018, I had the thought that it would be only one book. After my initial excitement of having my first book out in circulation waned, I thought, what now? After a few months, I grew restless with the idea forming about doing another book. Initially, I was going to write something completely different, then thought it made sense to continue with the first story which became my second book, *Operation Ameliorate*.

When I was toward the end of *Operation Ameliorate*, I didn't feel like I was finished, like I could continue. I didn't want the book to end, but it had to, thus giving me an excuse to add another book to the adventures of Sergeant Rees and his team. So now you have *Recoveries: A Clio Project Time Travel Story*.

I want to thank all those who have helped me through these years of writing. I want to thank my wife Lori for her patience listening to me babble about the book and watching me shut the door to the cave (what she calls the office) as I recluse myself from the rest of the world to write, only to be greeted with a smile when I emerge (usually around dinnertime) and drink ready.

I want to thank Julie Rogers, my editor, for taking the time to read, and re-read, then read again my manuscript. She is the one who painstakingly made all the corrections to my grammar and sentence structure. She did a fantastic job and is a wonderful person to work with.

Thanks to Mike Dauplaise of M&B Global Solutions Inc., for reading my manuscript and making a few tweaks here and there as well as giving me some suggestions as to make the book flow a little better and all the other things involved. Plus talk a little golf here and there.

I also want to thank my friends and fans who inquire about how the book was coming along, when the book was coming out, etc. This means a lot to me.

As with the first two books, this one is a work of fiction. Even though most of the places and historical figures are real, the timeline may have been altered a bit in parts. Think of it as an alternate universe. Many liberties have been taken with the times of events, areas the team travels, as well as the weapons used and descriptions of military facilities and personnel, both past and present. These things are results of the author's imagination, nothing more.

I hope you enjoy this book and, as always, enjoy the adventure and stay adventurous.

Mark S. Roberts

Chapter 1

1980

United States Air Force Chief Master Sgt. Joseph G. Black opens the door to his modest, but upscale Georgetown apartment. Placing his keys on a table near the door, he roughly pulls the sweat-soaked T-shirt over his head as he walks through the kitchen, grabbing a Gatorade from the refrigerator on his way to the bathroom for a shower. He had tossed and turned all night. His mind rehashing the conversation, almost an argument, he had earlier in the day with his commander. His troubling thoughts keeping him from shutting his mind down to get any sleep. Finally, around 0300, he climbed out of his bed, dressed in shorts and a T-shirt, and went for a run. He thought the exercise would relax him enough to get his mind off what transpired yesterday, and what he knew was going to happen later this morning.

The early morning run did not have the desired effect. His mind just will not shut off, and he is fuming over what the council did to him and his project. Thoughts of the conversation with his mentor and friend, who is also his commander, Gen. Richard Lucas, bother him.

"Chief Black!" Gen. Lucas shouted, following the chief as he left the office and made his way down the corridor. The chief continued until the general called again.

"Joe, stop, please."

This got the desired effect, not an order, just a pleading request from his commander and friend.

Chief Black turns to face the general. Lucas walks up and stares into his hardened face, then looks at the instrument in the chief's hands.

"Joe, I understand you're angry. Hell, I'm angry, but this is going to happen with or without you being there. It's just that I would prefer that you be there."

The chief raises the device he is holding. "Not without this."

The general looks again at the device, tilts his head slightly and sighs.

"Joe, come on, that's being petty. And you know, as well as I that it's not becoming of you. I understand you can disable the Inabular device, but I implore you not to. This project is bigger than you or me now. The wheels are in motion, everything is in place and it needs to go forward. I understand your position. You know I do. I fought the good fight; no, take that back - we fought the good fight - but lost."

The general stops, takes a deep breath and continues. "Chief, you know I could order you to give me the Inabular device. Even though you created it, as well as Clio, it is still the property of the United States Air Force. Our friendship means too much to me to do that. I am hoping you understand what is at stake and do the right thing right here, right now."

The chief shakes his head, grasping the device tightly, then stops, relaxes and puts his hand with the device out for the general to take.

The Inabular device was created by the chief after the first time-travel trials were completed. The chief thought it best if he had a type of key for the Clio Project, so only one person had the power to start up the time machine. The Inabular device is a simple, but complex instrument that needs to be inserted into the time machine to initiate startup procedures.

The device is about twelve inches long with a handle on one end, connected to a cylindrical tube containing the electronics that use a code to talk to the time machine. This tube has a rod extending from it with four prongs on the end that are fed into a slot located on Clio. Once the device is inserted, it is turned and locked into place, completing the connection that begins the startup sequence.

The code inside the tube changes after each use and only the chief knows the code. Unknown to the chief at this time is that in the future, microprocessors will be at his disposal and he will create a much smaller and smarter Inabular device when he rebuilds a new Clio.

"It's only because we have been in this from the beginning and that I, too, believe in our friendship that I am handing this back to you. Believe you me, I don't give a rat's ass about the committee, but do care about the lives of those men who are willing to sacrifice if something goes wrong," he says and turns to leave.

Lucas could have ordered him to stay at the Bank, the name of the top-secret facility that houses the project, but the general knew that would be a mistake. Lucas knew the chief was upset, and he had a right to be. He also knew having the chief stick around for the first project experiment, in his frame of mind, would be counterintuitive.

The project is called Clio. It's an appropriate name for the time machine that Chief Black created in the 1970s, when he was first assigned to work under the then-major. The future general saw potential in the younger sergeant and took him under his wing. The two men had dreams of the future. With the general's military and political pull, and the then-staff sergeant's brilliant mind, they created the world's first-ever time machine.

Soon after its creation, the first trial run of a smaller version of Clio was shown to a group of politicians and high-ranking military personnel. The test was a success, and not long after, appropriations came flooding in to build a full-scale time machine. A few years later, the chief had the larger machine built, and it was being tested daily. The tests were taken in baby steps. The chief wanted those tests to continue. He needed to be completely satisfied that Clio was fully operational before beginning human trials. The chief, being a perfectionist, wanted to ensure it was safe before being used for, well, for whatever the politicians and military wanted it for.

Millions of dollars had been thrown into the project. Oh hell, billons. And it took a few years for the chief to get the newest version of Clio up and running. By the time he did, the politicians and military were tired of waiting. As such for bureaucracy, those in power could be small-minded. This is how the chief thought of them. The political and military wants and needs were of no concern to him. Chief Black never considered why they wanted the machine; he just knew the machine had to be perfect before he, himself, volunteered to step into it and be sent to wherever or whenever he chose to go.

Not understanding how or why, the politicians and military joined together and created an oversight group called the Bank Council, or just the Council. Without keeping him or the general in the loop, the Council decided amongst themselves that it was time for the Clio Project to begin. The Council had already selected a group of Air Force personnel and had them all placed on a predetermined base and into the same squadron as well as the same unit. The general and the chief tried to dissuade the Council from moving forward until the chief could give the green light. Their pleas fell on deaf ears. The Council refused to listen and ordered the experiment to begin, and a date was set for the first mission.

Today is that day. Yesterday the chief had stormed out of the Council with no intention of being a part of the experiment. Even though he built Clio and knew more about her (as he thought of the machine) than anyone else alive, he was walking away. He was the most qualified to run the experiment, but he just could not bring himself to do it. If the experiment failed, fifteen men could die. He didn't want to be responsible for their deaths or worse, being kept in a time portal or a time loop or maybe some other time abnormality that would keep them trapped forever in space time. That and the moral aspect of using those fifteen airmen in a time-travel experiment without their knowledge, giving them no chance to prepare, did not sit well with the chief.

The chief finishes his shower, dresses, and goes into the kitchen for a cup of coffee. He takes the cup, walks into his library and retrieves a book he has been reading, *A Brief History of Time*, by Stephen Hawking. He moves to the living room, sits and flips open to the last page he read.

The phone rings, breaking into his concentration. He glances at the clock, then at the book. He hasn't read a single page in more than an hour. He sets the book down and walks to the table, seeing the flashing light on the black push-button phone indicating Bank. Black switches on the crypto scramble and picks up the phone, activating the automatic recorder.

"CMSgt. Joseph G. Black. Go ahead, Bank."

A hissing noise associated with a long-distance call fills the handset.

"CMSgt. Joseph G. Black, voice identification clear," a mechanical voice responds. "You may speak, Bank."

"Chief, Shelly here. The general wishes to see you. Priority Zero."

"Copy that, Shelly. I'll be there in approximately two hours," Black replies and hangs up.

He calls base operations at Andrews Air Force Base and ensures he has a flight ready, then changes into his uniform.

Priority Zero means the experiment had been scrubbed. *Good,* he thinks. *Maybe they came to their senses.* But in the back of his mind, he knows that's not the reason.

The chief grabs his car keys and exits his apartment.

***

Gen. Richard Lucas is standing in his office, staring through his picture window at the giant view screen located in the control room. The Clio Project was initiated, and all seemed to go as planned. The unsuspecting security police officers guarding the munitions area were seemingly sent back in time, but now there is a Civil War-era soldier, a captain, lying on the ground in their place. The bearded soldier rolls onto his back and sits up. The man winces in pain and looks around groggily, his head turning one way then the other, attempting to get his bearings. He suddenly looks directly into one of the hidden cameras, like he knows where it is, and yells, "Chief Black sent me. Stop Capt. Henries! DSI panel! Stop Clio!" He then falls onto his back, unmoving.

Gen. Lucas has always been a man of action and confidence. He learned a long time ago to trust his gut feelings; having done so in the past has been more beneficial than harmful. Reaching down to his desk, he turns on the speaker system to the control room.

"Capt. Henries, status?"

Capt. Hunter Henries is in charge of monitoring the DSI, or Degree Servo Instrumentation panel, which is responsible for the height the time-travel subjects reappear above the ground after transport. Chief Black estimated three inches above ground was a safe distance to fall without causing injury. The idea was to ensure all fifteen of the men would appear at the same height, no matter where they were when transported. This was especially important for the man assigned to the control tower, which was a good fifty feet above the ground.

Henries looks around, and upon hearing the general's booming voice over the loudspeaker, turns his attention back to the panel.

"Shit!" he exclaims as he frantically begins working on the computer.

The general watches the captain, then turns his attention to Maj. Frank Hess, who is in charge of the control room for this shift. The major is making his way toward Henries' station.

"Maj. Hess, shut Clio down. Capt. Henries, I'm waiting," Gen. Lucas announces over the intercom into a room of silent people, all continuing to do their jobs, but giving furtive looks toward Capt. Henries.

Maj. Hess stops, then looks around as the personnel stare at him.

"You heard the general. Shut it down!"

Though most in the room are baffled, they obey and begin the shutdown process.

Knowing it will take too long, the general's rumbling voice blares over the loudspeakers, shouting at the technician overseeing the Inabular Device.

"Pull the damned device!"

Without hesitation, the technician wrenches the device from the control panel. All the systems shut down instantaneously, then slowly begin coming back online.

"Capt. Henries?!" the general shouts.

Henries curses under his breath, focusing on the task at hand and ignoring the general. He was not paying attention when Clio began its maiden voyage, caught up as he was watching the screen and not his monitor. When the Civil War soldier appeared, saying Henries' name and something about the DSI, he was so enthralled that he neglected his station. Only when he heard the general shouting his name over the loudspeaker did he return his attention to his monitor.

Henries sees that his inattentiveness has allowed the DSI to run its own course and has not made any corrections. He realizes that the man assigned to the control tower is going to rematerialized at the height of fifty feet or so. Henries gives a cry of panic, then begins working furiously. He has almost corrected his mistake when his screen goes dead, then flickers back to life. He looks up at the general, whose face is taut, eyes narrowed as he stares directly at him.

"Yes, sir. There seems to be a problem with the DSI program. I believe I found the problem," he stammers. "Ah..." Henries begins, then closes his eyes, "I do not believe I was able to correct the problem before the system shut down, sir."

Hess is now standing over Henries, looking at his screen. His eyes widen while he reads. He looks up at the general.

"Sir, the man in the tower," he begins to say and shakes his head, "Oh."

"Damn it, major. What is happening down there?"

"Sir, the man in tower. If he rematerialized at all, well, he would have rematerialized at the height he was in when transported. It seems the tower would not have been under him when he did so."

Gen. Lucas looks hard at the major, then shifts his gaze to the captain, who is busy typing on his console, deliberately avoiding eye contact. Lucas turns to face the screen and sees Sgt. Rees lying on the asphalt, unmoving. The general starts to call for his secretary, Shelly Moore, but turns to see her already in the room, gun in hand. She, too, is staring at the screen, her eyebrows furrowed. She finally turns when she feels the general's eyes upon her.

"Sorry, general. You were yelling pretty loudly I thought there might be a problem," she says, feeling a little foolish holding the gun.

"No, Shelly, you were doing your job. That's not a problem," he says, pointing to the screen. "That's a problem."

He faces her, "Get the chief here right now!" he grumbles. Shelly nods and rushes to her office.

"And don't let him give you any excuses or grief!" he adds, his voice gruff.

"Yes, sir," she answers, shutting the door behind her.

The phone rings and the general sees the name of the caller from the control room. Maj. Hess. He snatches the phone up after the first ring.

"Yes, major?"

"Sir, what do you want us to do now? I mean, about the man lying in the Munition Storage Depot?"

The general looks at the screen. "Get a team out there to secure the area. I want medical there as well. Get the man any help he may need, then get him here ASAP. He is to be treated well, got that? If he comes to and is able to speak, don't ask him any questions, but take good care of him."

Maj. Hess nods. "Yes, sir got it. Another question?" he says and waits for acknowledgement from the general.

The general anticipates the question. "What happened to the men we sent back in time?" the general says and shakes his head, "Major, I know as much as you do right now. Get your people on it and see what the consequences of my orders may have had on those men," he says with a sigh. "Keep me informed."

"Yes, sir," Hess replies and hangs up.

God help me if I made the wrong call, the general thinks.

Chapter 2

S MSgt. Scott Rees wakes. He's lying face down on asphalt, his face slightly scratched from the impact. *Asphalt?* he thinks to himself, trying to recover from the all-too-familiar effects of time travel. He didn't take any pills to help with the nausea, so he wasn't at his best when he woke. He doesn't know where he is and ... "Shit!" he exclaims and balls his fists as the pain from the shotgun blast catches up to him. Luckily, he had the bullet-resistant uniform that Capt. Epstein had made him wear, but the impact from two barrels of buckshot was still enough to make him cry out.

He was with Capt. Farnsworth and his team, along with Sgt. Ian McGregor of the Union Army and Miss Emma Kelly. They were in a major fight with the local railroad baron and his ragtag army - more like an oversized, undisciplined gang than an army. They had beaten them and were in the process of being transported back to their own time when the baron, Joshua Walsh, charged and tried to shoot Emma. Rees dove toward Emma, who was standing next to Sgt. McGregor, shielding them just before the pellets were fired. The time machine must have kicked into full gear at that moment, as that's all he can remember before awakening here.

Pushing through the pain, nausea, and vertigo, Rees grunts and rolls onto his back, trying to gather his thoughts. *Asphalt!* his mind screams at him, and he instantly realizes that he has returned to 1980 and the Munition Storage Dump (MSD). He knows what he must do. Mustering his strength, he manages to sit up, legs sprawled in front of him.

Squinting from the harsh sun, he searches the area, looking for one of the hidden cameras he knows are around. Finding one he looks directly into it, trying to shout, but can only summon up a hoarse grunt. Knowing he is running out of time, he lifts his hand toward the camera, fingers spread, and waves it in a stopping motion, finally clearing his voice enough to be heard.

"Chief Black sent me. Stop Capt. Henries! DSI panel! Stop Clio!"

The pain from the gunshot as well as the effects of time travel are too much for him. Rees falls onto his back, unconscious.

***

SMSgt. Wright, Security Superintendent and Non-Commissioned Officer in Charge (NCOIC) of deployment, is sitting in his office when he hears a ringing in his desk drawer. Unlocking the drawer, he pulls out a phone. "Sgt. Wright," he answers and listens for a few seconds, "No sir, I haven't heard anything. I already initiated the recall. I assumed the project was on schedule and followed the procedure for the exercise as instructed. Personnel are already coming in to fill the vacancies left by the deployment."

Wright lights a cigarette and listens. Taking a deep drag, he walks over to the window and watches the commotion of incoming personnel arming and getting ready to go to the MSD. They had been told that this is an exercise and the men in the MSD were deployed without notification; a top-secret exercise to see how quickly the squadron could fill the void of the missing men. Other than Sgt. Wright, only the security police commander was aware of the exercise and only Sgt. Wright was aware of what really transpired. Wright is secretly a member of Sen. Dick Minten's private security organization, Military Intelligence Security Service, or MISS.

"I'm not following you. Not everyone deployed?" he asks, his brow furrowing. "No, sir, I can't stop the troops from going out there. Not letting them go would cause more of a problem than trying to explain why one person didn't deploy. I'll go out there right now and see what's going on. Yes, sir, I will," he says and hangs up, slamming the drawer shut and locking it.

Wright stubs out his smoke, grabs his beret and runs out of his office, exiting through the back door where he is greeted by troops milling around waiting to be transported to the MSD. Wright ignores the men and rushes to his dark-blue military Ford sedan. He turns the vehicle around and heads for the MSD as fast as he can. Before he can get there, he spots rows of government vehicles along the road, some blocking his way. As he approaches the roadblock, his radio squawks and he grabs the mic.

"Wright here."

"Sir, we just got notified that several outside security police, Office of Special Investigation and government agencies have entered the base without prior notification. The guard just called it in."

"No shit!" Wright remarks tersely. "They're blocking the road up ahead of me. Way to be on top of it, Control," he replies sarcastically and slams the mic back into its holder.

Wright slows the vehicle to a stop, well short of the roadblock. He exits his vehicle and begins walking purposely toward the SP and obvious civilian agent. As he approaches, a Blackhawk helicopter flies low overhead, flying toward the MSD and coming in for a landing.

"Morning," he says when in earshot of the two men and looks at the SP's beret crest. He doesn't recognize the unit and can only surmise that it's the Banks' official unit because only Bank personnel would be here.

"Sir, this area is restricted. You will need to get back into your vehicle and leave the area until it has been cleared," the staff sergeant tells him.

"Cleared? Cleared for what? We are conducting a base exercise and I'm in charge of the deployment. I need to get to the MSD to ensure it's secure and watch the replacements' arrival and disbursement," Wright explains.

The civilian agent, wearing his standard dark suit with dark sunglasses and the military-type of haircut that screams "G-Man" to one and all, purposely walks up to Wright.

"Sergeant, the exercise is still on, but we are overseeing it for now. Once we have ensured the men have been deployed, you will be allowed entry. But, for now, you will need to get back into your vehicle and head back to your station. You will be notified once we are finished."

"Okay, but why in the hell are *you* here? This is a military operation. What agency are you with that needs to be involved in a deployment?

And by whose authority?"

"Sergeant ...," the agent says, looking at Wright's nametag, "Wright. I am with the DOD and that's all you need to know. Now, please kindly vacate the area or we will be forced to apprehend you," he finishes, and the SP takes a step toward Wright.

Wright's face blanches and his jaw clenches. Little did these pricks know, he has an organization behind him, too, but he can't say anything. No, his best bet is to retreat to the station and call his non-military supervisor for instructions. Wright doesn't know what's going on, but something is amiss.

"All right then; I'm going. Please contact the squadron when you're finished so we can get the troops back into the area. This is a munition area, after all, and it does need security."

"That is being taken care of, sir. We will inform the appropriate authorities when the area is cleared for normal use. Thank you for your cooperation," the agent tells him.

Again, Wright fumes at the arrogant little man. "Yeah, you do that," Wright spats and stomps back to his car, slamming the door. Turning the vehicle around, he floors the gas, causing the tires to lose traction and throw gravel toward the SP and the agent.

Driving back to the squadron, he hears a helicopter overhead. He leans forward, looking up through the windshield to see the Blackhawk as it flies toward Ft. Bragg.

Chapter 3

Rees awakens again and still is lying on the asphalt, semi-conscious. He remembers this same feeling the first time he time traveled. They did it without taking the pills to soften the time-travel shock, so he knows it will take some time to recover. He hears voices and works himself up onto his elbows, wincing from the pain in his back from the shotgun blast. He cranes his neck to see where the sound is coming from. He watches as people in Air Force uniforms and others in civilian clothing run toward him. He closes his eyes, hoping to clear his head, and feels hands grabbing him. Weakly he tries to shake off the people fawning over him, helping him to an upright sitting position.

"Whoa, hey, let go of me. I'm fine, just give me a minute!" he grumbles, jerking his arms away from the grasping hands. "I've got to see Gen. Lucas."

A MedTech is trying to poke a hypodermic needle into his arm, but the point won't penetrate his uniform. Rees snorts. The senior airman stares at Rees, then instructs the others to remove the jacket. Once this is done, the MedTech rolls up the white shirt sleeve and jabs the needle into Rees' skin. "Ouch!" he says, suddenly slurring. Unexpectedly he is feeling better but is very tired. He feels himself being lifted and shifted before being laid on the rough material of a stretcher.

A bass thumping sound overrides the voices and he watches a helicopter come in for a landing. He is jostled as the stretcher is lifted and he is carried to the UH-60 Blackhawk, the downward thrust of wind from the propellers making a miniature tornado all around him. As he is placed into the 'copter, he happily realizes what is going on and the potion from the injection is really kicking in. *Oh, goody*, he thinks. *I love helicopter rides.*

The personnel holding the stretcher place it into the open bay, and a crew chief ensures it is secure before he climbs in with the MedTech. Rees shakes his head, trying to get back to the here and now.

As soon as the helicopter personnel are aboard, the machine lifts off and flies out over the base to take the time traveler back to the Bank. Rees is tired and fights it, but sleep overtakes him, and he misses enjoying the flight.

***

Gen. Lucas is pacing the floor in his office when Shelly opens the door, holding a cup of coffee.

"Any word on the chief?" Lucas asks, taking the cup from Shelly.

"No, sir. But I scanned the air traffic control net and heard his jet arrived a short time ago, so he should be on his way," she says with a smile.

The general nods. "Of course you did," he says grinning, "and thanks for the coffee, by the way."

Shelly walks to the door. "That's why you pay me the big bucks, general, and you're welcome," she replies, shutting the door behind her.

Shelly had just settled behind her desk when the door opens, and Chief Black enters the room.

"Good morning, Miss Moneypenny," he announces in his best Sean Connery accent, a joke between him and Shelly. He throws his beret a few feet onto a shelf reserved for covers, hats, caps, and berets, in typical James Bond fashion.

"Speak of the devil. Sorry, no time for pleasantries. Something is up, and the general is as uptight as a cat on a hot tin roof. You need to go right in."

The chief understands and nods to Shelly as he approaches the door, knocks once, and enters - not waiting for an invitation. The general, facing the window, whirls around when he hears the door open. He gives the chief a somber smile, one that shows he's glad to see the man, but also sorry to see him at the same time. The chief picks up on this instantly and walks directly to the general, saluting along the way. The general quickly returns the salute, then grasps the chief's outstretched hand in a welcoming handshake.

"I'm sorry, Joe, but you had to be called back."

"I understand, sir. A code zero, that's great, but why? The council get cold feet?"

The general looks at the chief for a few seconds, initially not comprehending the question, then realizing just as quickly that the chief has not been briefed on what is happening.

"Sorry Joe, but no. The council didn't back down. In fact, the experiment is going on right now. It's just that we ran into a snag," the general says with a frown.

"But a code zero?" the chief begins and the general nods and continues.

"The Clio Project was initiated, and everything seemed to be going as planned," the general says, walking around his desk. "But just as the men disappeared, being sent back in time, we were left with this," he finishes and turns a dial that changes the view screen to show Sgt. Rees lying in a bed in the hospital section of the Bank. "All fifteen men vanished, as expected, and this man was left in their place."

The chief squints and looks at the man.

"I can't be sure, what with the long hair and beard, but that looks like Sgt. Scott Rees."

"This man appeared almost exactly where Rees disappeared, but he was in a Union Cavalry uniform. A captain's uniform at that. He yelled at me, said that you sent him, and that the experiment should shut down. I made a command decision and had it done."

The general turns toward Chief Black, noticing the scowl on the man's face.

"I ordered the project shut down and seeing that it was taking too long to stop the process, I ordered the Inabular Device pulled."

Chief Black's scowl turns to wide-eyed shock. "Sir? You didn't!" he exclaims in alarm. "We hadn't worked on that scenario. We don't know what the outcome could be. Those men could be dead for all we know."

The general raises his hands in a gesture to calm and quiet the chief.

"Joe, I know, but I had a choice to make and only a few seconds to make it. A man in a Civil War uniform appears right after we send others to the Civil War, claiming that you ...," he says pointing at the chief, "that you sent him back here and to shut down the experiment. I had to do something and because you two haven't met, I could only assume he somehow met you in the future. Not only that, but he knew my name as well, and also seemed to know where the hidden cameras were. Too much was going on, so I did as he instructed. Hopefully when he awakens, we will get more out of him. He was well out of it when the teams got to him and one of the med techs gave him a sedative, so he's been out for a few hours."

The chief walks a little closer to the window and stares at the image of the sleeping man.

"I want to talk with him as soon as he awakens, general," Black says, more forcefully than intended. Realizing this, he turns to face the general. "Sorry, sir. I would like to speak with him as soon as he wakes," he amends in a more respectful tone.

Gen. Lucas nods and smiles. "Of course, Joe. We all do, but you and I will do so first. After all, he did mention you and I, so we all must be good friends, right?"

The humor is lost on the chief who is thinking about the men who were just sent into the past, and who - more likely than not - haven't made it there. *What has happened to them?* His mind is already thinking of what he needs to do. He looks up at the general, who is watching him, then shakes his head. "Sorry, sir. I was lost in thought. I need to get down there," he says, pointing into the control room, "and try to figure out what has happened to those men. I knew something was bound to happen, but this is one scenario I didn't count on."

"Of course, please get to it."

Black, still in thought, nods and turns to leave, his mind racing with all the things he needs to accomplish and accomplish quickly. He heads toward the door when the general calls him.

"Chief?"

Black stops and turns to look at him.

"I'm sorry for what the council did and for how this turned out. I should have been more forceful, and for not being so, I apologize. I just hope this wasn't a mistake that can't be rectified. Thank you for coming back here as fast as you did and thank you, in advance, for what you are surely going to do to make this right."

The chief smiles at the general, his friend, but it doesn't reach his eyes. "I just hope I can do something. It might take some time, but I'll do everything I can," he says and leaves the office.

Gen. Lucas suddenly remembers the situation with Capt. Henries and what may have happened to the control tower guard. He had forgotten to mention it to the chief.

Maybe for the better. At least for now, he thinks.

Chapter 4

Rees lies in the hospital bed in a drug-induced stupor, his mind reeling from the effects of the drug streaming through his body. Slowly, he opens his eyes and is rewarded with a sharp pain from the harshness of the overhead light. He attempts to raise his hand to cover his eyes, but the arm only moves a fraction of an inch until it stops. He looks over at his hand only to see it handcuffed to the hospital bed. He tries the other arm with the same results.

What the hell? he thinks.

He lifts his head to look around, then scoots up slightly until the handcuffs prevent him from any further movement. Looking to his left, he spots a heart-rate monitor and a drip bag that is giving him an infusion - of what, he has no idea. Hopefully just saline.

The room is sparse. He looks around for his uniform. Not seeing it, he curses, then starts yelling, hoping to get someone's attention, wincing from the pain it causes in his bruised back. A few minutes later the door opens, and a young, female captain enters, along with a senior airman security policeman and a sergeant orderly.

"What the hell is going on here? Why am I handcuffed to the bed? Where is my uniform?" Rees barks. "I need to see the general, the chief!"

The captain doesn't say a thing as she walks over to check the monitor and the drip setting.

Satisfied that Rees isn't going to die from high blood pressure, at least, she gives a weak smile and walks out of the room, the SP and orderly following.

"What the hell? Am I a prisoner?" he screams at their backs, "and I gotta pee!"

He blows out a frustrated breath and slams his head back into the pillow, yanking on the handcuffs a couple of times, finally settling down to await whatever comes next.

It doesn't take long. He hears the door open and a man he recognizes from photographs walks in along with a younger version of a man he personally knows.

"Gen. Lucas, Chief Black, glad to see you. Now, could you remove these handcuffs?" The general squints at Rees and walks around the bed, scrutinizing him. The chief stands to one side, also studying the young man.

"Gen. Lucas, please. Did you stop the time transfer? Did you stop it in time?" Rees implores.

The general and chief look at one another.

"Who are you?" the general asks, hands on his hips.

"What? I'm Senior Master Sgt. Scott Rees, security police," he answers.

The general looks at the chief again. The chief uncrosses his arms and walks to the other side of the bed.

"Okay, what's with the long hair and beard, and the cavalry uniform. Why are you here?" he asks, then furrows his brow. "Did you say senior master sergeant?"

Rees looks at the chief, then the general, then again at the chief, finally realizing what he must look like.

"Oh, yes, my appearance. Sorry, I forgot, still a little groggy. I was Tech Sgt. Rees when you sent me and my squad to the Civil War. Things happened and I was sent to the future. I then went on another time-travel mission and, when transferring back to the future, I was rerouted here to try to stop the first experiment from happening."

The general grows angry. "So, you are here to sabotage us?"

"No, no, sir, nothing like that," Rees replies defensively.

"Then what, sergeant?" the general demands.

Rees nods at the chief. "The future Chief Black had an idea that we could save the team from going into the past, where we had to fight our way back. We suffered some losses. He thought we could correct the mistake and not mess up the timeline."

The chief looks thoughtful for a few minutes before nodding.

"Yes, I could see how that might be feasible."

The general snorts. "Well I sure as hell don't. Sorry chief, this man is to be placed into our custody, and put in a holding cell until I can get a grasp of what is happening here."

"Gen. Lucas, please. I am not a threat to you or to the Clio Project," Rees begs.

"I'm sorry Sgt. Rees, but until I know more about you, you are to be detained and placed in confinement until I get this sorted out," the general says, then heads toward the door.

Rees suddenly remembers his uniform. "Sir, my uniform! The buttons on that uniform are explosive, plus I have a hidden pistol in the belt buckle, a knife in the lapel and other devices that could potentially hurt someone. I've got to retrieve them before something happens."

"We know. Your uniform has been placed in safe keeping. We know all about the weapons as well. It is unfortunate though, but your jacket is in bad shape. After it was taken off of you and thrown on the ground, no one took notice of it until we inquired about its whereabouts. It had been ignored until then. By the time it was recovered, it had been trampled and run over. A lot of your gadgets were broken, much to our dismay."

Rees stares. "Which gadgets, sir?"

"As far as we can tell, you seemed to have a very tiny camera and something that looks like a, oh, I don't know, a small electronic device of some sort. Something we are not familiar with, but our lab boys are looking into it."

"The buttons, sir. Don't mess with the buttons. They are explosives."

"Oh, we are quite aware of that, as well. Hence my question to you, again. Why are you here to sabotage us?" he asks, not expecting an answer, and walks out of the room.

Rees looks at the chief. "Chief, if your lab guys are looking at my gadgets and decide to reverse engineer anything, you could disrupt the timeline by creating something that doesn't exist yet."

The chief studies Rees for a few seconds. "Sorry," he says, then follows his commander.

A few minutes later, two SPs enter the room. They release Rees from his restraints, and one opens a closet door. Inside is a flight suit. The SP throws it to Rees and tells him to dress. The SP also tosses a pair of socks and boots at Rees' feet. Rees shakes his head, peeved at the situation. "What, no clean underwear?" he snarks, then dresses.

The SPs handcuff Rees and walk him out the door to an elevator, which they ride to the security floor. Rees is led into a processing room, then placed in a holding cell.

"Guess I don't get a phone call, eh guys?" he asks when the cell door clangs shut.

The SP doesn't answer.

***

As the general walks down the corridor toward the elevator, Chief Black catches up.

"Sir?" he asks, moving alongside the general.

"I know what you're going to say, Joe. That he is the sergeant who we just sent into the past. I do believe it to be the same man, but we don't know anything about *this* man, not like we know the man we sent."

They reach the elevator and Chief Black uses his card to call the lift.

"Yes, sir, that's what I was going to say. General, he knows who we are, called us by name, knows Capt. Henries' name. That can't be a coincidence. Somehow, he ended up back here, what, maybe a couple of weeks, months in the future. I'm thinking that something went wrong in the future because of something we did now so we sent him back to stop, hell, stop whatever from happening."

The elevator door opens, and the men enter.

"Joe, I know, and I really want to think that is the case. Okay, say I do believe that is the case, but until we know exactly what is going on, that man stays under guard. If, and I stress if, he is telling us the truth, we will let him out."

"Yes, sir." The chief replies as the door to the elevator opens and the men exit.

"Meanwhile," the general says walking toward his office, "You go have a talk to him. Get the full story. If it seems plausible, then we'll go from there."

***

Chief Black enters the security police section of the Bank and informs the senior airman at the desk that he is here to see the prisoner. The airman picks up his phone and informs Capt. Theo Smit that Chief Black is in attendance. A few seconds later Smit comes to the front desk.

"Hi, Chief, what can we do for you?"

"I'm here to talk with the prisoner, sir. General's orders."

Smit doesn't hesitate, indicating the chief should follow him.

"Any problems with him, sir?"

Smit purses his lips and shakes his head while unlocking the first door to the holding cells. "Not a peep out of him, chief. He's just been sitting on his bunk, hasn't moved, looks like the statue of *The Thinker*."

The captain opens the door and walks in, holding it open for the chief. Chief Black asks that the prisoner's cell be open so he can go inside. Again, the captain doesn't hesitate and does as he is asked.

"Want me to stay, chief?"

"No, that won't be necessary. I need to speak with him alone. I don't see him as a danger; this is just a precaution by the general. I'll let you know when I'm ready to leave."

The captain nods and pulls the outer door shut.

Rees sits up and watches as the cell door is opened, allowing the chief entry.

"You, okay?" Black asks, moving into the cell.

"I'm fine, chief. Couldn't be better."

The chief smiles at the sarcasm and leans against the cell bars.

"Okay, Sgt. Rees, and yes, I believe you are Sgt. Scott Rees, Technical Sgt. Rees. But now you say you're a senior master sergeant, huh?"

"Yes, chief, I am."

"How old are you, 22, 23? Kinda young for a senior."

Rees grins. "Just a little older now than when you sent me into the past, extenuating circumstances on the rank."

"Okay, fair enough. Why don't you tell me your story?" the chief asks, and Rees begins to explain. Fifteen minutes later the chief knocks on the outer cell door and Capt. Smit opens it. Smit sees Rees is still sitting on the bunk and moves to secure the cell door.

"That won't be necessary, captain," the chief says and Smit raises an eyebrow in question. "He'll be coming with me. May I use one of your phones, please?"

Smit points to one on an unoccupied desk and the chief picks it up, pressing a button to connect him to the general's office. After a few minutes of conversation, the chief places the handset back and smiles at the captain.

"Okay, sir. Sgt. Rees is now in my hands. Do you need to do anything for his release?"

"I can bypass any out-processing procedure, chief. I would ask that you have Gen. Lucas send me a release order when he gets a chance. Paper trail, you know. I don't want to get caught letting a detainee go without proper paperwork," he explains.

"You got it, sir," the chief replies. He walks back and sticks his head inside the holding cell room. "Rees, let's go," and turns to leave.

Rees jumps up, following the chief and nodding to the captain as he passes him. "Sir."

Chief Black stands in the hallway, waiting on Rees. "I'll take you to a room where you can get cleaned up. I'm going to go see the general while you're there."

The men take the elevator to another floor and Rees sees an SP standing outside a closed door.

"I take it that's where I'm going?"

The chief gives him a sidelong look. "Very perceptive. You must be a cop," he says deadpan.

Rees snorts and enters the room.

***

Twenty minutes later, Rees has showered, shaved, and is dressed in the same flight suit provided earlier, ready to see the general. He informs the SP standing guard that he is ready to leave. The guard speaks into a handheld radio. He acknowledges the answer and looks at Rees. Rees is grinning, looking at the radio they used to call *the brick* due to it being about the size and weight of one. The guard notices the look but doesn't say anything.

"Chief Black is coming down to escort you to the general's office," the SP explains, still holding the radio to his mouth.

"Actually, I know where it is," Rees informs his guard.

"Sorry sir, the chief will need to escort you."

Ah, so I'm still a prisoner? Rees thinks as he nods to the SP.

A few minutes later the chief comes walking down the corridor and spots Rees. He stops and motions for him to follow; Rees complies, thanking the young airman guarding his room.

Rees catches up to the chief and moves to walk beside him. Not saying a word, he looks around, checking out the various offices.

"I assume you have been here before," the chief says, watching Rees.

"Yes, sir. But when I came here, it was several years in the future. Some things have changed, he says. I assume that's where we're going, to the assistant's office then the general's office, which overlooks the control room for Clio."

The chief looks nonplussed as he opens the door and enters, holding it open for Rees. After closing the door, Black looks at the pot of coffee behind Shelly's desk.

"Is that coffee fresh?" he asks, pointing to the almost-full pot. This gets him an admonishing look from the secretary.

The chief raises his hand in surrender. "Sorry, should have known better than ask. Can you bring us three cups when you get a chance?"

"Of course, Chief. Sgt. Rees, cream or sugar?" she asks, smiling at him.

Rees is a little taken aback, not knowing who this woman is. "Ah, no. I mean, yes, cream, please. I can get it myself if it's too much of a bother," Rees tells the secretary, and now it's his turn to get an admonishing look. Rees just nods; this is her world and he's just passing through.

The chief walks to the next door, knocks once, and opens it to the general's office. Holding the door open, he looks at Rees and tilts his head, indicating that Rees should step inside, which he does. The general is standing behind his large, oak desk, a remnant from the Korean War era. He waits for the men to come inside, then has a seat in his overstuff, high-back chair. He leans back and rests his elbows on the arms of the chair, steepling his fingers while eyeing Rees. The chief walks over to a couch and sits, also watching Rees.

Rees moves to the center of the room, faces the general, and salutes. He feels like a schoolchild standing in front of the principal after having been caught in some indiscretion. Rees sees through the glass window into the control room and smiles.

"What's so funny, sergeant?" the general asks after returning the salute and seeing the smile.

"Nothing, sir. It's just I've stood here before with your successor. In this exact spot, with my commander sitting where you are and the chief sitting where he is. Kind of a deja vu feeling."

"And just when was this?" the general asks.

Rees takes a deep breath and lets it out. "2020," he answers, and his smile grows a little larger as he sees the general's eyes widen slightly.

The general leans back, staring at Rees. He is about to say something when there is a knock at the door.

"Enter," the general says, watching as Shelly strolls in with a tray holding three steaming coffee mugs. Behind her a service NCO brings in a tray of food, placing it on a table next to the couch. He leaves without a word. Shelly passes out the coffee and smiles warmly at Rees, who thanks her when she hands him one of the mugs. She turns to leave and notices the look on the chief's and general's faces. She then looks at Rees, standing in the middle of the room holding his coffee, looking like a fish out of water.

"I don't know what's going on, sir, but will you let the poor man sit down and have his coffee and some food?" Shelly asks with eyebrows raised in the way a mother asks a child to do something. The general scowls good naturedly at his secretary and tells Rees to grab a chair. Satisfied, Shelly leaves the office and closes the door. Rees softly chuckles to himself.

"Now what, Sgt. Rees?" the general asks.

"Sorry sir, your successor's assistant is a far cry from Shelly. She could learn a thing or two from her," he answers in a wry tone, "But I would never tell Sam that."

Lucas glances at the chief then back at Rees. "Eat, sergeant," the general orders, and Rees grabs a sandwich, consuming it with a flourish, along with a pickle and some of the chips. He wipes his face with a napkin and takes a sip of coffee.

"Thank you, sir." Rees says, setting down his coffee, "I know you have questions, but if I may, I would like to say a few things first, maybe answer some things you have on your mind. It may save some time."

Rees watches as the general and chief exchange looks. The chief nods. Rees now knows that what the chief told him in 2020 about him and Gen. Lucas' relationship was true. They can almost read each other's minds.

"Go on, sergeant," the general orders.

"Sir, you have a Capt. Henries who was operating the Degree Servo Instrumentation panel during the send-off, correct?"

"Yes, that is correct. Why?"

Rees runs his hand down the front of his mouth and neck. "If I am correct, you need to arrest him for dereliction of duty and espionage."

The general cocks his head and narrows his eyes at Rees.

"Explain yourself, sergeant. That's an officer you are wanting us to arrest, and without evidence."

"Yes, sir," Rees says, taking a breath. "Capt. Henries is working for his uncle, Sen. Minten."

At this revelation Gen. Lucas' eyes narrow further, and his face turns a shade red. Rees is taken aback by the transformation.

"Sgt. Rees, that is a grave accusation. Any proof?"

"No, sir, not physical proof, but, if you will allow me?" Rees implores, and the general nods for him to continue. "As I said, Capt. Henries was working the DSI panels during the send-off and he was derelict in keeping an eye on the readout. I know his job was to ensure that when everyone reappeared in the past, they were all on the same level with the ground. His inattentiveness caused the man in the tower, Sgt. Parks, to fall to his death."

The general's eyes grow wide, and Rees continues.

"That is why I asked you to stop Clio while in transport. Right now, everyone is in limbo, I hope, and are safe for the time being - again, I hope."

The general holds up a hand to stop Rees.

"Are you sure about this?"

"Yes, sir. If the chief would be so kind as to go check the printouts from the log, he will find what I say is true. If the men rematerialized right now, Sgt. Parks will die."

The chief stands and hurries out of the office and into the control room. While he is making his way downstairs, the general continues watching Rees.

"Okay, but why are you here?"

"Sir, if I may, can we wait until the chief returns and verifies what I said is true?"

The general nods. "Yes, of course."

It isn't long before the chief returns with a handful of printouts from the dot-matrix printer. Rees sees the amount of paper and smirks. The general notices.

"Sergeant?" he asks.

Rees looks at the general. "Sorry sir, just thinking about how different things are in the future."

The general eyes Rees some more, then looks at the chief.

"Got it!" the chief exclaims, eyes darting over the multiple pages spread out before him. "By damn! You're right, sergeant," he says, taking a sheet from the printout to the general. He points to some of the numbers and traces a line. The general watches but has no clue to what he is looking at.

"Chief Black, please. You know I have no idea what I'm seeing," Lucas says.

The chief looks at the general, and smiles. "Yes, right, sorry, sir," then looks at Rees. Rees raises his hand in surrender.

"Don't look at me, chief. I know the practical aspects of time travel, but this ..." he says trailing off while pointing at the printout, shaking his head.

The chief sighs and walks over to the couch to sit.

"You're right, Sgt. Rees, to a point at least," he says again and looks at the general. "Sir, he's partially right. If those men had materialized, Sgt. Parks would have fallen, but from around fifteen feet. Henries must have seen what was happening and tried to adjust the elevation but was only partially able to do so."

Gen. Lucas scratches his chin, looking at Rees. "Sgt. Rees?" he asks.

"Sir, I can only tell you what happened to me in my timeline. Maybe my arrival did something that caused Capt. Henries to realize his mistake. Parks may not have fallen to his death, here, now, but he would have if I hadn't arrived when I did. Fifteen feet is still pretty high though, but that is a moot point, I hope," Rees says with hope in his voice.

Gen. Lucas presses his intercom, "Shelly? Please locate Capt. Henries and have him report to me ASAP."

"Yes, general. Right away."

"Even if your sergeant is still alive, Capt. Henries may still have been derelict, but that's not what concerns me right now. What concerns me is him being here as a spy for his uncle, so you say. Anything else, sergeant?" the general asks, staring at Rees.

"Yes, sir," Rees replies. "When you found out about Henries, in my timeline of course, you and the chief had a talk with him. Capt. Henries didn't like it, so he decided to go to the press about the Clio Project. He didn't get his chance. Sen. Minten had his MISS agents intercept Henries and the news crew at the warehouse where the meeting was set and killed them all."

"Good grief!" the general says, shaking his head. The chief snorts, then chuckles.

"So basically, your coming here was just to save the sergeant's life?"

Rees tilts his head and looks at the ground. "Yes, I guess you could say that, sir. Or lives. This is strange. In my timeline, I know Sgt. Parks is dead, but now I know he is alive again. I hope." Rees looks at the two men. "I've got a little more to tell you, but I would like to wait until you speak with Capt. Henries, which is what you will want to do, too, I assume."

"Oh, I want more than that sergeant," the general responds. "If what you are telling me is true, I want more than that."

Chapter 5

Rees is sitting in a chair located across from the general's desk in a corner of the room, trying to be a fly on a wall, but he is too obvious not to be noticed by Capt. Henries.

Henries walks through the door, chin up, back ramrod straight, uniform impeccable. Rees detects the air of one who thinks he is superior to everyone, including the general. Rees thinks the man has more pride in how he looks than his job. The perfect specimen of a man using a military career as a stepping stone to a future in politics, who looks the part but does shit when elected.

Henries glances at Rees then at the chief, who is sitting on a couch near the door, then stops and stares at Rees for a few seconds more, not able to come up with where he knows this man. Still uncertain, he returns his attention to the general. He salutes and reports. Gen. Lucas returns the salute and points to a chair in front of this desk.

"Sit," is all he says.

Henries looks at the chair, brushes off a piece of invisible lint, then sits, deliberately taking his time as if he was the person in charge.

The chief looks at Rees and arches an eyebrow. Before the general can speak, Henries begins.

"What is so important, sir, that I have to be interrupted on my off time?"

The chief shifts in his chair. Rees sees him change from relaxed to tense and thinks the man is about to launch himself at the captain. He doesn't, but Rees sees his large arm muscles tense and jaw muscles twitching.

Would not want to make him mad if I was the captain, Rees thinks.

"Excuse me, captain?" the general asks, then stands so fast that Rees flinches, but the captain doesn't move a bit. "I don't know who you think you are, but you had better start showing me some respect. I know who your uncle is and believe me, I don't give two damn shits,'" he says with menace, his eyes ablaze and shooting daggers at the captain.

To Rees' astonishment, the captain doesn't seem fazed and looks at the general.

What is that? Rees thinks. *Disdain? Contempt?*

"Again, sir, why am I here?" Henries asks, sighing.

Chief Black is now off the couch and beside the captain before anyone can stop him. Rees thinks he's going to grab the officer, but the big NCO restrains himself.

"You were told to show some respect to the general, captain! Do it or I'll wipe that shit-eating grin right off your face." he says, then adds, "sir."

The captain stands up, getting into the bigger man's face as if daring him to do so. The general intervenes.

"That will be enough. Chief, captain. Sit down, both of you!" he barks.

The chief glares at the captain, curls a corner of his lip up into a sneer then returns to the couch. As he sits, he leans forward like a cat ready to pounce. The captain also sits and returns the gaze.

The general turns his attention to Henries.

"You were operating the DSI when the project was initiated?"

Henries narrows his eyes while answering. "Yes, sir."

"Look at me when I'm talking to you, captain, or I'll have you braced for the remainder of your time here. Is that understood?"

Henries turns and faces the general, his demeanor changing somewhat. "Yes, sir."

"And you were monitoring it the entire time, ensuring the calibration for the correct height requirements were met for the personnel being transported?"

"Of course, sir. Please tell me what is going on?"

The chief starts to say something, but the general raises a finger in warning. The chief closes his mouth, his lips pressed tightly together and the muscles in his neck tightening.

"Capt. Henries, the DSI printouts show differently. Plus, I was there, remember?"

Now he has the man's attention as Henries turns his head slightly toward the general.

"I don't understand what you're getting at, sir?" he replies, but with a twinge of something showing in his face. *Uncertainty,* Rees thinks.

"Chief Black studied the printouts, and it revealed that, if we had carried through with transporting those fifteen men, one of them could have been seriously injured or killed. It seems the DSI wasn't being monitored well enough to stop the tower guard from falling. Granted you reverted your attention in time to keep him from falling fifty or so feet, but not soon enough to have him rematerialize at ground level," the general finishes, his voice having risen.

Capt. Henries shakes his head.

"Sir, you were there. Maj. Hess was there. You know what happened. There was a glitch or something. You know I was working on the panel. I couldn't ... I couldn't fix the problem before the transportation process was interrupted. You saw it!"

The general sits down in his high-backed chair and watches, giving the man time to squirm.

"Why would you even need to be looking at the printouts anyway, sir? The mission was scrubbed. You, yourself, gave the order to have the Inabular Device pulled. If anything went wrong, it would have been on your end."

The chief is standing in front of the captain, again, before anyone can say or do anything. The large man backhands the captain across the face, making the captain's head snap around in what looked like a painful angle and the chair leans back precariously for a second before it and the captain tumble to the floor. Rees stands in surprise and knows the chief must have restrained himself from using all his force, otherwise the captain's head would be rolling across the floor. But it still looks bad.

Henries rolls onto his back, an astonished look on his face as he reaches his hand up, holding it to the red mark forming on his cheek. It takes a few seconds before he realizes what just happened. Finally, the downed man awkwardly comes to his feet to face the chief. The general yells at the chief to stand down and move away from the captain.

"I'll have your ass for this, sergeant!" Henries tells him, wavering on his feet, his voice loud and quivering, face flush and the red mark growing more pronounced. He removes his hand, seething. "Striking an officer ... you're through, sergeant. Kiss those stripes goodbye!"

"That is quite enough from both of you!" Lucas commands, "Chief, I'm ordering you to stand down and get your ass back to the couch and sit! As for you, captain, you are in no position to do shit! In fact, if there any charges to be brought, they will be against you!"

Henries forgets the slap and turns to stare at the general.

"What?" he screeches. "What charges?"

"Dereliction of duty for a start. Then we will be looking into possible espionage charges. We got word that you have been spying for your uncle, something we were already looking into."

The blood drains from Henries' face and his eyes widen with the sudden realization that he has been discovered. He quickly recovers, sticking his chin out. "Do your worst, sir. I have done my duty and I do not work for the senator. Granted he helped me get this assignment, but that is it. I will not stand for this."

The general leans his head back, raising his eyebrows and chuckles.

"Fine, captain. Have it your way," he says and presses the intercom. "Shelly, have the SPs come in. I need them to arrest Capt. Henries, please."

The general had preplanned the arrest and already had things in place to do so.

The door to the office opens and a security police captain enters, followed by two SP NCOs.

"Capt. Smit, please place Capt. Henries under arrest for dereliction of duty and espionage."

The captain acknowledges the order and tells the two NCOs to handcuff and search the captain.

Henries' eyes shift and his jaw tightens. He turns to run but is grabbed by the two burly NCOs and placed in cuffs.

"You can't do this. I haven't done anything wrong. You have no proof; you have nothing to charge me with," he yells and tries to make a move toward the general.

Smiling, the general looks at Capt. Smit. "Please add conduct unbecoming an officer, threats to a superior, attempted assault on a superior, and I'm sure we'll find some more charges to hold him for a while. Now get him out of my office, please."

The captain salutes and the three men march Capt. Henries out the door with him yelling that they cannot do what they are doing, and that his uncle will hear about this, yada-yada-yada.

The general turns to Rees. "I guess that's enough proof for me that you're here for a reason, and that Capt. Henries is working for his uncle, no matter what he claims."

Before Rees can respond, the phone on the general's desk rings. Lucas walks over and picks it up, looking into the control room.

"Yes, Maj. Hess?"

"Sir, we may have a problem."

Chapter 6

2020

The open grounds on the army base seem to move by an invisible force, shimmering like a heat wave rising and blowing though the grasses.

If someone was standing and staring at the trees, they would swear the trees were moving inwards then outwards, like looking through a magnifying glass and pulling the lens toward then away from your eye.

Without any sound, and looking similar to the special effects used in many science-fiction movies, a group of people appear out of thin air in the same positions they were in when transported from the farm in 1862. As soon as the transformation is complete, the group begins to slowly move, some trying to stand, others just rolling on the ground, while still others fall to the ground as they lose their equilibrium. Most are moaning, some retching, others sounding off with various degrees of cursing, including a gruff-sounding, brogue-accented, "Oh, shite!"

As the bodies of the dark blue- and gold-colored uniformed men, and one woman dressed in light blue, try to recover their senses, a group of Humvees come rolling across the open fields and stop well short of the group. Armed security-force members exit the vehicles and fan out, watching over the group of people trying to recover from their time jump.

A major cautiously approaches the group, trying not to worry them, but at the same time needing to speak with the officer. Capt. Farnsworth is still lying on top of Emma and looks into her glassy, emerald-colored eyes, but she doesn't seem to notice. *Delirious,* he thinks, then realizes he is still on top of her. Remembering what has just occurred, he swiftly pushes himself up and rolls off her, wincing in pain from where a couple of buckshot rounds struck him. He looks around, his eyes blurry. He sees the others in different stages of disorientation as well: a couple lying on the ground, some in kneeling positions, and others standing gingerly.

The major recognizes Farnsworth and takes a few more steps toward him.

"Welcome back, captain," he says and gives Farnsworth his hand to help him stand.

Farnsworth blinks a couple of times, takes a few quick breaths, clears his throat, then reaches for the hand.

"Where are we?" he asks, looking around as he stands. Before he can ask anything further, a wave of dizziness hits him and he bends over, placing his hands on his knees and taking a deep breath. Once the bout of lightheadedness is over, he continues. "Where is Rees?" he asks, searching, forcefully blinking, and trying to adjust his sight, still taking gulps of air.

The major holds onto Farnsworth's elbow and turns him around.

"You're back at Bragg, captain. Rees didn't come back with you."

This causes Farnsworth's head to clear instantly as he stares at the major.

"What? Why not? Where is he?" Farnsworth demands.

"Sorry, captain. My orders are to get you all back to the Bank for a debriefing, and all will be explained then."

Farnsworth then realizes they are back, and that Emma and the Union sergeant came back with them.

Oh, shit! Not again, he thinks.

While he is processing this, a medical unit arrives as well as a transportation vehicle. Staff Sgts. Jack Bouvier and David Kriger amble up, both still recovering and also asking about the situation and the whereabouts of Sgt. Rees. The rest of the team members are slowly adjusting and approach the group as well. Only Emma and Union Sgt. McGregor are left on the ground, both awake but bewildered.

Farnsworth sees the distress in their eyes and moves toward them.

McGregor raises his hand and points at Farnsworth.

"What in the devil's name is this, colonel?" he asks in an accusatory tone. "What has happened to us? And, what in blazes are those contraptions there and the strange men in ... in whatever they are wearing? And, why is that man calling you captain?"

Farnsworth squats, looking at both Emma and McGregor. He takes a deep breath.

"This is going to be hard to understand and I should probably not say anything, but ..." He stops and looks around, seeing everyone watching him. "You have just traveled about 150 years into the future."

McGregor stares at Farnsworth for a few seconds then looks at Emma and begins laughing.

"You got us good on that one, sir. No, please. What is this? Last I remember we was a-fightin' at the O'Tooles' farm when that arse Walsh attacked us, then some strange feeling came over me and ... and I wake up here," McGregor utters, sweeping his hand around the site. "And this sure ain't where we were."

Emma is looking around as well and breathing hard, as if she is about to have a panic attack. Farnsworth notices and calls for a medic, who runs over and kneels beside the woman. Farnsworth stands, as does McGregor. Emma jerks away, then begins to wave her hands and fight off the MedTech's attempts to check her. Farnsworth sits next to her, wrapping his arms around her. She settles and leans into him, her face buried in his chest. Farnsworth nods at the MedTech, who administers a shot. Emma jerks her head around as the needle pricks her, then she relaxes and closes her eyes.

McGregor looks on, then raises his hands in surrender.

"Now, don't be gittin' any ideas about sticking me with that thing, boy," he tells the young MedTech.

"I'm a woman, sergeant," the female MedTech corrects McGregor.

"What?" is all he can say.

"And it's sergeant to you," she admonishes further and walks away, leaving him with a dumbfounded look on his face.

Farnsworth looks at McGregor.

"If you can be calm about this, sergeant, we won't have to. I will need you to trust me and do as I say, as well as anyone else here," he declares to the group, speaking a little louder. "I promise you are safe, and all will be explained. This wasn't supposed to happen, but it did, and we will just have to work it out.

"For right now, I need you to go with the team," he explains to McGregor and Emma. "We will be going to a place where you and Miss Kelly can be checked out by a doctor. You just have to relax. Now, please go with the team," he finishes and looks over at Bouvier, who motions for McGregor to come to him.

McGregor looks at Farnsworth and slowly makes his way to where the team members are waiting, his eyes full of fear and confusion. Farnsworth helps Emma to her feet, talking softly and reassuring her that all is well. Bouvier tells the other team members to help their nineteenth-century guests into the waiting vehicle. Satisfied they are in good hands, Bouvier and Kriger make their way to where Farnsworth and the major are standing.

"Okay, major, what is going on?" Bouvier says, suddenly bending over and using his hands for support on his legs as a wave of nausea washes over him. Kriger reaches in a pocket, produces a couple of pills and gives Bouvier and Farnsworth one each.

"This will help," he tells them.

What is it?" Farnsworth asks.

"Just take it, sir," Kriger says forcefully, shoving the pills into each man's hand, in no mood to be questioned. Satisfied the men will comply, he turns toward the major.

"Well, sir, what is going on, where is Sgt. Rees?"

"Like I told the captain, you all will be debriefed once we are back at the Bank. I don't know any more than you, I'm afraid. My orders are to collect all of you and get you back there ASAP."

Kriger nods and pats Bouvier on the back while looking at Farnsworth. Bouvier stands up and takes a deep breath.

"Better?" Kriger asks.

Farnsworth nods.

Bouvier stands straighter and blinks. "Much, thanks." Farnsworth looks at the major. "Lead on, sir," and the four men move to the Humvee.

Chapter 7

1980

Gen. Lucas' hand tightens around the phone, his eyes narrow as he listens to Maj. Hess on the other end.

What kind of problem, major, as if we don't have enough already," he says in a terse tone while staring at Rees.

Maj. Hess is not fazed by the general's question and tone of voice, as he is used to the man's ways, having worked for him for many years.

"Sir, when we pulled the Inabular Device, I believe we were too late to stop the transportation."

"What!" the general exclaims, then, stern-faced, points first at the chief then into the control room, indicating the NCO should make his way there. Chief Black understands and heads to the control room. Rees stands and the general shakes his head. Rees returns to his seat.

"Yes, sir. From preliminary readings, it looks like we were off by a split second before stopping transportation. If we are right, and I have no reason to think we're not, then the men are in 1862 as planned."

The general lifts his chin and looks at the ceiling, taking a deep breath. He turns and looks at the large screen encompassing one wall. He frowns at the black-and-white scrambled static snow covering it.

"Major, if they made it through, why are we not receiving any visual?"

"We don't know, sir. All our people are working on it, as well as auditory."

"Very well, the chief is on his way down. He'll sort it out." The general finishes and drops the receiver into the cradle.

Gen. Lucas rests his hand on the phone and seems lost in thought. Without looking up, he addresses the room, speaking his thoughts aloud.

Well, apparently, you and your team made it there after all. Now we are in a conundrum. If they are there, how is it you are here?" Lucas asks, absently.

Rees stands and clears his throat. "Sir, if I may?"

The general slowly looks at Rees, his thoughts elsewhere. He blinks, as if just remembering the man was in the same room.

"I'm sorry, sergeant. What?"

"Sir, the future Chief Black had a theory on that. He felt that it doesn't matter who is sent where, or when, that person will continue to exist, no matter what, in a different timeline, unless he is killed in that timeline."

"I'm not following, Sgt. Rees."

"Yes, sir, believe me, it's something I have a hard time comprehending as well, but the chief told me I might run into something like this if I was too late to stop the time jump. Even if I did stop it, there would still be two of me."

The general stares at Rees, trying to figure out just what in the hell he is talking about.

"Sir, when Chief Black returns, maybe I can tell him, and he can possibly clarify what I'm saying and explain it better."

The general nods in agreement. "Yes, that would be a promising idea, but before that, let's see what is going on down in the control room. First things first, shall we?" he says and makes his way toward the door. Rees beats him to it and opens it for him, then follows the man out.

They reach the control room and walk over to where the chief is talking to Maj. Hess.

"SITREP Major?" the general asks, stopping in front of the man, requesting a situation report.

"Sir, we were right. We didn't stop the time jump. The team made it to where they were destined to be. Sorry, sir."

Gen. Lucas looks at the chief, who nods in agreement. The general shakes his head.

"Not your fault, major. No need to be sorry. What we need to do right now is to sort out what is happening and why it is that I do not see anything useful on that screen," Lucas says, pointing to the large wall-mounted monitor that continues to show nothing but flickering black-and-white specks, like old televisions did when the signal went off the air for the night. "And will somebody please shut off the damned audible! The white noise is getting on my nerves!" he finishes, waiting until the hissing noise stops before looking at the major.

The major shakes his head, replies that he is not sure what has happened, and again, ensures the general they are working on it.

The general turns to the chief.

"Chief, do what you can and get me some comms. I want to know the status of those men."

"Yes, sir," Black replies.

Sgt. Rees is listening, not wanting to interrupt their conversation, but a smirk slowly comes across his face, and he raises his fist to his mouth and clears his throat.

The small group of men turns as one and look at him. The general raises his eyebrows and tilts his head.

"You have something to add to this conversation, Sgt. Rees?"

"Ah, yes, sir. If you would permit me," Rees answers, looking at the chief. "Chief Black, I believe if you check the DSI, you'll find the problem there."

The two officers, the chief and a couple of lab technicians stare at Rees. The general narrows his eyes, glaring as if Rees just took the Lord's name in vain inside a church.

The chief moves toward Rees. "I looked at the printout earlier, remember?"

"I know, Chief, but you need to check the DSI itself," Rees replies.

"How in the hell would you know that?" the general grumbles.

"The chief told me, sir. One of the many things he told us in our debriefing when we returned to 2019."

The general starts to reply, but Chief Black beats him to it.

"That would make sense, sir. Let me look."

The general nods his approval, and watches as the chief walks off, then looks back at Rees.

"Okay, what does the DSI have to do with this?"

Rees walks closer to the men.

"It was being manned by Capt. Henries in my timeline, as it was in this one. The captain failed to adjust the coordinates for the control tower during the jump, so it somehow threw the sequencing out of whack, as I understand it. The chief compared what is happening here," he said, pointing his index finger over his shoulder toward the screen, "to listening to a sports program on the radio while simultaneously watching it on TV. One of the programs is usually a few seconds ahead or behind the other. Same principle: the time difference between the cameras in 1862 is not in line with the equipment here.

"Again, sir, so I was told," Rees says with a grin. "Chief Black discovered the mistake and corrected it, thus allowing you to have contact with me and my team. The only problem is you will only have visual and one-way audible. You won't be able to talk with the squad, but you can listen. When I was sent back from 2020 to 1862, we still had the same problem. We used one of the cameras to answer yes and no questions. It was the one time I wish I had taken a course in Morse code."

The general walks over to where the chief is working and watches. Within minutes the screen flickers, then comes online. They now have a full view of the time travelers in 1862.

Chapter 8

1980

The men in the Clio Project control room watch the screen as a few of the security police officers mill around in the woods in the year 1862. The small group of airmen are discussing where they might be and what might be happening to them.

One man is lying on the ground, being treated for what looks like a head injury. Several others are forming a security perimeter.

"I don't see Staff Sgt. Parks," Rees mutters, staring fixedly at the screen.

Chief Black walks up beside Rees.

"I don't believe anything has changed. Sgt. Parks still may have died."

"That could be true, but we brought him back. We didn't bury him until later," Rees says, then notices something. "No, wait, they are getting ready to go look for Parks and the others. There's still a chance."

Rees turns and looks at the chief, with hope in his eyes.

"We don't know what is happening yet Sgt. Rees. Let's wait for a while, okay?" the chief asks.

Lucas takes in a deep breath and slowly exhales.

"Sgt. Rees, I am sorry, but right now there is nothing we can do about this situation. So, for now, sergeant, chief, in my office," he orders and moves toward the stairs, the two men following. "Maj. Hess, keep things under control and get me some damn comms!" Lucas shouts over his shoulder.

Once in the office, Gen. Lucas tells the men to have a seat. He strides over to a cabinet and pulls out a decanter. Grasping the neck, he brings it, along with three glasses to his desk then dispenses a dollop of the amber liquid in each glass. Offering each man a glass, he takes a sip from his and sets the glass on his desk.

Lucas leans on his desk and purses his lips.

"Okay, Sgt. Rees. Do you have any ideas on what we do now?"

Rees pauses, then looks at the chief. "Sir, you told me that it took you a day or two to fix Clio so that she would be able to transport the men back. But you were able to send a tape-recorded message to them ...," Rees stops as another thought enters his mind. He looks at the general, his eyes large.

"Oh, shit. I forgot," Rees says and rubs his face.

"Forgot what?" Lucas demands.

"My girlfriend, Nora. We were to be on three-day break after our shift at the Mud Dump. Nora, her sister Skylar, and another friend, Ivy, will be waiting for me and McAdams and Nionee. They expect us to be at their home when we get off work. From what I have been told, as well as read in the after-action reports, is that Nora, Skylar, and Ivy come to the base looking for us and get the runaround from SMSgt Wright, who is on Minten's payroll, by the way."

As Rees explains, the general interrupts.

"You're just now telling us this?"

"Sir, there's a lot going on. It just slipped my mind. Plus, I have to be careful about what I am telling you. I may have told you something already that can affect the timeline. Unless, of course, the chief's theory of alternate worlds is correct, then it doesn't matter."

The general eyes Rees then turns his attention toward the chief. Chief Black's face is an unreadable mask. Not getting any sense from the man, the general just nods. "Continue, sergeant."

"Yes, sir. Sen. Minten sends his goons to Nora's home with orders to kidnap them. This results in some of Minten's men, as well as some SPs, being killed and injured.

"Early tomorrow morning, I," Rees says pointing to the Rees on the screen, "will take a patrol out to an area where we saw and heard artillery. That's where we lost McAdams and Steele. Steele was killed by a cannon blast and McAdams dies from a gunshot wound."

"After the girls get the brush off from Sgt. Wright, they go to Ivy's brother for help. Her brother is a lieutenant assigned to the Base Personnel Squadron. He ended up being taken by MISS agents and held prisoner. The girls then go to the newspaper and recruit a local reporter, who agrees to help them.

"A local TV news crew is to secretly interview Capt. Henries, who decided to be a whistleblower about the Clio Project after you reprimanded him, sir. I was told Chief Black was here during your questioning, and a physical altercation ensued between the captain and him," Rees says, looking at the still stone-faced chief. "I guess some things didn't change."

Not receiving any feedback from the general or the chief, he continues. "MISS agents find out about the secret meeting and kill the TV crew, as well as Capt. Henries, in an attempt to stop the story from being aired."

Rees begins pacing. "The girls and the reporter do more digging, so they all come under the MISS radar and the attempt to kidnap them goes south, as I said earlier. They were brought here after the debacle at Nora's house and that's when Sen. Minten and his team attempted to take control of this facility."

"What?" Lucas shouts, his face going red with rage. "That sure as hell ain't happening!" he bellows.

Rees shakes his head. "It didn't in my timeline either. The chief disabled Clio and took the Inabular Device. He, along with the girls and the reporter, escape. I can't say any more about the chief. The girls and the reporter signed a gag order..."

"A what?" Lucas asks.

"Ah, a non-disclosure agreement."

"Oh. Carry on."

"Yes, sir. That's about it. They then went on with their lives."

"Okay, what about you and the team?" Chief Black inquires.

"Chief, when you disabled Clio, me and my guys were all stuck in limbo. Something you only knew about in theory but took a gamble, granted a gamble with our lives," Rees grins at the chief, "but the other outcome could have been worse, especially if Minten had gained control of the project. As it turned out, you were correct about limbo, about us floating around out there," Rees says waving his arms in the air. "And when you built another Clio, you brought us home, granted 38 years in the future, but hey, what's a few years."

Chief Black grunts, stands and walks over to the large window overlooking the control room, staring at the screen. The technicians are flipping through different camera angles. He watches as each scene shows an area at different angles as well as the men and equipment. He turns back to Lucas and Rees.

"Okay, so we may have already changed the timeline. But to what effect? Where do we go from here, other than to stop Minten and get Clio up and running?"

"I can either lie to Nora and tell her we're all going on a classified TDY mission," referring to a Temporary Duty Travel, "or we can bring them here. I have a feeling they're going to find out one way or another. Besides, it's what was going to happen anyway. So far, we haven't lost anyone, other than possibly Sgt. Parks. If you can get a message to the men, you can stop them from venturing out and getting killed."

The general walks around his desk and Rees moves to allow him access. Lucas pulls out his chair and sits. He takes another sip of his drink and indicates the men should have a seat. He turns and watches the security policemen on the screen. The screen glows an eerie green, brought on by the camera's optic using what light it can find and amplifying it so they can see in the dark. Just like Night Observation Devices, or NODs, or what they used in their timeline, a Starlight Scope.

Lucas turns around and studies Rees.

"All right, Sgt. Rees, Chief, here's what we will do. Rees, you and the chief will fly out to the base, then go see your girl. I prefer you see her in person. I am requesting an OSI team to keep an eye on the reporter just in case he somehow gets wind of this. No sense taking any chances. You will talk your friends into coming here. That shouldn't be too much of a problem, should it?"

Rees shakes his head, his bangs falling over his eyes, reminding him he is still out of regulation.

"No, sir. The girls will understand. They are all military brats."

"Good. I'll make the arrangements for you two to leave in about ...," the general looks at the wall clock, "two hours. That should give you time to get some rest and get yourself in 35-10 regs. Sergeant, we don't have a uniform for you, so you'll just have to wear the flight suit."

Rees laughs, "Sir, when we get to the base, we can make a detour to my place, and I can grab a uniform."

"Yes, I suppose so. Safe trip."

Rees takes this as being dismissed so he stands, salutes, and follows the chief through the door, stopping and asking the chief to hold on. Rees turns his attention back to the general. "Sir, what about contacting the squad?"

The general looks up at Rees. "What? Oh, yes, right. How did we do it last time? I mean in your time. You know what I mean."

Rees smiles. "Yes, sir. Drives you crazy if you try to think on it too much. Ah, the chief ordered some drones and ...," Rees stops talking, seeing the general's furrowed brow and squinted eyes. *Must stop using terminology they don't understand.* Rees thinks, then corrects himself. "Sorry, sir, tiny helicopters equipped with cameras. I think he called them heli-cams, if I remember correctly. Anyway, you made a cassette tape and sent it through. Clio was operational enough to send small items to us, just not enough power to get us back. If you could do that now and inform the team to stay put, it might work. Granted we were pretty pissed off when we found out what had happened to us."

Chief Black has been listening and re-enters the room.

"Yes, I could order those right now. And better yet. Why don't we let Sgt. Rees do the talking."

Rees recoils and raises his hands, "I don't think that's a good idea, chief. I would prefer they didn't know I was here. We were under enough stress and, at this time of our journey, we still hadn't figured out where we were. It wasn't until we ran into the Rebels that we started grasping our situation. I suggested it was time travel, but we weren't sure until the end of the day and, only then, after losing two men. Having 'me' talk to 'me' just might be a little over the top for the guys. It is probably best if the general just sends a cassette tape. I wouldn't even wait on the heli-cams. I would just send the tape."

The chief looks at the general. Lucas nods.

"I agree. I'll make a tape and send it while you two are gone. But how will they know there's a tape? If it just appears in the area, they might not see it. It could just appear somewhere in the woods or tall grass, and they won't know."

"Sir, we used a boom-box, a cassette player we had with us, to listen to the tape," Rees responds. "Why not send a player with the tape running. Loud enough for the men to find it if it appears close to their location. If they hear the noise, maybe they can find it."

"Good idea."

"Also, sir, tell them about the cameras, too. Explain that they are being monitored and can be seen and heard, but that we can't respond. We felt betrayed once our people started dying."

"Understood, and I will. Anything else?"

Rees looks at the chief, then at the general. "Sir, there's also the situation with Sgt. Wright and Sen. Minten. As they really haven't done anything wrong as of yet, I know they can't be arrested. I would suggest that you set up a meeting with the base police chief and base commander. We could say that Sgt. Wright is needed on a special project or something like that, and he could be quietly removed from his office and brought here."

The general shakes his head. "How do you suppose we do that without making a spectacle? He's gotta know something is up. He was on scene when you did your magic act and we sent in the Blackhawk. I was told he was not allowed entry to the dump and was mad as a hornet. I'm sure, by now, the good senator is aware that something is up. Granted he doesn't know what it is, of course. At least I hope not, but the way things are going, according to you anyway, they both probably do."

Rees rubs his chin as the chief chimes in.

"Sir, he had to be getting information from a secure source, which I would say was Capt. Henries."

"You're probably right, but I'll worry about that a little later. Right now, you two have a mission to carry out."

Rees adds, "Sir, I know there are several delivery vans being used by MISS. You see one around anyone involved with the project, or near where Nora and the girls are, that will more than likely be them. They were monitoring everything electronically and using teams to follow the girls as well as base personnel involved with the project. I know vans aren't allowed near here, but they can still monitor personnel who live off base."

"That's good to know. I will have teams discreetly comb the area and monitor anyone involved with the project as well. You two should get some rest and get ready to depart."

Both men salute and leave the office.

***

Rees and the chief stop by the barbershop where a bleary-eyed barber, who has been awakened and told to report to the barbershop for an emergency haircut, waits for them. Stationed at one of the most secret facilities in the world, and knowing what goes on here, the young buck sergeant didn't think twice about this unusual order. Rees climbs into the chair and is kind of sad to have to cut his hair. He was getting used to it. The beard had to go, but he enjoyed the long hair. Oh well, military life.

Once shaved and shorn, Rees rubs his head as he leaves the barber shop and is taken to a dorm-type room. The chief instructs him to get some rest, indicating he will be back in a little while. Rees takes advantage of the time. He showers, brushes his teeth, then sits on the couch in the main room and falls asleep.

***

Twenty minutes later Rees is awakened by a knock on the door. Groggily he sits up and yells, "enter!" The door opens and Chief Black walks in.

"Up and at 'em, sergeant," Black says, staring at Rees. "Tired?"

Rees shakes his head. "My adrenaline rush must have worn off. Had to crash for a minute. I feel fine now."

"Time to make history or change history or stop history from changing. Something like that," the chief tells him, clapping his hands.

Rees' eyes sting from the harsh florescent light and his ears ring from the loud, chipper voice of the chief.

"All right, all right, chief. Give me a second."

Rees stands, walks to the bathroom and splashes cold water on his face, combs his hair and checks himself in the mirror. Satisfied, he walks back into the room where the chief is standing by the open door.

"What time is it?"

"Time to get moving. We've got an hour to catch our flight. Just enough time for us to get a cup of joe and a doughnut. Let's go. Day-light's burning," and they leave the dorm room.

Rees shakes his head as they walk down the hall. "Damn, I was hoping for another helicopter ride; kind of missed the first one."

The chief snorts. "Yeah, well, maybe one day I'll get to fly in a fighter jet."

Rees smiles, knowingly, as they continue toward the chow hall.

***

The chief and Rees go through the exit procedures and finally find themselves outdoors. Rees inhales the pine-scented air and scans the immediate area. "Good ol' North Kackalacky," he says, following the chief to a waiting Jeep. They climb in and move out to the flight line.

Rees is still disappointed that he couldn't fly in a 'copter, but a C-21, basically a military Lear Jet, is just as fun. They climb aboard and are soon in the air and, in a very short time, are already landing at their destination.

Upon exiting, they watch as a dark-blue sedan, with US Air Force stenciled in gold lettering on the door (along with a serial number and the words, "For Official Use Only"), pulls up to the aircraft and a security police staff sergeant emerges from the driver's side.

"Hey, Sgt. Rees," SSgt Chris Jensen says as he holds the door open. His eyebrows are furrowed, and he has a quizzical expression on his face. Rees notices and knows that Jensen believes him to be on a classified TDY.

Rees smiles. "I know ... you're wondering why I'm here and not with the rest of the team that disappeared, right?"

"Yeah, I guess I am," he says, staring at the flight suit, "but that's really none of my business."

Rees points to Chief Black. "The chief is part of the exercise. He asked for me to work with him behind the scenes. I can't talk about it, but I did want to talk to you about something else."

Jensen's eyes dart from Rees to the chief, then back to Rees.

"Okay, what about?"

"Nothing earth-shattering. You wouldn't, by any chance, have seen Nora, or her sister, or Ivy today?"

Jensen nods. "Yeah, earlier today, in fact. They were leaving the cop shop and waved at me as I was pulling into the side lot. The desk sergeant said they were there to see SMSgt Wright. I assumed it was because of the mess made when your squad didn't come back from the Mud Dump after your shift. Which, then, made a mess for the squadron, security side of course. The law enforcement side was unaffected," he says with a smirk.

Rees nods. "That's fine. I was just wondering. I thought they might be worried since we haven't had time to talk before or when the exercise kicked off."

Jensen snorts, "Guess not."

The chief clears his throat, indicating they needed to be on their way. Rees takes the hint.

"Okay, Sgt. Jensen, thanks for delivering the car. Drop you off somewhere?"

Jensen shakes his head, "Naw," and looks over his shoulder just as a white law enforcement unit enters the flight line. "Got my ride coming. See ya later," and he walks toward the approaching LE car.

Before Jensen gets into the patrol car, Rees shouts at him.

"Sgt. Jensen!"

Jensen stops and turns back towards Rees.

"Yeah."

Rees hesitates, not sure what to say now.

"Listen, keep on your toes. I mean it. Be careful."

Jensen looks confused then offers Rees a crooked smile, then a thumbs up. "Every day, Scott. Every day." He shakes his head as he climbs into the patrol unit.

Rees looks at the chief, who is staring at him.

"What?" he asks, "Just covering bases, chief. He apprehended a couple of the MISS agents and was involved in the shoot-out at Nora's."

The chief shakes his head and opens the passenger side door.

"You drive. That is, of course, if you can remember where to go. You have been gone awhile, haven't you?"

Rees chuckles as he sits in the driver's seat and puts the car in gear. "I got it, sir. This place is still here, even when and where I come from."

Chapter 9

1862

Tech Sgt. Rees stands in the middle of a forest, mostly of pine trees, surrounded by several of the security policemen who were transported with him, each silently watching him, waiting.

"Right now, we need to scout the area and find the others," Rees says, breaking the silence. "We'll split up into three teams. Sgts. Bouvier, Shepard, and Airman Tucker will be one team. They will take the Jeep to locate Tosseti. Sgts. Kriger, Montoya, Airman McGuire and I will go on walking patrol to look for SSgt. Parks, who is – was – in the tower and shouldn't be too far away. I'm surprised he isn't here already. Airmen Nionee and McAdams will stay behind to watch the camp and take care of Green. Airman Harris is still looking a little green around the gills, so he also will stay close to Green while the rest of you will secure the perimeter."

Rees looks up at the sky and checks his watch. Damn, still working. Not bad for seven dollars. It's 1832 hours, or 6:32 P.M. civilian time. It will be dark in a couple of hours and the group will be spending the night in the woods. Rees is not worried about finding AIC Matthew "Matt" Tosseti unless he has wandered off in a different direction. And with Tosseti, you never know.

Squad members grab radios and conduct radio checks to ensure they are working. One airman on each team has one turned on, while the others remain off for power preservation. The call signs are all 15. Sgt. Bouvier's team is 15 Bravo, and the base camp is Security 15. These are the regular call signs, so they stay with what they know.

Rees tells the teams that they are to return to camp in one hour, no matter what. Kriger gives some last-second pointers regarding Airman Green to the men staying and then joins his team.

McGuire takes point, followed by Rees, then Kriger, who is carrying the M-60, and Sgt. Ben Montoya who has the M-203 grenade launcher. They arrive where they believe the tower should be and fan out. The silence is interrupted by a person making a groaning sound. Each man cautiously moves toward the noise. They find Sgt. Isaac Parks lying on the ground in obvious pain.

"Damn, Sgt. Parks. You okay?" McGuire asks, running to the downed man. Kriger brushes by McGuire and bends over Parks.

"Isaac, what happened?" he asks, looking the man over.

Grimacing in pain, Parks is holding his leg and Kriger can see blood and a protrusion in the uniform where the shin bone is located.

"I don't know what happened. One minute I'm in the tower, feeling a painful pressure in my ears, then I wake up on the ground with this," he says between clenched teeth.

Kriger drops his pack and pulls out a pair of scissors to cut the pants leg open. Doing so reveals the shin bone pushing tightly against the skin. Parks looks down and yells a curse, then falls onto his back, his hands grasping pine needles and dirt.

McGuire gives a choking sound and turns away from the sight. Montoya looks at the wound, then to Kriger.

"*Santa Mérida.* You able to fix that?" he asks Kriger with a grimace.

"Yeah, I need a few things," Kriger says, then pulls out a tape measure and measures the length from Parks' foot to his groin, then from his foot to his arm pit, then looks up. "McGuire, pull yourself together and go get me some branches to use as splints," he says, then turns to Montoya "Sgt. Montoya, go with him. I need them both to have a Y shape and these lengths," and he tells the men the measurements.

McGuire nods and takes off into the woods with Montoya in tow. Kriger yells, "And make sure they're strong."

"Sure thing," McGuire answers, still running.

"What do you need me to do?" Rees asks.

"Nothing right now. Just keep watch. I'll give him something for the pain," he says and rummages through his pack, coming out with a morphine syringe.

"Isaac, I'm going to give you a shot of morphine. This should help with some of the pain, but when McGuire returns, I'm afraid we're going to have to set that leg, and that is not going to be pleasant."

"Just do it, David. Give me the damn shot, please," Sgt. Parks pleads, and Kriger injects the man, watching as his face relaxes and his body slumps. Within a couple of seconds, the man is resting quietly.

"He going to be all right?"

"Yeah. Luckily the bone didn't break the skin; that would have been cause for possible infection. I'm going to need everyone's help on this. Even with the morphine, setting that leg is going to be a bitch."

Rees pulls out his radio, calls the base camp and explains the situation, informing them they will be returning shortly. He receives an update on the other team, noting that they have yet to find Tosseti. Rees lets the base camp know his orders stand and all teams are to return in one hour. He signs off and squats down next to Kriger, watching the man work.

A few seconds later they hear running footfalls, and they turn to see McGuire and Montoya heading in their direction with two large branches. They are both winded when they reach the three men.

"This is all we could find. Will they do?" Montoya asks.

Kriger takes one branch, tests it for durability. Satisfied, he throws it on the ground and checks the second one. Again, satisfied they will work, he places them next to Parks' leg, one on the inside of the thigh the other on the outside. He grabs some elastic bandages and duct tape from his pack. He tears off two large sections of the tape and attaches them to his clothing. He sets the bandages next to Parks. He looks around and finds another small stick and places it at the base of Parks foot. Using the duct tape, he attaches the small stick to the two branches.

With the help of Rees, McGuire, and Montoya, they lift Parks up slightly so Kriger can wrap the bandages around his body to attach the branch. He does this around the leg also, making sure both branches are secure.

Kriger takes another bandage and wraps it around Parks' ankle and, using the two open ends, he ties them to the bottom stick. He places another stick in between to use as a twist.

"Okay, guys, I'll need you all to hold him down. I'm going to tighten this so that the bone sets, and it's going to hurt."

"Can't you just give him some more morphine?" McGuire asks.

"No, I already gave him some and I can't take a chance of overdosing him. I need to set the bone or he'll be in worse condition. Now hold him down good. He's going to want to thrash about and that could do him more harm. Now, are you three ready?"

The men acknowledge and Kriger begins to tighten the bandage, which pulls on the ankle causing the broken bone to slowly move back into place. Parks immediately awakens and begins screaming. He tries to get up, but the combined weight of the three men keep him in check. He curses them and threatens them all with bodily harm and yells disparaging things about their mothers, sisters, and such.

Kriger keeps tightening, apologizing, but refusing to stop. Finally, the bone sets and Kriger wraps the leg as tightly as he can. Finished, he sits back, sweat pouring down his face in tiny rivulets, stinging his eyes.

Parks has passed out again, thankfully.

"What now?" Montoya asks.

"Montoya, McGuire, run back to camp and get a Jeep and bring it back," Rees orders and the two men begin running.

"Now we wait," Rees says as he and Kriger stand over Parks. Kriger sighs and looks around the area, spotting something not too far away. Going to the object, he looks down at it for a second then picks it up. He chuckles looking at the object, which is a military cap, a Confederate Kepi at that.

Some kid must have dropped this, Kriger thinks.

He shows it to Rees and makes a comment about giving it to Sgt. Tomas "TJ" Shepard, since he's a hillbilly and his grand pappy probably fought in the war.

Two minutes later they hear the M-151 Jeep approaching. They load Parks into the Jeep and head to camp.

Back at camp they place Parks next to Airman Steven Green and AIC Wallace "Wally" Harris. Rees checks his watch as he listens to the men talking. Bouvier and his team are still out there, and the deadline is drawing close.

Just as he begins to worry, Bouvier's voice comes over the base-station radio announcing they have found Tosseti and are returning to camp. Rees breathes a sigh of relief.

A few minutes pass and Montoya tells the group that he hears a Jeep. A few seconds later the rest of the squad hears the engine noise as well. Bouvier's team arrives with Tosseti in the back of the Jeep being his usual jovial self, cursing up a storm. After all the reunion pleasantries are through, Rees orders the men to again set up a security perimeter. He watches as the men grumble and begin the task of preparing the camp for their first night in ... wherever they are.

Chapter 10

2020

A time travel device very similar to Clio was ordered constructed by Senator Helen Hellberg in 1997. The new time machine was named Janus.

The Clio Project had been moth-balled in the 1980s, and Hellberg recruited several disgruntled former employees who worked on the project. With their knowledge, as well as being in possession of stolen blueprints, she was able to construct her own time machine in an area of the southwest desert. Her intention was to change the course of history so she could stop her senator father from making the fateful mistake of attempting to forcefully take control of the Clio Project facility in the 1980s. He failed at his endeavor and was subsequently removed from office, and soon after committed suicide. There were some theories and speculations that the CIA had actually killed her father, theories Hellberg completely agreed with, so she created Janus.

As fate would have it, the US Government got wind of the time machine and sent in a Special Forces team to capture it. They were successful, but not before Hellberg and her brother, retired Col. Aeson Minten, were able to use the time machine to escape just before its seizure. After the government took control of Janus, it became a backup for the Clio Project as well as a training facility.

***

Hellberg and her brother were in their father's office, attempting to stop him from executing his plan to take over the Clio Project. They don't know if he heeded their pleas as they were whisked away, grabbed by some unseen force that could only be the time machine taking control.

Hellberg doesn't understand what happened as she rematerializes somewhere else. It takes her a few seconds to realize she is back in the disembarkation room at Janus. She spins and sees a large window where there wasn't one before.

Her brother is next to her, but he is fading in and out. Checking her hands and arms, she sees she is doing the same. The room is there one second, then gone. She tries to see as much as she can and even yells at the people in the control room. They can't hear her, of course, but they all stare in amazement, some pointing, others looking up into the observation room where Cedric Novell, director of the Military Intelligence, Law Enforcement and Security (MILES), should be watching. Looking to the room herself, she doesn't see Novell. It's full of military personnel. Looking back in the control room, she realizes it, too, is full of Air Force personnel.

She is confused. What has happened? What is happening? This can't be Janus. The only military personnel working for her were for security and espionage. The room is the same, except the equipment looks different -- newer, more streamlined, fewer lights, and she spots color computer screens. Color!? She glances at Janus, her eyes widening. This isn't Janus. It's too small and doesn't look the same. She sees large screen showing ... what? Another time period? She isn't sure.

She turns to her brother, who looks just as confused. As she is trying to wrap her head around what is happening, they both suddenly disappear.

***

The personnel in the control and observation rooms don't have time to dwell on what they just witnessed. Everyone knows who they saw. The colonel orders everyone back to their stations; they have men in trouble in 1862 and that is their priority.

Chapter 11

1862

TSgt. Rees gathers the men together on their first morning in the unknown area. They are discussing what they believe to have been a battle earlier that morning. They decide Rees will take two Jeeps with a team and scout the area to the north where they heard what sounded like artillery fire. They will stay in radio contact as long as they can, then report their findings.

Rees, Sgts. Shepard and Montoya, and Airmen Alex Steele, Ray Nionee, Eric McAdams and Nathan "Nate" Tucker climb into the vehicles. Tucker sets an azimuth reading and they are on their way. They keep their security call signs, 15 Bravo and 15 Charlie. The base camp is using the larger radio in the armored Cadillac Commando, or more lovingly known as the "Duck," and will use the call sign Security 15. After the plan is formulated, the men assigned for the recon set off.

***

SSgt. Bouvier is leaning on the outer door of the Duck, talking with Amn. Tosseti, who is manning the radio. The team has called in a couple of times, but Tosseti fears they are getting out of range.

Sgt. Kriger is attending to the wounded and McGuire is performing perimeter duty. Kriger is talking to Greene, even though the man is unconscious, and in the middle of a sentence, Kriger stops. He thinks he hears something and becomes still, squinting in concentration. He can hear a voice, a very faint voice. Tosseti's loud voice isn't helping so Kriger rises and yells for Bouvier and Tosseti to quiet down.

Bouvier looks at Kriger, who is walking in circles, eyes closed, his face a mask of concentration, his head tilting like a confused puppy.

"What in the hell are you doing, Dave?" Bouvier asks, pushing off the Duck and walking towards Kriger. Tosseti leans out the door and watches the scene.

"Youse been taking some of your own medicine there, sarge," Tosseti says in his loud, Bostonian accent, followed by an even louder laugh.

Kriger sternly looks up at both of them, and pushes the palm of his hand out to them in a stop motion.

"Will you two shut the fuck up and listen?"

Bouvier walks slower and begins listening, trying to hear what Kriger is hearing. He stops walking, then perks up as he, too, hears something.

"I hear it, Dave. What is it?"

"I don't know but if you two would stop yapping, maybe we can find out."

Being rebuked a second time, Bouvier gets a little agitated, but lets it slide. Kriger lifts his head and walks briskly toward the wooded area, outside the perimeter. Bouvier follows, hearing the voice get a little louder.

"Hey, where youse guys goin'?" Tosseti shouts, but he is ignored.

Kriger and Bouvier pick up the pace. McGuire is coming around on his perimeter check and sees the two sergeants jogging to the woods.

"Hey, Sgt. Bouvier. I thought I heard someone talking out there," he shouts.

"Stay on security. We got it," Bouvier replies.

The two men can definitely hear a voice and it sounds like it's repeating itself. It is becoming clearer as they continue walking. Finally, they see a cassette player lying in a small opening among the trees.

"What the ..." Kriger says, not finishing his sentence. They stop and stand over the player, just watching it and listening.

"This is Gen. Lucas of the Clio Project. If you hear this, do not leave the perimeter of your camp. You are in danger if you do. Turn the tape over for further instructions. This is Gen. Lucas of the Clio Project. If you hear this, do not leave the perimeter of your camp. You are in danger if you do. Turn the tape over for further instructions."

The message keeps repeating. Bouvier retrieves the cassette player and turns it off.

"What does this mean?" Kriger asks.

"No idea."

"We should at least listen to the other side."

"Dave, I don't know any Gen. Lucas. And the Clio Project? Sounds like something that may have to do with where we are. Again, I don't know, but I am going to contact Rees and see what he says."

Bouvier and Kriger run back to the Duck, passing a confused-looking Amn McGuire along the way.

As they reach the Duck, they hear Tosseti talking with someone whom they assume is the patrol.

"That Sgt. Rees?" Bouvier asks, a little out of breath.

"Yeah, sarge. But the transmission is breaking up."

Bouvier sticks his hand out and waggles his fingers, indicating he wants the mic. Tosseti hands it to him.

"Security-15 Bravo, Security 15, come in."

"15 Bravo ... ahead."

"Listen. We received a message and I think you should return and hear it. There's more to it than what we have heard, but we haven't listened to it entirely. I think this might be important and, from what we heard, it's a warning not to leave our camp perimeter."

There's a long pause.

"Security-15 Bravo, do you copy?"

There is another long pause and Bouvier is about to repeat the question when 15 Bravo answers.

"Security-15 ... not copy..."

"Security-15 to Security-15 Bravo, you need to terminate the patrol and return ASAP."

"Security.... Bravo ...."

"Negative 15 Bravo, return to base."

No reply.

"15 Bravo, do you copy?"

Static.

"Fuck!" Bouvier exclaims, squeezing the mic and glowering. He straightens, exhales and hands the mic back to Tosseti. He looks at Kriger, then at a confused Tosseti.

"Let's just hope that general is wrong."

Chapter 12

2020

Col. Joe Black is in his office, staring at a blank screen and observing the technician and Air Force personnel going about their duties in the Clio control room. His father, Chief Joseph Black, is pacing the room, deep in thought.

"You're wearing a hole in my new carpet, dad," the colonel says without turning around, "And making me nervous."

Chief Black stops and looks at the back of his son's head.

"And don't stare at the back of my head either."

Chief Black chuckles and shakes his head.

"You know you would have been branded a warlock for doing that in the 1600s."

"Well, it's a good thing I don't live in that era, and I wouldn't even use Clio to try to see what happened then. Popping out of thin air would probably get me burned at the stake a hell of a lot quicker than knowing what someone is doing behind my back. I just know you is all," the colonel, says turning to face his father.

The Chief has a despondent and agonized expression on his face. The colonel can't tell which is more profound.

"Okay, I know you're worried about Rees, and I know you think you made a mistake sending him back to 1980. And I agree, that was a dumb thing to do on your own, but it's done. Now we have to work on finding him, or at least getting in contact with him. I'm sure he's fine."

The Chief takes a deep breath and releases it, staring at his son.

"Listen, I know I should have told you, but I wasn't sure you'd go for it."

The colonel's eyes harden. "You're damned right I wouldn't have. After all the crap we went through to get this project back up and running, only to have it sabotaged, with people getting killed. No, I would not have added another kink in the chain of events already in play. We had enough information from the last jaunt, and everyone made it back safely, except for Rees. Granted we brought back two nineteenth-century people this time instead of one, so we have that to deal with, on top of finding Rees and hoping he doesn't do anything to screw up the timeline."

The chief opens his mouth to speak but the colonel shakes his index finger at him.

"No, I already heard your reasoning for it, and I understand, but we could have tried that experiment later. One thing at a time, dad. One thing at a time."

The chief takes another deep breath and releases it, slightly embarrassed by being chastised by his son, but knowing it is deserved. This lasts only a few seconds before the chief stands taller and looks back at the colonel.

"Yes, sir, of course you're right," the retired chief says, reverting back to his military bearing, but the colonel notices a mischievous look in his eyes, like he knows something.

The colonel waves his hand dismissively.

"No, forget about it. Like I said, it's water under the bridge. We will work on both problems at the same time. And don't ever call me, sir. You're my father for Pete's sake; it gives me the creeps and besides you're a damn civie now!"

The older man chuckles at this. Col. Black watches his father for a second. *What's he not telling me?* He thinks then turns once again to look at the large screen in the control room.

"Now, let's go down to meet our newest guests."

The two men leave the office, making their way to the bank of elevators. The ride down to the medical floor is a quiet one, both men silent with their own thoughts. The trip is quick, and the doors open to reveal Capt. Farnsworth waiting for a lift. Neither man was expecting to see the captain so they both are a little surprised.

"Capt. Farnsworth!" Col. Black says, reaching out his hand. "Good to see you back."

Farnsworth shakes the colonel's hand.

"Thank you, sir. Believe you me, it's good to be back," he answers, then looks at the chief and nods. "Chief."

"Capt. Farnsworth, nice vacation?" he asks deadpan.

A crooked smile forms at the corner of the captain's mouth.

"Let's just say it was a very interesting one, how about that?"

The Chief returns the grin.

The colonel takes back the conversation.

"Captain, ah, I'm ... we're sorry about your mother's passing. The fact she died in an accident while you were in 1862 makes it that much more tragic. I don't know what else to say. I'm sure you'll want to take time off, of course."

"Thank you, sir. And thanks for offering some leave, but I came to terms with that while I was gone. I had time to grieve, in a sense. As I told Sgt. Rees, I knew my mother was up to something, and that she was using me to get whatever it was she was really after. As much as I loved her, I could not be the treacherous son she wanted me to be. From what I was told, her body has been cremated and her ashes placed in the family cemetery. So, no, sir. I don't need time off. I need to be here to see this mission through, if that is all right with you."

The colonel watches Farnsworth for a few seconds and nods.

"That's your call to make captain. But, if you change your mind, let me know. No questions asked. Okay?"

"Yes, sir. Thank you, sir."

Then the colonel decides to break the morose mood by clapping his hand together and rubbing them briskly. He smiles at Farnsworth.

"Now, how are our guests?"

"They are fine, sir. Both are being seen by the doctors. Separately, of course. They are in mild shock, as I'm sure you understand. Physically both are fine. Once the doctor releases them, I'm sure they would love to meet you both. They do have some questions, I might add."

"Oh, I'm sure they do. I'm sure you and the men have some, too."

"Yes, sir. In fact, I was on my way up to your office."

Col. Black smiles. "I will be answering all of your questions when we have the debriefing. You and the whole team. We are just here to see the new guests and, hopefully, reassure them that they are safe. Once the doctors release you and you've had time to get some chow and clean up, we will set up a debriefing time."

"Yes, sir. I've been released from medical, and I guess I should shower and change into my regular uniform. I will be in my quarters, waiting, sir."

"Good. We will talk soon, captain."

Farnsworth nods to the chief and makes his way to the open elevator.

Col. Black and Chief Black continue on to the medical bays, where the two newest time-traveling guests are being examined. Col. Michelle Thompson, the chief medical doctor, and Capt. Mary Wells, one of the psychologists, are standing in an observation room that has two-way mirrors looking into the separate room. One of the rooms is occupied by Sgt. McGregor and the other by Miss Emma Kelly.

Thompson and Wells turn at the sound of the door opening and watch Col. Black and Chief Black enter.

"How are our patients, colonel?" Col. Black asks, walking over to the two female doctors.

Col. Thompson looks at Col. Black then nods toward the room where Union Sgt. McGregor is apparently yelling and cursing. They can't hear him as the intercom is muted, but from the way his mouth forms when speaking, and the body language he is making, it's obvious he is none too happy. The doctor, as well as the med-tech in the room are standing far away from the irate man. McGregor isn't restrained and isn't making any physical moves to indicate a hostile act, but they aren't taking any chances.

Thompson turns and nods to the room where Emma is sitting on the edge of the bed with a blanket wrapped tightly around her. Col. Black asks Thompson if the young woman is cold. Both women chuckle.

"No, sir. She is modest. She was sedated for a little while when she was brought in and we changed her into a hospital gown. When she woke, she was none too pleased to see her clothes had been removed."

Col. Black and the Chief snap their heads toward Thompson. Thompson raises her hand to ward off what she knows they are going to say.

"I know, sir. We weren't supposed to sedate her, but as you can see with Sgt. McGregor," she says, turning halfway toward the other room and pointing at McGregor, "neither of them are being cooperative. We didn't put them under too long, just enough to get them into hospital attire and into the rooms. When they woke, it was apparent they were not happy knowing someone had removed their clothes. I do apologize, sir. It was a mistake on my part."

Col. Black doesn't answer so Col. Thompson takes that as a cue to continue. "Emma is embarrassed and won't let anyone near her. The sergeant, on the other hand, is angry and also won't let anyone near him."

Capt. Wells clears her throat. "Sir, if I may. The trauma of being transported to another century, well just being transported, is enough to cause some mental trauma on anyone, even someone from our time period. But, for these two, it is especially traumatizing. They haven't had time to deal with what is happening, and it might take a while."

Col. Black stares at the captain.

"Suggestions?"

"Well sir, they both have been asking ... demanding to see Capt. Farnsworth and Sgt. Rees. Of course, they referred to them as colonel and captain."

The chief nods. "Of course. They know them. Why wouldn't they?"

Col. Black agrees and asks why that hasn't been done.

"Waiting on you, sir," Col. Thompson tells him. "Both Capt. Wells and I think it's a good idea. We just wanted your blessing."

"By all means. I'll let Capt. Farnsworth know," he advises, then turns toward McGregor's room. "Turn on the intercom."

Col. Thompson takes a breath. "You sure sir?"

He stares at Col. Thompson and she reaches over and turns the volume up. The room is instantly filled with McGregor's strong Scottish accent booming into the small observation room with all sorts of vile language.

"Bamba Bassa! Keep ya fuck'n distance now, ya hear. Buncha Doaty Dobblers, the whole lot of ya."

Col. Black waves at Col. Thompson to shut it off.

Chief Black is shaking with laughter, drawing a stern look from Capt. Wells.

"Oh my, he's a colorful one. Don't really know what he's saying, but I can guess he's not wishing them peace and long life."

Col. Black shakes his head and walks to the door.

"I'll get Capt. Farnsworth and Sgt. Bouvier down here ASAP."

"Sir, they asked for Sgt. Rees."

The colonel nods his understanding.

"Rees isn't available right now, so Bouvier will have to do," he explains, then smiles as he watches McGregor continue to strut around the room, still mouthing what he can only assume are more choice words for the hapless doctor and technician.

Chapter 13

Capt. Farnsworth had not been in his room for more than ten minutes when the intercom buzzes. He is partially undressed and wanting a shower. He tells the voice-operated intercom to connect whoever is calling.

"Capt. Farnsworth," he answers when prompted.

"Captain, this is Samantha from Col. Black's office."

"Yes, Samantha. What can I do for you?"

"The colonel would like you to go back to the infirmary and talk with our guests. It seems they are not very happy to be here and are being uncooperative with the staff. Sgt. McGregor is being especially outspoken, and both are demanding to speak with you."

Farnsworth laughs. "Of course they are. Tell Col. Black I will be down there as soon as I clean up and change, if that is all right with him."

"I'm sure it will be, but I will inform him. About how long, captain?"

"Give me fifteen and I'll be down."

"Very good, captain," Samantha says, then continues before Farnsworth can disconnect. "Captain?"

"Yes, Samantha?"

"Ah, how was Scott when you last saw him? I mean ... was he well?"

Farnsworth is a little taken aback by the question from the colonel's assistant, then remembers the kiss she planted on Rees before they time-jumped, and it dawns on him.

"Samantha, to be honest, I don't know. He was fine up until we were all shot by that asshole, then we jumped. I have no idea. I hate to say it, but he took almost the full brunt of the shotgun blast. Our bullet-resistant clothing saved us numerous times, so I am hoping that this time was no different. I pray he is well, wherever he is, and I'm sure the colonel and the chief will be getting him back soon. Sorry I can't tell you anymore."

Samantha is silent for a few seconds. "Of course, captain. Thank you, and I'm sure you're right," she says softly, then her old voice returns. "I'll inform the colonel you will be down shortly," and ends the call.

Farnsworth hangs up, finishes undressing and makes his way to the bathroom, thinking about Rees for a few minutes.

I do hope he is all right, he thinks.

Fifteen minutes later, he is making his way to the elevator and sees MSgt Bouvier waiting.

"You coming along, sergeant?"

Bouvier nods. "Yes, sir. I was asked to join you in seeing if we can calm Sgt. McGregor down and reassure Miss Kelly that she is going to be fine. Should be fun. Last time I did this was with Corp. O'Toole, but he was more cooperative with the medical personnel and had been here for a while before we spoke with him. He had a good adjustment period."

The elevator door opens and both men walk on.

"This bringing people back from the past is getting to be a habit. One I hope we don't keep doing. The last one didn't work out as planned. Not sure what we are going to do with these two," Bouvier says, staring straight ahead.

Farnsworth watches Bouvier for a minute as they ride down. They reach the medical floor, and the door opens. The men step out and Farnsworth reaches out his hand and places it on Bouvier's arm. Sgt. Bouvier stops, looks at the hand, then at Farnsworth.

"Listen, sergeant. I didn't really get to know you before Rees and I left, but he said a lot of good things about you and Kriger. Hell, he said great things about all of you, except for two sergeants," he says with a concerned look on his face, "one of which I haven't met, and the one missing a leg."

"Sgt. Shepard," Bouvier informs him.

"Yes, him and that Bostonian, but I digress. Anyway, I want you to know I got to really trust Rees and his judgment of people. So, if he says you're a good NCO and a good person, I believe him. I just want us to be able to work together."

Bouvier stares at the captain, trying to form his words.

"Sir, I am a professional NCO. You are an officer. I can work with just about anyone. You're right, I don't know you. There was a point where I wanted to kill you. Sorry, but we thought you had double-crossed Rees, no offense."

"None taken. I quite understand."

"Rees is my supervisor and my friend. Rees told us we could trust you while we were at the O'Toole farm, so I will trust you. As for the other men, that's up to them. If you are assigned to us, they will follow your orders as they would any officer. So, we are good, sir."

Farnsworth grins. "Good to hear, sergeant. Now shall we go and try to make some really old people welcome into a new century?"

***

The two men enter the observation room. Capt. Wells is there alone. She introduces herself to Farnsworth and just looks at Bouvier. Farnsworth feels a chill in the air between the two. He knew Rees had a run-in with the captain, so, Bouvier must have been there as well. He puts the thought away for possible discussion later with Bouvier.

"Capt. Wells, we understand our guests aren't too happy with us," Farnsworth says.

"No, they most certainly are not. They asked for you and," she looks at Bouvier, "Sgt. Rees."

"Well, Rees is currently indisposed, as I'm sure you are aware. How about Sgt. Bouvier and I try to calm Mr. McGregor down first, then go assure Miss Kelly that she will be fine?" he says, looking at the doctor. "If you will excuse us."

"Capt. Farnsworth, I do believe I should be in the room as well. As the Bank's resident psychologist, it is my job ..."

Farnsworth raises his hand, making Wells stop talking. He smiles.

"No captain, your job is to evaluate from here. They asked to see us, not you. Now if you will excuse us," he finishes with finality.

Wells stares at them as they leave. Bouvier turns and gives her a smile and a thumbs up.

Farnsworth opens the door to McGregor's room and sticks his head in to see McGregor, as well as hear him, pacing back and forth in front of the doctor and the med-tech.

"Mind if we come in?" he asks.

The two medical personnel turn at the sound of Farnsworth's voice. McGregor stops his pacing and his cursing at the interruption. All three men stare first at Farnsworth, then at Bouvier as they enter.

"Colonel, darlin'. Good to see ya!" McGregor announces in his heavy accent.

"Good to see you, too, sergeant. You remember Sgt. Bouvier, I hope."

"Ah, yes, I do lad. How are ya, sergeant. Good to see you, as well."

"I'm fine, McGregor, thanks."

Smiling, Farnsworth turns his attention to the Air Force personnel.

"If you don't mind. We got it from here," he says, dismissing them.

The two men happily, but quietly, leave the room, shutting the door behind them. Farnsworth turns back to McGregor, giving him a stern look. McGregor's smile falters upon seeing the captain's expression.

"Sgt. McGregor, you told me you would behave and here I find you giving my people bloody hell."

McGregor comes to attention. "Sir, they gave me something that made me feel funny. Not my fault I cannot handle what it is they gave me," he says, then grins. "Felt pretty good though, I give ya that, sir."

He grows serious again. "Then they put me in this here manky hen clothing with me bum out!" he shouts, turning to show his posterior to the men.

"Woah there, sergeant. Not something we really want to see," Farnsworth chides, and both men laugh.

McGregor, nonplussed, continues. "But then they wanting to poke me and do other ungodly things to me that no man should be doing to another man, if you know what I am meaning, sir."

"All right Sgt. McGregor. At ease."

McGregor relaxes, stares at the men and raises an eyebrow in a questioning manner. "Ah, sir, where is your uniform? I mean, oh never mind, everything is a dream here."

"No sergeant, it's not a dream. We are from your future. These are our uniforms from our time. Also, I'm a captain, not a colonel," he says, then adds, "Maybe one day."

McGregor looks even more confused.

"I tell you what. If you can be patient for a little longer, and not give the people here - who are trying to help you by the way - any more grief, I will bring you along with us and explain everything to you and Miss Kelly. Can you do that?"

"Aye, sir, that I can, but can I get some damned clothes, please? Don't like having me arse just flapping out here out for someone's jollies."

"Yes sergeant, I'll see what I can do. We will be back shortly, so, just hang in there."

"What?"

Farnsworth looks perplexed, then gets it. "Be patient."

"Oh, aye, sir."

Next, the two men go to Emma Kelly's room. Farnsworth knocks, then slowly opens the door, peeking into the room, eyes averted from Emma, and announces himself.

"Miss Kelly, it's Farnsworth and Bouvier. May we come in?"

Silence, then, *Bang!* as something bounces off the door. "You most certainly may not! I am not decent and will not be treated like a big-city hussy! I won't be havin' any of it. Now go get me some clothes, damn you, sir!"

Farnsworth and Bouvier are, again, chuckling. "Yes, ma'am. Be right back."

He shuts the door, and they make their way back to the observation room where Capt. Wells is standing with a stern look on her face, the clipboard across her chest.

"You two are not qualified to be interacting with our guests. You don't know the psychological damage you could have on them not knowing how to say the right things. That and, as it's possibly too late, letting them know too much. We can't send them back if they know too much."

Farnsworth looks at the doctor. "Capt. Wells, is it?"

She nods.

"Captain, we have been dealing with the good sergeant and Miss Kelly for some time, granted in 1862, but still. Now, here we are again in a situation where we accidentally bring two more nineteenth-century people back. I also dealt with Corp. O'Toole for quite some time while taking him home. I understand you had some misgivings about him as well," he says, looking to Bouvier who faintly nods, "and the young man adjusted very well. He accepted the theory of time travel and didn't make a fuss over it at all. He just carried on like the good soldier he was and did not misuse his knowledge or act out of sorts. So, captain, we will continue to interact with these two good people until someone in higher authority says we can't. Also, it's not your call regarding if they are sent back or not; that I know is not part of your job description."

Capt. Wells' face flushes with a look of controlled anger and starts to speak, but Capt. Farnsworth raises his hands to stop her. He continues.

"I ... we are not here to step on your toes or undermine your position, Capt. Wells. We know you have a job to do, just as we do. Right now, our job is to see to these two peoples' needs, then work on a solution to this dilemma. I hope you can understand our position. As you can see, Sgt. McGregor is taking it well."

They turn to look into the room where McGregor has his hand underneath his gown, scratching himself, all the while pacing and cursing.

Wells looks at Capt. Farnsworth and raises an eyebrow. Farnsworth smiles at her.

"Believe me, captain. He is taking it well. Now, if you will excuse us, we need to find some clothes for Miss Kelly and Sgt. McGregor. Apparently dressing in a hospital gown is not something a nineteenth-century woman or man are used to."

Giving Wells one more smile, he makes his way to the door and opens it. Just as he is stepping through, he adds, "I just hope it doesn't psychologically damage them." He closes the door quickly behind him, but not before he hears Capt. Wells saying something about arrogant and maybe even asshole, but he is not sure.

Chapter 14

1862

Capt. Conroy Absher of the 6th Artillery Battery, North Carolina Volunteers, tugs on the red collar of his officer's uniform. He swivels his neck, trying to gain some relief from the constant itching of his collar, along with a feeble attempt to cool off from the heat and humidity. Even the cotton lining his wife sewed on the inside of his uniform isn't helping. He releases the collar, reaches up and removes his straw hat, wiping his brow with the sleeve of his jacket.

Sgt. Jedidiah Baine silently appears beside him.

"Another scorcher today, sir."

Absher looks at the sergeant and sees the man's uniform is still in impeccable condition, even after the battle they fought earlier in the day. Baine is wearing the grey jacket of the Confederate artillery, with the red stripes running along the jacket sleeve. His light-blue pants also carry the red stripes on the outside of the legs. His red kepi is tilted at a cocky angle, reminiscent of the young men in his unit.

How does he do that? Absher thinks, *Keeping neat and tidy in these conditions?*

"Yes, sergeant, it is," he replies, looking at the sky and using his hat to block the sun. He replaces his hat and looks around at the big guns lining the hill. "How are the men holding up?"

"Oh, the boys are fine, sir. Not losing any artillery boys in the fight is always a morale booster. And to see Billy Yank hightail it out of here is always a treat for the fellas."

The captain listens to the sergeant and looks down the hill where the bodies of both blue-and-gray, and butternut-clad men are strewn about. Dark spots cover the clothing where blood spilled from the men's injuries. The wounded infantry had been removed not too long ago, both Rebel and Yank, taken to the rear hospital area. But the dead have not been attended to.

"Yes sergeant, we were a lot luckier than those boys down there."

Sgt. Baine stares at the dead infantry, saying a prayer under his breath.

"Sgt. Baine, make sure the men are fed and have plenty of water, and ammunition should be replenished as soon as possible. That was just a Yank reconnoiter unit. I have a feeling they will be back."

Sgt. Baine watches his commander as he speaks. When he knows the captain is finished, he informs him that the men have been fed and given water and that the ammunition is being replenished as they speak.

Capt. Absher stares at the sergeant.

"You are a God-send for me sergeant. Bless you. I thank you for being here and ensuring the men are always on their toes."

"Yes, sir. Thank you, sir."

Absher is looking down the hill again when he notices movement coming from the tree line more than a quarter of a mile away. He can hear an unfamiliar noise coming from the same direction, a rumbling sound. Absher takes a couple of steps forward and looks around for his glasses, which Baine dutifully hands the officer. The gesture doesn't go unnoticed, but the young officer's mind quickly switches gears to the scene in front of him.

Absher moves to stand next to one of the Napoleon cannons, raises the binoculars to his eyes and begins scanning for the source of the movement. Turning his head slightly left, then right, then up, he finally locates the source. He swiftly lowers the glasses, then raises them again. Once again, he moves forward, not understanding what he is looking at.

"Sgt. Baine!" he yells, and the sergeant appears in an instant.

"Sir!" Baine replies, standing behind the officer.

The captain turns and hands the binocular to the older man and points toward the tree line.

"See that movement just below the trees, before the clearing?" he says, watching the sergeant place the glasses to his eyes. "Look there and tell me what you see."

The grizzled NCO moves the binoculars around, then stops and moves back to his right a fraction. He emulates the captain's earlier movement by dropping the glasses, looking at the captain, then raising them back for another look.

What he thinks he sees are two small wagons with four men in each, but the wagons are operating under their own power, or so it would seem, as they are moving and there are no horses pulling them. He takes another look and notes the men are all wearing dark-green clothing, with blue and white markings on the sleeves. And some are wearing what looks like round buckets on their heads, while others are wearing blue caps without a brim or green caps with a brim. He is confused as to who they are.

"What in tarnation are ...?" he exclaims, not finishing. He drops the binoculars to his side and faces the captain with a quizzical look. "Horseless wagons, sir? When did the Yanks get horseless wagons?"

Capt. Absher takes the binoculars from the sergeant for another look and sees what the sergeant is talking about. The men in green stop the wagons and some of them climb out. They are all carrying some type of weapon ... *a fancy looking musket, or are those Spencer rifles?* Now the captain is as confused as the sergeant. He watches the men for a little while, trying to understand who they are and what they are doing. These aren't Confederate troops; of that he is certain. So, they have to be Union soldiers.

He watches as some of the men go through the belongings of the downed soldiers. Growing angry, he observes items being removed from the dead. The captain has seen enough. He doesn't care who they are; they are desecrating the bodies of fallen soldiers and stealing from them. Gripping the binoculars until his knuckles turn white, he angrily tells the sergeant, "Tell Lt. Peters to get his men ready to attack and then have our boys prepare to fire."

"Sir!" The sergeant shouts and hurries over to the gunners, shouting, "Prepare to fire on the captain's order." He locates the lieutenant and relays the captain's order. The lieutenant does as he is told and yells at his NCOs to get the men ready. It only takes a few shouts from the NCOs before the men are up and moving. The lieutenant rushes over to the captain for clarification. The captain explains the situation and advises the lieutenant to disperse some men down to the tree line to the north. Once they hear the cannons fire, they are to charge the area where the enemy has been spotted. He hands the lieutenant the binoculars and points to the area he wishes the men to attack.

"The rest will stay on the hill until the cannons have fired, then charge making it a pincher move."

The lieutenant acknowledges, salutes and retreats.

While the captain is briefing the lieutenant, Sgt. Baines is pacing behind the cannon, watching the young men ready their weapons. He occasionally takes a peek down a barrel to ensure the elevation is correct and makes adjustments as needed. When he is satisfied all is in order, he shouts to Capt. Absher.

"Ready for your order, sir!"

Capt. Absher is still watching the scene below and doesn't move.

"Fire!" he shouts and, within three seconds, five Napoleon cannons belch flame as their five-pound iron balls sail down the hill toward the unsuspecting men. Once the firing has stopped, the lieutenant and his men charge, weaving around the cannon and screaming the Rebel Yell as they rush toward the unknown enemy.

Capt. Absher watches as the first couple of shells explode short of the group of men. Then he flinches slightly as one round makes contact with one of the wagons and it explodes in a shower of flames and sparks. He is astounded at what he sees next. The wagon is not made of wood, as it doesn't disintegrate into splinters, but crumbles into a heap of metal.

My God! We are going to be in serious trouble if they have more of those.

He is still watching the scene when he hears one of his cannoneers scream. He turns to find a soldier on his back, a rapidly spreading pool of blood soaking the wool uniform. He hears pings and thuds and realizes it can only be bullets striking his men and equipment. He returns his attention to the area below and catches a glimpse of a man standing in the back of one of the wagons firing a Gatlin Gun, but unlike any he has ever seen.

The other men in green are firing back as well, and somehow their rounds are making it this far and accurately! The men racing down the hill are dropping as round after round finds its mark.

The enemy is scrambling around now and loading their wounded into the last wagon. One of the men shoots what looks like a large-bore shotgun toward the advancing Rebels and, within a couple of seconds, an explosion tears through several Confederates. Those within the blast zone die or wounded, falling and tumbling down the hill where they lay either unmoving or moaning in pain.

The other Rebels come out of the woods, screaming and shouting as they attempt to overcome the men in green and their horseless wagon. The wagon is fast, too fast for the men to catch. He watches as the men in green move away, still firing and causing more of his men to fall.

Capt. Absher lowers his glasses once the horseless wagon is out of sight. Sgt. Baines is standing beside him with his mouth slightly agape, wanting to speak, but at a loss for words.

"Sergeant," Capt. Absher says, returning his binoculars to his eyes once more.

The sergeant comes out of his reverie instantly.

"Sir?"

"Get our horses. We are going down there. Those men took the lives of some of our boys, but they left something behind."

"What may that be, sir, if I might'n ask?"

The captain drops his binoculars, giving the sergeant a sad smile and pointing down the hill.

"The remains of their wagon, sergeant. A prize for Richmond."

Chapter 15

1980

SMSgt. Wright drives his vehicle back to the Security Police station as fast as he can, still fuming from the rebuke he received from that pretentious asshole civilian agent.

How dare that puny ass runt try to tell me what to do. I'll fix his wagon. Let's see what he thinks when my people get wind of this, he thinks.

He pulls into the cop shop parking lot, exits the vehicle and makes his way to the building, ignoring several people trying to talk to him. Forcefully opening the back door to the station, the sergeant storms down the hall to his office, slamming the door behind him. Standing in front of his desk with his hands on his hips, Wright takes a couple of deep breaths while staring out the office window. Out comes a cigarette. He lights it, inhales deeply, then sighs, releasing a cloud of smoke. The action relaxes him slightly.

He walks behind the desk and unlocks a drawer, reaching in, removing the hidden phone and placing it on his desk. He lifts the receiver, placing his cigarette in an ashtray and taking another calming breath before dialing.

One ring. A voice answers. "What have you got?"

Sitting down, Wright leans back in his chair and swivels to look outside.

"Something has gone wrong."

"Explain."

"The MSD is full of civilian agents, as well as Bank security. They would not let me near the site. A chopper flew in, and I believe they flew someone out."

"Who?"

"I don't know. Like I said, they've got it locked down and no one is allowed entry."

"Okay, I'll let the boss know. If you find out anything else, let me know," the voice says, disconnecting the call.

Wright places the phone back in the drawer and locks it. Still looking outside, he smokes his cigarette and fumes.

A few hours later his phone rings. The desk sergeant tells him there are three young women here who would like to speak with him.

Now what? he thinks. "I'll be right up," he says and hangs up. Wright walks to the front desk. He puts on his best fake smile and approaches the three women.

"Hi. I'm Sgt. Wright. I'm in charge of security and personnel deployment. What can I do for you?"

Before Nora Miller can say anything, Wright stops her.

"I'll tell you ladies what. Why don't you come back to my office where it's a little more private? Then you can tell me what's on your mind."

The women thank him, filing through the door and down the hall to Wright's office.

Once in the office they explain that they are looking for their boyfriends, Rees, McAdams and Nionee. Wright gives them the cover story about the team being sent on a secret Temporary Duty exercise and assures the women that the men are all okay and should be back soon. He apologizes but explains that he can't give out any details.

Standing to indicate the meeting is over, Wright leads the women to the door then watches as they leave the building. His fake smile disappears as he shuts the door and returns to his desk.

Opening the desk drawer, he again removes the phone and holds the receiver to his ear.

"Listen," Wright says into the phone as he swivels his chair to point away from the door. "We may have another slight problem we didn't foresee. There were some young women here asking questions about their boyfriends, guys who are on the assignment."

He listens briefly before continuing.

"No, no, of course I gave them the cover story, but I could tell that at least one of them remained suspicious."

He listens again and stirs uncomfortably in his seat.

"Yes, I agree, but something has to be done about this. We will keep an eye on them and see what transpires. We will handle it if need be," he says, then listens.

"No, we have enough agents here running surveillance and undercover. It won't be a problem."

The sergeant ends the call and replaces the phone in the drawer. He takes a deep breath and exhales, a look of stress-induced fatigue evident on his face. Picking up a folder, he throws it onto the desk and turns back toward the window with his hands behind his head. A heavy sigh is all he can muster as he loses himself in thought.

***

Nora Miller, her sister, Skyler, and their friend, Ivy, leave the cop shop, thanking the young desk sergeant for his help. The three women are very familiar with the base police and know a lot of the SPs by name.

Once outside Nora's demeanor changes.

"That son of a bitch is lying or hiding something," she says as she looks for her car keys.

Ivy shrugs. "Seems like a perfectly good reason that the boys are gone. I mean, come on Nora, we grew up as military brats. This stuff happens all the time."

Nora finds her keys and unlocks the door to the vehicle. She looks over the roof at Skylar and Ivy.

"Yes, Ivy, they do. But that asshole, with his fake smile and his condescending attitude, is lying.

"To what end, Nora?" Skylar asks.

"I don't know, but when we get home, we'll discuss it some more. If need be, I'll get in touch with the newspaper. They love looking into whatever the base is doing."

With that they climb in the car and leave the base.

As Nora drives down her street, she sees a dark-blue USAF vehicle parked in front of the home she shares with Skylar.

"Now what?" Nora says and pulls into the driveway.

She shuts off the engine and sees a chief master sergeant on the front porch. He turns to look as the vehicle pulls in. Nora exits the car, noticing as her boyfriend, Scott Rees, moves around the chief and walks down the porch steps. She smiles at him, then frowns.

"Hi gorgeous. Surprised to see me, I take it?" Rees says as he approaches with a huge grin on his face. He stops in front of her and kisses her, hard. Nora is taken aback.

"Huh, hello to you, too, handsome. What's with the kiss. I mean, I really like it but, wow."

"Oh, just haven't seen you in a while is all."

Nora gives Scott a peculiar stare. There is something off about him. Skylar and Ivy walk up. Both say hello to Scott, then look over at the chief as he approaches.

Rees sees them staring at Chief Black, so he introduces everyone.

"I am working for the chief," he explains.

Nora furrows her eyebrows. "We just left the station after talking to Sgt. Wright. He said all you guys are TDY."

Ivy bounces on her tiptoes. "Is Eric with you?"

"Ah, no, no he isn't," Rees tells her, then looks at Nora. "Why don't we go inside and talk?"

Ivy puts on a pouty face and walks toward the house. Skylar falls in line behind her and, as she passes Rees, she asks him, "I suppose Ray is gone as well?"

Rees nods. "Let's go inside. I'll explain everything."

He begins walking toward the house, watching as a delivery van drives up the street and stops a couple of houses down. Rees stops on the porch as the rest enter the house. Chief Black walks past Rees. "Are you coming?" he asks. Rees doesn't respond, still watching the van. He can't see inside due to the glare off the windshield. No one comes out to make a delivery and he finds that curious.

"Chief?"

Chief Black stops. "Yes?"

Rees looks at the chief, then looks at the van. The chief follows his gaze, spotting the van.

"You think it's MISS."

"I don't know, but my guess is ..." Rees stops, The two men watch as the passenger-side door opens, and a man dressed in a company uniform steps out with a package and a clipboard and makes his way to one of the houses.

The chief pats Rees on the back. "Paranoid or coincidence?" he asks.

Rees makes his way to the door and smiles. "Neither chief. You know better than that."

The chief follows Rees into the house. "Oh, I know. Just checking to see if you did."

Once inside Nora asks Skylar to make some coffee. Nora and Ivy sit at the kitchen table with Rees and Black. Nora is looking at Rees and can't put her finger on it, but something is different about the man.

"Scott, hon. What is going on? Why did you need to come here?"

Rees looks at the chief, then each girl in turn. "Nora, ah, damn I don't know how to say this without sounding crazy. But just hear me out and I can prove what I'm going to tell you."

Rees hesitates, takes a breath, and looks out the back window in thought.

"Okay, I am Scott Rees, just not your Scott Rees," he begins and looks around the table for everyone's reaction. The girls look dumbfounded. Nora tilts her head slightly and gives Rees a slight scowl.

"What are you talking ..." she says, but Rees raises his hand to stop her.

"Let me finish, Nora, please. Okay, again, I am Scott Rees, but from the future."

This causes Ivy to snort, and she blows coffee out her nose.

"Dammit Scott, look what you made me do."

Skylar grabs some napkins and hands them to her.

Nora's scowl deepens. "What the hell are you talking about, Scott? What? What is really going on? A future you? Bullshit."

Rees looks at the chief for support and only gets a sardonic smile, then nods.

"Miss Miller ..."

"Nora, chief, please."

"All right, Nora. Sgt. Rees is correct. What we are about to tell you is top-secret. None of you have been cleared, officially, but we have good reason to trust all of you. I am with a special branch of the Air Force called the Bank. We work with time displacement," he says, then quickly adds, "Time travel."

This causes Ivy to again snort, with the same results. Skylar hands out more napkins and frowns at the two men.

"Dammit to hell. Will you two stop with the jokes? My sinuses can't take it," Ivy complains.

"Sorry, but it's true and we will prove it to you."

Rees takes over. "Nora, the Bank sent me and the entire team, including Ray and Eric, back in time. To 1862 to be exact. There were some complications and when we returned, it was 2019."

Nora stares at Scott; Skylar is slack-jawed; and Ivy blows her nose, waving her hand in a gesture for them to stop. They all continue staring at Rees.

"Riiiiight," Nora finally says slowly and leans back in her chair.

"When we were sent back, it was during the Civil War, and we ran into some problems. We had to fight Rebels and Yanks. We accidently returned with a Union Cavalry soldier and we went back again to return him. Again, some complication arose, and when the team and I were transported this time, I was sent here to try to correct some things that went wrong the first time."

The room is silent until Nora leans forward, her hand in her lap, staring into Rees' eyes.

"So, let's say any of this is real, and I really don't think it is but I'm giving you the benefit of the doubt, you're saying you're you, but if that's so, where is the other Scott Rees?"

Chief Black leans forward.

"He is now in 1862."

"Bullshit!" Skylar finally interjects. "Scott, are we on *Candid Camera*? Is this some type of USAF mind game? Come on. Time travel? Again, I call bullshit." She turns away in disbelief and snatches up the used napkins.

Rees sighs. "Sorry, Skylar. It's true. That's why we came here. The Bank is located on another base. We flew out here to retrieve all three of you. I can explain more on the way, but we need to go."

Nora straightens at that. "On the way? On the way where?"

The chief looks at Nora.

"Miss ... sorry, Nora. We need you all to come with us to the Bank. Once there we can prove what we say is true. Look at Scott. Can you see any difference in him at all?"

Nora and the two other women now look at Rees more intensely. Nora stands and tells Scott to stand. She looks into his eyes, turns him around and, still holding his arms, she stands back and gives him the once over.

"Yes, as a matter of fact, I can. Scott, you have a different look in your eyes, more intense, haunted, aged; I can't put my finger on it. Another thing is your hair cut is different from the last time I saw you and, unless you have some instant super fitness program going on, you've bulked up some, "she says squeezing his biceps. "Leaner. Your uniform doesn't fit right. There is something else changed in you. Maturity? I don't know, but that doesn't prove a thing."

Rees nods. "I know, but if you come with us, we can show you proof. Nora, I love you and I have missed you for some time now. I know that's hard to believe, but I haven't seen you for more than a year," he says, leaving out that he has seen the older version of herself and still talks with her occasionally.

"Another thing. You went to see SMSgt. Wright today?"

"Yeah, so?"

"I know what went on in there. You three went to ask him where we are. He gave you some story about us being on a secret TDY mission and couldn't tell you anything. You don't believe him, and rightfully so. I'll explain that later, too." Rees grins and jerks his head towards the living room. "Follow me," he says and walks to the window. Pulling up the blinds, he chuckles and looks back at the chief. "Still there."

Rees points to the van still parked along the curb about two houses down.

"See that van?" he asks and watches her from the corner of his eye as she leans over his shoulder.

"Yes."

"I'll bet anyone twenty bucks that the van belongs to the Military Intelligence and Security Service organization - MISS for short. In my timeline, once you three went to see Wright, you came under their radar and they started monitoring you. Again, we will explain all that to you later."

"Really? MISS? You call them MISS?" Ivy asks.

Everyone turns to look at her.

"Hey, not my acronym," Scott replies and turns to the chief.

"Sir, can you call that in and see if OSI can check it out?"

The chief beams. "My pleasure. Nora, may I use your phone?"

She nods and he goes into the kitchen. Rees hears the sound of the home phone being picked up, dialed, then the chief's voice. A few seconds later, he returns.

"Done."

Rees looks at the women. "Now we wait."

The women bombard Rees with questions as they wait, but he insists on not revealing any answers until they get to the Bank.

Ten minutes slide by, and Rees spies movement on the street. A local police cruiser is driving slowly along the road with an unmarked, dark-blue sedan behind it.

"Here we go," Rees says and they all go outside to watch, as do a few of the curious neighbors. Rees chuckles to himself. *Damn nosey neighborhood.*

The vehicles park behind the still-idling van and two police officers exit the patrol car while two civilian-clothed men exit the sedan. The two officers are carrying revolvers and the civilian-clad men brandish modified Colt 1911s. Rees recognizes the men as Special Agents Eric Von and Christian Beltrane from the Office of Special Investigation (OSI), the Air Force equivalent of NCIS.

The four men spread out as they approach the van from the rear, with weapons at the low ready or at their side, pointing down. One officer and Von cover the back of the van as the other officer moves to the driver's door and Beltrane goes to the passenger side. Once the officer reaches the driver's door, he takes a quick peek inside, doesn't see anything and looks again until he is sure there is no one in the front seat. Beltrane does the same on his side. They hand signal to the two in back that the front is clear.

Agent Von goes to the back door and beats on it, but no one answers. One of the officers walks up and grabs the handle and pulls. The door is unlocked and, as he is about to open it, the door flies open. The officer staggers backwards as the door strikes him. Before regaining his balance, shots ring out of the back of the van from a submachine gun and strike the lawman once in the face, once in the neck, and once in the chest. He is dying as he hits the ground, blood spewing into the air from the neck wound. His heart pumps a few more times as the arterial blood flowing profusely slows with each dying heartbeat.

The scene becomes chaotic. One neighbor screams. Agent Von is caught off guard and is a split-second late in returning fire, as are Beltrane and the surviving officer. As Von begins firing, the rear doors slam shut, his bullets deflecting from the armored metal.

Beltrane and the officer run to the back of the van as the shots are fired, leaving the front uncovered. Someone inside the back of the van had time to climb into the front seat and place the large vehicle in reverse, flooring it. Von jumps out of the way as the van smashes into the patrol car, crumpling the front end and hood. Steams hisses and rises from the shattered radiator. The patrol car, in turn, rams into the front corner panel of the OSI vehicle. The impact crumples the sheet metal like aluminum foil. The corner of the fender is driven down into the tire, puncturing it and disabling the car. The person in the van places it into drive and floors it, tires screeching before rubber grips the asphalt, propelling the vehicle forward.

All three men shoot at the van, but the bullets don't penetrate what should be thin-skinned sheet metal and safety glass. The glass cracks, but doesn't shatter, even after multiple hits. The men stop firing and run to the fallen officer.

Chief Black and Sgt. Rees are both angry and horrified. Ivy is wide-eyed with shock, her hands covering her mouth. Nora and Skylar stand open-mouthed, not believing what has just happened.

Rees and the chief run down the steps and across the lawn. Rees calls out to Von, who looks up, mildly surprised.

"Sgt. Rees, what are you doing here?"

Rees quickly explains that they called this in, believing it was a surveillance team watching the house. Von confirms that that's what he was told.

"You think this was MISS?" Von asks.

"Yes, I can't tell you much, but we believe they were monitoring my girlfriend, her sister and another woman. Call your commander. I'm sure he can fill you in. I've got to get the women out of here."

In the distance everyone can hear sirens approaching. The officer comes over.

"I got the description out on the van, and it shouldn't take too long to locate the bastards. I've never seen anything like it. Bullet-resistant glass on a delivery van? I'm sorry but that wasn't just any delivery van. And who was that inside? Machine guns? Now my partner is dead. What the hell is going on here, flyboys?" the officer angrily asks, then looks at Rees and the chief. "And who the hell are you two?"

Von and Beltrane pull the officer aside and Von tells the chief and Rees to go do what they have to; he will handle this.

They two men return to the porch, where the women are waiting.

Nora looks at Rees. "So, you were right about the van. I assume you know a lot since you say you're from the future. What about that man lying there dead? Why didn't you know about that, Scott?"

Rees sighs. "Look, Nora. Things have already changed. From what I was told, this didn't happen. I was told that you three were almost kidnapped by the same organization that those in the van work for. The MISS agents attempted to take you three. Sgt. Jensen and a few others stopped them, but not without loss of life on both sides. So, things are not the same in this timeline."

She looks at him and then comes over and hugs him.

"Okay, Scott. What next? I believe you, but now I want you to show me definitive proof."

He smiles. "Definitive proof. Chief, you hear that? My southern belle is learning fancy words here. Impressive."

She playfully punches him in the arm, then looks at the dead man in the street and grows solemn. She watches as rescue and police units, their lights flashing and sirens wailing, screech to a halt. She takes in the grim scene for a few more seconds, a tight expression on her face. Rees sees it and gently leads her back into the house as the others follow.

***

The driver of the van recklessly speeds through the residential neighborhood with no regard to pedestrians who might get in the way. An agent is talking on the radio through a set of headphones, explaining the situation to their headquarters.

The man wearing reflective sunglasses is securing the MP-5 he used to kill the police officer. He has a crooked smirk on his face as he places the submachine gun in a rack. Hanging on to an overhead rail, he steadies himself and makes his way to the front of the van, kneeling next to the driver.

"Always wanted to blow a cop away. Would have rather it been one of those damned OSI agents. Never could stomach those condescending assholes," he grumbles to the driver.

The driver ignores his boss's banter, watching for police cars.

"Where to, sir?" he shouts a little too loudly, adrenaline still flowing through him.

The other man removes his sunglasses and begins to clean them. He looks at the road in front of him. "Well, first off, slow it the hell down."

The driver complies.

"Good, that's better. Now keep going on this road and pull into the mall parking lot. We will drive around to the loading area and back the van in, so the shattered glass won't be seen. We'll look like we're delivering something."

The driver acknowledges this and does as he is told, turning the vehicle into the parking lot. Just as they are driving around the back of the mall, a patrol car passes them. The driver tenses and Sunglass Man grabs his arm.

"Steady, just keep driving. We're a delivery van, just going about our business."

The patrol car glances at the van as it passes, then moves on as if nothing is wrong.

"See, it's all good. Just some hick cop, doesn't know shit from Shinola. Now do as you were told," he orders, making his way into the back of the van where the radio operator sits.

"You notify HQ of the situation?"

"Yes, sir. I told them where we would be, and they are sending an extraction team for us and a tow for the van."

"Good, good," Sunglass Man says, rubbing his hands. "Okay, once we park, we leave the van and make our way to the mall where we will blend in with the drooling idiots and wait."

Once parked, all three agents exit the van. They haven't made it around to the front of the mall when the police car they saw comes back, and it is trailed by another vehicle.

The three MISS agents stop, then turn to walk back toward the van. As they turn, they see two more police cruisers coming from the opposite direction.

Sunglass Man curses, then makes a dash for the van. The two other agents hesitate just a second, then do the same.

The police cars speed up and one stops directly in front of the van, blocking it in.

"Stop right there and put your hands up," a voice orders over a loudspeaker.

The driver and radioman both stop and do as they are told. Sunglass Man keeps running and jumps into the van, grabbing his MP-5. He ensures there's a round in the chamber and opens the driver's side door. He jumps down and begins firing on the two patrol cars nearest him. The drivers of both vehicles are caught by surprise and die in a hail of bullets.

Sunglass Man moves around the vehicles and makes his way toward the other police vehicles, grinning like a psychotic hunter and shooting as he is walking. Before he can move any further, he hears the distinct sound of a helicopter right before an AH-64 Apache reveals itself, flying sideways over the roof of the mall and hovering in front of him.

All three agents are stunned, but Sunglass Man is defiant. He gives the pilot of the 'copter the middle finger and curses as he raises his submachine gun. He fires ineffectively as the bullets ping off the armored helicopter. The copter doesn't waver, and Sunglass Man doesn't pay any attention to the police officers still alive. While he is shooting the helicopter, two officers take aim with their service revolvers and unload all their rounds at the agent. Sunglass Man flinches as he is hit once, twice, three, then four times, falling onto his back but still managing to hold the trigger, firing off the last few rounds harmlessly into a stack of wooden pallets.

The two other agents drop to the ground and lay flat with their arms out in surrender.

Chapter 16

2020

Capt. Farnsworth and Sgt. Bouvier make their way to the clothing shop where they acquire two plain uniforms for McGregor and Emma. Bouvier holds one of the uniforms up and looks at Farnsworth.

"I hope Miss Kelly doesn't mind wearing pants, but I don't think she will like this century's current dress style. It's not as modest as she prefers."

Farnsworth grins. "I'm sure she'll be fine with it. We'll just ask Col. Thompson and Capt. Wells to explain the limited access to nineteenth-century clothing."

The two men separately pack up the uniforms, underwear, socks, and shoes and take them back to the observation room, with Farnsworth holding the brasserie up and wondering if they even had those in 1862.

"Stop playing with that," Bouvier says when he notices what Farnsworth is doing, "Sir."

"Did women wear these back then?"

"I think they wore corsets, sir. I could be wrong, I'm just thinking of movies I've seen, like *Gone with the Wind*."

Farnsworth looks at the item, shrugs and adds it to the rest of the clothing.

Thompson and Wells are both present when the two men arrive. Farnsworth hands the bag with Emma's clothing to them. Both women understand the men's concerns and their slight embarrassment. Thompson assures them it will be all right as they leave with the clothing.

The two men take the other bag into the room where McGregor is still pacing. They toss the bag to McGregor, and he catches it. Wearily he opens it and pulls out the camouflage uniform. Looking it over, he does the same with the rest of the items. When he spies the pair of boxer briefs, he raises his eyebrows in question.

"What in tarnation is this?" he asks, holding the underwear up for the men to see.

"Boxer briefs," Bouvier said.

McGregor fixes him a quizzical look. "Again with ya talking nonsense."

"Drawers," Farnsworth says, and glances at Bouvier, explaining, "What they called underwear back then."

Bouvier nods "Ah, gotcha."

McGregor drops the bag to the floor and holds the boxers up with both hands as he squints. "Kinna small."

Farnsworth's chuckles and Bouvier looks at him and whispers, "I don't think he means *that* captain."

Farnsworth whispers back. "I know, it just struck me as funny is all." Then, looking at McGregor, he explains. "Things have changed, sergeant. We don't wear the long underwear anymore. Only when it's cold. Trust me, you'll like them."

McGregor looks at each man in turn, smiles, removes his smock, and begins dressing. Bouvier has to assist him with the T-shirt as McGregor is having a difficult time getting it on. And he puts the boxers on backwards. Once he is correctly dressed, he laces the boots, again with some help.

Fully outfitted, the Scotsman stands and looks down at himself, then walks over to the two-way mirror.

"Not too shabby, if I do say so myself. And I do say so myself. This feels nice, better than that bleed'n wool uniform. I like the different colors, like the woods, I say."

"That's the intent, camouflage," Farnsworth explains. "Come on sergeant, let's get you debriefed ... I mean let's inform you as to what is going on."

The three men exit the room.

They walk into the observation room and McGregor turns and stares at the room he just left. "Weren't we just in there?" he asks, touching the glass. "What kind of magic is goin' on here?"

Bouvier moves beside him. "No magic. This is a two-way mirror. You can't see into this room from the other side. Just more modern things we have that you don't. There are other things as well."

McGregor looks offended. "You tell'n me you've been watching me in there. I mean, that's downright embarrassing, sirs, what with me scratching me arse and such. "

Bouvier claps McGregor on the back and bends close to his ear. "And the worst part is that there were women in here watching as well."

McGregor's mouth drops open, and he stares at them in shock.

Bouvier can't help himself and continues. "And we filmed you."

McGregor is puzzled, staring blankly at Bouvier.

"What is film?"

Bouvier smiles. "Oh, you'll see it someday. I might even put it out on YouTube," he adds and turns away. McGregor slowly shakes his head and whispers. "Daft is what you are, bleed'n daft."

The window that shows Emma's room has the drapes closed so the men can't see inside. They explain to McGregor that that is where she is being kept and is probably getting dressed.

"Aye, and you couldn't have thought to be that kind to me, what with women folk in here?" he asks, looking insulted.

A few minutes later, the curtain opens and the men see the two female officers and Miss Kelly. She is wearing a light-blue Air Force blouse, dark-blue pants and black shoes. She seems a little uncomfortable, but the uniform looks nice on her. The women walk out of the room, and the men leave to meet them.

"Ah, Miss Kelly," Farnsworth says when he sees her. "Looking very nice. How are you feeling?"

She hadn't noticed the men and looks up, surprised.

"Ah, thank you. I'm feeling better, especially now that I am more decent. These clothes are quite different than what I'm used to, but these two ladies tell me that most women wear pants now. I like that idea and will miss being in a dress, but not the damned corset!" she says with a smile, which causes the rest of the group to smile as well. Bouvier nudges Farnworth knowingly.

"It will take a little getting used to though, what with the ..." she hesitates, "unmentionables they wear now."

The USAF officers and NCO smile at that; McGregor remains stone-faced, still fuming over the window situation. Farnsworth holds his arm out to Emma.

"I'm glad to hear that. Now if you don't mind, we will escort you and the good sergeant to another area where you can meet the commander and we can try to answer any questions you may have."

Upon hearing this, Capt. Wells clears her throat. "A word, captain, if I may. Colonel, will you join us?" she asks and walks a few feet away from the group. Bouvier just shakes his head.

"What is it, Wells?" Col. Thompson asks.

"Ma'am, I do have my concerns about these unqualified people talking with the guests."

Thompson raises her hand to stop the captain.

"Capt. Wells, your objections have been noted, on more than one occasion, I might add. As you have been told, Col. Black makes the decisions on how the guests are treated, what information they are told, and what they are shown. That is not for us to decide. Granted I, too, have some reservations, but our job is to advise, not dictate. I trust Col. Black and that's all there is to it."

Farnsworth looks at Wells and she gives him a hard stare. "Yes ma'am, I understand. Capt. Farnsworth, please, if you will, keep me informed on their status."

Farnsworth looks at the captain. "I will make sure you get a copy of our daily reports, if that's all right with you. I will be too busy to personally give you an update, but I do have to file my dailies."

"That is fine, thank you. If you will excuse me," she says and leaves the two other officers in the hallway.

"Capt. Farnsworth, don't be too hard on her. She is just doing her job and she is very good at it. A little overzealous at times, but she means well," Thompson says.

Farnsworth smiles. "Oh, I don't have a problem with her, but I can't say the same for Bouvier and Rees. But I'll talk to them."

"Very good, captain, and good luck."

"Thank you, ma'am," and he returns to the group.

***

Col. Black and retired Chief Black are sitting in the conference room along with the rest of the team. Sgt. Shepard and Tosseti are at the far end of the table, bickering back and forth, entertaining those immediately around them. The colonel and his son are talking quietly with Kriger and Nionee when Capt. Farnsworth enters the room. He is followed by Emma and Sgt. McGregor with Bouvier bringing up the rear. Both the displaced guests are staring all around, wide-eyed with wonder and a little fear. Neither knows what is really happening or what their futures hold. Everyone in the room stops what they are doing and turns in their chairs to face the newcomers.

Both Emma and McGregor smile at some of the men, recognizing them. Col. Black rises from his chair and makes his way to them, the chief in tow.

"Miss Kelly, good to meet you. I am Col. Black, commander of this facility. Welcome," he says by way of introduction, then turns to the chief. "And this man is CMSgt. Black, retired, who also happens to be my father."

The chief shakes both their hands. "Good to meet you."

The colonel points to the table. "Please, have a seat and we will get this show on the road."

Both McGregor and Emma look at each other, confused and slightly intimidated.

Farnsworth walks behind them and points to a couple of chairs close to the head of the table. He takes a seat next to Emma while Bouvier sits next to McGregor.

Bouvier leans over to McGregor, who looks a little uneasy.

"Sergeant, relax. You know most everyone here and you just have to listen. Let the colonel speak. When he is finished, he will ask if you have questions. Okay?"

McGregor turns to Bouvier and smiles. "Aye, lad. I know me place and won't be causing no problems."

Col. Black stands and, before he can do anything, Sgt. Shepard speaks.

"Col. Black?"

The colonel looks at Shepard. Shepard stands, wobbling a little on his new artificial leg, and looks around the table.

"Sir. We've been back a little while now and no one has told us where

Sgt. Rees is."

Col. Black smiles then looks at his father.

"Dad, you want to take this?"

Chief Black stands, slowly making eye contact with everyone in the room.

"If things went as planned, Sgt. Rees is back at the Mud Dump in 1980. He should have arrived immediately after you were transported. He is or was supposed to stop the experiment from happening."

The room comes alive as everyone begins talking at once, throwing questions at the chief. The chief lets this continue for a minute then raises his hands, shutting down conversation.

"All right, all right. That's quite enough. I know you have a million questions, but for now, let's allow the colonel to conduct the debriefing." He returns to his seat as the colonel moves forward.

"Gentlemen, and ladies," he says, nodding at Emma and Sam, "When we decided to send Corp. O'Toole back, we did so because we thought we would corrupt the timeline if we didn't do so. Mainly, stopping the chief from being born, or me for that matter. And, of course, the Clio Project would not have come about. We were under the impression we were descendants of the corporal, but discovered we are the descendants of his sister, Kailee O'Toole, so it didn't matter."

Emma looks at Farnsworth, her mouth opens as if to ask a question. Farnsworth whispers in her ear. "I'll explain later. Let the colonel finish," and pats her arm.

Unaffected by the side conversation, the colonel continues. "Unfortunately, Corp. O'Toole was killed, and that, in itself, is a great tragedy." He looks at Emma and can see her eyes beginning to tear up. Capt. Farnsworth reaches for her hand and holds it. Emma presses her lips tightly together and lifts her head. She is proud and will not let these people see her being weak.

Farnsworth leans over. "Miss Kelly, no one here will fault you for crying. We all understand."

She looks at Farnsworth and gives a sad smile.

"No, colonel," she whispers, and Farnsworth doesn't correct her. "I have grieved, and this is no time to start that process again, and not in front of strangers." She squeezes Farnsworth's hand, then releases it.

Col. Black had stopped talking and Emma looks at him.

"Please continue, sir."

Col. Black smiles. "Thank you, Miss Kelly. As I was saying ..."

The colonel speaks for an hour, going over the details of the mission, including a PowerPoint slide presentation. He explained what went right, what went wrong, asking questions periodically about how the equipment works, taking suggestions, etc.

After the debriefing and after all questions had been asked and answered, he turns the floor over to Chief Black and takes his seat. The chief stands and scans the room.

"As I told you earlier, we believe Sgt. Rees is in 1980, back where this started. By now he should be in contact with me, as well as Gen. Lucas. This was all my doing and neither Col. Black nor anyone else had knowledge of what Sgt. Rees and I agreed to do."

"To stop the first project from happening?" Tosseti asks.

"Yes," is all the chief says.

"Chief, why?" Montoya asks, which is followed by head nods and murmurs around the table. "The timeline and us? If he did that, we wouldn't be here. So, since we are, it must not have worked."

Chief Black paces, raising his hand for their silence. "I have three theories, and Sgt. Rees agreed to help test those theories. One, I believe the timeline does not allow a vacuum. That means once something happens, no matter what we do, it will still happen. Maybe not in the same order, or the way it happened the first time, but it will happen."

Tucker speaks up. "You mean we would still be here no matter what, and the deaths of Sgt. Parks, and Airmen Steele and McAdams would still happen?"

The chief points at Tucker. "Correct Sgt. Tucker. And that is one theory. The second theory I have is that we have created an alternate universe."

This suggestion causes a small uproar and, again, the chief allows it for a minute, then calls for silence. The noise level drops immediately.

"And the third, sir?" inquires Airman Harris, who is usually very quiet.

"The timeline changes, but we don't know it."

"Oh, that's the best one, chief. So, we just go through life, it changes, but we are unaware of it?" McGuire asks.

"Essentially, yes," Black answers.

The room is buzzing again. The chief lets them fuss for a couple of minutes then clears his throat to regain their attention.

"Thank you. Once we send someone back in time, and if they are sent back when their former selves are in that timeline, that means there are two of the same people in the same time period. Now, let's say the future self does something that changes the course of history during that timeline, then they return to their timeline. Nothing will have changed for them except that now there is another earth moving in a different historical direction."

"Oh, like in *Star Trek: Mirror, Mirror*, where there is another universe, only with an evil bearded Spock!" Shepard exclaims, causing the others to stare at him. He notices the looks. "Hey Sgt. Rees isn't the only one who watches *Star Trek*."

Green stands. "So, you're saying that no matter what goes on, we will always end up here?"

"No, not at all. Where we are now will not change whatsoever, but the alternate timeline could be changed so that you don't end up here. It was our hope that Rees made it in time to stop the Clio Project and stop your past selves from transporting. You all would still be here, but your past selves would remain at the base and those men would go about their lives making a different history for themselves."

McGregor leans over to Bouvier, "What on God's green earth is this man yammer'n about, sergeant?"

Bouvier smiles. "I'll explain later."

Now it's Nionee's turn to ask a question. "Okay chief, we got that. Now, how come you don't know if Scott made it or not. Are you in contact with him?"

The others again nod.

Col. Black stands. "We know he made it, but that's all. We lost comms with him not long after he transported."

The colonel picks up a remote and aims it toward a viewing screen. He presses a button, replacing the PowerPoint with a video.

"This is from Sgt. Rees' jacket camera."

A U.S. Air Force logo appears, followed by the Bank logo and a legal warning about the video being top-secret, then the screen turns black. Movement can be seen as the camera is jostled and then they hear the rustling of clothing. The men see a quick view of asphalt followed by a clear, blue sky. This lasts for a few seconds before the picture moves again and sections of the MSD come into view. The men hear moaning and an utterance of "Shit!" from the voice they recognize as Sgt. Rees', and he sounds like he is in pain. The men know he probably is because, just before transporting, he and Farnsworth were shot. The picture jerks some more, then stops.

Bouvier turns to look at their two guests, both wide-eyed in wonderment at seeing moving pictures. He smiles. McGregor turns to face him and Bouvier points at the screen, mouthing, "That is film." McGregor eyes grow wide, realizing that this is what Bouvier was talking about earlier, being filmed in the hospital room.

The colonel speaks, bringing their attention back to the screen.

"This is where we believe Sgt. Rees finds a hidden camera he was told about. There were several in the area covering most of the MSD during the initial transport," Col. Black explains just as Rees begins to speak.

"Chief Black sent me. Stop Capt. Henries! DSI panel! Stop Clio!"

The picture moves once again to reveal the blue sky. There is quiet for several minutes before the camera is jostled and the room fills with the sound of a helicopter rotors, then of running footsteps. There are quick flashes of uniforms and faces, sounds of people talking all at once. The camera movement becomes jerky. They can tell Rees' jacket is being removed, then the picture spins and stops suddenly, the camera pointing at Rees being loaded onto a stretcher. The camera moves once more, then the screen goes black.

Col. Black shuts the video off and turn toward the men.

"We believe when the jacket was thrown on the ground, it damaged the camera."

The chief looks at the people in the room, "And the transponder, as well?"

The colonel nods, "Yes, that, too. The video is available for review by each of you. But for right now, we need to see to our guests and answer any questions they may have. Everyone except Capt. Farnsworth, Sgts. Bouvier and Kriger, Sam and our guests are dismissed."

At this, Farnsworth stands and orders the room to attention. The men move as one to stand and he dismisses them. The men file out, greeting Emma and some shaking McGregor's hand or slapping him on the back. Once everyone is out, the chief shuts the door. Col. Black looks at Kriger,

Sergeant, if you wouldn't mind, you know where the refreshments are?"

"Yes, sir," Kriger replies and asks Sgt. McGregor to help him. Confused, McGregor warily stands and follows Kriger to one of the walls. Kriger presses a button. The wall slides away, and a well-stocked bar moves out of the opening.

McGregor's eyes widen in disbelief, some because of the magical wall but mostly at the sight of all the bottles of what he knows as Bug Juice, Joy Juice, Bust Head, Ole Red Eye or plain old booze lining the shelves.

He reaches out and tentatively touches a bottle of Basil Hayden, then stops and looks at Kriger. Kriger, still smiling, tells him to go ahead. McGregor takes the bottle and Kriger holds up a glass. The old soldier has the top off and is about to take a swig when he sees the expression on Kriger's face. Kriger holds the glass up a little higher and McGregor, looking sheepish, takes the glass from Kriger, pours about four-fingers worth of the amber liquid into it, then downs it. Smacking his lips, he looks at the glass then at Kriger.

"Ahh laddie, that is good. Thank you, me boy, I be needing that," he says and pours himself another.

"Take 'er easy there, sergeant. We don't need you getting pie-eyed in the meeting."

"No need to worry your wee self about that, lad. I'll be fine," McGregor tells him with a mischievous smile and sways back to the table, glass in one hand, bottle in the other.

"Hey, I thought you Scotsmen drank, well, Scotch?"

McGregor turns back to Kriger, still smiling. "Hey, I'm an American now, laddie. Got to be acting like one."

The people at the table laugh and give Kriger their drink orders. Emma refrains from alcohol, so the colonel orders a carafe of coffee and a pitcher of sweet tea from the chow hall.

The group sits to talk, more relaxed now.

Chapter 17

1980

Sen. Minten is sitting in his high-back leather chair behind his impressive maple-wood desk. He is sipping his drink, his mind reeling from the encounter he just had – or was it some sort of hallucination? Two people claiming to be his children from the future? They wanted to warn him about something, but before they could get it out, they simply vanished into thin air, just as they appeared.

Both looked like his children, but much older. The one claiming to be his daughter yelled, "Dad, don't go through," before she disappeared.

Don't go through. Don't go through, he repeats to himself, *Don't go through. What? A door?* Then he arrives at what he believes is the correct conclusion. *No, she meant Clio! That's got to be what she was trying to tell me!*

Minten straightens with what he thinks is utter clarity. "She meant Clio!" he shouts to an empty room. Taking a gulp of his drink, he spins his chair around and hastily sets the glass on his blotter, sloshing a bit over the rim and leaving a dark stain on the material. It goes unnoticed by the senator because he is too busy in thought.

Following his logic, he surmises they must have been sent here by his future self. That was it. He sent his children back in time through Clio because his plan to take over the Clio Project worked, and he oversees the entire program. In the future there must have been a problem with him using the time machine, something that would affect his future self, and not for the good, so, his older self sent his children through

Clio to warn him "not to go through Clio," he says aloud. He is not to use the time machine himself. For what reason, he has no idea, nor does he care. He will listen to himself, but by God he will take over that facility and kick out everyone involved in the program, especially those two troublesome hacks Gen. Lucas and Chief Black.

While contemplating this scenario, he doesn't hear the intercom buzzing on his desk. He finally comes out of his trance when his secretary knocks on his door.

"Come in!" he shouts.

The door opens and his secretary peeks around the door, taken aback by the roguish look on his face. The almost sinister smile, the corner of his mouth turned up and one eyebrow arched. Recovering her composure, and not daring to ask why he didn't hear the intercom, much less if he is feeling all right, she informs the senator that John Clayborn is here, as requested.

"Well, send the man in," he orders, almost jovially, and she turns and says something he can't hear. A few seconds later Clayborn strides into his office.

"Senator, we need to talk," Clayborn announces as soon as he is through the door, his face flush.

"Oh, we do, do we?" Minten replies, all joviality gone in his voice. "Clayborn, you need to calm down is what you need to do. Look at you, man, red-faced, perspiring like a pig." Minten stands and comes from around his desk to tower over the smaller man. "You been drinking, Clayborn? I certainly hope not because now's not the time to become slack or let up on the job,"

"No, no sir, nothing like that. We have problems."

Sen. Minten's face grows dark. "*We*," Minten says, the palm of his hand pressed against his chest, "don't have problems, John. You might have problems, but you were hired to take care of *your* problems, not bring them to me and make them *my* problems. I've got other things to do, and they don't include babysitting you.

"If you can't do your job, John, I will get someone who can," Minten warns sternly, knowing this tactic always works on Clayborn, who sees potential problems everywhere.

Clayborn, who is usually stammering by now, sets his jaw and stares at the senator.

"Sir, your nephew has been arrested."

This causes Minten to pause, and he softens his look as he stares at Clayborn. "Go on, John, you have my attention."

"Senator, something has been going on at the base. It seems there was some sort of commotion after the Clio Project was initiated. We have some reports about the incident ..."

"God dammit, Clayborn," Minten interrupts, becoming choleric, "what about my nephew? Why was he arrested? By whom? What charges? Where is he?"

Clayborn's initial wave of confidence has quickly evaporated, and he shrinks from the other man's stare.

"Yes, yes sir, if you will, I'm getting to that," he says, clearing his throat. "One of our operatives claims that someone in a civil war uniform was flown out of the weapons area by helicopter. Later in the day, your nephew was placed under arrest by orders from Gen. Lucas."

Clayborn stops talking, watching the senator's reaction. Minten looks up towards the ceiling at the mention of Lucas, his jaws tight. He looks down at the far wall, his eyes moving as if in thought, and it seems to Clayborn that the man is trying to remain calm, which he hopes he will, for his sake.

"A civil war uniform?" he mutters, then looks at Clayborn. "Continue."

"Yes, sir. The details are sketchy; we're still gathering information, but I was told he was arrested for treason, espionage, and other charges. He is being held in the Bank's holding facility."

"God dammit!" Minten shouts again, startling Clayborn, who takes an involuntary step back. Regaining his composure, he takes a few steps forward, berating himself for being so easily cowed.

"How? How did this happen? What did my idiot nephew do to bring this down on himself. He was just supposed to observe and report. He must have done something to bring attention to himself, that ... that, ahhhhh!" Minten shouts, turning around and stomping to his desk. He leans on it, his back to Clayborn, his knuckles pressed against the top so hard that Clayborn can see them turning white. After a few seconds the senator relaxes, straightens, and moves around the desk and takes a seat.

"All right Clayborn, what else?"

"Ah ...," he begins then stops as the senator cocks his head and gives Clayborn a warning look.

"Grow a fucking pair, for God's sake, and tell me what is going on? Don't fucking hem and haw. Be a man and spit it out!"

"Another operative reported that some of the men sent on the classified mission have girlfriends who are asking about them."

Minten glares, "So what?"

"Sir, when the background checks were conducted on these men, they were picked because they had no ties with close family," Clayborn continues. "They didn't have girlfriends at the time. If you remember, you specified that if they disappeared, you wanted to make sure there would be no one to search for them. Well, since the project took longer to initiate than projected, the men had time to get acquainted with the women. Now that they are on assignment, the girlfriends are asking questions concerning their whereabouts."

Clayborn finishes and waits uneasily for an eruption.

Minten stares back for several minutes, not moving. Clayborn is getting worried when Minten suddenly blinks.

"Clayborn, this is what I'm talking about. Don't come to me with this bullshit. You are paid to handle it, quietly and without me knowing about it. You were right coming to me about my nephew. That I needed to know. But worrying me about a few girls asking about their boyfriends?" he says, arching his eyebrow. "You fucking know better. Now get the hell out of my office and do your job!" He finishes and turns his chair around, presenting his back to Clayborn, essentially dismissing him.

Clayborn gives the man the evil eye before turning to leave.

"Oh, and Clayborn," Minten calls out, still staring at the wall.

"Sir?" Clayborn says, wincing while holding onto the door.

"Don't ever come to me with that type of bullshit again. Understand me? Just. Handle. It!"

Clayborn grips the door harder, a scowl on his face. "Yes, sir," and leaves, almost slamming the door, then thinking better of it.

Chapter 18

1862

TSgt Rees is watching the rear area as the Jeep bounces along the rough terrain. He holds on for dear life as the vehicle swerves and dodges around pine trees in the thick forest. He doesn't believe the men who were shooting at them are following, but he occasionally takes a quick glance over his shoulder. He listens to McAdams' curses. Rees has had enough of this.

"Airman Tucker, stop the Jeep," Rees orders, and Tucker complies.

The small squad exits the vehicle. Nionee begins working on McAdams' and Steele's wounds as the others scout the area to ensure there's no danger. Once the men believe they are secure, they return to the Jeep and watch Tucker and Nionee work.

McAdams curses again as Nionee begins removing part of his uniform to get a better look at the wounds. When he removes the shirt, he sees a piece of shrapnel lodged in McAdams's shoulder, another in his back. Both pieces are relatively small. Tucker grabs hold of the piece in the back, which he thinks is the worst of the two.

Montoya checks on Airman Steele, who is thankfully still unconscious from the earlier Jeep explosion. Steele's weapon had jammed and he couldn't clear it, so he grabbed his M-16 and was moving away from the Jeep when it exploded from the cannon ball strike. The explosion threw him several feet and left some serious burns and cuts on his body. Montoya isn't sure, but he doesn't think the burns are life threatening.

Nionee calls Montoya over to assist him with McAdams.

"Eric, this is gonna hurt, but I'm going to remove the shrapnel on the count of three. You ready?" Tucker asks.

McAdams grits his teeth and nods.

"Okay, one, two," Tucker says and pulls the metal shard out as quickly as he can. "Three."

"Ahhh! Dammit, you said three," Eric screams.

"I lied," Nionee says grinning. "Let me patch this up, then we'll get the other one out. How's the leg?"

Nionee rips open McAdams' pants leg and sees a deep gash where a piece of shrapnel sliced into Eric's thigh.

"The leg isn't bad, as far as I can tell. The gash is pretty deep. You're going to need a lot of stitches. But it looks to have missed the femoral artery, but just barely."

Nionee finishes cleaning and bandaging Eric's back and moves around to look at the shoulder wound.

"Sgt. Rees, listen, I'd like to give Eric some morphine. He's hurting."

"I'm fine," McAdams moans.

"You are not, so shut the fuck up," Nionee tells McAdams and turns back to Rees.

Rees nods. "Go ahead."

Nionee gives him shot of morphine, just enough to knock off the edge. Once he does, Eric relaxes. Nionee pulls the piece of metal from the shoulder wound and McAdams winces, moans, but doesn't cry out. Nionee finishes patching the young man up and they place him across the seat so he can rest.

Sgt. Shepard has a radio in his hand and is attempting to contact base camp. He walks around, getting louder with each call, not receiving an answer.

"God damn you, answer me. I know you can hear me!" he yells.

Rees walks over and tries to take the radio. Shepard yanks it away and faces Rees with a snarl, yelling at the man.

"Get the fuck away from me, Sarge," he hollers, walking backwards, away from Rees.

"They can hear me. Why won't they answer? I know they can hear me."

"Sgt. Shepard, you need to calm down. We are still out of range. We need to get closer, and you know it."

Shepard breathes heavily and looks at McAdams and Steele lying in the back of the Jeep.

"What the fuck, Sarge? What the fuck is going on? Who were those people? Rebels and Yankees? Look what just happened to us," he demands, pointing to the Jeep. "Look what they did Eric and Alex. Why are we here? What in God's name are we doing here?" he yells, anger almost overtaking him.

Rees walks over and stares at the bigger man.

"TJ?" No response. "Sgt. Shepard!" Rees says in a more menacing tone, "Get it together, sergeant. It's going to be all right. We're going to get through this ... whatever this is. I need you to hold it together. We need to get Eric and Alex back so David can look at them. Can you do that for me?"

Shepard clears his throat, spits, then nods, appearing calmer.

"Yeah, sarge, I'm good. I'm good. You're right, let's get them back."

The others ignore the performance, instead using the time to make a couple of litters. When Rees and Shepard get back to the Jeep, they find Steele's litter secured to the hood with McAdams' on the rear of the vehicle. The rest of the men climb in, finding what little space they can and sit. Tucker starts the Jeep and, once he's sure everyone has a good grip, drives off.

***

SSgt Bouvier has all the team members gathered in camp and they are listening to the message they received earlier from Gen. Lucas. After hearing it a couple of times, Bouvier turns the tape machine off.

"Okay guys, you heard it. Questions?"

"Who is this clown, Sarge?" McGuire asks, scratching his head before replacing his helmet.

"You heard what we all heard. He says he is the general in charge of this so-called Clio Project. What that is I have no idea."

"Sgt. Rees may have been right. Maybe the Clio Project is a time machine," Parks says.

"Youse can't be serious, still believing that load of horse manure," Tosseti chimes in.

"Well, what answers do you have, Airman Tosseti?"

"Well, I don't, but that doesn't mean it's time travel for crying out loud."

"Let's get back to securing the camp. The guys should be radioing in soon," Bouvier says, looking at his watch.

As the small group of men disperse, they hear a noise coming from the denser-wooded area to the southwest, followed a few seconds later by a gun report and, a split second, later a *ping* as something strikes the side of the Duck.

Everyone is stunned as they hear more gunshots, more pings and some thuds as rounds strike the ground and trees.

"Oh, shit!" Kriger and Tosseti yell at the same time, scrambling for their weapons and diving for cover even before Bouvier begins yelling for them to get their asses in gear.

Kriger sprints to Harris and Green.

McGuire! Airman McGuire, get over here and give me a hand."

McGuire is dazed, staring into the woods. Upon hearing his name, he turns, seeing Kriger attempting to lift Green. Coming out of his stupor, he runs over to help. They begin moving the wounded into the Duck and out of harm's way. Bouvier and Tosseti give them cover fire while moving behind the Duck. The armored vehicle gives them excellent cover as it reflects the lead shot away from them. Parks grits his teeth and forces himself up, painfully limping to the Duck. McGuire sees the man struggling and jumps out to help.

"Jeez, Sarge. Who's fuck'n shooting at us?" Tosseti yells just before unleashing a full magazine of 5.56 mm rounds into the woods toward an area where he sees tendrils of smoke floating up and around from a slight breeze. Not bothering to take aim, he is still rewarded with a scream.

Bouvier moves slightly around the front of the Duck and takes a couple of shots, not knowing if he hit anything or not. He can spot movement in the woods through the smoke. Staring harder, he sees people and they look like ... no, it can't be. Confederate soldiers??!!

He moves around the Duck as more rounds strike the metal and shatter or fly off in a harmless direction. With his back against the vehicle, he stares off in the distance, not believing what he just saw. He takes another peek and, sure as shit, the men shooting at them are dressed in Civil War Confederate grey uniforms, and they're actually firing muskets. The entire front section of the tree line is now filled with smoke from the weapons' black powder. Again, he ducks behind the armored vehicle and looks at Tosseti.

Tosseti sees the expression on Bouvier's face.

"What? What is it, sarge?"

Bouvier's mouth is slightly open in disbelief.

"Rebel soldiers," he says, eyebrows furrowed.

"What?" Tosseti asks, not sure he heard Bouvier correctly.

Bouvier looks directly at him.

"They are dressed in civil war uniforms and shooting muskets at us."

Tosseti snorts. "Come on, Sarge? You're joking."

"Take a look for yourself."

Just as Tosseti looks, he hears a blood-curdling scream coming from the woods. At the same time, he hears McGuire yell, "Holy shit!"

Tosseti steps back and finds McGuire in the turret atop the Duck manning the M-60 machine gun.

Kriger must be inside because the Duck's powerful engine roars to life. He hears Kriger yelling for them to get inside. Tosseti looks to Bouvier who is opening the passenger door and climbing in. Tosseti takes the hint and runs to the back and climbs inside himself. He pulls the hatch closed and yells at Kriger that they are all in. He then takes position at one of the ports and sticks his M-16 barrel through and stares in awe at the sight of civil war soldiers charging the Duck and screaming like a bat out of hell.

McGuire is still in the turret but drops down when Minié balls come too close for his comfort. Tosseti pulls him out of the way and hands him his rifle. He climbs up into the turret, checks that the M-60 is ready to shoot, and pulls the trigger. The distinctive chatter of the machine gun reverberates inside the vehicle. Holding the trigger down, the weapon releases its 7.62 mm rounds at a sustained rate of 100 rounds per minute with every fifth round being a tracer.

The results are devastating.

Tosseti aims just in front of the mass of human bodies charging toward them. When the rounds leave the barrel of the gun at a velocity of

2,800 feet per second, they strike the ground, sending up tufts of dirt, leaves and pine needles. He tilts the weapon up slightly, walking the red stream of lead until the rounds find human flesh. Each shot that strikes a soldier either kills him almost instantly or mortally wounds him. Tosseti begins sweeping the weapon left and right with nearly each round finding a target. The soldiers are so close together, he can't miss. *Fish in a barrel,* he thinks.

The bodies begin to fall and fly apart as rounds shatter arms and legs, removing them in gory detail. Men begin falling at an alarming rate, yet the soldiers behind the ones that fall keep coming. Some rounds hit the men in the head and the tops turn into a red mist and meaty gore as the blood and brains disintegrate, spewing matter onto those behind them. Tosseti winces as one man's head completely disappears in a bloody spray from a couple rounds to the face, but the body keeps moving a few feet as if not knowing the brain is no longer working.

The uniforms of the dead are more red than grey due to massive blood loss through gaping wounds. Tosseti's face is a mask of anger as he continues his onslaught. Soon the yelling stops and Tosseti realizes he has been screaming as well. He releases his finger from the trigger, the barrel of the weapon glowing red. Breathing hard he watches the remaining soldiers scamper, limp, and crawl back into the woods. Some of the men are dragging comrades with them, disregarding their own safety. Tosseti calms down for a second as he takes in the results of his handy work. His breathing becomes more intense and finally the Tosseti anger again lashes out.

"Fuck youse, you fucking arseholes. You want some more? Come on back, you fucking twits. Fucks with us, will ya? Ya fucking backwoods, whatever the fucks youse is." A haunted look comes over him as he realizes what he has done. For all his bravado, Tosseti has never taken a life. He is a brawler, a fighter, but in all his street fights, he has never killed anyone until today. Now he is staring at dozens of broken and bleeding bodies. He reminds himself; he is a security policeman, and he is protecting his life as well as that of his fellow airmen, his friends. He calms again on this reflection.

He jumps when a hand grabs his pants leg and yanks. He comes out of his self-pitying mood and returns to his Tosseti mood in an instant.

"Hey, fuck'n don't be trying to pull my pants down jerk off."

The Duck begins moving slowly. Kriger was in such awe of the grisly scene before him, he didn't think to drive off. Sgt. Bouvier was just as shocked and didn't think to tell Kriger to drive off either. When the shooting stopped and it became quiet, only then did Bouvier come to his senses and tell Kriger to get them out of here and to the fallback location. That's when he reached over and grabbed Tosseti's pants leg to get his attention.

"All right Matt, it's just me. Come down out of there."

Tosseti slowly drops down into the vehicle, leaving the hatch open to allow some air into the vehicle, which reeks of body odor due to the sweat from fear and adrenaline. It is mixed with the stench of the pro-pellant left over from firing the weapons.

Bouvier eyes Tosseti and notices a slight change in the man, but it only lasts a second before the old Tosseti comes back, but with a more subdued attitude.

"Hey sarge, you see them stupid wannabe soldier boys go down. Shit, fish in a barrel babe, fish in a barrel. They blew up real good, too. What were they thinking coming at us like that? And what's with the civil war garb?"

Bouvier stares at Tosseti for a few seconds.

"I don't know, Matt, but you did a great job up there. You took charge and protected the squad. I'm proud of you; hell, we're all proud of you."

When he said this, Kriger looks at Tosseti in the rearview mirror and nods. McGuire slaps Tosseti on the back.

"Real Audie Murphy shit there, Matt."

Parks grunts and gives a thumbs up.

Tosseti grins proudly. "Yeah, real Audie Murphy stuff. Hey Sgt. Bou-vier, ya think Sgt. Rees will put me in for the Medal of Honor or some-thing?"

Bouvier sighs, shakes his head and returns to the front seat.

"Sure Tosseti, sure."

Chapter 19

1862

Capt. Absher dismounts his horse when he reaches the destroyed Jeep, his eyes never leaving the mangled vehicle. As usual, Sgt. Baine is right beside him, also staring in awe at the wreckage, still burning from the ignited fuel tank.

"Sergeant, have the men douse that fire. I want to get a better look at this contraption."

The sergeant turns and orders the men to extinguish the flames, which they dutifully do to by throwing canteens of water and handfuls of dirt on the burning heap until it is reduced to a smoldering hulk.

Once the fire cools, the captain and sergeant walk near the Jeep for closer inspection. The captain tentatively extends his hand and touches the metal lightly, checking for heat. Seeing the metal is cool enough, he rubs his hand over a smooth section of the hood that is bent upwards, revealing a partially destroyed motor.

"My Lord, sergeant," he says, (he hears his wife's voice scolding him for using the Lord's name in vain) leaning in closer to see the motor. "I believe that is a small steam engine, a small type of train, or something similar." Squatting, he uses his knuckles to tap on a tire that is still intact and inflated. "My goodness, they have a wheel made up of some type of hardened rubber and, instead of spokes, they have a solid metal ... whatever this is that wraps around it."

Baine is busy looking at what is left of the M-60, still attached to the pole mounted in the rear of the Jeep, barely hearing the officer.

"Sir, look at this. It's one of those damn Gatlin guns they were shooting at us."

Capt. Absher stands and moves to the back of the wreckage to look. He smiles.

"Sgt. Baine, I think we just struck gold with this here capture. If our boys in Richmond can figure out how these things work, and can duplicate them, by God I think we may be able to whip the Yanks, or at least put us on equal footing if they have these in production."

Absher smiles broadly at the sergeant. "Have the men load this onto the wagon. We need to get this to the train depot for transport."

Baine salutes. "Yes sir," then orders the men to get to work. It is difficult at first as the Jeep is heavy. Soon, they work out a block and tackle, and after some trial and error, get the Jeep carcass loaded.

"Good job, sergeant," Absher says.

"Thank you, sir. We are taking this down to Kingston?"

"No, sergeant, head west until you locate the tracks, then north until you find the depot. Find Maj. Carter who runs that small depot. Those tracks are not in heavy use. I would not expect Billy Yank to be in that area." Then he looks at Baine and adds, "Yet."

Absher walks around the wagon inspecting it again. "I want this horseless wagon covered. I do not want anyone to see what we have. You will oversee its safe delivery. Take a couple of men and make haste," he orders as he is writing something on a piece of paper. "As I said, Maj. Carter oversees the train station. Here is a note for him. I'm sure he will want to see what is so damned important, and by rights he should. Show him, but explain that secrecy is most dire. I am sure he will understand and will do whatever he needs to ensure its safekeeping and delivery. Now go, and God's speed, sergeant."

Baine takes the note and places it inside his jacket breast pocket and salutes. "You can count on me, sir," he answers, then picks two soldiers to follow him as he climbs onto the wagon, taking the reins and urging the horse on. When passing the captain, he again salutes and sets out toward the train station.

***

The next night, Sgt. Baine and his escort arrive at a train depot being used by the Confederate Army. Baine stops the wagon and climbs down, ordering the escort to guard the wagon with their lives. The makeshift train depot is nothing more than a shack that was hastily erected, along with a platform for loading and unloading troops and equipment.

Baine asks a Rebel private where to find the major and he points to the shanty. Baine walks into the small building and watches the major cursing and shuffling papers, a cigar hanging out of the corner of his mouth.

Baine clears his throat. "Maj. Carter, sir?"

Carter doesn't even look at whomever is interrupting him. "Go away unless you're here to tell me the troops' transport has finally arrived after being five hours late! If not, then get out of my office!"

Baine isn't fazed in the least and grins. "Compliments of Capt. Absher, sir."

At this Carter stops and looks at the sergeant, then smiles.

"Capt. Absher, you say. How's that young scoundrel doing?" The major turns toward the sergeant. "Okay, what can I do for you sergeant? Need some supplies, I gather? I do not have much left. Still waiting on a train that should have been here quite a while ago."

Baine shakes his head. "No, sir," he says as he hands the paper to the officer.

Carter stares at the sergeant, then at the paper for a second before grabbing it and reading.

"What the ...," he says, then looks suspiciously at the sergeant. "Okay, sergeant ...?"

"Baine, sir."

"Okay Sgt. Baine. Have you read this note?"

"No, sir. I have not," Baine replies a little indignantly.

The major nods. "Well, let's go see this important find you have."

Carter moves out of the door, past Baine, and stands on the platform looking around. He doesn't see the wagon and turns to Sgt. Baine, who walks up to him and points to the area where the wagon is somewhat hidden.

"This way, sir." The major follows him down the stairs, toward the wagon.

When they arrive, Baine tells the guards to lift the cover enough so the major can look underneath. Once they do, Carter leans in for a glimpse.

"Can't see diddly squat. Go grab me that lantern over there," he says, pointing to a lantern hanging on a pole not too far away. Baine looks at one of the guards and jerks his head in the direction of the lantern. The young soldier runs over, grabs the lantern and returns, holding it up so the major can get a better look at the Jeep.

When the light hits the metal, revealing a tire and part of the motor, Carter's eyes widen. He reaches in and reverently strokes the metal, trying to understand what he is seeing. He takes the lantern from the soldier and uses it for closer inspection. Satisfied, he steps back and looks at Baine.

"Sergeant, what am I looking at?"

Baine explains the happenings of the day up to him leaving with the Jeep.

"If this is true, then you just may have given us an advantage over the blue bellies. Good job, sergeant. Now, what is the plan?"

"Sir, Capt. Absher said I was to bring it here, where you could secure it and he thought you would best know how to get it to Richmond."

Carter thinks for a minute, then nods. "Yes, yes. I can do that. Take the wagon over there, sergeant," he says, pointing to the adjacent loading ramps for the cars, "so we can load it onto a flatcar. I don't have anything to use for transportation until the next train arrives, but we can have it ready. I will send a messenger forthright with the information. I do not trust the telegraph with this. Now, get on up there so we can load and secure it for the evening. Once the next engine comes in, we will reroute it to take this ... this whatever-it-is back to Richmond."

Sgt. Baine salutes the major, climbs into the wagon and moves it to the platform where a flatcar awaits. The major instructs his soldiers to help and writes a message for his division commander, explaining in as much detail as he can as to what they can expect to be delivered. He gives it to a messenger and sends him on his way. Once that is finished, he goes to the flatcar to ensure the Jeep is secured and covered to keep prying eyes from looking. He gathers the men who helped and threatens them with court martial or firing squad if one word gets out about what they saw.

Once Baine is satisfied everything is taken care of, he tells the major that he and his men are going to get some food and rest for a short period, with his permission, of course. The major assures him the secret gift is secure and to go take care of his and his men's needs.

When Sgt. Baine returns, he can see the flatcar has been moved from the platform area onto a set of tracks about thirty yards away, parked on its own and away from the rest of the troops. He finds the major in his small office.

"Ah, sergeant. You get some food and rest?"

"Yes, sir, some food. I'm too nervous about the horseless wagon to sleep. My men, though, had no problem."

The major chuckles. "Ah to be young and ignorant, eh sergeant?"

Baine grins. "Yes, sir. If you don't mind, I'm going to wander down and keep an eye on the wagon. I will feel better when it is off my hands, but for now I want to keep an eye on it."

"Yes, yes, sergeant, by all means. I received a telegraph that said my next train should be here tomorrow, delayed as usual, so hopefully you shall not have too long to wait."

"That is good news, major. Thank you," he says.

He walks to the waiting flatcar and stands next to one of the guards.

"Quiet?" he asks the guard.

"Yes sergeant. Nothing is going on. May I ask why we are standing here?"

"You just never mind, boy. But be assured, it is important. One day you may know how important, but for now, you have no need to know. Just do a good job and keep it safe."

Clapping him on the back, he walks back to the major's office.

"Excuse me, sir?"

"Yes, sergeant?"

"When will this," he asks, pointing over his shoulder to the flatcar, "get to Richmond? Once the train arrives, of course."

The major thinks for a minute. "I can't rightly say off the top of my head. This ain't the regular railroad anymore. Could be quite some time. Depends on any hold up along the line."

"Okay sir, it's just that the captain believes this will help in our defeating the Yanks, if our boys in Richmond can figure it out, so the sooner the better."

"I quite understand, sergeant, and I will do my best to see it gets there as soon as possible."

"That is good, sir. I am sorry to have bothered you. Thank you."

The major waves him off and goes back to his business.

Sgt. Baine checks again on the soldiers guarding the flatcar. Satisfied it is in good hands, he decides to get some rest. He finds an area away from the noisy bustle of the train yard and sits on the ground, leaning against a pine tree, but still facing toward the wagon. His mind is reeling, and he thinks he won't be able to rest, but within two minutes his head is resting on his chest, and he is softly snoring.

Much later, Baine wakes suddenly, thinking he is under attack. He startles, then realizes where he is. He blinks away the sleep and sees the tangerine hue of the sun coming up. "Damn!" He curses himself for sleeping all night. He stands and makes his way to the wagon and sees the two guards still doing their job.

"You men go get something to eat and get some sleep. I've got this for now."

The grateful sentries leave.

While Baine is keeping an eye on the wagon, Maj. Carter walks over. "Sgt. Baine," he calls out. Baine turns toward voice and salutes the officer as he approaches.

"Sir, any word on the train?"

Carter nods. "That is why I'm here. The train should be here late tonight, or in the morning. It seems the engine has some mechanical problems, and they will not be able to get it rectified right away. I do apologize, and I will assign some more men to help keep this wagon under guard."

Baine shakes his head in disappointment. "I was hoping to get this to Richmond sooner than that, sir. I know it is not your fault, but this thing makes me nervous. I keep thinking the blue bellies are gonna come for it any time now."

"Do you think they know about it?" Carters asks, concerned.

"I do not know, sir, but there are spies everywhere, as well as scouts and patrols. I just don't have any idea."

"Well, there's not much we can do but wait."

"Yes, sir," Baine answers and salutes the major as he leaves.

Sgt. Baine tells his men to go eat and waits at the wagon until a couple of men amble over, informing him they were sent by the major. Baine leaves the two men to guard the wagon and walks over to where his men are having breakfast. When his troops see him, they hand him a plate with some fried pork, beans, and hard tack. Since they didn't have coffee available, they brewed ground chicory root, peanut and Dandelion flowers as a substitute. Baine quietly eats his meal, anxiously waiting for the next train to arrive.

That evening they have uninvited guests, and early the next morning those guests become quite a nuisance.

Chapter 20

1980

Capt. Smit is having lunch in the chow hall, talking with some of his subordinates about trivial matters ... cars, sports and such. He is smiling and being polite, but internally he is on pins and needles. He is waiting for a phone call; one he is dreading. Earlier he was ordered to place Capt. Henries under arrest and the man is currently resting his heels in a holding cell, awaiting his fate.

As if reading his thoughts, the overhead intercom squeals to life.

"Capt. Smit, you have a phone call in your office."

The man winces. Only important phone-call notifications are made over the loudspeakers. He nonchalantly wipes his mouth with a napkin, stands, excuses himself, and heads for his office. The walk is a short one, but enough to cause him more anxiety. He knows why he is being summoned. He puts on his best smile as he passes people and enters the front section of the security police offices. Airman Choi informs him that there is a secure call waiting. Smit thanks Choi, rapping his knuckles on his desk as he passes, and continues down the hall to his office.

He closes the door and moves to his desk, taking a deep breath before picking up the receiver.

"Capt. Smit," he says.

"Smit, Sen. Minten."

Smit shuts his eyes and squeezes the bridge of his nose between his thumb and forefinger, trying to ward off a headache.

"Yes, senator?"

"Smit, what the hell is going on down there? Why is my nephew in lockup?"

"Sir, he's being charged ..." he tries to say, but the inevitable, abrupt interruption cuts him off. Smits sighs.

"I don't give a flying fuck what he's being charged with Smit! I want to know why he's in jail!"

Smit attempts to calm himself; he hates this man and wishes he had never gotten involved with him.

"Sir, I don't know the details. I was called into the general's office and told to place him under arrest. The general told me what to charge him with, and that's what I did."

Smit waits for more abuse, but none comes. The phone is quiet, and he is beginning to think he might have lost the connection. A few more seconds tick by before Minten speaks.

"Capt. Smit. I do not care what he did. He is going to be released. Do you understand me?"

"Sir, I can't ..."

"DON'T!" Minten screams. Then, in a calmer, more menacing tone, he says, "Don't you dare tell me that you can't, captain. You will be receiving orders that give you permission to release him and I expect them to be followed."

"But sir."

"No, captain. Don't 'but sir' me. Never 'but sir' me. Now shut up and listen. You will receive orders from Gen. Lucas. Capt. Henries is to be released pending, I don't know, his trial or whatever it is you call the damned thing. Anyway, he is to be released on his own recognizance. Being an officer and a gentleman, his word is gold. Got it?"

"I don't know about this, senator."

"God dammit, you're not listening to me. It will happen or, by God, I'll have your ass. You know what I'm capable of, captain. I put you there and I can take you out, but not in a good way. Am I making myself heard, captain?"

"Sir, are you threatening me?" Smit asks, feeling a flash of irritation.

"My good captain, what do you think? You are just a small cog in my giant machine, and cogs wear out their usefulness. They get replaced and discarded, never to be seen again, if you get my drift. Now, get my nephew out of jail. I will send the paperwork over shortly. It will have the general's signature, and it will be sent when he has gone for the night, so you don't have to check with him. Get it done, captain. I'm counting on you," Minten states, abruptly hanging up.

Smit holds the phone for a few seconds, then drops it into the cradle. Growing more agitated, he snatches up the phone, yanks the cord out of the wall as he screams and throws the phone across the room.

One knock on the door and it is flung open. Senior Airman Choi is standing there with his hand on his .38. He sees Capt. Smit, then does a quick check of the room, doesn't see any danger, and looks back at the captain. Smit has his hands on his hips and is breathing heavily, eyes shut. He slowly opens them and, raising both hands, he gives Choi the calm down gesture. Choi removes his hand from his weapon.

"You okay, sir? Sorry, I heard you yelling and then a crash. I thought you were under duress."

"No, no, Airman Choi. No, all is good. Sorry. The phone call didn't ... well, never mind. I'm fine. You can go. Please, shut the door. Thank you. Good response though," he says with a dry smile and a double thumbs up.

Choi warily watches the captain for a couple more seconds then shuts the door. Choi sighs. *Wait till the guys hear about this,* he thinks as he walks back to his desk.

Smit watches the door close, looks at his thumbs up and shakes his head. "Really, a double thumbs up?" he asks himself, then pulls his chair out and sits. All manner of thoughts run through his head. What has he gotten himself into? What is he going to do? Does he do what the senator tells him to do and take a chance on being caught and arrested, jailed, court martialed, dishonorable discharge, or worse - Fort Leavenworth - or should he disobey the senator and have the same thing happen, plus the added bonus of possibly being assassinated? This makes the decision for him.

An hour later his phone buzzes and it's Airman Choi.

"Sir, there's a fax for you in the Crypto office. Your eyes only."

"Thank you, Airman Choi," he replies, hangs up and exits his office. Smit takes the stairs to the next floor and enters the Crypto office. Opening the door a staff sergeant greets him and hands him a release form. Smit dutifully signs the form and receives an envelope.

Smit opens the envelope and removes the single sheet of paper with the release information for Capt. Henries, signed by Gen. Lucas. Smit looks at the sergeant who is watching, thanks him and, still reading the orders, exits the room. He goes directly to the holding cell area and shows the orders to the on-duty Non-Commissioned Officer in Charge. The technical sergeant reads the order, calls one of the guards and tells him to release the captain from his cell.

Capt. Henries is sitting on the lower section of a bunk bed, his elbows resting on his knees, his head down. The man is sad, angry, self-pitying, and scared all at the same time. *How did this happen? I didn't do anything wrong. That asshole chief master sergeant and that jackass general did this to me. They've had it out for me since I got here,* he unrealistically thinks.

Henries is trying to come up with a plan or, more likely, an excuse to give to his uncle. Somehow, he must place the blame on those in charge of the project. Maybe he could say that the general knew that Henries was Minten's nephew, so they set him up to make him and his uncle look bad. Yes, that could work.

Before he can continue concocting his scheme, the outer cell door opens with a clang, and a guard walks in.

"You're being released, captain," the guard says, opening the cell door. Once open he points to the open outer door. "Through there, sir. You can get your belongings in the next room."

Henries sits there for a few seconds, stunned. *Is this some kind of joke or maybe a test?* He thinks, then jumps up and scurries out of the cell. After he gathers what little things he had in his possession at the time of his arrest, he walks into the main room and sees Capt. Smit.

"Capt. Henries, come with me," Smit says. He walks out of the office, Henries in tow.

"What's going on? Why am I being released?"

"Orders," Smit says and continues walking.

"Where are we going?"

"We received orders to release you, so I am taking you to the Bank gate where you will be released."

Henries is still confused.

"Okay, then what?"

Smit turns, takes a step toward the man and, with narrowed eyes, looks directly at Henries.

"Captain, I don't give a damn what you do then. Go home, go get drunk, run to your uncle, die. I don't care. All I know is that once you are out of that gate, you better make yourself scarce."

"And just what does that mean?" Henries asks angrily.

Smit snorts in disgust, then continues walking, ignoring Henries the rest of the way, refusing to talk or answer any more questions. True to his word, he takes Henries to the Bank's main gate and sets him free.

Henries looks dumbfounded, and keeps looking over his shoulder, waiting for something to happen. What if the SPs suddenly know he shouldn't be out and chase him down. Or worse, shoot him? He becomes afraid and begins to trot down the road toward the main base, continuing to look behind himself every so often. He knows he has miles to go before he can even see the lights of the main base, but, once there, he can make some calls and get to relative safety.

Chapter 21

1980

Rees and Chief Black escort the young women onto the base and drive straight to Base Operations, located on the flightline. The plane that will take them to Pope Air Force Base is fueled and waiting.

The Chief leads the way, and everyone boards the aircraft and prepares themselves for takeoff. The C-20F or, commonly known as a Gulfstream IV in civilian terms, lifts off smoothly and reaches its cruising altitude rapidly. The flight will be a short one. Along the way the chief explains to the women that they will have to go through security screening. It will be more of a formality, but still a requirement.

Upon landing, everyone exits the aircraft and are met by a small group of security police officers, who will drive them to the Bank in two Jeeps.

The chief looks at the women. "Sorry, I guess they couldn't part with the nicer vehicles for our guests."

Everyone chuckles, the girls doing so more warily than Rees and the SPs. The party climbs in the vehicles and are taken to the Bank. Once through the secure doors, the group is escorted down several floors and exit the elevator on the security processing floor. As promised, the women are swiftly cleared, issued badges, and then ushered to the general's office.

"Ladies, make sure you keep these badges on you at all times, and please do not wander off on your own. Make sure that if you go anywhere, either one of us, Shelly, who you will meet, or a guard is with you," the chief explains as they approach the stairs leading to Shelly's office.

Shelly looks up as the door opens and smiles as the chief saunters in, in his usual manner.

"Hello, Miss Moneypenny," he says, throwing his cap on the shelf.

"No time for that now, chief, I want to meet our guests." Shelly stands to greet the girls.

"Oh, my, what a lovely looking group of visitors," she says, smiling.

Nora smiles and Skylar and Ivy flush slightly, still in awe at what is going on and a little embarrassed by the attention.

"Now, ladies, if you need anything, you come to me. My name is Shelly and, as I am sure these men don't have a clue about us women, I will take care of you. Now, would anyone like a refreshment, soda, coffee?"

The girls settle for sodas and Shelly informs the general the guests have arrived. Chief Black opens the door to the general's office and enters, followed by Nora, Skylar, and Ivy. Rees brings up the rear.

"Ah, Chief Black, Sgt. Rees. Welcome back."

The two NCOs salute, but the general waves them off, moving around his desk as he does to meet the women.

Introductions are made and everyone takes a seat.

"I assume the chief and Sgt. Rees have filled you in on our little operation?"

The women look at each other and Nora nods. "Yes, general, but we still can't believe it. I know there is something going on, I can't deny that, not after what we witnessed in front of our home. And I've been around the military my entire life, but I've never seen anything like this place."

The general shakes his head. "Yes, nasty business," he says, acknowledging the incident. "We are looking into that, and I can assure you that all of you are safe here. And as for here, no you have never seen anything like it because there has never been anything like it. You are in a one-of-a-kind facility. But enough on that for now."

"Thank you, general, but I want to see and understand what is going on with *my* Scott Rees," Nora says, while looking at SMSgt Rees, who is wearing technical sergeant stripes for now.

The general looks at Rees.

"Sir, I explained that I am not *her* Scott Rees. That I'm from the future."

The general shakes his head. He is still having a hard time believing it himself. He stands and opens the blinds that cover the large windows overlooking the control room.

The three women stand as one and walk over to look into a cavernous room filled with personnel scurrying about, walls lined with computers, large reels spinning, stopping, then spinning again, and the largest screen they have ever seen inside a building mounted on the wall.

The screen shows a small group of military personnel, most of whom they recognize. The men are standing in a small group talking, none looking pleased. Nora looks at the general.

"Okay, what are we looking at? I ... we know those men. They are in the woods somewhere. So what? They could be on maneuvers anywhere on the base," she says, then stops, walking to the window for a better look. Her mouth is slightly open, as if to speak, then she closes it. On the screen is Scott Rees, technical sergeant, talking to the group. Nora turns to look at SMSgt Rees, then back at the picture of him on the screen.

Turning back around, she shrugs. "Still doesn't prove a thing. You could be showing me a film you made."

Rees shakes his head. "No, Nora, that is a live feed from the year 1862. That is me ... well, another version of me."

The camera changes views a couple of times, showing everyone in the group, except ... Rees moves toward the window. His eyes grow wide as he realizes what he is seeing.

"Ah, general, can I have a word with you and the chief, please. And can you have them turn the view screen off for a few minutes. Please. It's important."

Everyone looks at Rees, a feeling of despondency overcoming him.

"Okay sergeant. What is?"

"Please. Gen. Lucas, the screen. Please shut it off and I'll explain to you and the chief."

The general picks up the phone to call the control room.

Nora comes to Rees. "Scott, what is it? What is wrong. I know you, well the other you, never mind ... what is going on?"

Rees places his hand on her back. "In a minute, Nora. I promise, but I have to talk to the general and chief first. I'll be right back." Removing his hand, he walks to the door, opens it and holds it open for the two men who glance at him as they pass. Rees shuts the door behind him and places a hand over his mouth and sighs.

"All right, sergeant, what is so damned important?" Lucas asks.

"Sir, what we were seeing on the screen is all of us talking about the deaths of McAdams, Parks and Steele. I didn't say anything about this before because I was hoping when I arrived and interrupted the experiment, things might have been different. I was hoping that those three men didn't die."

"What are you talking about, Sgt. Rees?" the general asks, concern showing on his face. Rees explains what happened when he took the team out for reconnaissance.

"Sir, as I said, I was hoping for a better outcome this time, but I did not see those three men anywhere on screen. I assume that the chief's theory about no matter what happens, a void has to be filled, so they must have been killed in this timeline, just like in my timeline."

"My God. What have we done, chief?" Lucas asks, his face drawn.

"Sir, we knew this could happen."

"I know, but shit!" he says and looks at Rees.

"Any more deaths I need to know about, sergeant?" he asks in a not-too-friendly tone. His anger is not directed toward Rees, but at himself and Rees just happens to be someone he can use as a release.

"No, sir. If the timeline hasn't changed, even though we tried, Parks, Steele and McAdams are the only fatalities. Green has a severe head wound from falling. Harris has some time-travel sickness, we thought. Tosseti has his face cut open by a saber. Sgt. Shepard gets shot in the leg, and Montoya gets a mighty concussion from a Minié ball to his head."

The chief realizes why Rees wanted to come into Shelly's office.

"So, McAdams is Ivy's boyfriend?"

"Yes, chief. I didn't want her to hear me talk about his death."

The general catches on. "Yes, very commendable and the right thing to do. I apologize for my anger, sergeant. You don't deserve any of it."

"No need to, sir. I understand."

The chief and general look at each other, then at Rees.

"You are their friend. What do you want to do?" Lucas asks.

"I'll take the women to another room and explain the situation, if that is all right. The conference room down the hall will work."

"All right. Go. Take care of this. I am sorry, sergeant. Really, I am, as well as angry, though not at you. I will have to have a guard stand outside the door."

"Yes, sir. Thank you, sir," Rees replies. He opens the door and asks the women to follow him.

Rees escorts the ladies to the conference room and shuts the door. A few minutes later the guard hears the women wailing and sobbing.

Chapter 22

1862

"Security 15, come in," the radio squawks in the Duck. Tosseti quickly presses the mic button, "Security 15. Go ahead."

"Security 15, Security 15 Bravo. We are close and coming in, three miles out," the voice says. "And have Kriger standing by for wounded."

Tosseti frowns. "Security 15 Bravo, copy, three miles out. Good to hear your voice. The lights will be on. Security 15, out," Tosseti finishes and leans out the Duck's door. "Sgt. Bouvier," he yells and sees Bouvier already moving toward him, pushing up his glasses.

"That them?" he asks.

"Yes, sir. Three miles out," he answers and moves out of the Duck. "Said to have Kriger standing by for wounded." He looks at Bouvier. "That can't be good."

Both men walk to where they believe the Jeep will be coming from and Bouvier yells for Kriger to join them. Kriger is checking Parks' leg. He finishes what he is doing, then he makes his way to them.

"What's up?"

"15 Bravo is coming in and we were told to have you standing by."

"I hear the Jeep," McGuire says. A few seconds later, the Jeep and all its occupants come into view. The Jeep jostles and bounces as it runs over depressions and rocks, finally slowing to a stop next to where the others are waiting.

Kriger swiftly moves to the vehicle when he see the two injured men. Cursing, he immediately checks on McAdams, then Steele.

"What the hell happened? Move these guys over there," he orders, pointing to where the other wounded are laying.

Rees walks over to Bouvier, lighting a cigarette on the way. "I guess from the mess we found back there," Rees says pointing his thumb over his shoulder referencing Bouvier's squad's battle, "that I don't have to tell you what we ran into."

"Rebel soldiers?"

Rees nods and exhales a cloud of smoke. "Found a few dead Union soldiers as well. McAdams and Steele nearly got blown to bits. Eric got some shrapnel wounds and Steele has significant burns, maybe a concussion," he says, watching Kriger work on the men. "What about you?"

Bouvier watches Kriger as well. "Group of Rebels came out of the woods like Banshees, shooting and screaming. We were able to get everyone into the Duck, and Tosseti," Bouvier says and looks at the man and chuckles, "well, Tosseti turned into a demon himself. Took the 60 and wreaked havoc on those poor bastards."

Rees looks at Tosseti and shakes his head. "So, we have an Audie Murphy wanna-be with us, huh?"

Bouvier laughs slightly. "That's what McGuire called him. Tosseti thinks he's getting the Medal of Honor."

"Bullshit!" Rees exclaims.

"I kid you not. He wants you to put him in for it."

Rees snorts a laugh. "Only Tosseti would think that." He looks around the area. "Right now, we have bigger fish to fry, such as what are we going to do with the wounded and how are we going to get out of here?"

Pinching the flame off the cigarette, he places the unused butt back into the only pack of cigarettes he has. Bouvier watches with a grin, Rees notices. "What? It's the only pack I have and there's no telling how long we'll be here."

Bouvier raises his hands in surrender. "Preaching to the choir, Scott. I'm in the same boat. Gotta conserve."

Bouvier suddenly remembers the tape. "Oh shit, almost forgot. You gotta to hear this," he says and jogs over to the Duck, retrieves the tape recorder and returns.

Rees frowns. "Where did you get this?"

Bouvier shakes his head. "Another story. Listen," he says and plays the tape.

Rees listens, then has him play it again. "What the hell? Who is this guy?"

"I don't know, but we got this right after you left. That's when we tried to contact you, but you were moving out of range. Maybe if we got it sooner ...," Bouvier says, his sentence trailing off.

Rees looks around. "Well, yes, maybe. Water under the bridge now. Maybe he knew somehow, but I don't get it. I don't get any of this."

***

Gen. Lucas and Chief Black are still watching the screen. They're listening to the conversation coming from the men on the screen. Lucas grunts and goes back to his desk and chair.

"Well, I guess sending that tape didn't work," he says dejectedly.

The chief is about to turn from the window when something catches his eye.

"Oh, my," he says, getting the general's attention.

"What?"

"Sir, look," Black says, pointing to the screen.

"Okay, I see two makeshift stretchers with two men on them and," he hesitates, "who is that?" pointing to a sergeant sitting on the ground with a broken leg.

"Yes, sir," Chief Black says. "We need to get Rees back up here." Black makes his way to the conference room, where he hears the faint sounds of crying. Hesitating for a brief second, he opens the door.

"Sgt. Rees, ladies, I think you may want to see this," and holds the door open for them.

"Chief?" Rees asks, confused.

The chief gives Rees a peeved look. "You may have jumped the gun, sergeant."

"I don't understand. Jumped the gun on what?'"

"Just come with me and I'll show you," he orders. Black leads them into the general's office, then points to the screen. It depicts the area where Airmen Green and Harris are lying. Rees' eyes widen as he sees Airmen McAdams, Steele and Sgt. Parks lying beside them as well, alive.

"Oh, shit!" is all Rees can say. "Oh my God!"

The chief and general look at Rees, who is staring at the screen where McAdams is groaning and moving slightly as Kriger checks the young man's wounds.

Gen. Lucas shakes his head. "You told us they were ...," he starts to say, then stops and looks at the women.

Nora turns to Ivy. "Ivy, Eric is alive!"

Ivy, who refused to look when she came into the room, sniffles and stares blurry-eyed at the screen, then moves from Skylar closer to the window. She places a hand on the glass. "Eric?" she says softly. "He's alive? He's alive!"

Everyone except Ivy turns toward Rees and stares at him.

"Hey, chief, general, Nora, I swear Eric and Alex were killed. I don't know what to say. I'm glad they are alive, but believe me, when we were there, Eric died in the Jeep from a bullet to his leg and Alex was killed by a blast. This is not what happened in my timeline. Look," he says, pointing to McAdams. "His wounds appear to be his shoulder and back, as well as his leg. When I was there, he took one round and it hit his femoral artery. We couldn't stop the bleeding before we made it back to camp."

"Also, is that who I think it is?" Lucas asks, pointing to the screen that now shows Sgt. Parks sitting on the ground with a makeshift tourniquet wrapped around his leg. The man is in obvious pain and is rubbing his thighs and grimacing.

Rees looks and a grin appears on his face. "Isaac!" he exclaims. "Ah hell, he made it." Then he looks closer. "Looks like he fell after all."

The chief takes everything in and starts tapping his chin with a fist, thinking.

"So, apparently, somehow, your arrival here has made a difference in how things turn out. But now that we see that Airman McAdams is alive, how does that affect your timeline?"

No one answers as they don't know what to say.

Rees look at the chief. "What about Parks? He didn't fall to his death? A fall from that height would have caused more damage than a busted leg."

The chief nods. "No, of course not. I will go over the logs, but I will take a guess that Capt. Henries may have gotten lucky and was able to adjust before they rematerialized."

"You mean he may have only fallen a few feet instead of the forty or so from the top of the tower?" the general asks.

"Yes, sir, precisely. As I said, I'll look at the logs. But for the time being, I think we need to work on what to do now."

***

Sgt. Kriger removes the bandage from McAdams' shoulder and checks the wound.

"Who did this bandage?" he asks, looking at the group of men standing around.

"Ah, I did," Tucker admits, walking closer.

"Good job with what you had available."

Kriger checks the other wounds, nods, then stands as Rees walks over.

"Sgt. Rees, Tucker did a good job, but these are serious wounds. If we don't get these men to a real hospital or, at least, to a clinic, they are going to die. I'm limited in my knowledge, as well as short on medication and equipment to handle these injuries. We don't have any antibiotics or real antiseptics. I don't know what else to tell you, but with these types of wounds, infection is sure to set in and then ...," he trails off.

"Gangrene," Rees says staring at Kriger, becoming lost in thought for a few minutes.

"Okay, we don't know exactly what is happening, but if I'm right, and we are in the mid-1800s during the Civil War, I will take a gamble and say we are where we were in 1980, only in the year 1861 or sometime around then. If that's so, then the town of Hendricks Hill is somewhere in that direction," he says waving his hand to the northwest.

Bouvier shakes his head, his arms crossed over his chest. "I know what you're thinking, but even if we are and the town is there, do you think they got a doctor or hospital? I wouldn't think so. Even if they do, 1800s medicine. Come on. Open wounds, burns, compound fractures, concussions?" he says cocking his head toward the wounded men.

Kriger stands. "Sgt Bouvier is right, Sgt. Rees. The doctors of this era were under trained, and they didn't find out about antibiotics for another fifty years or so. Plus, I'm running low on morphine."

Rees paces while thinking, stops and looks at the men.

"I still want to go into the town. We need some answers as to where we are and when. Nionee, TJ, Tosseti and I will take the Duck and head in the direction of the town. We can scout it out and, hopefully, get some answers."

Bouvier shakes his head. "I don't think we should leave again. You heard the tape, Scott. He warned us not to leave the camp area, and said we were in danger if we did. Look what happened when you left. Somehow that general knew something."

Rees smirks. "Well, the hell with that general. I don't know if he is even real. Did his warning advise you of those Rebel soldiers wandering into camp? Don't you think he might have mentioned that?"

Bouvier looks away and sighs. "Yeah, I guess he would have."

"Okay, now I intend on getting some answers, and this is how I'm going to go about it. We are just going to take a quick look and, hopefully, gather some info. I don't know exactly what, but anything we find out may be useful. I'm taking the Duck this time for better protection in case we come under fire again."

Rees looks around and tells the men to keep security tight and maintain radio silence unless an emergency arises. He doesn't want the radio squawking if he is near the town.

With that he and the three men load into the Duck and head off to Hendricks Hill.

***

Gen. Lucas looks at Rees. "Forgot to mention that battle, didn't you?"

Rees looks non-plussed. "I'm sorry, general, but there is so much information, I didn't think about that skirmish. I apologize, but everything was moving so fast when I arrived that I missed it."

The general crosses his arm and looks at Rees, then the chief. The women are still watching the screen.

"All right, I can accept that. But from now on, I want to know what is happening before it does. Maybe we can prevent any more casualties."

"Ah, sir. Things have already changed. McAdams, Steele, and Parks being alive is the main thing, and I did go into town. It is important that Rees still does, but I took Kriger and Tucker along as well."

"Is that going to make a significant difference?"

"I have no idea. We parked the Duck a little ways from the town, and only Kriger, Shepard and I went into town. Tosseti, Tucker and Nionee stayed with the Duck. That's when we ran into some trouble with one of the townsfolk and he was killed. That apparently did nothing to our timeline, but while we were in town, a boy came across the Duck. Tosseti and Nionee held him, didn't hurt him, just kept him there and entertained him with ...," Rees looks at the girls, then back at the general, a little embarrassed, "a *Playboy* magazine and some rock music."

The chief snorts, and Nora rolls her eyes. Lucas' expression remains neutral.

Rees shakes his head. "I know, I know, but it's Tosseti, sir. You have to know the man. Anyway, the boy's last name is Olsen. He has a great, great grandson named David Olsen."

The general pulls his head back in mild surprise. "You mean Judge Olsen from Dansburg?"

"Yes, sir. You know him?"

"I do. Very well in fact. Okay, you have my attention."

"Yes, sir. Anyway, young Olsen steals Tucker's beret crest and passes it down throughout the years. In 2019, after I returned, I was approached by a Sen. Olsen, another descendant, and he returned the crest."

"Okay, so what's the senator's story?"

Rees blows out a breath. "When Sen. Minten attempted to take over the facility, Chief Black escaped," he turns toward the three women, "along with these three ladies and the reporter I told you about."

Nora, Skylar, and Ivy all look at each other, not following the story completely. Rees continues. "We were in transit when Clio was shut down, so we stayed in a suspended animation, or limbo as we call it, for thirty-eight years. The senator became fascinated by the story of travelers from a different time visiting his ancestors, and when he came to power, he found out that the stories were true. The Clio Project had been shut down, moth-balled is a better analogy, and he lobbied to have it restarted. When it was up and running, we rematerialized in the twenty-first century."

"So, those men need to make contact with Olsen, or your timeline will not exist?" Lucas asks.

The chief takes the question. "Not necessarily, sir. If you remember, one of my theories is about the possibility of multiple universes. Rees' timeline might not be affected by the events going on right now."

Rees looks at the chief. "That is one theory, chief, but now that I'm here, I kinda worry if that is true. Of course, I am here, so ... oh hell, my head always hurts trying to figure this stuff out."

The general looks at the screen. "Well, there's nothing we can do about it right now."

***

TSgt. Rees and the team drive the Duck the few miles to town. They park the vehicle several hundred yards from the settlement in a denser section of woods. The men pile out and gather at the rear of the vehicle.

"What's the plan, sarge?" Tosseti asks.

Rees looks toward the town, then back at the three men. "Well, we know the town is there, so we'll take a look. Tucker, you'll guard the Duck while Tosseti, Shepard and I check out the town."

"Oh, sure, leave the black man behind, by himself, nothing could go wrong," Tucker muses.

Rees thinks about it. "You're right. Tosseti, you stay as well. Shepard and I can handle this."

Tosseti grows red. "Fuck that. I'm going with youse guys."

Rees stares down Tosseti. "Tosseti, you'll do as you're told. One thing I don't need is a loudmouth Yankee Italian Irishman yacking away in a small southern town in the mid-1800s. Now stay here and help Tucker."

Tosseti fumes and grumbles as he walks to the back of the Duck, opens the hatch, and sits. Tucker chuckles and shakes his head. "Should be fun, sarge, thanks."

Rees look down at his uniform, then starts unbuttoning his shirt to reveal a dark-green T-shirt.

"TJ, take the uniform shirt off. We might blend in better with just the T-shirts and green pants. Unblouse the pants, too, and leave your beret behind."

"What about our weapons?" Shepard asks.

Rees hands his M-16 to Tucker and leaves his web gear and .38 revolver on. He grabs the shotgun from the Duck and hands it to Shepard.

"Not perfect, but maybe it won't draw so much attention."

When both men are ready, they begin making their way toward town.

They cover the distance quickly and are soon at the back of one of the wooden buildings. Cautiously, they move through an alley and stop before the street opening. Rees glances up and down the dirt streets at the buildings. He leans further out and looks at the building on his immediate right, then steps up on the porch area. He keeps an eye out for trouble, and peeks through a large window. He spots a man behind a counter, and a teen-age girl walking into a back room. There are shelves with assorted goods, so Rees figures it for a hardware store. He thinks he can probably get some information here. Rees signals for TJ and they casually walk into the store.

A small bell chimes as the door opens and the man behind the counter looks up with a smile.

"Welcome," is all he says, his smiles falters slightly as he looks at Rees and Shepard. He recovers and his full smile returns. "What can I do for y'all?"

Rees tells Shepard to watch the door and then he walks over to the counter. The man notices the strange clothing, as well as the web gear, but doesn't say anything. Rees catches on and smiles back.

"Hello! Sorry to bother you."

"No bother at all, strangers," he says and takes a furtive glance at the back room.

"My apologies, I'm sure we look a little different from your regular customers. We're, ah ...," Rees says, not sure what else to say. "We're a special unit of the Confederate Army. We have different uniforms than most, to blend in with the woods."

The man nods, a little skeptically. "Ah, makes sense, I guess. Okay, what can I get y'all?"

"I know this may seem strange, but what is the year?"

"What?" the man asks.

"What year is it, if you don't mind?" Rees says holding his smile.

"You're telling me you don't know what year this is?"

"Please sir, humor me?"

"Ah, 1862," he answers, thinking something isn't right with these men.

Shepard turns from the door and looks at Rees, shrugs and turns back to the door window.

"August?"

"Yes, sir."

"Okay, great, and this is Hendricks Hill, I take it."

"Yes, sir, it is. I'm David Olsen, proprietor of this store," he says proudly, just as the girl walks back in. Rees smiles and nods politely. "Ma'am."

Mr. Olsen looks a little alarmed then grudgingly introduces his daughter, Sarah.

Shepard looks at the girl, then back out the door, grinning.

"Mr. Olsen, we won't take up much more of your time, but I was wondering. Do you have a doctor in this town?"

"Oh, sure. Doc Hayes is just down the street, about four buildings, on the other side of the street. You boys all right?"

"We're fine, just wanted to know in case something happens. Never know when you may find trouble and we're not close to any of our sawbones."

Shepard spots a man approaching and clears his throat. "Ahem."

The three turn at the sound and Shepard cocks his head at the door.

"Someone's coming," he says as he steps away from the door, moving to the side. The door opens and a man enters, greeting the Olsens then staring at Rees, not noticing Sgt. Shepard towering behind him.

"Mr. James, good day, sir. How are you?" Mr. Olsen asks.

James approaches the counter, taking furtive glances at Rees. Rees nods, smiles, and moves out of the way. James looks at Rees' outfit and finally rests his eyes on the web gear and holstered .38.

"I was wondering if you still had some of those fancy glasses for drinking? Might want them for my wife."

Rees walks over to where Sarah is standing by the door leading to the back room. Olsen watches nervously. James must have noticed and takes it upon himself to help. He draws his Colt revolver and aims it at Rees, believing him to be robbing the place or about to. He isn't sure, but something is amiss here.

Rees has his back to the counter and doesn't see the gun being pointed at him. James takes a couple of steps from the counter, pistol still on Rees, and raises it higher.

"Drop the gun!" Shepard yells, pointing the Remington 870 at the man.

The voice startles James, who turns toward the source of the warning and aims his pistol at Shepard. Shepard pulls the trigger at the same time as James and there is a tremendous *boom* as the weapon sends a load of buckshot into James' chest, flinging him back about six feet. His body slams against the counter, shattering glass and sending items rolling across the floor. The lead pellets rip open his chest, sending blood in a wide spray, blotches of red painting the walls and countertop with some landing on the Olsens and Rees.

James' shot is off target by several inches. The Colt's bullet strikes the large front window of the shop, shattering it into pieces. Shepard ducks to avoid the glass shards and scurries over to Rees.

Sarah screams and flees into the back room. Rees had turned at the sound of Shepard's voice, seeing the pistol in James' hand. He dropped to the floor and was reaching for his own weapon when the deafening shotgun explosion filled the air. He watched in slow motion as James was thrown against the counter, crumbling into a bloodied heap, his feet twitching in death's throes.

Rees slowly stands and looks at Shepard.

Shepard stares at the body, then Rees.

"He was about to shoot you in the back!" he howls in defense.

Rees stares for a few more seconds, then looks into the back room.

"There a way out of here?"

Olsen drops the glass container he was holding and shakily points into the back room.

"Window," is all he says in a shaky voice.

"Ah, shit, we got company coming, and one looks like a cop," Shepard yells and heads for the back room. Rees is already ahead of him, opening the window and climbing out, holding it for Shepard. Shepard scrambles through the opening right behind Rees. Both make haste down the alley.

Before they can clear the town and make it into the brush, they hear yelling and then gunshots from behind them. A few rounds zing past, motivating them to run faster. They flee in the opposite direction of where the Duck is parked, hoping to lead whoever is hunting them on a wild goose chase. When they are several hundred yards away, and a good distance from their pursuers, they hide. Soon they hear the sound of men shouting and running through the woods, away from where they are hiding. They wait a few more minutes, then make their way back to the Duck.

Rees is breathing hard and shaking his head. "I've, I've ...," is all he says and stands, taking deep breaths, "gotta quit smoking."

Shepard snorts, breathing hard as well. "Speak for yourself, sarge."

When they arrive at the Duck, they see Tucker has his rifle trained on them. He lowers his weapon once he recognizes them and shakes his head.

"Trouble, I take it?" he asks, spotting the looks on their faces and the sweat-soaked T-shirts, Rees's with a few spots of blood on it.

"Yeah, you could say that," Rees answers, his hands on his knees taking another deep breath. He looks up and notes a peculiar look on Tucker's face, then hears a young male voice coming from the back of the Duck, followed by Tosseti's gruff laugh.

Tucker smirks. "Yeah, about that."

Rees straightens, looking at Tucker. Curious, he walks to the back of the Duck and sees a boy, about fifteen or sixteen, dressed in clothing of the era, sitting next to Tosseti and looking at the centerfold of a *Playboy* magazine. Rees is dumbfounded.

Shepard comes around and begins to laugh, then sees the magazine. He reaches over and calmly takes it from the boy, who hasn't seen the new arrivals until that point.

"Hey!" the boy blurts.

Tosseti is smiling. "Hey, sarge. Look what we done found. Or rather he found us."

Rees is still staring at the boy, then looks at Tucker, who just shrugs. "Hey, you know Tosseti."

"Boy, who are you?" Rees asks.

The young man smiles broadly. "My name is Billy Olsen."

Chapter 23

1980

Capt. Henries walks for a few hours before getting a ride by a supply sergeant. It is early morning, and the area is void of heavy traffic, so he is lucky. As they near the main base, they pass an army military police (MP) vehicle and he tenses, nervous fluttering upsetting his stomach. They probably aren't looking for him, yet, but he doesn't want to take any chances.

Henries needs a ride to his apartment so he can make plans. He also needs to contact his uncle. The sergeant drops him off at the gate and drives away. Henries approaches the guard standing outside the shack and sees another guard sitting behind a desk inside. Henries spies the telephone on the desk.

"Good morning," he says, approaching the back side of the gate.

The MP notices the captain bars on Henries' uniform, comes to attention and salutes.

"Good morning, sir."

Henries returns the salute, smiles, and asks to use the telephone, official business of course.

The guard tells the other MP, and he relinquishes his chair for the captain, then walks outside, removing a cigarette from a pack and offering one to his partner.

Henries watches them as he dials the number to John Clayborn's home. Henries knows his uncle won't be in his office for a few more hours, and he doesn't want to wake him. But John, on the other hand, is his lackey and will jump when told to.

The phone rings a couple of times, then a raspy voice answers. "Hello?"

"Clayborn, this is Capt. Henries."

"Yes, I've been expecting your call. I thought it would have been sooner," Clayborn responds, all hints of sleep gone.

"You were?" Henries asks, confused, then thinks about it for a second. "Of course, you were. My uncle. I was released some time ago, but they made me walk from the Bank to the main base. I'm at the Honeycutt Road gate."

"I can have someone there in, ah, twenty minutes or so."

"Have them meet me on the outbound lane by the railroad tracks, and make it sooner than twenty minutes, damn it," Henries demands and hangs up.

He says the last part a little louder than he intended and both guards look at him. The second MP comes into the gate shack as Henries hangs up.

"Everything all right, sir?"

Henries smiles and stands. "Yes, everything is just peachy," he says, thanking the guards as he makes his way toward the railroad tracks. The guards watch him leave, both curious as to why his uniform is a little rumpled and why he doesn't have a vehicle. Something they will discuss later.

Twenty minutes later, Henries is in the passenger seat of an MISS vehicle and on his way to his apartment.

***

After releasing Capt. Henries, Smit returns to his office, gathers his things, and informs Choi he is leaving, but should be back in a few hours.

He decided he needs some rest before he has to answer to Gen. Lucas once he discovers that Capt. Henries is missing.

He drives to his home, about thirty miles from the base, parks, then fumbles with his keys. After a few seconds he locates the correct one for the front door. He enters his home, closes the door, and flips on the living room lights. Two men are waiting for him. Smit sighs, drops his briefcase, and can only stare at the two pistols aimed at him. He only has time to think, *Ah, so that's what a silencer looks like* before four rounds fling him against the front door. His body slides quickly down the door, which now has four bullet holes and a large swath of red blood streaking it like a bad Pollack painting.

***

"What do you mean he's gone? On whose authority?" Gen. Lucas yells into the phone.

"On yours, sir," SrA Choi nervously answers.

"What? I never gave an order to release Capt. Henries."

"General, I have the signed copy of the order right in front of me."

"I want to see Capt. Smit right now!"

"Sorry, general, but Capt. Smit went home," Choi explains.

"Well, get him back here."

"Yes, sir. Right now, sir."

Lucas slams the phone down and looks at the chief.

"What in blue blazes is going on here, Joe?"

The chief raises his hands in a gesture of surrender and shakes his head.

"Don't look at me, sir. I just work here."

The general gives Chief Black the stink eye. "Not a time to be funny, sergeant."

"I know, sir. Sorry, but we have other things to worry about. I need to get Clio operational so we can get those men back. We need to figure out what we are going to do about SMSgt Rees as well. When we bring those men home, I can't see us with two Sgt. Reeses on our hands. Plus, what are we going to do with the men when they return? We just can't pat them on their backs and say, 'Great job, boys. Thanks for letting us use you and getting some of you killed all in the name of science and national security.' "

Gen. Lucas paces. "I know, I know. You get to work on Clio; I'll figure out what to do about the other situations."

A little over an hour passes when the general receives a call from Lt. Munn.

"Gen. Lucas here."

"Sir, this is Lt. Munn, sir."

"Munn, I wanted to speak with Capt. Smit. Were you able to find him?"

"Yes, sir. I'm sorry, sir, but Capt. Smit is dead."

"What? How? When?"

"We couldn't reach him by phone or radio, so we dispatched a patrol to his residence. When the SPs arrived, they found bullet holes in the front door. They called for backup and searched the outside of the home. Looking through one of the windows, they saw Capt. Smit lying on the floor by the front door, unresponsive to their calls and in a large pool of blood. They broke in through the back door and checked the captain and found he was dead."

"Was it a burglary? What?"

"We don't know, sir. Local authorities and OSI are on the scene. Preliminary reports say it looks like an assassination. No bullet casings, nothing taken, no prints as of yet, nothing to indicate a motive."

"Jesus, Mary and Joseph!" Lucas swears. "All right, lieutenant, get me a report as soon as one is available."

"Yes, sir. Ah, sir?"

"What?"

"What about Capt. Henries?"

"Yes, thank you, I almost forgot. I want to see that order I supposedly issued, and I want Capt. Henries located and arrested. I'll contact OSI myself."

"Yes, sir, understood. I'll have someone bring the order up right now. You will have to sign for it."

"What for?"

"It's now evidence, sir. It's in an evidence bag and we must maintain a chain of custody on it."

"I understand, just get it to me," Lucas says wearily.

"Sir, one more thing," Munn says, then provides the general with all the information he has on Henries' release.

Lucas thanks Munn, hangs up, then asks Shelly to have Col. Grayson of the OSI call him. A minute later she informs him that the colonel is on the line. He picks his phone up.

"Ed?"

"Yes, Gen. Lucas. What can I do for you?"

"I've got a situation here that I need your help with."

"Capt. Smits' murder?"

"You already know?" Lucas sighs. "Yes. It is something that probably ties in. It seems someone forged my signature on a set of orders to release Capt. Henries from our custody. I was informed that Capt. Smit personally took Capt. Henries to the Bank's gate and released him. The guards at the gate said there was no one waiting for Henries, and, after a short phone call, he just walked off down the road in the direction of the main base. Not long thereafter, Capt. Smit himself left. I need Henries found and captured. I did not order a release. I'm having the order brought to me as we speak. I want to look at it for myself but would appreciate it if you could come get it and find out who did this."

"Of course, sir. I'll have an agent come right over and pick it up. We'll do our best to find out who made the forgery as well as locate Henries for you. Anything else?"

"No, that's it for now. Thank you, colonel. Talk soon," and Lucas hangs up.

A few minutes later, Shelly advises the general that Lt. Munn has arrived.

Munn enters the office, reports and hands the evidence bag and release form to the general. He takes both, signs the evidence bag and release, and hands it back. Turning his attention to the orders, he begins reading. When finished he looks at the lieutenant and shakes his head.

"Damn fine job of forging my signature. Someone went to a lot of trouble to ensure the release of Capt. Henries."

"Yes, sir. Anything else I can do for you, sir?" Munn asks.

The general is re-reading the fake orders and doesn't immediately reply. He finishes and looks up at the lieutenant, realizing he had been asked a question.

"Hum, ah, no lieutenant. No, that will be all. Thank you," he says, adding, "OSI is coming and will take this." He raises the evidence bag.

Munn salutes and, after receiving a return salute, he retreats. When he opens the door, Chief Black is standing there with his hand out, reaching for the doorknob.

"Oh, chief," Munn says, startled.

"Lieutenant," the chief responds and holds the door open for the young officer to move past him. Once out of the way, Black enters Lucas' office.

The general looks at the chief and holds up the fake orders. Black takes the orders, reads them and smirks.

"Good job, I must say. Who has the time, effort and need to do this, I wonder?" He looks at the general with a cheeky expression.

"Oh, we both know who and why. That's another problem we have to take care of, but very carefully. Just can't be accusing a senator of breaking the law. Especially one who is the head of the Council and has the president's ear," Gen. Lucas says dolefully.

"Any thoughts as to what you're going to do?"

Not yet. But I'm working on it," he says, then changes the subject. "You got some good news for me, I hope."

"Yes, sir. We are making headway on getting Clio up and running. Shouldn't be too much longer."

"Good, just let me know when we can bring our boys home."

Chapter 24

2020

Capt. Farnsworth, along with Sgts. Bouvier and Kriger are walking the different levels and corridors of the Bank, sightseeing since Farnsworth hasn't been here long and hasn't had time to explore. The sergeants are giving the captain a tour of some of the places he hasn't seen. The men drive a golf cart down a section that is on the same level as Clio. At about a quarter of a mile from the control room, they discover a door none of them are familiar with - CPX-1.

"What's in there?" Farnsworth asks.

Bouvier and Kriger look at each other.

"No idea, sir. I have never been inside," Bouvier says.

Kriger shakes his head, "Me neither."

"You're telling me there is an area you didn't know about?"

Bouvier chuckles. "I knew about it, but we don't come down to this area much. I just never thought about it."

"Huh," is all Farnsworth says, exiting the cart and walking to the door. "Curious. So, neither of you have been in there?"

"No, sir," both men say in unison.

"Owe me a Coke," Kriger says.

"Fuck off. Grow up!" Bouvier answers.

Farnsworth ignores the jabs between the two and studies the door.

"That's strange. I wonder what's in there?" he says almost to himself, then looks at the two sergeants and the corner of his mouth turns up in a devilish grin.

"Maybe we should check it out," and he reaches for his badge and places it on the scanner. Nothing happens. He tries again, then looks at Bouvier. Bouvier tries his with the same results. Kriger, the same.

"Now I am damn curious," Farnsworth says.

"As am I," Bouvier adds.

"I know who to ask," Farnsworth says. The men climb back into the golf cart and make their way to Col. Black's office. "Besides, we need to check on Scott's status anyway."

***

Capt. Farnsworth enters Samantha's office, with Sgts. Bouvier and Kriger right behind him.

"Hi, Samantha. How are you?"

"I'm fine, captain, and you can call me Sam. Don't be so formal. I only make Rees talk to me like that; keeps him on his toes."

"Ah, yes, Sam, and I've seen how you keep the good sergeant on his toes."

"Not recently, captain. Not recently."

"Yes, I know. We're working on it, but in the meantime, would it be possible for us to see the colonel?"

"Oh, I'm sure he is available for you gentlemen," she says reaching for the intercom button. Kriger, being Kriger has to interject.

"Hey, who you calling a gentleman?"

Sam isn't fazed the slightest and presses the intercom button. "Sir, there are two gentlemen and one asshole here to see you."

Kriger's eyes grow wide and the other two men scowl at him. Kriger shrugs sheepishly. "Hey, I was joking, Sam."

"And just for that, you now need to call me Ms. Johnson until otherwise so informed."

Kriger just stands there, mouth open, imploring the two other men to help. They ignore him.

Sam then presses the correct button on the phone and informs the colonel that the men are here to see him. The colonel acknowledges and she turns back to the officer and two sergeants.

"You may go in now," she says and gives the men a sly smile, then squints menacingly at Kriger.

Once they enter, Bouvier leans back and whispers to Kriger, "You're screwed now buddy, and you know she can probably kick your ass as well."

Kriger gives Bouvier a quick sneer, then straightens up as they approach the colonel's desk.

After reporting, Farnsworth asks if the chief can join them. The colonel says he sent the chief to his room for some rest, but he should be back in about half an hour. While waiting, the men have a drink with the colonel and talk about the project, Sgt. Rees, and the chief. The men are still curious about how the chief thought that sending Rees back to 1980 wouldn't mess up the timeline. In the middle of the conversation, retired Chief Black knocks and enters the room.

"Ah, my ears were ringing. Ya'll talking about me?" he asks, smiling, then walks to his favorite chair and sits.

The colonel looks at Farnsworth and nods towards the chief. Farnsworth understands the gesture.

"We are still wondering if you feel the same about sending Rees back. Do you still think it won't mess up the timeline?"

The chief clears his throat then leans forward, his elbows on his knees. "Yes, I do. But here's another thing about that. We wouldn't know if it changed or not. I still believe there are multiple universes out there and, no matter what Rees does, we will still be here and everything that is happening will still happen."

Farnsworth looks at the colonel. "Sir, we haven't heard anything about Rees. Is he okay? Are you bringing him back soon? We would just like to know what is going on."

Col. Black leans back in his chair, fingers steepled.

"As you know, we don't have contact with him right now."

"Yes, sir, but we're not just going to leave him there, are we?" Farnsworth asks. "I mean, can't you send one of us back to get him? I'll volunteer to go, sir."

"As will I," replies Bouvier.

"Me, too," Kriger adds.

The colonel raises his hands. "Listen, men. I know you are worried, but believe me, it will work out. I don't really want to send anyone else. It's already screwed up enough as it is." He glances at his father. "But we may not have any other choice. If it comes down to that, we'll decide who goes. I'm sure everyone on the team will want to go, but we'll get to that if the time comes. Okay?"

"Yes, sir," all three men reply, dejectedly.

"Ah, sir, we also came for another reason," Farnsworth says, changing the subject.

"Okay, I'm listening."

"Col. Black, we were driving down one of the corridors and came across a door that we do not have access to. None of us," he says. He watches for a reaction from the colonel and gets one in the form of a slight smile.

"I assume you mean room CPX-1?" the colonel asks, smiling slightly.

The men all look at each other.

"Yes, sir. It's on this level. CPX-1," Farnsworth tells him.

"Been waiting for one of you to ask about that," the colonel says as he stands. The chief stands as well. "Shall we?" the colonel asks, grinning, and moves around his desk and toward the door.

The three men look at each other in confusion, not sure what just happened, and without a word, follow the two men.

The colonel stops at Sam's desk and utters something quietly to her, then he and the chief exit her office. Farnsworth, Bouvier and Kriger, again, look at one another in confusion and proceed on, with Sam giving them a wry smile.

***

The five men are walking down the hall, the colonel saying something about exercise, when they are met by Sgts. Montoya and Tucker. Further up the corridor, Sgts. Harris and McGuire are driving a cart in their direction. When the procession gets closer to the door, they see Sgts. Shepard and Tosseti already there, standing by their cart. The colonel stops in front of the door and looks around at the men circling him, all with curious looks on their faces.

"Everyone here?" he asks, still looking around.

"Nionee and Green are missing," someone says.

"Okay, we'll wait." Everyone turns when they hear the sound of running footsteps and look to see the two missing team members coming at double-time down the hall, boots slapping against the white tiles.

"Whew!" Nionee says, catching his breath. "Sorry, I'll blame it on

Airman Green. He didn't do anything wrong, but I'll blame him anyway."

Tosseti can't resist. "I thought youse Indians could run faster than us white guys, yet we beat youse here."

Nionee takes a deep breath, straightens, and looks at Tosseti. "I'm a Native American to you, you sawed off ..."

The colonel interrupts. "All right, gentlemen, that'll be enough. You men can hash that out later. We are here to show you something you haven't seen. We aren't hiding this from you, we were just waiting for the right time to show you," he says as he uses his badge and security code to unlock the door. When he opens the door, the overhead lights blink, then stay on.

Before they enter, he turns to look at the men, a serious scowl on his face.

"Sgt. Tosseti?"

"Sir," Tosseti answers.

"If you and Nionee want to race, I'll place my wager on him," he says, the scowl turning into smile.

The men ooh and ahh and heckle Tosseti, who smirks, and bobs his head. "Yeah, yeah, yuck it up," and gives everyone the middle finger of both hands.

"All right men, come on in," the colonel announces and walks into the room with the chief, ten security force members and one spec-ops man following.

Chapter 25

1980

Chief Black has been working almost non-stop repairing Clio. Not being able to talk with the men in 1862 is frustrating, but not as frustrating as not being able to get them back to their correct timeline.

His mind is reeling as he ponders what they have accomplished, and how there are now two Sgt. Reeses, one in 1862 and the other currently here inside the Bank. The chief gets a chill and looks up to see Sgt. Rees and the three young women watching him ... or is it his imagination? Maybe they're watching everyone, he can't tell, until the woman called Nora waves at him. He waves back, then they all wave. He smiles and gets back to work.

Nora looks at Rees. "Do you think he'll get it working soon?"

Rees nods. "The chief is a genius, and it is his creation. He'll have it back up soon, if the timeline is still moving as it did when me and my guys were there. I'm just glad no one has died this go around." Then he glances at Nora, "I can't wait to get back to my timeline though, if I can."

"Why couldn't you?" Nora asks.

"When they destroyed my camera and transponder, they took away my chance to be found."

"But when the machine is fixed, can't they send you to the future?"

Rees thinks for a minute, then nods. "I suppose that's possible," and he look again at Nora. "Be hard to leave here. Leave you, I mean. Again."

Nora gives Scott a sad smile, then Ivy jumps in.

"Hey, Nora, just think, you can have two boyfriends at the same time. When one is away, the other can be with you. You'd never be alone. Think of all the possibilities, my goodness, the sex!" she says gleefully.

"Ivy, that's sick. Even for you. Yuck," Skylar says.

Ivy gives Skylar a blank look. "Huh?"

Skylar closes her eyes and shakes her head in resignation. "Never mind, Ivy, you're incorrigible. Let's go get something to drink," she says as she pushes Ivy toward the door.

"But I don't want a drink," Ivy protests.

Rees smiles as he and Nora watch Ivy. Nora lets out a breath. "That girl." Then she looks at Rees. "I'm sorry about that."

"No, no, that's just Ivy being Ivy. Wouldn't want her any other way. I'm sorry I brought it up ... about being hard to leave. It's just good to see you again, in this decade, I mean."

"So, I'm alive in your timeline."

Rees nods. "Yup, and you will do well for yourself. I'm not going to tell you any more though. I wouldn't want you to do anything differently."

"Isn't it already too late for that? I mean, from what you said, I have already made different decisions as far as what happened in your timeline and what happened here."

Rees looks intently at Nora. "I guess that could be true, but I think you will make the right decisions, just like the Nora in my timeline did. I think you will do the same."

The door opens and Gen. Lucas walks in. He stops when he sees Scott and Nora.

"Oh, sorry. Am I interrupting you?"

"Oh, no, sir. This is your office. We are the ones trespassing."

The general waves it off. "Nonsense. You all are part of this project, in some fashion or another. Now, how's it going down there?" Lucas asks as he wanders over to the window. "I see the chief is still at it."

"Yes, sir, that he is. I wish I could help, but I'd be a fish out of water amongst all the big brain matter running rampant in the room."

The general chuckles. "You and me both, sergeant. You and me both."

Rees turns to the general. "Sir?"

"Yes?"

"Nora brought up something. I'm not sure if it would work, but when Clio is back up, do you think you could send me forward in time? Back to my time?"

Lucas watches Rees, then looks at Nora. He turns toward his desk, pulls his chair back and has a seat.

"I would have to check with the chief first, but I believe that would be possible. We had a quick discussion earlier about you, and what we were going to do with you. I can't see us having two Sgt. Reeses running around the base. Be worse than having twins stationed together in the same career field on the same base. Worse because you would be exact copies of one another. Here I go again, thinking too much about this time travel stuff. Gives me a headache."

"I understand that completely, sir," Rees replies.

"We'll talk to the chief when he has time," the general tells Rees.

Chapter 26

Capt. Henries is livid. He was expecting the MISS driver to take him home. Instead, he is being taken to the airport where he is to fly to Washington, D.C., to meet with his uncle.

The car drives straight to a hangar where a civilian government jet is parked, engines running and ready for departure. Grumbling under his breath, he exits the vehicle. The driver looks straight ahead, showing no emotion. Henries slams the door and, like a petulant child, stomps over to the aircraft. He climbs the stairs and enters the aircraft. Even as the stairs are being withdrawn and the door shut, the aircraft begins taxiing.

An hour later he lands at Andrews Air Force Base, where he is met by another MISS agent and driven to his uncle's office. He exits the vehicle and is met by yet another agent, who escorts him to the secretary's office. The agent announces Henries' arrival and is told to send him in.

Henries straightens his uniform the best he can. He was hoping to go home and clean up. He knew he eventually was going to see his uncle but wanted to be presentable at least.

The agent opens the door for Henries, and he marches into Minten's office. Sen. Minten is leaning back in his chair, facing the door. His feet are stretched out in front of him, ankles crossed. Not saying a word, he stares at Henries as he enters the office.

Henries stands in the middle of the room, looking around like a tourist. "Haven't been here in quite some time. I like what you've done with the place."

Minten continues to stare at Henries, causing the younger man to become uncomfortable. He then he comes off the chair in a flash, closing the distance between him and Henries in a second, his face within inches from the younger man's. Henries involuntarily takes a step back, then stops.

"Tell me why I shouldn't take you off the face of the earth, you self-centered, sniffling excuse of a man?" Minten screams, his breath hot and smelling of Scotch.

Henries' mouth starts to open, then he closes it quickly as he sees the anger in his uncle's face. Minten's features are a mask of rage. "Don't even think of answering that question you, you total fuck up!" he yells, then turns and storms back to his desk. He keeps his back to his nephew and stares at the *I love me* wall.

In what seems like an eternity to Henries, but actually is only about a minute, not one word is spoken. Then he sees his uncle take a deep breath and his shoulders relax. Henries has a lump in his throat, his stomach begins to ache and, suddenly, he needs to pee. He jumps as his uncle suddenly turns to face him.

In a calmer voice, Minten asks, "What the hell happened that got you arrested nephew? This had better be good, because you have put a monkey wrench in my plans, and I don't like monkeys and I hire others to use wrenches."

Henries swallows hard. "Uncle, when the experiment was executed, something strange happened."

Minten takes a step forward, his head cocked and his eyes menacing. "I asked why you were arrested, not about the experiment."

Henries raises his hands in defense. "Yes, but it is part of the reason. Please, hear me out."

Minten slowly nods.

"When the time machine was activated, it worked, and the entire team disappeared, but there was a man lying on the ground afterwards."

"What man?" Minten inquires.

"It was one of the sergeants on the team."

"But you said they all disappeared."

"Yes, uncle, they did. This man was wearing a civil war uniform, a captain's uniform, and he had a beard and long hair. But it was one of the sergeants who just left."

"Well, how do you know it was the same man?"

"I didn't at first, but he used my name, told the general to stop me."

"What? What are you talking about?"

"He looked at one of the cameras and told the general to stop me. He said that Chief Black sent him."

Minten's attention is now piqued, but patience is not one of his virtues. "Stop babbling and get on with it. Go on."

"They flew him out of the MSD, the munition ammo ..." is all he gets out before Minten screeches, "I know what MSD stands for, you nitwit."

Henries is stunned for a second, then continues. "Yes, yes, of course you do, uncle. Anyway, they took him to the Bank. Later, when I was off duty, I was summoned to the general's office. When I got there, the sergeant was in the room. He had shaved and was in a flight suit, no rank. I didn't recognize him at first, took me a few minutes," he sputters, then continues. "There was a glitch with the system I was operating and one of the security policemen may have been killed," he says, then quickly adds, "It wasn't my fault, uncle, I swear, but they accused me of dereliction of duty."

"What glitch?"

"I don't know, the panel wasn't working correctly, and I couldn't adjust the altitude of the man in the tower," Henries lies. "Anyway, the general said I was being arrested for that and for espionage."

"Espionage, how ... why that?"

"Gen. Lucas said he knew I was working for you. That's why all of this is a mistake. They somehow knew we were related and had it in for me since day one," he stammers, hoping this will appease his uncle.

Instead, Minten's face grows red with fury. "And just how in the hell did he know that? You get drunk and start bragging about who you are and who I am? Big man on the base whose uncle is a senator?"

Again, Henries raises his hands defensively. "No, no uncle. I never said a word. I swear! I don't even talk to people when I'm not at my post. I go straight home after my shift."

"Are you sure you didn't go out to a bar, tie one on, pick up some base whore and brag about who you are, or run your lip within earshot of some of the base personnel? Come on, tell me -- you did a little bragging didn't you?"

"No uncle, no. I was careful. I have no idea how he knew, but … but that sergeant said to stop me. He just knew. Something. It was the same man who was transported, but he was wearing the civil war uniform. I don't know, but he must have known about the glitch and told the general. If he knew that, then maybe he knew about you."

Minten stares at Henries for a few minutes, watching sweat form on his nephew's forehead,

Good, he thinks, *just the way I like him. Maybe there is something to his story. Who is the mysterious sergeant and how much does he know? Can he know about my plans? Shit, what if he does?*

Minten comes out of his reverie and looks at his nephew. "I'll have a man take you to the guest house. Someone is already gathering your things and will bring them here. Now, get out of my sight so I can think. And don't you go anywhere but the guest house. Wait to hear from me, is that understood?"

"Yes, uncle. Perfectly."

"And clean yourself up. My God, you're a disgrace to that uniform. And you smell!"

Henries looks down at his soiled uniform, slightly embarrassed as well as angry at not being able to get cleaned up before his uncle dragged him here.

"I will," is all he can say as he walks out the door. *I don't see how Clayborn can put with that man all the time. I was only here a few minutes and that was enough for me,* he thinks, following the MISS agent to the car.

Chapter 27

2020

The men follow Col. Black and Chief Black into the cavernous room, each man taking note of the items in the room until they round a corner and see the Duck. It is perched on a platform about a foot off the ground. Some of the men walk over to it, patting it like it was a giant pet. They touch the areas where Minié balls left small dents or scratches and they stare at the indentation where a cannon ball struck the slanted side.

Capt. Farnsworth and Sgts. Bouvier and Kriger stand with the colonel and chief, watching the others.

"I had completely forgotten about this," Bouvier says.

"Me, too," Kriger replies.

"We kept everything that was brought back with you," Col. Black says, pointing to the vehicle on the other side of the room, "as well as your weapons," again, pointing to a rack with M-16s, M-60s, and a cabinet containing ammo, LAW rocket tubes, and other assorted items.

"But that's not what I really wanted you to see. Come with me," Black says, walking further into the room.

A couple of the guys see them leaving and get the attention of those still walking around the Duck. The rest of the team follows. They walk into another room and see one of their Jeeps, also on a raised platform. It, too, bears the scars of battle and, again, some of the men wander over and touch the machine with reverence.

Col. Black, the chief and Capt. Farnsworth stand by the entrance, allowing the men some time to reminisce.

Nionee and Montoya walk a little further into the room where they see another platform, except this one is empty.

"Chief, what is this one for?" Nionee asks.

The others in the room stop and look at Nionee, and then at the empty platform.

The chief points at a small plaque. Nionee bends over and reads it.

"M151 Jeep. Destroyed 1862 by Confederate artillery," he reads aloud. He looks up at the chief, confusion on his face. "Ah, sorry chief. I don't get it. Where's the Jeep?"

By now the entire team has walked over and are staring at the plaque.

"Well, as you can see, it's not here," the chief tells them, "yet ..." This is met with a barrage of questions, which he ignores. "A team will be going back to locate the Jeep and bring it back."

"I still don't understand," Nionee says.

"We are sending a team back tomorrow to retrieve the Jeep."

"Tomorrow?" Harris asks, a little loudly.

The room once again erupts with questions from everyone until the colonel orders them to quiet down.

"Listen, men. For the last couple of years, I wondered why the Jeep was never a factor in the timeline. We couldn't fathom why it wasn't even mentioned in any documents. We thought that maybe it was abandoned and just rusted away or was covered by growth and never found. We weren't 100 percent sure where it had been left after your encounter with the Rebels. Oh, we had the general vicinity, and even sent search-and-recover teams to the area in an attempt to locate it, then the chief told me not to worry about it. He said that if it was never mentioned, then it was never found, so why worry? At first, I didn't understand."

"So, you say it was never found? That seems very unlikely," Bouvier observes.

The chief smiles at Bouvier. "And quite right you are, sergeant. The reason it was never found is because we found it and brought it back here."

"What are you talking about, chief?" Shepard asks. "If we went and got it, why ain't it here? You put it someplace else?"

"No, Sgt. Shepard. We brought it here ... tomorrow," he finishes and looks around at the stunned looks on the squad members' faces.

"Tomorrow? Why tomorrow?" Montoya asks.

The chief smiles. "Well, Rees and I talked about it, and he said that when I thought it was time, I should send you back to get him and the Jeep. Well, I think it's time."

Everyone is bewildered, except the colonel and chief.

They watch the men, understanding their puzzlement. Then the questions begin.

"What are you talking about, chief?" Bouvier asks.

"How would you know?" TJ shouts.

"Where is he?" Kriger implores.

"Just what are we talking about?" Tucker asks.

The colonel moves further into the room and orders quiet.

"Okay, men. I know this is a shock. Believe me when I say it was for me as well, and it will be explained to all of you. But first we need to get a team ready to go. Once this mission is over and we have retrieved the Jeep and Sgt. Rees, the entire situation will be explained. Hopefully with Rees filling in a lot of the blanks for all of us."

While the colonel informs the men, he can see they want to push the questioning further but have enough discipline not to. The colonel checks his watch and glances at the chief. Chief Black steps in.

"Okay guys, we can carry on more about this later, but right now we need to prepare a team for departure as well as inform Miss Kelly and Sgt. McGregor that they will be going home. I know you still want answers and I know all of you want to go on this mission. Answers will be forthcoming, but not all of you will be going on the mission. You all will be involved with this in some way or another, but only a few will be transported. I will hand out assignments as soon as I can. I want everyone to be prepared for tomorrow."

Col. Black takes over. "Capt. Farnsworth, Sgt. Bouvier, Sgt. Kriger, Sgt. Tosseti, and Sgt. Nionee, I want to see the five of you in my office after we leave here," he says and heads out the door.

The small group comes to attention as the colonel leaves, then relax once he is gone. The men moan, then grudgingly disperse from the rooms that contain some of their history.

***

The colonel, chief, Farnsworth, and the others walk up the stairs and enter Sam's office. Sam looks up from her desk and smiles, faltering as she sees the serious expression on the men's faces.

They pass by her desk one by one. As Kriger passes, she reaches out, grabbing his arm. He stops and looks down at her hand, wiggles his eyebrows and gives her a coy smile. The smile fades as he receives a glaring look in return. He waits until the others file past him, then turns his attention to Sam, giving her a somber look and shrugs his shoulders. She releases her grip, and he continues on, shutting the door behind him.

Once all are inside, the colonel tells them to find a seat or grab a wall and listen.

"All of you will be going on this mission. The first priority is to find the Jeep and place a transponder on it, then find Sgt. Rees," he announces, carefully watching the men's faces. "Now, about how Rees told the chief when you were to go. I'll let him explain."

The older man looks each man in the eye. "I'll give you the *Reader's Digest* version for now. If you think about it, it will make sense. Rees and I decided to send him back in an attempt to stop the first time-travel mission. I knew he had arrived because, of course, I was there, so naturally I knew I had to send him back again," he explains and begins pacing.

"At that time, we did not know if he could be sent back to this timeline without it killing him or sending him too far into the future or any such scenario. Hell, we still don't know. Anyway, back in 1980 we decided to send him to 1862. Since I sent him there, I knew when to send you back to retrieve him. When he left here on the last mission, I knew what was going to happen. He didn't, nor did any of you."

The men in the room are silent and the chief is stunned. "No questions?"

Farnsworth looks at the men, then back to the chief. "Chief, of course we have questions, but I think we understand. I also think we will wait until we get back with Rees to delve deeper into this," he explains, looking at the others, who nod. "I take it you have a date for us in mind already."

The chief nods. "I do. You will appear not long after the Jeep was destroyed."

Farnsworth interrupts. "Chief, won't that be around the same time we took O'Toole back?"

"Yes, and that's the beauty of it. By the time you and the team find the Jeep, retrieve Rees and make your way to Mount Airy, the former you, all of you," he says sweeping his hand indicating the entire team, "will have already transported back here."

"I don't get it," Kriger interjects.

"You see, when you get there, Miss Kelly will have been brought back here. You will adjust your timing, so you arrive shortly after you already left. You will bring her back and no one will be the wiser. Even if you're late, you can say you took her with you for protection or something of the sort."

The men look at each other.

"So, let me get this straight," Bouvier tries to summarize. "While we are there, the other *us* will be coming back here? They are going to do the same things we are doing now? So actually, this is a time loop of sorts?"

"That's essentially correct," the chief answers with a grin, "and you'll really like this. You will also be there at the same time you were there the first time."

Tosseti looks lost. "My head is going to explode if y'all don't stop talking."

Everyone laughs and relaxes a little.

"Anything else?" the chief asks and they all shake their heads or say no.

The colonel moves behind his desk.

"I have already instructed Capt. Epstein to get your uniforms and equipment ready. Capt. Farnsworth, you will now be Gen. Farnsworth. After watching that general pull rank on you during your last mission, I think a general rank will make it easier for you to move around, along with an adjutant captain," he says, looking at Bouvier, "and lieutenant," he nods at Kriger. "As for you two, you will go as sergeants," he tells Nionee and Tosseti.

Everyone turns to face Tosseti, who is surprised to see them staring. "What? I didn't say anything."

"That's the problem," Bouvier says. "We thought you'd complain about being a sergeant and not an officer," he finishes with a smirk.

"Oh, hell no! Don't want to be no damn officer. You kidding?" he says, then realizes who is in the room. "No offense, sirs," he adds sheepishly. "Besides, I only like to complain when Shepard is around. Drives him fuck'n crazy, oops, sorry sirs, I just meant crazy, not fuck'n crazy, I mean."

"That's fine, sergeant," Col. Black says, stopping Tosseti from rambling.

Farnsworth looks at the colonel. "Where are we going, sir?"

"Chief?" the colonel says, looking at his father. "You want to take this?"

The chief picks up a remote and faces the large wall monitor. He clicks once and a map appears. Everyone stares at it for a few seconds. Chief Black walks over to the picture and points at a spot not too far from a set of railroad tracks.

"What you are looking at is an area where we believe the Jeep is located. We took a chance and sent a reconnaissance drone into the past to take some pictures." The chief presses a button on the remote, which changes the topographical map into an aerial map showing a sparsely wooded area. "The drone flew over this area where Sgts. Shepard, Tucker and Montoya all agree looks to be the spot where they were attacked. The pictures we obtained show the ground in the area had a lot of activity and you can see a scorched area. That may be where the Jeep exploded and burned," he explains, pointing to the spot on the screen.

He switches to a close-up of the area. "Also, the ground is torn up and it looks like there are wagon tracks moving away from the scene."

"Wagon tracks?" Kriger asks, moving to the screen for a better look.

"Correct," the chief answers. "And if you look closely, you can tell one set of tracks appear deeper than the other set. This, I believe, is because they placed the Jeep onto a wagon."

"Where would they take it?" Bouvier asks.

The picture changes again to show a small building next to railroad tracks, along with loading docks.

"This is, or was, a Confederate depot used to receive troops and equipment. We believe the wagon will be brought here. You will need to locate it, identify it and, once you are certain, attach a transponder and we will do the rest."

"And what about Sgt. Rees?" Kriger asks. "How are we going find him?"

Chief Black clicks to another view of the area. "We sent him about here," the chief answers, pointing to an area west of the tracks. "At the time, we did not know where the Jeep was. Rees had a pretty good idea, but we couldn't just drop him in the middle of an area swarming with soldiers, so, we decided he would be transported to this area with the hopes I would remember and send a team to get him."

"Okay, so we have a plan, and hopefully we can find Rees. What can go wrong?" Kriger announces sarcastically.

The colonel moves behind his desk and sits. "Now, if there are no more questions, you men go see Capt. Epstein and get your equipment. When you're ready, Capt. Farnsworth, let me know. I will let you all inform our guests of the good news."

"Yes, sir," Farnsworth replies, taking this as their dismissal. The men salute and leave the office. They walk past Sam's desk, and each man smiles at her. She looks at Kriger, who stops and looks at Farnsworth. Farnsworth looks from one to the other, then nods. "Not too long, Dave," he says and walks out.

"Well?" she asks, trying to look serious at Kriger, but failing. He can see the advantage he has now.

"Nothing. The colonel just wanted to have a morale talk with us. Probably bring the others in later for the same. No big deal," he says and sits on the corner of her desk.

She gives him a look that usually makes Kriger shiver, but not this time. She wants something and he wants her to beg. It doesn't happen.

"Sgt. Kriger. You know what I did before I got this job, don't you?"

He nods.

"Well, you had better start talking or you're gonna see what I am capable of. If I want information, I can damn well get it, so you better start talking or I am going to put a world of hurt on you. Now get off my desk and tell me what is going on!"

Kriger looks at her for a minute, wondering if she is serious or not, then decides not to press it and removes himself from her desk.

"Shit, sorry Sam ...," he starts to say and sees the warning in her eyes, remembering what she said. "Ms. Johnson. Sorry. We're going on a mission to get Scott."

She relaxes and sighs in relief. "It's about time, no pun intended. Thank you, sergeant, I appreciate that. I have been very worried about him," she says and seems to wander off in thought. She looks up at Kriger. "You bring him back, you hear me?"

"Oh, I plan on that S ... Ms. Johnson. He's one of the best friends I've got, and I don't let my friends down."

She watches his face and realizes he is just as concerned for Rees as she is. She nods.

"Okay then, thank you for the update," she says and goes back to work.

Kriger takes this as his dismissal, smiles again and opens the door.

"Sergeant?" she calls out, her back to him.

"Yes?"

"You can call me Sam again."

Kriger grins and starts to leave when she adds, "As long as you bring him back."

Still grinning Kriger begins to close the door but swears he hears a sniffle coming from Sam and opens the door a little. He starts to say something, then decides not to. He watches her for a couple of seconds, then shuts the door.

Chapter 28

1980

Rees slowly shakes his head in denial. Frustrated, he presses his lips together, his hands balled into fists at his side.

"No, chief. There has to be a way."

Just a few minutes earlier the chief explained that he couldn't send Rees to his future timeline, or, rather, he wouldn't.

"Sgt. Rees, listen. We haven't done anything like that. We haven't done enough experimentation to try that with a living being. One slight miscalculation and we could send you into a future that doesn't even exist. That or we could scatter you into oblivion, or put you into limbo. We just don't know and I'm not willing to take a chance with your life to do it."

"But it's my life, chief. I sure as hell don't want to stay here, as great as it would be. I foresee you getting these men back, and I don't want to be hidden away as my other self goes on with my life."

Gen. Lucas moves toward him. "Sgt. Rees, I agree with the chief. If we can't get you back to the future timeline, we can make you comfortable here. Hell, look at all you can teach us?" he explains to Rees, "some things that may help us with the Cold War or medical research."

Rees shakes his head. "And then what, general? I stay here, a prisoner, so I can tell you everything I know about the future? Oh, I'm sure that would work out. You ever read the book *Replay*? No, wait, you can't, it hasn't been written yet. Anyway, it's about a man and woman who keep reliving their lives. In one of their lives, they are being held prisoner by the government who wants information about the future. Of course, the government takes what they tell them and completely screws up the world by trying to change things. The point being, in that replay of their lives, they were kept prisoners the entire time, never free until they died."

Gen. Lucas stares at Rees then nods. "We wouldn't want that, sergeant, but we won't send you to the future either, and that's final."

"Well, what about fixing my transponder or camera?" he asks.

Lucas looks to the chief who, in turn, looks at Rees.

"The lab is looking at it now, but we don't have the technology to fix either of them. They were pretty well busted up."

"You can create a time machine, but can't fix a small electronic device?" Rees asks sardonically.

The chief looks at the ground and walks around the office, thinking. Rees watches him. The chief smiles, then looks up.

"Sorry, trying to figure out what we can do to help, but I've got nothing. I am sorry, sergeant."

Nora places her hand on Rees' shoulder. Rees looks at her and sadly shakes his head.

"Nora, sorry, but I can't be here."

"I can say I understand, but I really don't. To me, you're Scott Rees. In my mind we were just together a couple of days ago. I can look at you, then see you on that screen, but to me, that's like a movie, but you're real. I believe that there are two of you, but I just can't wrap my head around it. Sorry."

"No need to be. I get it. But when that Rees," he says, pointing at the screen, "comes back, he is the one you need to be with."

Nora leans back and eyes Scott, a mischievous smile coming across her face.

Rees sees it. "What?"

"Oh my," she says and laughs. "Do you have another girl in the future?"

"What? No. Don't be ridiculous," he sputters and looks away.

"Oh my God. You do. And here I was thinking I was the only one," she replies, laughing.

Scott turns to look at her. "You are, I mean you were, I mean, shit!

Nora."

She begins to laugh.

Scott shakes his head. "I don't have anyone. None of us do. We don't meet many people," he says, thinking he is just as much a prisoner in his future timeline as he is here.

"I'm messing with you, Scott. How could we be together in your future? I'd be an old woman and probably married or something."

He looks away.

"Ah, I'm married. Children?" she inquires.

"Nora, I can't tell you your future. I told you that. I can tell you that we are still friends. That's it, so don't ask."

She is still smiling and comes up behind him and wraps her arms around him, kissing his neck. Scott closes his eyes and feels emotion taking control of his body. She breathes into his ear and whispers something that causes Rees' eye to widen. He turns to look at her, but sees the colonel and chief watching. His face grows red from embarrassment.

The general breaks the awkward silence. "Sgt. Rees, why don't you two take a break and let the chief and I discuss what we can possibly do to help your situation. "

Rees cautiously nods.

"Good, good. Why don't you two go and talk, relax? We'll let you know if anything comes up."

The chief snorts at the unintended pun. Nora places a hand over her mouth, stifling a laugh, and Rees, well, he just becomes more embarrassed.

The general is puzzled for a few seconds, then realizes what he said, "Shit," is all he can say and, to cover his embarrassment, he calls Shelly to get him some coffee.

Chapter 29

2020

Capt. Farnsworth and his team make their way to the lab where Capt. Epstein, their resident mad scientist, or as Kriger calls him, Q from the James Bond series, spends most of his time. As usual they find Epstein tinkering with some project that none of them could possibly understand.

They approach the captain and surround him, just watching. The man is so engrossed with what he is doing he doesn't notice them. Farnsworth clears his throat. "Ahem!" This gets Capt. Epstein's attention.

He stares at the men, not really seeing them. After a couple of seconds, he finally recognizes the group and smiles.

"Ah, Capt. Farnsworth, Sgts. Kriger and Bouvier." He closes one eye in thought. "Sgt. Niomee."

Ray corrects him. "Nionee."

"Ah, yes, my apologies," he says and looks at Tosseti. Tosseti saves him the trouble. "Sgt. Tosseti."

"Yes, yes, thank you for that, again I do apologize," he says, still smiling, "I take it you are here to get more of my goodies for another exciting mission?"

Farnsworth nods. "That's right, captain. What do you have for us this time?"

Epstein motions for them to follow and he takes them to a wardrobe area where there are numerous civil war uniforms hanging in open lockers. Each locker contains the name of each team member.

"Looks like my high school football locker room," Tosseti says, walking over to the one with his name.

"I have updated and improved the uniforms. They are even more resistant to artillery fire. I took your old uniforms and performed an analysis on the damaged areas, and, I must say, you put them through quite the testing."

Farnsworth looks at Epstein. "Sorry about that, but it couldn't be helped. I will tell you though, they saved our asses quite a few times, even though we were bruised and battered from the results."

Capt. Epstein lifts both his hands and simultaneously shakes both index fingers at Farnsworth. "Yes, I know, and I have added some nano technology as well as strengthened fibers to assist with that," he says excitedly.

All the men stop examining their uniforms and turn to listen to Epstein. Tosseti looks confused. "Nana, what's a nana?"

Epstein is excited, "Nano, Sgt. Tosseti. Nano ... microscopic robots!"

"Huh?" Tosseti says, confused.

Kriger looks at him. "Nanos, Matt. Don't you watch or read any sci-fi stuff?"

Tosseti shakes his head. "Naw, that's Sgt. Rees' bag, not mine."

Epstein continues. "This material is made from a genetically engineered material, similar to a spider's webbing but far more resilient and lighter. Our scientists then introduced nano technology with polymeric amyloid, or spider silk as Prof. Fuzhong Zhang, the inventor, calls it. We were able to make a material that is stronger than steel and able to withstand a projectile larger and faster than what you were shot with in 1862. The material can even stop a cannon ball!"

"Bullshit!" Bouvier exclaims.

Epstein raises his hand to stop Bouvier from continuing. "I know, I know. What I'm saying is that the material can stop a cannon ball, but the blunt force trauma would still kill you. You would be smashed to bits, but my material wouldn't get a scratch!" he says happily.

Farnsworth strokes his improved uniform. "Well let's just hope we don't have to stop any cannon balls. Anything else for us?"

"Also, the material is super cool."

"I'll say. The uniforms definitely do look cool," Nionee says.

Epstein looks confused for a second, then shakes his head. "No, you misunderstand, the material is super cool. I mean, it's not hot like the other material. This material is better than wearing a nylon golf shirt! It will pull the sweat from your body and allow adequate airflow, and the nano technology makes it so that your body stays cooler or, if it becomes cold, it will become warm. It's modified to adjust to weather to keep your body temperature as close to 98.6 degrees as possible. Also, it resists getting soiled. Just a bonus that came with the technology."

"Well, that is a bonus!" Kriger says. "I hate a dirty uniform."

The others stare at him, and Farnsworth turns back to Epstein. "Anything else?"

Epstein is still all smiles as he walks out of the room and leads them into another, this one the armory.

"I've updated your weapons. The Colt Army 1860 pistol can now fire ten rounds. I finally had time to make it so you can use clips now," he tells the men, picking up one of the altered pistols. He gives it to Farnsworth, who turns it over in his hands. He sees the ejector button and pushes it, releasing a clip from the butt of the gun. Epstein takes it back from him.

"This is, of course, a little bigger than the 1860 Colt, but shouldn't be too noticeable. It fires just like any semi-automatic pistol in our arsenal today. Of course, I can't do anything about the clips though. You'll just have to keep them hidden inside your jackets. You'll find pockets that can hold several clips," he explains as he grabs a couple and walks out of the armory toward the firing range. "Follow me."

He points to a box of noise-cancelling ear plugs and each man grabs a set. He hands the weapon to Farnsworth, who picks up a clip and inserts it. He studies the weapon for a few seconds then figures out the charging handle. The entire top of the revolver slides back and, when released, a round is chambered.

"Like I said, it works like any semi-auto. There is no safety, so please be careful. I'm afraid the charging handle will lock back when empty. Sorry. I can only do so much. The weapon looks like a Colt Army 1860 from a distance, but not up close, as you can see."

Farnsworth nods. "That's fine, Capt. Epstein. I assume you will have a self-detonator in these as well."

"Oh, of course. Can't have people in 1862 getting their hands on one of these, now can we?"

"No, of course not," Farnsworth says. He raises the pistol and fires off all ten rounds into the center ring of the target. The charging handle locks back, and Farnsworth swiftly picks up a second clip as he is releasing the other from the weapon. He inserts the new clip, lets the handle slide forward and begins firing rapidly, again all shots inside the center ring.

Tosseti whistles. "Hot damn, sir, that was awesome."

Farnsworth looks over his shoulder at Tosseti and grins as he clears the weapon, placing it on the table. "Good balance and very well-sighted, Capt. Epstein."

"We do strive to please, Capt. Farnsworth," he replies.

Farnsworth looks at the others. "Anyone else?"

Bouvier shakes his head. "I think we should see what else is available from Capt. Epstein, then we can come back later and get some practice."

Farnsworth nods. "Sounds good." He looks at Epstein. "What else?"

"The earplugs now have intercom capability, so you may talk with each other for short distances, around one hundred yards, give or take." Epstein shows a set to the men. "Sorry, but without radio towers and such, that's as far as you can transmit."

He then walks over to another area of the lab. "The food rations are about the same. You all seemed okay with what you were given. We added a few more nutrients and vitamins, but that's about it."

"Just make sure you have a lot of hard tack. We can use that as a bartering tool if needed. The soldier boys loved them," Farnsworth adds.

"So did Sgt. Rees," Kriger adds, then shakes his head. "I mean does."

Epstein moves right along. "We still don't know why we couldn't communicate with anyone in the past. We have a lot of people working on it, but for right now it's just going to be one way for verbal communications. We have come up with a better typing system," he says, moving to a table containing several pocket watches. "Please, gentlemen, pick them up."

Each man takes a pocket watch and examines it. Epstein also picks one up. "Open them," he instructs, and each man does. The interior looks like the face of a watch, with the small second-hand moving at the bottom. The only thing they noticed was that the face of the watch did not look quite right. It looks like a projection of a watch face. Before the men can react, Epstein moves over to where there is a microphone and leans into it.

"Can you read this?" he says.

The men look at him, and he points to watches they are holding. "Look," he says. The men look at the watches and the face of the watch transforms into a black background with gold words scrolling across it. *Can you read this?*

"Oh, shit, that is rad!" Tosseti says.

Farnsworth looks at Tosseti, snorts, then turns back to Epstein. "So, you all can talk back here, and we will get the message on these watches?"

"The watch will vibrate when a message comes in. A little more discreet than carrying the obvious electronic device we gave you last time."

"This is awesome, Capt. Epstein. You never cease to amaze us. Thank you!" Farnsworth says with a wide smile of his own.

"Oh, that's not all it does," Epstein says beaming. "We added another feature. One I think you will like." He turns the watch over, turning the back about a quarter of an inch. The knob located on top and used to wind the watch pops up.

He looks at each man. "Press this down," he says, using his thumb to press the knob. "Now you can come back when you want."

"What?" Bouvier asks.

"Let me explain," Epstein begins and shows the watch to the men. He demonstrates the procedure again. "If any of you desires to return, all you do is what I just showed you. Turning the back of the watch ring a quarter of an inch is the setting for just one person. If you turn if further," he says, demonstrating, "the area of transport widens with each quarter of a turn. The maximum transportation range is twenty feet. This is in case one of you is incapacitated or, God forbid, loses his watch. This was Chief Black's idea. Not the technology, just the idea."

Each man takes a turn with the inert watch.

"My head is going to explode with all this stuff I have to remember," Tosseti grumbles.

"Ah, speaking of explode," Epstein says, still all smiles. "We've increased the explosive power of the buttons. We improved the Semtex and now use something invented in our labs called P166 or Pix. It is much more powerful than anything we've had before. We made hand grenades for you that look like canned milk, and smoke grenades that look like canned soup, so don't try to open the stuff to eat," he says, chuckling at his own wit.

He continues. "We placed notches on the cans, so you don't have to actually look at them to know which is which." He picks up a can of condensed milk and shows it to the men. "There is one a small notch located on the top, bottom and side of the grenades," he says, showing the notch to each man. He does the same with the can of soup. "The smoke grenade has two notches. Make sure you know which is which before using."

Epstein selects a can of condensed milk and throws it to Bouvier, who is startled. He fumbles with it for a few seconds, almost dropping it, but manages to hold on. He gives everyone who is laughing the stink eye.

"All you need to do is hold the bottom and turn the top. The center of the can will turn until you hear a pop," Epstein says and nods at Bouvier indicating he should do it. Bouvier complies and when the can turns about one quarter of the way, they all hear a pop.

"What now?"

"Oh my God, throw it! Throw it!" Epstein yells. Bouvier doesn't hesitate and throws the can down the range. It hits the floor, bounces twice then rolls a few feet. All the men drop, covering their heads and waiting for an explosion. Epstein doesn't move. The can fizzles, then makes a small *Pop* sound. A little smoke drifts out of the cracks and dissipates. No huge explosion and no shrapnel.

Epstein is chuckling. "Sorry, just a little laboratory humor."

The men, still crouching, look up at Epstein, then slowly rise. Everyone looks a little peeved, then Farnsworth starts laughing and the others join.

"Hell, professor. I didn't think you had it in you," Nionee says, still laughing.

"Professor?" Epstein asks, a confused look on his face. "Ah yes, because I invent stuff; good, very good," he adds, finally understanding.

"Is that it, captain?" Farnsworth asks.

"Yes, that was my grand finale, as they say."

"Okay then. Again, thank you."

Epstein nods. "Yes, yes, anytime. My pleasure working with you all," he says, walking away from the team. He stops, then turns and watches as they begin filing out of the lab. "Oh, and good luck to you all."

The men smile and wave.

Chapter 30

1980

Sen. Minten is pacing his office, waiting for his nephew and Clayborn to arrive. His mind is reeling with a new plan to take over the Clio Project. His first plan was good, but due to the incompetence of his dimwitted nephew, he had to scratch it. He just can't waltz in like he planned: going in under the guise of an unannounced readiness inspection, then methodically take over the entire facility. It *was* a good plan, a brilliant plan because, well, it was *his* plan.

His intercom buzzes and he presses the button.

"What?"

His secretary announces the arrival of Clayborn and Capt. Henries.

"Well, send them in," he tells her in the authoritative voice she is used to. A few seconds later, the door opens, and Clayborn and Henries enter.

"You wanted to see us, sir?"

"No Clayborn, I just called you here because I was bored. Of course, I want to see you!" Minten barks. Clayborn tightens his lips and thinks, *When will I ever learn?*

Capt. Henries stands beside Clayborn and, when Minten turns his back to move to his desk, Henries looks at Clayborn and rolls his eyes.

Minten pulls out his high-back chair and sits. He leans backs and steeples his fingers, staring at the two men like they are annoying insects.

"Oh, please have a seat," he finally says, bored with intimidating them -- for the time being.

Both men do as instructed and this time Clayborn doesn't make a peep, not even a thank you.

Minten eyes the men, then leans, the corner of one side of his mouth curls into a vicious smile.

"I have come up with a new plan to take over the Clio Project," he says, staring icily at his nephew, "and you're gonna love this, nephew. You get to see the inside of the Bank again."

Henries blinks. "I don't understand, uncle."

"Of course, you don't fucking understand, you boob. You don't understand much, but I know you don't understand now because I haven't told you anything. Now just sit there, shut your blow hole and listen."

***

Rees is sitting up with his back against the headboard. Nora has her head against his chest, kissing him as he strokes her head and back with his hand.

That was nice, Scott. You have changed. Seemed a little aggressive there."

He chuckles. "Sorry, it's been awhile."

She turns and looks up at him. "Oh, so you really don't have anyone where you come from?"

He smiles and looks down at her. "I told you, I'm too busy. I'm a senior master sergeant and in charge of some made-up section where all the guys are assigned to me. I don't leave the facility much."

"But you got embarrassed when I said something."

"Oh, that? Naw. The colonel's secretary, I mean assistant -- I don't dare call her a secretary! Well, she seems to have taken a liking to me. It's just banter back and forth, and it won't lead to anything. But let's not talk about that. I just want to stay here for a while and enjoy your company."

Nora smiles and sits up, facing him, the sheet falling away from her. She smiles coyly at him. "You going to talk or enjoy?"

Rees smiles as he moves toward her.

***

Later, Scott and Nora are relaxing in each other's arms, Nora resting her head on his shoulder.

"You know," Nora, says, "After a performance like that I could just forget about the other you and keep this you here."

Rees untangles himself from her embrace and raises himself up on one elbow to look down at her. His face grows serious as well as concerned.

"Nora, don't say that," he chides.

Nora looks up at him, her eyes wide in surprise. She reaches up to touch his face, "Oh, no, no, no, no, no! I don't mean that. I was, I was making a joke, I was trying to compliment you, but it came out wrong. I am sorry."

Rees lets out a sigh and looks back at her. He presses his lips in a sad smile.

"I am sorry, too. I didn't mean to get uptight. It's just that this has been nice, and I won't ever forget our time here. I miss you and if I can help the other me out of this mess and keep him from going through what I went through, I will do what I can to make it happen. Maybe you two can have a life together at least," Scott finishes with a depressed smile.

Nora gently strokes his face, looking into his eyes and realizing she is falling in love with *this* Scott Rees. She is about to say something when the telephone rings, interrupting her. Nora is silently glad for the disruption, stopping her from telling the man about her feelings and, possibly, regretting it later. She reaches for the phone.

"Hello?" she says and listens. "Yes, he's right here, Shelly," and hands the phone to Scott.

"Sgt. Rees," he says and listens.

"Yes, Shelly, give me about ten minutes."

Scott hands the phone back to Nora, kisses her quickly, and climbs out of bed. "Duty calls," he says, standing and looking at Nora with a tight smile. She grins at him and wiggles her eyebrows. He shakes his head and sighs, muttering, "Incorrigible," and makes his way to the bathroom.

Nora watches his naked backside and gives him a wolf whistle. Scott snorts a laugh. Scooting herself up against the headboard, she listens as the shower comes on and a different thought comes to mind. "Hey?"

Scott sticks his head out of the bathroom door, toothbrush in his mouth. "Yeah?"

"You haven't had a cigarette since I've seen you."

She hears him spit out toothpaste right before he laughs. "One of the after effects of time travel, I think. I haven't wanted one since I returned to 2019. No one smokes anymore, except TJ for some odd reason. But no, I don't smoke anymore."

"Well, good for you," she replies, watching his naked form as he gets in the shower.

She stares for a few more seconds. *Oh hell*, she thinks as a solicitous grin forms on her face. Throwing off the rest of the sheets, she climbs out of bed and heads to the bathroom.

Ten minutes, my ass.

***

The general and the chief are all smiles as Scott and Nora enter the office. Rees doesn't know if it's good news, or if they are perverts thinking about him and Nora.

"Sgt. Rees, we may have figured it out. We won't attempt to send you to the future, but we can send you back to 1862," the general says.

"Okay, sir," he says, puzzled. "But what good does that do for me?"

The chief stands and walks the room. "First, I have a question. When you finally returned to 2019, did everything you took with you make it back with you?"

Rees shakes his head. "No. Of course not. We left the bodies of our comrades, as well as their weapons, helmets, whatever, behind. Buried of course. Why?"

"Did you return with both Jeeps and the Duck?"

Rees has a confused look on his face and, again, he shakes his head. "I'm not understanding these questions, chief. What has it got to do with ...," he starts to say then is silenced by the chief raising his hand.

"Scott, please, hear me out. It may be important."

Rees shrugs. "Sorry, chief. Please continue."

"Thanks. Now think. Did you bring back all the vehicles?"

Rees looks at the floor in thought, then raises his head to face the chief. "Sir, I really don't know. I never asked about them and just assumed they were brought back. The Duck had some of the men in it, including O'Toole, so it obviously came back," he says, then furrows his eyebrows. "Didn't it?"

The chief shakes his head. "We wouldn't know."

Rees snorts. "Of course not. How could you?"

"We thought maybe you did. The reason I ask is that you probably left the destroyed Jeep behind. The cameras were probably all destroyed, so we wouldn't know its exact location. When we do bring the squad back from 1862, we will only be able to bring back the men, their equipment and the two remaining vehicles, using this scenario."

"Ah, shit," Rees says, finally understanding.

"Yes. The destroyed Jeep will have to be left behind."

Gen. Lucas steps in. "I could have another message sent back, asking them to return there and give us the coordinates."

The chief shakes his head. "Not a good idea, sir. They might run into more trouble by going back there. Besides," he says, and looks at the screen, "I have a feeling it's not where it was when it was destroyed. I mean, whoever was firing on them had to see it. I can't believe they would just leave it there without checking it out. And once they do, they will realize a trophy was just handed to them."

"But chief," Rees interjects, "Wouldn't that cause something to change in the timeline if the Rebs got ahold of the Jeep? Don't you think new technology would have been developed, like the invention of the car years before it actually happened? Or the South developing some technology that affected the war's outcome? I mean, even now, we would have noticed something, wouldn't we?"

Chief Black smiles. "That's why I asked you those questions. And yes, I would think something would have changed, unless one of my theories is correct and we wouldn't notice the change, but I don't think that's the case here. Anyway, that's where you come in."

Rees just stares.

"I think we send you back to find the Jeep, from here. You locate it and get a message back to the future. Now, the future me will know it when I see it and we will send your Capt. Farnsworth back to find you."

"Hell, yes," Rees says enthusiastically, then starts thinking, suddenly looking confused.

The general notices first. "What's wrong, Sgt. Rees?"

Rees isn't listening as he stares at the floor.

"Sgt. Rees?" the general asks again.

Rees looks up and realizes the general is talking to him. "Oh, sorry. What, sir?"

"Are you okay? You went somewhere for a second."

"Yes, sir," he says and looks at the chief. "I'm just wondering, chief, why is it that, if you know what is going to happen, you didn't say anything about this in the future?"

Chief Black stares at Rees, then shakes his head. "I have no idea, Sgt. Rees. Maybe something happens that keeps me from remembering, or maybe I decide not to talk about it. Maybe I'm trying to keep from changing the timeline even more. I just don't know," he says, shaking his head, "but I guess when you get back, you can ask me, huh?"

Rees watches the chief, still wondering why the man never spoke of this. He decides he will just have to get the answer at a later time. "I guess so, chief. All right, then. When do I go?"

"First, we need to figure out the approximate location of the Jeep. We can get a good idea of where you were when attacked, but we need to estimate the time between the attack and where they might take it. We'll work on that while you get ready to go. Clio is almost ready. If all checks out, probably tomorrow."

"Sounds good to me. I would appreciate getting my cavalry uniform back for the trip."

Gen. Lucas nods. "It's in the works as we speak. Should be in your quarters soon. We left everything as is or put the things back after we examined them. Some pretty impressive gadgets you have there, as well as the uniform itself, not a material any of our science boys have seen before. I especially liked the hidden pistol as well as the hollow heels. I guess whoever invented those liked that old '60s show about cowboy secret agents."

"*The Wild Wild West*," Rees says with a smile. "One of my favorites."

"Is that what it's called? I never saw it. I just remember hearing about it. Anyway, your uniform will be ready. We even cleaned it for you."

"Thank you, sir. I appreciate that," Rees says. "I guess I would like to see Skylar and Ivy for a bit, if that's all right with you?"

"Oh, of course. I believe they are in the chow hall. At least that's where they said they were going."

Rees looks at Nora. "Care to join me?"

"Of course," she replies, and, with that, Rees salutes and they leave the room.

The general and chief watch as the door closes. The chief turns to his superior. "Any word on Henries? Or Minten?"

"Nothing yet. OSI has been keeping me updated, but no sign of him since he left the main gate. I figure he is either dead or his uncle has him. I don't know which is worse," the general says impassively, then straightens in his chair. "So, Clio should be ready in the morning?"

"Yes, sir. The teams have done a great job and, after we run diagnostics and a few tests, God willing, she should be operational," the chief replies.

Lucas turns his chair toward the window, watching the view on the screen. "Good," is all he says.

Chapter 31

2020

Capt. Farnsworth is walking to Emma Kelly's quarters to give her the news about going back to her time period in just a few hours. Sgts. Bouvier and Kriger are on their way to inform Sgt. McGregor of the same.

Farnsworth nods at the SP standing outside of Emma's quarters, then knocks and waits for a reply.

"Please, come in," a soft, Irish-tinted voice says from behind the closed door. Farnsworth enters.

"Hi," he says as he walks in, leaving the door ajar for her peace of mind.

"Oh, Col. Farnsworth. How are you?"

Farnsworth smiles and lets the rank slip slide. "I'm well and I'm here to bring you good news." He watches as she gives him a quizzical look. "We are taking you and the good sergeant back to your time period."

The quizzical look turns to happiness. "Do you really mean it? I can go home?"

"Absolutely. In just a few hours, you will be back where you belong," he says, happy for her.

Emma jumps up and gives Farnsworth a hug. He is slightly taken aback, as he didn't think women from her time did things like that to someone they didn't know well, so he involuntarily tenses. Emma feels his body go rigid and releases him, taking a step back.

"Oh, I am sorry. I was just so happy ... I ... I am sorry, sir," she apologizes, turning red. "How impolite of me."

Farnsworth recovers quickly. "Oh, no, no. I just wasn't expecting it, is all. I was hoping you would be delighted with the news, so I'm pleased by your reaction."

"Well, as long as you don't think of me as being a hard tick," she says, still embarrassed.

Farnsworth isn't aware of that phrase, but can take a good guess. "No, no, of course not. Now, Col. Thompson and Capt. Wells will be here soon with your clothing and personal items," he tells her. "I just wanted to let you know first."

"And I do thank you, colonel, and I am so happy to be going home."

"My pleasure. I will let you know when it's time," he finishes, leaving her room and shutting the door behind him.

As Farnsworth walks toward the bank of elevators, he meets Thompson and Wells. Both female officers are carrying large boxes.

"Col. Thompson, Capt. Wells. I take it you are on your way to see Miss Kelly?"

"You are correct," Thompson replies. "Knowing you will be traveling through some rough territory, on horseback no less, we had some britches made for her."

Farnsworth grins. "Britches, huh?"

"I just like that word. Anyway, we figured she needed something a little more rugged than a dress, which, by the way, we had made for her, as well. Something she can wear when she gets home. That along with some other goodies and a carrying bag. Took a little doing getting the right materials and all, but we got it done."

"That is mighty thoughtful of the both of you. Miss Kelly is excited to be going home and I am sure she will appreciate the gifts. Now, if you will excuse me, I must get ready for the mission," he says, then notices Capt. Wells staring at him. She looks like she is resigned to what is happening but not happy about it. *For a shrink, she sure is bitter,* he thinks. Farnsworth smiles, nods, and turns to leave.

"I probably won't be seeing you before you leave, so good luck, captain," Thompson says to his back, then she and the captain make their way to Emma's room.

Farnsworth proceeds to the elevator. He takes the car to the Clio floor and heads for the colonel's office.

Col. Black is watching everyone make preparation for the departure. When Farnsworth enters, Black nods and waves him over. Farnsworth stands next to him and they both watch the commotion below them. They see the chief walking among the personnel, talking with some while pointing at various things in the room. The colonel chuckles. "He can't help it, has to give advice, or make corrections. But it is his baby."

Farnsworth nods. "A true professional."

"Speaking of professionals, your team ready to go?"

"Yes, sir. Just stopped by to let you know the guests have been informed and are getting dressed, and the men are in the locker room changing. I'm on my way to do that as well."

"Good. Your horses and equipment are in the staging area waiting for you. I'll be watching from here, so I want to wish you all good luck and God's speed. Be careful and do bring our wayward sergeant home, as well as yourselves." He reaches his hand out, which Farnsworth shakes.

"Thank you. Hopefully we'll see you soon," Farnsworth replies, releasing the colonel's hand.

The colonel raises an index finger for Farnsworth to hold a moment, then presses the intercom button for the control room. "Chief?" he calls, and Chief Black looks up into the general's office. "Capt. Farnsworth and his team are about to leave for the departure zone." The chief nods, then finishes his task at hand. Satisfied with the way the control room is running, he makes his way to the general's office.

"Sorry, last-minute preparations," he says, walking into the room.

"For my sake, I'm glad you're such a perfectionist, chief," Farnsworth tells him. "Everything good to go?"

Before the chief can answer, the colonel interrupts. "No, captain. It's never good enough for my dad. Like you said, a perfectionist. He would tinker with that thing until the end of time, no pun intended, and still find something to fix or improve."

The chief smiles at his son, then shrugs. "What can I say?" he says, then looks at Farnsworth. "This is going to be strange, sending you all back during the same time as when you and Rees are taking O'Toole back to Mount Airy."

Farnsworth nods. "You're telling me! I don't foresee us crossing paths, but it is strange."

The chief shakes his head. "If planned correctly, you will be taking the sergeant and Miss Kelly back just after your return transportation here from Mount Airy, so you shouldn't run into yourselves. Our guests will not have been missed for long. Just think. You, Rees, O'Toole, and the rest will be on the way to Maryland while you," he says, pointing to Farnsworth, "will be trying to find the Jeep and take Miss Kelly and McGregor back there as well. Wrap your head around that one."

Now it's Farnsworth who shakes his head. "No, Chief, I won't. I just want to complete the mission and get back. Hopefully this goes well and there's not another future me running around there trying to fix something we did wrong on this mission."

The colonel throws up his arms. "Enough, enough. You two are going to give me an aneurysm. Just go on the mission and get the coordinates of the Jeep, get our two visitors home and find Sgt. Rees. Now, get going, captain," the colonel orders and reaches his hand out once again.

Farnsworth takes his hand, then shakes the chief's hand as well. He salutes the colonel and walks toward the door.

"Again, good luck, captain," the colonel adds and Farnsworth smiles back at the two men as he leaves the office.

***

The ride to the staging area is uneventful except for Tosseti farting, laughing as he excuses himself, only to do it again. McGregor gets a kick out of it; the others, not so much.

"Whatcha been eaten lad? You smell like the sulfur of hell fury, ya does. We should send ya to the graybacks as a secret weapon. You could kill 'em all with that stench and win the war for us single handedly."

Farnsworth is shaking his head in dismay, pinching his nose. "Sgt. Tosseti, are you going to be okay? I mean, you could give away our position with that smell. Rebs won't have any trouble finding us," he says to the laughter of the others.

"Youse don't have to worry, sir. I'm fine. Just ate too many burritos for supper. I'm sure glad Miss Kelly is up front!"

The vehicle they are driving is a specialized armored passenger transport that has a separate compartment for the cab, which is sealed off. It's similar to the army's MRAP (Mine Resistant Ambush Protective vehicles). They allowed Emma to sit in the front so she wouldn't be crammed into the back with the men.

"I'll say! Hey, Matt. You just gave a new meaning to the word Boston Butt," Nionee says with a smirk.

Everyone laughs, then Kriger adds, "Our own human biological weapon."

All laugh even harder, except Tosseti, who tells the others to ... well, what Tosseti always tells people to do to themselves.

The vehicle bounces a few times, then slows to a stop.

"Thank God," Bouvier says as he quickly opens the back door, jumping down and moving away from the idling vehicle while taking deep breaths and waving his hand in front of his face. Soon all the men are out, doing the same, and Farnsworth moves to the front passenger door and opens it for Emma. She smiles as he helps her down from the seat.

"I wish we had these things in my time. Comfortable seat, cold air, my goodness," she says in awe, looking at the transport. "I will never be able to ride in a buggy again without thinking about this."

"No ma'am, I don't think you will either. I know I missed this luxury after a few days of riding a horse," Farnsworth says, taking her elbow and leading her around to the back of the vehicle.

Emma stares at Farnsworth for a few seconds and suddenly notices his change of rank. "My goodness! They made you a general. How wonderful. Congratulations," she says happily.

Farnsworth smiles. "It isn't permanent, Miss Kelly. We thought it might be helpful when dealing with the other soldiers. Last time, I had rank pulled on me and it cost us some time getting ...," he trails off, not wanting to bring up the memory of O'Toole, "getting us through the lines."

"I see," she replies in a tone that clearly indicates she doesn't.

Farnsworth changes the subject by focusing on the team. "Everyone got their stuff?" he asks. The squad replies in the affirmative. "Okay, then let's go," he orders and they make their way to where the horses and a wagon are waiting.

The horses are tethered to poles, each about ten feet apart. They have been blindfolded and given a slight sedative to help them during the time transition. Being this is only the second time they have transported horses, the veterinarian thought the blindfold and sedative would help keep them calm.

Each person moves in front of their assigned horse and sits on the ground. Emma and McGregor are looking around anxiously. Farnsworth walks over to assure them that everything will be okay.

"Listen, just relax, and close your eyes. There will be a shock-like sensation, nothing bad, and there will be some pressure on your ears," he says. "Sorry, but if you can remember from when you came here, it will hurt. Hopefully the pills you were given will work and you won't be any worse for the wear."

"Huh?" McGregor asks. "There ya go again yammering about things I do not understand."

Farnsworth smiles. "Sorry. You should not feel as ill when we arrived. Okay?"

"Yes, sir," McGregor replies.

Farnsworth kneels beside Emma. "You, okay?" he asks softly.

She smiles. "Could you sit with me and hold my hand when we do this?"

"Of course, Miss Kelly, it will be my pleasure," he replies. He sits and reaches for her hand.

"Thank you and, please, call me Emma."

"Okay, Emma," he says with a smile.

Farnsworth can feel eyes on him and hears the chuckles from the other men. He looks and sees Nionee, Kriger and Bouvier with grins. Tosseti, however, is too busy talking to his horse.

Farnsworth gives them the evil eye and then the middle finger.

"Oh my, sir. Not very gentlemanly of you," Kriger says. "You picking up bad habits from Tosseti? Or is that normal Spec-Ops training hand signals for the IQ?"

Upon hearing his name, Tosseti looks back. "Huh?"

"Nothing, Tosseti, go back to ... whatever you're doing with your horse." Kriger says, pauses, then looks back at Tosseti. "Just what are you doing to your horse?" Kriger asks, thankful he can divert attention away from the captain.

"I'm explaining to him that if he doesn't do what I tell him, I'll sell him to the soap factory."

Nionee looks at Tosseti. "They don't make soap ..." is all he gets out before being interrupted by Bouvier.

"Ray?' he says, and when Nionee looks at him, Bouvier shakes his head. "Don't bother."

Nionee nods and lets out a breath. "Yes, you're right, of course," and he turns back around.

"Sgt. Tosseti, have a seat. We are ready to go," Farnsworth orders, then points a finger at Kriger while nodding in an *It's on* gesture.

When everyone is in position, they notice the sky growing hazy with a tint of gray, as if a storm is rolling in. The sounds of buzzing insects, birds chirping, even the light rustling sound of waving grass moving in the wind disappear. The air fills with static electricity and seems to move as if alive. McGregor looks at his arms, then to Farnsworth.

Emma grasps Farnsworth's hand harder and he pats it with his free hand and winks at her. Before he gives her reassurances, he begins to feel the pressure in his ears. He places his one hand over his ear. He wants to use both but doesn't want to let go of Emma's hand. Emma moans and presses her face against Farnsworth's chest. He drops his hand from his ear, placing his arm around her. He attempts to cover her ears but can't think clearly enough as the pressure builds to a crescendo. The horses become skittish, pulling on their tethers. They begin whinnying in fear and pain, the sedative not seeming to help. The small group of people on the ground begin to moan and holler.

Then they are gone.

Chapter 32

1980

Sen. Minten's personal jet lands on the runway at Pope Air Force Base and taxis to Base Operations. The senator walks down the steps to the tarmac where he is greeted by Gen. Beck, the USAF base commander.

"Welcome to Pope, senator."

Minten puts on his practiced political smile and shakes the general's hand.

"Gen. Beck, great to see you," Minten says in an overly friendly tone. "Sorry for the short notice. I was already airborne as we were heading back from Patrick Air Force Base and thought I would stop in. Again, my sincerest apologies."

"Not a problem, Sen. Minten. Always glad to have our civilian leadership stop by. Keeps us on our toes. We are here at your pleasure, sir. Now if you'll come with me?"

The general gestures for the senator to take the lead as they walk toward the Base Ops building.

"Gen. Beck, can we speak privately for a minute?" Minten asks in a hushed tone.

The general's smile never wavers.

"Of course, sir. Why don't we step inside and find a room? Quieter there, away from the flight line noise and inquisitive ears."

"That's fine, general. Please, lead the way."

Beck does as he is instructed and walks into the building. The personnel inside stand at attention until the general waves them off. He points to a door leading to a small conference room, telling his escort to wait until he returns as he and Minten step inside.

Minten walks to the far side of the conference room and gazes out the window. Clasping his hands behind his back, he studies the aircraft that has just delivered him to the base and watches his MISS agents, dressed as Air Force police and OSI agents, unloading equipment and gear.

"Gen. Beck, again I'm sorry for the intrusion," Minten begins. "Don't worry, I'm not here to conduct any inspection or look at your soldiers. No tour, no escorts needed."

"Okay senator, what is it we can we do for you?" the general asks, irritated that the senator doesn't have the decency to learn the difference between a soldier and an airman.

"Well, you see, my nephew, a captain who is assigned to the Bank," Minten starts saying while walking over to another window to stare at the planes. "Well, let just say he got himself into a predicament." He turns to face the general.

"There is a warrant, or whatever the military calls it, out for his arrest. Some misunderstanding, I'm sure, as he was arrested, then released, but now they want to arrest him again. Utter nonsense, I assure you. The thing is, I can't be seen as showing any favoritism toward him."

The general eyes Minten, wanting this blowhard politician to get to the point and get off his base.

"I understand, senator. Now, again sir, what can we do for you?"

Minten's face grows dark for a split second, the bogus smile faltering, then returning just as quickly.

How dare this subservient military ass patronize me, Minten thinks briefly, then moves on, keeping his composure.

"You see, Gen. Beck, my MISS agents have captured Capt. Henries and, at this very moment, are bringing him here, or, should I say, to the Bank, to be released into their custody. I would like it if you would be so kind as to loan me a vehicle so that I might go there and see him first. I just want say a quick goodbye. You know, without any fanfare or people seeing me, other than those who have him in custody," he says, then asks, "Are you a family man general?"

Beck remains impassive as he listens to the senator. "Yes, I am senator; married, three children."

Maintaining the swarthy smile, Minten nods at Beck. "So, you see, good sir, I'm quite sure you understand my predicament?"

Beck doesn't trust the man, but he can understand the need for secrecy when dealing with such matters. And he can understand loyalty to one's kin. "I'm sure that can be arranged, sir."

Minten's smile grows even wider, if that is even possible.

"I knew I could count on you, Gen. Beck. I always liked you; you're a good officer. I do have my own security police escorts along, so the acquisition of a couple of vehicles is all I need to bother you with."

Beck takes a quick glance out the window, watching the senator's personnel unload from the jet. *What a waste of tax dollars and good Air Force personnel,* he thinks, but outwardly remains impassive. "Yes, sir. Whatever you say."

"Ah, good man. Two vehicles should do the trick."

"Two vehicles it is, senator. I can have them here in about fifteen, twenty minutes."

Minten clasps his hands together. "Very good, general. That'll give me time to get everyone off the plane and ready to go."

Gen. Beck nods and leaves the room. Minten's smile collapses instantly as he watches. He follows a short time later, walking over to the Base Ops counter where a staff sergeant is working.

"Sergeant?" he asks, the practiced smile returning.

The young sergeant looks up from his task. "Can I help you, sir?"

"Yes. Can you, or someone, radio my aircraft and have my escort debark and join me in the room back there?" he asks, pointing to the door from which he just emerged.

"Of course, sir."

Minten thanks the sergeant and heads back to the room. *What a bunch of idiots they have here. Why isn't there a guard at this door to hold it open for me? What incompetency,* he thinks as he opens the door himself.

Eighteen minutes later, two USAF dark-blue Ford four-door sedans park outside Base Operations. The fake SPs open the door for the senator, then pile into the sedans and drive off in the direction of the Bank.

***

Capt. Henries is sitting in the back of a security police-marked van with several counterfeit security officers and OSI agents. Following behind them is a USAF security police patrol vehicle with more bogus SPs inside.

The van stops at the gate leading onto Fort Bragg and the soldier on guard duty waves the vehicle through. Henries chuckles to himself. *Sure, let them through. One big happy military family.*

One of the MISS agents pulls out a set of handcuffs.

"Need to put these on before we get there," he tells Henries, who dutifully presents his hands.

The agents secure the cuffs loosely, ensuring they aren't too tight.

"Good?"

"Yeah, good."

Several minutes pass before Henries feels the vehicle slow. He leans forward and looks through the windshield, where he can see the Bank's main gate. He inwardly shudders, then smiles, knowing he is helping his uncle, and this time he will get it right.

The van slows even more as it approaches the gate, finally coming to a complete stop. Two guards emerge from the shack as the personnel in the vehicle begin departing.

"Hey, sergeant. What's this?" the first guard asks one of the fake SPs wearing technical sergeant stripes.

One of the men dressed in civilian clothing moves forward and pulls out his badge wallet.

"Agent Von, OSI. Capt. Henries was captured, and we have him in custody. We need to turn him over."

The guards look at each other and the first one shakes his head.

"We weren't informed of this."

"No, you wouldn't have been. It was sudden, so we haven't even called it in to the Bank," the bogus Von says.

"We'll have to contact security control first," the guard says.

"By all means," Von replies and looks at the two faux SPs standing beside him. He nods and they follow the two Bank guards into the shack. One false SP looks around and spots the camera, he lifts his hand slightly, flipping a switch on a small device that wirelessly connects with the electronics of the camera, shorting it out.

"Hey guys, you mind waiting outside until ..." is all the first Bank guard gets out before a needle is stuck in his neck and he quickly collapses. The second guard fares no better as he receives the same treatment. The two false cops move the unconscious men into the cleaning closet and take their place. They open the second gate, and the van and police car enter the Bank parking lot.

Just as they are driving through the gate, Sen. Minten's vehicles pull up at the rear. They had parked down the road and out of sight of the guard shack until told the area was secured.

A malevolent smile creases the senator's face as his vehicle passes through the gate.

***

SMSgt Rees changes into his Union Cavalry uniform. All his accoutrements are properly in place, except the transmitter and the camera, which he thankfully finds in a pocket. Or what's left of them anyway.

He makes his way to the general's office, where the women, chief and general are waiting. Nora whistles, Skylar just laughs, and Ivy gives a sexy, *ohhhhhh!* upon seeing him.

Nora walks up to him, smooths the front of his jacket and starts preening over him. Being from the south, Nora shakes her head as she finishes and takes a step back.

"Wrong uniform there, soldier boy," she says, laughing.

"Hey, I'm neutral in this matter. Remember I'm from Arizona."

"It doesn't matter. I think he looks handsome in that uniform, Nora," Ivy interjects.

"Down girl, this one is mine. When Eric gets back, you can dress him up and play southern belle all you want," Nora scolds and wraps her arms around Scott's neck.

Gen. Lucas clears his throat. "You ready to go, Sgt. Rees?"

"Yes, sir," he says and looks at Nora. "I will miss you. But you will have me, or the other me, back very soon."

"I know, but it just seems too weird."

He nods and leans into her, and she kisses him hard. They stay that way for a little while until Ivy, being Ivy, interrupts. "Jeez, get a room," she says with a disgusted look.

Skylar punches her in the arm. "Ivy!"

"Ouch, that hurt," she says rubbing her arm. "I was just saying they ...," she begins to say, then closes her mouth upon seeing Skylar's glare.

The general moves toward the small group.

"Sgt. Rees, good luck. Hope everything works out and you find your way back."

"Thank you, sir. It was good to meet you, and I thank you for helping me. The chief said you were a good man," he says and shakes the general's hand, then turns to the chief. "Chief, I'll see you in 38 years, God willing."

"I'm sure I'm looking forward to it. Still not sure how that will work out, but hopefully we will see," he says and also shakes Rees's hand.

Rees hugs Ivy and Skylar, then squeezes Nora's hand once more and walks out the door. He makes his way out of the building and to a waiting Jeep. He climbs in and the two SPs smile at his uniform.

"Ready, sir?"

"Let's do this," he tells them, and they leave the area.

They drive down the road toward the embarkation area. They make a turn onto another road and miss seeing two USAF vehicles driving up the road toward the Bank.

Chapter 33

1862

Capt. Farnsworth blinks as he slowly opens his eyes. A slight wave of vertigo hits him, so he closes his eyes again. When the feeling passes, he reopens his eyes and looks down to see he is still tightly holding Emma. He smiles and doesn't move. Several seconds later she, too, opens her eyes, blinks a couple of times, then sits up abruptly.

"Ohhh," she says with one hand covering her face, the other on her stomach.

"Whoa, whoa, it's okay," Farnsworth tells her. "Take it easy. The feeling will pass."

Emma takes a couple of deep breaths then looks around, confused for a couple of seconds until she remembers what happened.

"We ... are we back?" she asks.

"Yes, ma'am," Farnsworth replies and stands up, holding an outstretched hand to assist her. Emma stands, wobbling a bit. Farnsworth gently grabs her arms to steady her.

"You're okay. Just a side effect of the jump. You should be fine in a second or two."

When he sees she is all right, he releases her arms.

McGregor has awakened and, from his sitting position, flops onto his back. "Ah, damn lads, I would rather be fight'n a hundred Rebs by myself than havin' to go through that again. You should have let me at least had a drink before we left, then I woulda had an excuse for this bottle-ache."

Kriger walks over and nudges the man with his foot. "Get up. It ain't that bad," he says, then leans over and whispers, "besides, I brought a little bug juice with me." He looks at the others to see if they are listening, which they are. He grins and looks back at McGregor. Opening his jacket, he reveals the top of a flask in his pocket. "Shhhh. Just between us," he says with a wink, then helps the now-grinning older sergeant to his feet.

The team begins checking the horses and their gear. Gen. Farnsworth places his slouch hat on his head and looks around. He pulls out a compass and map, then looks at Emma and McGregor. He ponders for a few seconds, then pulls them aside. "This might get dangerous and has nothing to do with you two. You can stay here until we get done; then we will come back for you."

Emma and McGregor look at each other, then at Farnsworth. McGregor speaks first.

"I'm sorry, sir, but I'm a soldier. I go with you."

Farnsworth nods, already expecting that answer, then looks at the chagrined Emma.

"Gen. Farnsworth, I am quite capable of taking care of myself, thank you. I might not have all that fancy training and equipment that you boys do, but you just try to leave me out of this."

"Oh, I wouldn't dream of it, Miss Kelly, but I had to ask. I have no wish to place you in harm's way, but I also won't be the one who stands in your way," he says with a grin. "Okay, let's get to work then."

Farnsworth calls the group together. "Okay, here's the plan," he says, unfolding the map and spreading it in the ground. "If the Jeep is here," he says, pointing to a location on the map, "the train transporting it will travel north on these tracks at about fifteen miles an hour."

"You're kidding! I can run faster than that," Tosseti interrupts.

Bouvier gives him a look and Tosseti shrugs. "Just saying sarge, ah, captain, ah, whatever. Damn it gets confusing trying to keep these ranks straight."

Farnsworth shakes his head. "As I was saying," giving a warning look at Tosseti, "the train will take this route at about fifteen miles an hour. I'm sending a recon team to the depot and, when they return, we will move to here," he says, pointing to another spot several miles from their current location. "Once there, we will attack the train and place a transponder on the Jeep and then be on our way to find Rees."

"But they are going to have armed guards on that train," Bouvier adds.

"Of course, but how do you think they will fare against us?" Farnsworth asks. "There will probably be some shooting, but we have superior firepower and equipment, as well as the element of surprise."

"Why don't we just go to the depot and put the transponder on it there?" Bouvier asks.

"First, we are not one hundred percent sure it is on that wagon. That's why we recon first. Second, we are vastly outnumbered around the depot. We'd have a better chance of pulling off an old-fashioned train heist."

"Hot damn, a train robbery," Tosseti says, then looks at Emma. "Sorry."

She shakes her head dismissively.

Bouvier still looks worried, but nods. "Okay, looks simple enough, except for the shooting part, which is what you SpecOps guys like to do, I guess. Oh, and the trying-to-stop-a-train part, or are we going to do the old ride beside it then jump onto it off our horses?"

Farnsworth laughs. "Of course, Capt. Bouvier. What is the fun in robbing a train if we can't have a shootout?" Slapping Bouvier of the back, he says, "I'm kidding, sergeant. Hopefully we can catch the train from behind, board it and disarm the troops guarding it without any casualties. And no, you won't have to jump off your horse," he finishes, then turns to Kriger and Nionee.

"Okay, Nionee, you and Kriger are going on the reconnoiter. First, you need to find the depot and see if the Jeep is there. It's almost dark, so you should leave now. I don't want you to get too close; just see if it, or anything that might fit the description, is there and then get back here. Got it?"

"Yes, sir," the men answer in unison and move toward their horses.

"No heroics guys, just recon and get back," Bouvier emphasizes.

"Yes, dad," Kriger answers with a half salute using his middle finger, followed with a crotch salute before the two men ride off.

McGregor leans toward Emma. "I don't understand these men at all.

Why would he call him dad? And salute him with his middle finger?"

Emma, arms folded, shrugs. "I don't know, and what was that other gesture?" she asks, imitating it.

"I dunno. Maybe you should ask the general."

Farnsworth calls the rest of the squad together. "How about we set up camp, place some EWDs and wait for Lt. Kriger and Sgt. Nionee to return?"

"We going to need an LPOP?" Tosseti asks.

Farnsworth shakes his head. "Naw. The EWDs should suffice. Besides we don't have enough manpower."

McGregor looks confused. "Sir, I wish you'd talk plain 'cause I don't understand half of what yer saying."

"EWD is short for early warning devices; things we put out to let us know if intruders are near. LPOP is a listening and observation post. Nothing to worry about, sergeant. We've got it covered."

"Yes, sir."

"Now, go help set up camp, if you would."

With that, McGregor salutes, with the middle finger, and with the other hand gives him a crotch salute, then wanders over to help Tosseti.

Farnsworth, confused by the gestures, just shakes his head.

***

Kriger and Nionee ride through the woods until they hear commotion. Stopping, they climb off their horses, tying them to a nearby tree. Both men slowly make their way toward the sounds and soon spot the small depot. They lie on the ground and low crawl toward the area for a closer look.

"You see anything that looks like a Jeep?" Kriger asks.

"Not yet."

Both men scan in front of them, then Nionee points. "Wait. Look over there at your two o'clock, that flatcar with the tarp-covered wagon with two men guarding it. That's got to be something important, like a Jeep. Can't tell from here though."

Kriger brings out a set of binoculars and looks. The area is dark, except for some spots where lanterns are glowing, giving off faint light. He flips the binoculars to night-observation mode and looks at the scene. He hands the binocs to Nionee, who tries to get a better view.

"I can't see much, even with the night vison. That tarp is completely covering whatever is in there."

Kriger agrees. "I know that's it, but we need to be sure. We need to get closer and have a look under the tarp."

"Capt. Farnsworth said not to be heroes, remember? Just find something that looks like the Jeep," Nionee reminds him, still looking through the binoculars.

"Well, we can't say for sure if that's the Jeep or not unless we see it with our own eyes. We're here to recon, so let's recon."

Both men scoot back until they are sure no one will see them, then make their way back to the horses. To lessen the weight, as well as minimize any noise, they remove most of their gear.

"Okay, I'm going over there," Kriger says, pointing his thumb over his shoulder, "and make a distraction. Hopefully the guards will move toward me or at least divert their attention away from the wagon. I'll let you know when I get there. Check your watch, and let me know when you're ready. Get in there, get what we need and get back to the horses," he says.

"Listen, if I can get that close, and it is the Jeep, why don't I just put a transponder on it?" Nionee asks.

Kriger stares at him for a few seconds, then bites his upper lip in thought. "I don't see any reason why not. If we're going to disobey orders and be heroes, let's be heroes," he says with a broad grin. "Besides, aren't we supposed to improvise, adapt and overcome?"

"Sounds good. Once I confirm the Jeep, I'll attach the bug then hightail it back to the horses," Nionee tells him.

Kriger grins. "Aim high."

"I'll be waiting for your signal. And you be careful."

"Hey, I got the easy part," Kriger says and moves away.

It takes Kriger a few minutes to get to a spot he decides is a good place to create a distraction. Once set up, he alerts Nionee. About a minute later Nionee says he is ready as well.

Kriger pulls out a small flashlight, turns it on and off in the direction of the guards. He does this several times until he hears one of the guards call out to the other. The second guard moves from his position on the far side of the wagon and comes to stand at his side.

Nionee is crouched in the bushes near the flatcar when he sees the second guard move. Taking this as his cue, he stealthily makes his way to the car and climbs on, rolling under the wagon. He crawls to the back wheel, watching the feet of the two guards and listening to them discuss the light.

"Go see what it is," one guard says.

"Naw, I ain't leaving my post. Go get the sergeant and let him figure out what to do," the second guard says.

"Oh, no. The sergeant will have my ass if'n I wake him."

"Well, he'll have both our asses if that turns out to be something he might want to know about. Now go get him."

Nionee watches the guard run off and the second guard begins to make his way back around the wagon. Nionee crawls to the front side of the wagon and stands. He is now visible to anyone who might look his way. He hopes the darkness hides the color of his uniform from a distance at least. He quickly reaches up, lifts the tarp and sees a section of the Jeep. He smiles and reaches into a pocket, searching for the transponder. Silently he curses himself for not having it in hand already as he wastes precious time searching for the device. He is so intent on getting the device, he doesn't notice that the guard has come back around the wagon.

Nionee is pulling the transponder out of his pocket when he hears, "Ray, your six!" in his ear, then "Halt!" from behind him. Both voices startle him, and the transponder slips from his fingers, hits the flatcar, and bounces around. Nionee turns to face a young man aiming a musket at his chest.

"Hands up, blue belly," the guard orders and Nionee complies. As the guard moves toward him, Nionee begins to back up. He looks at the ground, searching for the transponder, but it's too dark. After a couple of steps backwards, the guard continues to move forward and Nionee hears *crunch* as the guard steps on the device. Nionee closes his eyes. *Shit.*

"Now, Yank, turn around and head toward that there shack," the guard orders.

Nionee turns. "Not today," and takes off in a run. He barely registers the sound of the musket firing as the .58 caliber round strikes him between the shoulder blades. The pain is not as bad as Nionee would have thought, the nano technology spreading the impact evenly across the uniform jacket, but the force of the impact throws him forward and, as he is trying to maintain his balance, he trips over a rock. Nionee spirals face first and hits the ground hard. He has just enough time to get one arm in front of him to lessen the impact, but not in time to stop his head from striking the ground with enough force to cause stars to flash before his eyes.

Nionee is able to get to his hands and knees while sucking in a lung full of air. He makes a feeble attempt to rise, but the guard has already caught up with him and, before Nionee can get to his feet, he is kicked in the head. He sees a bright flash of light and pain engulfs him. Rolling around on the ground, disoriented and in agony, he hears yelling and cursing before he feels hands grasp him, roughly pulling him to his feet.

"Well, lookey here, boys. We done caught ourselves a Yankee spy," a southern-accented voice drawls. Blearily Nionee sees a light in front of him as a lantern shines on him. "And what is this, an injun as well. Is them damn federal boys so distressed they have to draft injuns now?" the voice says to the laughter of others.

Nionee is none-too-gently led to the train depot, where his hands are tied behind his back. Maj. Carter heard the commotion and appears in the doorway of the shack. Sgt. Baine and the first guard are running up just as Nionee is brought to them.

"What in blazes is going on here?" the major demands.

The second guard comes to attention and salutes. "Sir, I found this Yank looking under the tarp of that there wagon," he says, proudly, as he points to the wagon. "Yank tried to run, so I shot him," he explains then looks confused. "I shot him square in the back, sir. But he just falls down, nary a mark on him."

"Nonsense son, you must have missed and he just fell from being scared is all," the major says, making his way along the platform for a better look.

Sgt. Baine walks up to Nionee and looks at his face. "Who are you soldier? Where did you come from and why are you here?" he demands, then looks at the group of men standing around. "Don't just stand here you idjits, get out there and find out if there are more of them. And somebody secure that damn wagon!" he orders.

Men scramble and begin fanning out, some making their way into the woods, others to the wagon. Baine walks Nionee over to the major. "Sir, I'll lock this man up for the time being. I assume you have a prisoner-holding area here."

The major looks at Nionee, then Baine. "Yes, sergeant we do," he replies, then orders another soldier to escort them to the where prisoners are held until transported to Salisbury.

Nionee grins as he's being led away. "Hey Dave, I'm going to a prisoner pen. Let Farnsworth know. Don't worry about me, I got this."

Sgt. Baine stares at Nionee. "Who are you talking to?" he asks.

Nionee just smiles. "My great spirit."

***

Kriger turns off the light when he sees Nionee stand up and lift the tarp on the wagon.

"Oh, shit!" he mutters when he spies the second guard returning. Kriger turns on his mic. "Ray, your six!" he whispers, but it's too late. He looks up in time to see Nionee take off in a run, then hears, as well as watches, the musket discharge. He stifles a curse when he sees Nionee fall violently to the ground. Fearing the worst, he moves forward, wanting to help his friend.

He continues to watch as Nionee is snatched up by some soldiers and perp-walked to the depot. Kriger curses and tries to think of what to do. Before he can come up with a plan, he hears the sound of men shouting as they make their way into the woods, some coming in his direction.

"Ah, hell!" he says and runs deeper into the woods, ashamed he is leaving behind his comrade, his friend. He runs a half circle through the trees and makes his way back to the horses. As he mounts his horse, he hears Nionee in his earpiece. He mumbles a curse, then grabs the reins of the other horse and gallops off as fast as possible to the encampment.

Chapter 34

1862 – Woods Near Hendrick Hill

TSgt. Rees and the men are, again, gathered together in the fallback encampment.

"Okay, so we are back at square one, only now we are pretty certain we are in the year 1862, in North Carolina and smack dab in the middle of the Civil War. We have several wounded and we're limited on medicine. How are we on ammo, food, water?"

Bouvier looks at McGuire who answers in his Tennessean accent. "We have plenty of ammo, as well as grenades, LAWs, and plenty of c-rations. We are short on water, but the river is close so we should be able to resupply with no problem."

Rees nods. "Good," he says and looks at Bouvier. "Jack, can you take care of that?"

"We have two water bladders in the Duck," Bouvier says, then finds two men to accomplish the task. "Shepard and Tucker, go grab the bladders and whatever canteens we have and take the Jeep to the river. You should be able to get a couple of days' worth of water. Just one of you collect water, the other keep security. You see anybody, stop what you're doing and retreat here. We're trying to stay out of sight until we can get out of here."

***

Shepard and Tucker drive until they locate a good area to gather water and stay out of sight while doing it. Tucker maintains guard while Shepard fills a bladder at the river and carries it back to the Jeep. As he places it into the back of the Jeep, both men hear shouting and then gunfire.

Tucker is already moving toward the ruckus as Shepard grabs his M-16 and follows. Staying low, they crouch behind some bushes and watch as a Rebel cavalry squad and a small Union cavalry patrol skirmish. The Yanks are outnumbered two to one and don't put up much of a fight. In fact, they try to flee the scene but are gunned down in their retreat, all except one fella whose horse is shot out from under him. The rider can't get off the animal as it falls, trapping his leg under the weight of the beast. The young blond-haired corporal howls in pain.

The Rebel cavalrymen surround the Union soldier, and a confederate sergeant orders his men to get the Yank out from under the horse, to which they readily comply by lifting the horse and jerking the man from underneath. The Union man hollers in pain and grabs his leg, yelling at the Rebels, his Irish accent very distinct.

They tie a rope around his wrists and one of the Rebels grabs the end of the rope and climbs onto his horse. The squad moves out, pulling the wounded man behind them. He tries to keep up but falls several times.

Both Shepard and Tucker feel sorry for him.

"I know I don't like Yankees much, but that's no way to treat a man," Shepard says. Tucker looks at Shepard then back at the man being pulled behind the horse until they are out of sight.

"Come on TJ, we've got a job to do. Let's finish it and get going," Tucker says, slapping Shepard on the back as he stands.

Shepard watches for a few more seconds then follows. They both walk back toward the Jeep when Tucker kicks something metallic. He reaches down and picks up one of the canteens.

"Damn. Thing must have bounced out of the Jeep. That wouldn't have been good leaving this for someone to find."

They make their way back to the river, finish filling the containers and go back to the camp with a story to tell.

***

Sgt. Holt of the Confederate cavalry rides into the camp near a train depot where they bring prisoners to be held for either exchange or transportation to Salisbury prison. He orders his men to secure the Union prisoner. Satisfied his orders will be followed, Holt makes his way to the command tent to report.

He opens the tent flap and knocks on the post, getting the attention of Capt. Butler.

The captain is sitting behind a small table, reading what appears to the sergeant to be field reports. Butler looks up at the sergeant and beckons him to enter.

"Well, Sgt. Holt, what have you got for me?" the captain asks, taking a last glance at a report and setting it aside.

Holt salutes the captain. "Sir, we ran across a Yank patrol in this area here," Holt says, pointing to an area on a map lying on another table.

Butler stands and walks to the map.

"We killed them all, except for one, who we took prisoner."

Butler looks at the area where they ran into the patrol. "A prisoner, you say. Haven't had one for quite some time. They must be part of the brigade we heard was moving down this way. A scouting party maybe, looking for our brigade. I'll be wanting a word before he is taken to the depot. Good work. That will be all for now, sergeant."

Holt comes to attention and salutes. "Yes, sir," and leaves the tent.

Butler walks over to where prisoners are kept and finds the lone Union cavalryman. "What is your name, son?"

"Andy, Cpl. Andy O'Toole, 3rd Regiment Maryland Volunteer Cavalry, 1st Brigade."

***

Sgt. Baine holds Nionee's arm tightly as they follow a private toward the area where prisoners are secured. Nionee is mad at himself for getting caught, for letting the others down. Now they will have to either postpone retrieving the Jeep to get him, or they might continue the mission and try to get to him later.

He is too deep in thought to even pay attention to the other prisoner already inside the fenced-in area. The gate is opened and the private shoves Nionee inside. He stumbles, can't catch his balance and falls, twisting at the last second to land on his shoulder. He feels hands lifting him, helping him get onto his knees as he to turns to stare daggers at the young soldier who pushed him.

Baine looks at Nionee. "I'll be back, sergeant. Got some questions for you. Make yourself at home," he says and walks away.

"Here now, let me help you, sergeant."

A familiar voice, with an Irish accent.

He is helped to his feet and feels the ropes on his wrist being loosened. Once free, he turns, rubbing his wrists and stares into the face of O'Toole. He is stunned for a second, then recovers.

"Jesus, Andy? What in blazes are you doing here?"

O'Toole stops what he is doing and furrows his eyebrows. "You know me, sergeant? I don't remember meeting you. What cavalry unit are you with?" Andy asks, studying Nionee's uniform.

"Ah, ah," Nionee stammers, "ah, no, no we haven't met. Sorry. You were, um, pointed out to me when I was with your brigade a few weeks ago. I was told you were an up and comer."

"A what?" Andy asks, confused by this strange NCO.

"Never mind. I am Sgt. Nionee of a special cavalry branch out of Washington. My unit works directly for the president," he says, using the cover story given to them and reaching out his hand.

Last question already forgotten, Andy shakes Ray's proffered hand.

"You work for President Lincoln?" Andy asks, skeptical.

Nionee drops his head and sighs. "Listen, Cpl. O'Toole. I am with a special unit that was sent here to recapture a piece of experimental equipment taken by the Rebels. That particular device is on a wagon near the train depot and will soon be on its way to Richmond. We were sent here to retrieve the item. Unfortunately, I got caught trying to identify the piece."

O'Toole continues to stare. "What is this experimental piece?"

Nionee shakes his head. "Sorry. I can't tell you. But trust me, it's important."

Andy just nods. "All right, sergeant."

"I'm sure my general and the others ...," he starts to say.

"Your general?" Andy interrupts. "You are here with a general?"

"A general, captain, lieutenant, and two other sergeants and ..." he almost mentions Emma. Should he say she is with them? How would he explain that? "And that's it."

"Well, if you are that important, I will believe it when they come to rescue you," Andy says sarcastically.

Nionee is taken aback, then smiles. "Is that sarcasm I hear from you, young corporal?"

Andy smiles back. "Not from me, Sgt. Nionee. Not from me."

Still smiling, Nionee leans toward Andy and whispers, "Don't worry, we won't be in here long. If they don't come for me soon, I have a way out. Trust me." Nionee walks over to a fence post and sits.

Chapter 35

1862

The displaced time travelers are again discussing what to do next. TSgt Rees is tired, as they all are, and has no idea what of next steps. That is frustrating as an NCO, especially one in charge. For now, he needs the men to perform their assigned duties: security, eat, rest, weapons maintenance, and care of the wounded. He pulls Bouvier and Kriger aside.

"Okay, guys, I need help here. We don't have a clue as to what is going on other than that we're in 1862, and for what reason?"

"Someone's sick fucking joke," Kriger blurts out, then looks around to see if anyone else heard him.

"That's not helping, Dave," Bouvier admonishes. "Look, Scott, we don't have to do anything except survive this. Meanwhile we just use our training and wait it out."

"Jack, those men over there," Rees says pointing to the wounded, "can't just wait it out."

Before they can continue their conversation, the report of an M-16 shot echoes and they all turn toward the sound, which originated from Sgt. McGuire's position.

"Now what?" Rees exclaims and tells Kriger to come with him. The rest are told to stay put until he returns. Staying low, they approach the foxhole and climb in with McGuire.

"What are you shooting at McGuire?" Kriger asks.

"I saw a Rebel."

The men stare into the woods across the wide-open field. "Where?" Rees wants to know, kicking himself for not having his binoculars.

McGuire points to a small grouping of pine trees. "Right there, those pines next to that clump of fallen trees, by the stump. He just stepped out into the open and was using binoculars. I thought he might be checking us out, so I took a shot. He moved back behind the trees just as I pulled the trigger."

"You sure?" Rees asks.

"Come on Sgt. Rees, I'm not jumpy like that. I know what I saw."

"Shit! We have got to move before they come at us again. Let's go," he orders, telling McGuire to stay put and keep his eyes peeled. He will send someone over to help. Rees and Kriger jump out of the trench and run back to the Duck.

When they arrive, they find those not on sentry duty already geared up and securing the inner perimeter.

Good men, Rees thinks. "All right everyone. We're outta here," he shouts and turns toward Tosseti. "Tosseti, radio the perimeter guards in." He looks for Montoya. "Sgt. Montoya, go help McGuire until we call for you two get back here. Now go!"

Before he can give any more orders, Airman McGuire's voice comes over the radio. Having lost his radio discipline, he says in a sing-song voice like the young girl from *Poltergeist,* "They're here."

"Dammit! Kriger, get the wounded into the Duck. The rest of you get up there and help out until we can get the vehicles loaded and moving. Go! Go! Go!" he orders and runs over to help Kriger and Nionee collect Green and Harris. When they get there, Airman Harris is already up and trying to help Green himself. McAdams' arm is in a sling and he is limping, but carrying his M-16. Parks and Steele also are moving around, every man looking like death warmed over.

"Airman Harris, what the hell?" Rees asks, astonished that the man is moving at all.

"I don't know, Sarge, I just woke up. I feel fine."

"You sure? I can't have you flaking out on me in the middle of a fight."

"No, sarge, I swear."

"Okay, but be careful." Rees points at the three other walking wounded. "You three, in the Duck."

"We can fight, Sgt. Rees," Parks says.

"Not here. Get in the Duck. We're heading for the lines to get the others. Now move! Go!" he yells, and the three men limp to the Duck and crawl in.

After ensuring everyone is doing as told, Rees runs toward the Jeep, calling for Bouvier, Tosseti and Shepard to join him. By the time everyone scrambles into the Jeep, the others are either in the Duck or on the front line.

Before they can move out, Rees and the others hear sounds of multiple gun shots, all M-16s, then the ominous bark of cannon fire.

"Get us up there!" Rees shouts, and the two vehicles move forward.

1980

Chief Black walks into the control room with Nora, Skylar and Ivy on his heels. The guests try to watch everything at once. Black approaches Maj. Hess, who assures him everything is a go.

Black opens the box containing the Inabular Device, the crucial piece of the transportation process, and removes it. He issues final instructions to everyone in the room, then walks to the main terminal.

"Please, watch the screen. We will conduct this in two parts. First, we send Sgt. Rees," he says, pointing to a long-distance shot of Rees kneeling in full cavalry uniform. "Then, when we are sure he has transported safely, we will begin the transfer sequence to bring the others home."

"Where will you send them, chief?" Nora asks. "I mean, they aren't where they were when you transported them the first time."

"We'll bring them here, on this base," he assures her. "In fact, they will appear at the same spot where Sgt. Rees is transported."

Looking at Maj. Hess, he asks him to split the screenshot.

Hess instructs a junior officer to do so and the screen blinks, then displays two scenes. The left view shows the men in 1862 getting ready for battle and the right screen is a view of Rees.

Chief Black places the Inabular Device into the computer and the room itself seems to come alive. The system runs through its transfer sequences, the large reel-to-reel magnetic tape drives spinning, filling the room with whirling sounds, the multiple clacking sounds of technicians typing on their keyboards, various multicolored lights flashing and blinking.

The women are fascinated by it all, then they turn their attention back to the screen. They watch as the sky around Rees grows grayer, hazier, the air surrounding him seemingly moving as if alive. Nora places her hand to her mouth as she sees Rees covering his ears, opening his mouth in what can only be a scream, bending over in obvious pain, then she gasps as he just ... disappears.

"Shut down the computers and reboot for the second phase!" Chief Black yells so everyone can hear him.

The shutdown and reboot process takes less than a minute and, when he is sure everyone is ready, he re-inserts the Inabular Device, waits and watches the screen.

***

Sen. Minten and his men move with purpose as they escort Capt. Henries through the front doors of the Bank. Using identification badges manufactured after hacking into the Bank's unbreakable computer systems (or so the Bank thought), the team opens the secured elevator doors and enters.

They wait patiently as they descend deeper into the supposedly secured facility. Minten is giddy and inwardly giggles, thinking of the look on Lucas' face when he takes control of the facility. He looks back at a couple of the SPs who are working on electronic devices that will scramble any communications within a fifty-foot radius. Another device also will cause any cameras to white out.

The elevator's voice announces they have arrived at their destination and the doors slide open. Henries, still handcuffed, is escorted to the front desk where a surprised security police officer looks up at their unannounced arrival.

"What's this?" he asks.

Fake Von shows his ID. "Bringing back a prisoner."

Fake Beltrane, grasping Henries' arm, brings him forward for the guard to see.

"I had no notification that a prisoner was being brought in. I'll have to inform my supervisor," the SP sergeant says, reaching for the phone. A fake SP leans forward and plunges a syringe into the sergeant's neck, quickly rendering the man unconscious.

Minten moves to the front of the team. "Take the handcuffs off my nephew," he orders, then looks at Henries. "When you get to the security section, make sure you incapacitate them quickly. Do not fuck this up."

Without waiting for a reply, he turns and moves toward the elevators. The doors open, and the insurgents enter.

***

The Jeep and Duck move toward the sound of fighting. Rees and the others jump out of the Jeep and watch in fascination as a battery of Rebel soldiers walk across the field in their direction.

The SPs are in awe of the sight of the soldiers silently moving toward their position. *This can't be just for us*, Rees thinks before his reverie is abruptly interrupted by cannon fire, followed by explosions in front and behind them. Some of the cannon shots explode in front of the foxholes, sending clumps of dirt and grass over the men and iron shrapnel whizzing by, some pieces embedding into tree bark. Other cannon balls explode in the tops of the trees, shredding wood and sending broken pieces flying in all directions, splinters that are as deadly as metal shrapnel.

The Duck comes to a halt a few feet from the Jeep and a cannon ball bangs off the armored side, making a dent in the thick metal and triggering the men inside to yell from the loud impact. The deflected piece of steel makes a whirling sound, flying further into the woods, shearing off the limbs of a pine trees like a surgeon amputating an arm.

McAdams climbs out of the Duck, followed by Steele. Both men make their way to where the other men are gathered.

"We are leaving!" Rees screams at the men. He looks at McAdams and Steele, who are hobbling toward him.

"Eric, dammit, get your asses back in the ..." An explosion sends him flying backwards.

Rees lands roughly on his back, the wind knocked out of him. He slowly rolls over, his ear ringing so loudly he can only hear muffled sounds. Tosseti runs over, shouting something unintelligible and trying to get him off the ground. Tucker makes his way over and helps push and drag Rees toward the Jeep.

Rees shakes off the fuzziness and looks at the area where McAdams and Steele were standing. He coughs from the acrid smoke and stares. Once he realizes what he is seeing, he fights the urge to throw up. Both men are lying in bloodied heaps on the ground. They were closest to the shell when it hit, so they received the brunt of the explosion, with the force of the blast and the resulting shrapnel tearing through their bodies.

The ringing in his ears lessens and he catches his breath. He jerks his head around when he hears a scream and sees Sgt. Shepard writhing on the ground, holding his leg, which is bleeding profusely. Kriger is already out of the Duck, running to help.

Rees finally realizes he is being shaken and notices that Tucker has a hold of him and is looking into his eyes. His mouth is moving; he seems to be asking him something. Finally, Rees snaps out of his daze. "I'm fine. We need to get out of here. Get Eric's and Alex's bodies into the Duck, now!" he shouts.

Rees looks at Tosseti, then points at Tucker. Tosseti understands and runs to help.

Montoya is in the turret, manning the other M-60. Minié balls are pinging off the Duck as the Rebel soldiers move within firing range. The Rebels shoot blindly into the grove of trees where the Air Force men are gathered.

McGuire and Harris also are out of the Duck, assisting with the bodies. Kriger ties off the wound on Shepard's leg as best he can and looks at Rees.

"He is losing blood fast. We have to get someplace where I can do a better job because I can't do it here."

"Get him in the Duck," he tells Kriger, then yells for McGuire, Tucker and Tosseti to get their asses in the Jeep. The three men do as they are told. Tucker jumps in the back with Tosseti on his heels. Tosseti stands and grabs the M-60, preparing for battle. McGuire jumps into the driver's seat as Rees climbs into the front passenger seat.

Once Rees is satisfied that all are accounted for, he orders the squad to move out. They drive through the pine trees, bouncing and shaking as they hit depressions and swerve around trees, shrubs and bushes.

It doesn't take them long to run out of forest and into open territory. The surface does not become any smoother, but McGuire is driving like a mad man. Rees looks back and can see the Duck has fallen far behind. Rees assumes Kriger is keeping the speed down due to the wounded on board.

"Airman McGuire, slow it the hell down. We're losing the others," Rees yells.

McGuire nods and does as he is told, taking a second to look behind him as well. Suddenly he slows to a stop and Rees is about to say something when he sees why.

Off in the distance there are hundreds of blue-clad soldiers moving in their direction: infantry, artillery, and cavalry spread as wide as they can see.

Rees stands in the Jeep and looks around. The Duck stops as well, and Bouvier and Kriger jump out, running to the Jeep.

"What is going on, Scott?" Bouvier asks, squinting as he tries to make out the Union soldiers in the distance. "Is that the Union Army?"

"Yes, it is," Rees answers, looking back to where they came from. "Those Rebels weren't here for us. They must have been heading this way to meet the Union boys and we just got caught in the middle. They probably thought we were scouts or something."

"Okay, what do you want to do?" Kriger asks.

Rees spies a small hill with a cluster of trees northwest of their position, and he points. "We go there and set up. Hopefully we can stay off the radar until they finish killing each other. Now move!" he orders, and the two sergeants run back to the Duck. Rees looks around again, finds where he wants to go and, using the flat of his hand in a chopping motion, he points in that direction. McGuire gives the Jeep some gas and they move again.

***

Lt. Stockman is in the Bank's central security control room standing behind Sgt. Lewis. Lewis is working feverishly trying to get a feed from the video cameras.

"What is the problem, sergeant?" Stockman ask.

"Sir, we lost video from all the cameras."

"That can't be. All of them?"

"Yes, sir. There's nothing wrong with the equipment, just not giving us a view."

The two men keep scanning the screens, but nothing except static shows. Stockman turns to SrA Gaskill, who is monitoring alarms systems. "Are the alarms all working?"

"Yes, sir. I don't seem to be having a problem. I was just about to run a systems check anyway."

"Do it," Stockman orders and turns back to the monitors.

Just as Stockman is about to run the problem up the chain of command, he notices the feed clear for just a second.

"Wait, what was that?" he asks pointing to one of the screens. He and Sgt. Lewis stare at the screen and it, again, clears for a brief instant.

"Those were security police personnel in the elevator. But why?"

Lewis looks up at the lieutenant, knowing the lieutenant was thinking out loud. Stockman reaches for the phone and finds the line dead.

"Oh great, now what? Is all our equipment on the fritz?" he utters, slamming the phone back in the cradle. Next, he picks up the base station radio and clicks the mic. He calls to one of the guards. No response. He depresses the mic and asks for everyone on duty to check in, but again receives no reply. This doesn't sit well with him.

"Something is going on. This doesn't just happen," he mumbles and makes his way toward the door. Before he can open it, it opens from the outside. He is startled as two SPs with weapons drawn move into the control room.

"What the ...," is all he can say as the first SP strikes him across the face with the pistol. Stockman falls to the floor, stunned and bleeding from a busted nose. The SP points his gun at Gaskill and the second SP trains his weapon on Lewis.

"Uh uhhhh" he taunts when he sees Lewis reaching for the duress button. "If you want to live, I wouldn't," he tells the controller and motions for him to stand. Lewis does and is handcuffed, then shoved back into his chair. The same is done to Gaskill and both men are wheeled to a corner of the room. The fake cops then drag the wounded lieutenant to the same corner, handcuff him and prop the moaning, semi-conscious man against the wall. Pulling out a roll of duct tape, they rip off pieces and place them over the men's mouths.

"Now, is everyone comfortable? Good," the first SP says without waiting for an answer. "We won't be long, so just relax and we'll be out of your hair in no time. Get it? No time. Time." He snorts at he own joke.

The two men in the chairs just glare. The fake SP shakes his head. "Tough crowd."

***

Sen. Minten steps out of the elevator, onto the Clio Project floor with his group of MISS agents posing as SPs and OSI agents. They make their way down the corridors toward Gen. Lucas' office and the main control room.

Before they can arrive, two Bank SPs, SSgt Castillo and Sgt. Harte, pass by and nod, saying hello to the senator and the others. Both men instantly recognize Capt. Henries and know he is supposed to be under arrest. Harte frowns, but figures since Henries is with the senator and being escorted by fellow police officers, it's OK.

But Castillo's gut says otherwise. He stops and studies the SPs for a couple of seconds before saying, "Excuse me?"

The group keeps walking.

"I said, excuse me?" he says a little louder and with more authority in his voice.

Three of the fake SPs stop and turn to face Castillo, while the others continue.

"I need all of you to stop," Castillo orders, walking toward the three fake SPs and looking at Henries.

"What seems to be the problem sergeant?" one of the men dressed as a 2nd lieutenant asks.

"Sir, Capt. Henries is supposed to be under arrest," he says, still watching as Henries continues down the corridor. Then several things happen.

Castillo notices the SPs are wearing semi-automatic pistols. He knows that SPs carry .38s. The lieutenant's name tag is on the wrong side of his shirt, and the two other SPs are out of regulation as well. Capt. Henries pauses to look back and smirks.

Castillo places his hand on his weapon and Harte follows suit. Both men take a step back. "I am ordering you to stop right there," Castillo shouts, drawing his weapon, but the two MISS agents standing beside the lieutenant draw as well.

The two SPs and three MISS agents face each other, weapons aimed.

"Now what?" the lieutenant asks, crossing his arms over his chest.

"Drop your weapons. You are all under arrest. I don't know who you are, but you're sure as hell not security police."

The lieutenant looks at the two other agents. "I told you to get haircuts."

"While you're at it, lieutenant," Castillo says sarcastically, his head tilted, "why don't you learn some 35-10 yourself," Castillo says, referring to the grooming and uniform regulation, then taps his own name tag.

The MISS agent, poised as the lieutenant, looks down at his own name tag and shakes his head. The two other agents smirk. The phony LT turns his attention back to Castillo and Harte.

"Guys, you might as well just holster your weapons and relax. We're not going anywhere and there is no backup coming to help you. We have this place in lock down until we finish what we came here for."

"And what is that?" Castillo asks.

"You'll see soon enough. So, for now, we will all just stand here like this until we receive orders to do otherwise. I suggest you just relax. It'll be over soon."

The lieutenant gives the two SPs a smile that sends chills down Castillo's spine.

***

Sen. Minten ignores Sgt. Castillo's order to stop. In fact, he does the opposite. Picking up the pace, he walks faster. Once he reaches the stairs leading to the general's office, he dashes up the steps. Unceremoniously, Minten barges into Shelly's office with his men behind him. Shelly reaches for her pistol but stops inches away as she sees weapons pointed at her.

"No, no, no. I wouldn't do that if I were you," Minten says, brushing by her desk on his way to the general's door. "She has a .45 under the desk," he adds, opening the general's door and entering.

Gen. Lucas is watching the proceedings in the control room and jumps at the unexpected sound of his door banging open. He turns, his eyes growing wide for a second, then narrowing just as quickly when he recognizes Minten, with Henries in tow.

"What's the meaning of this, senator?" he asks, venom in his voice.

"Oh, I think you know what this is, general. I'm here to take control of this project, your facility, as well as exact a little revenge on you for fucking with my nephew."

Minten begins walking around the room, nonchalantly looking at pictures and plaques.

"We're in the middle of an operation, Minten. I'm calling security," Lucas says with malice in his voice, reaching for his intercom.

Minten swiftly moves to the desk and grabs Lucas by the wrist, squeezing and twisting. Lucas glowers at Minten, not giving him the pleasure of making a sound from the discomfort.

"Move away from the desk and plant your ass over there, general," Minten orders, releasing the man's arm and pointing to the where Henries is holding a chair. Minten straightens, then notices the view screen in the control room.

"What is this? A live feed of the dumbass Air Force pukes getting their asses kicked. This is great," he says. "Why in the hell you and the Council chose this time period is mind boggling. And to send unqualified Air Force men on such a groundbreaking and important mission. Good God. You should have at least sent real professionals who could handle themselves," he says in disgust, reveling in the scene unfolding before him.

***

Maj. Hess looks up into the general's office and sees the senator and Henries. He also spots others brandishing weapons. He calls out to the chief.

The room is alive with the humming of electronics, the whirling of computer reels and the crackling of static electricity. The chief hears his name and looks around until the spies Maj. Hess. Hess looks up to the general's office and Black follows his gaze.

Minten notices Hess' stare, and he looks around the control room until he sees the chief standing by a console with three women, all of whom are staring at him. The senator makes eye contact with the chief and realizes what is happening. He turns to his men and orders them to get down to the control room and stop the time jump.

The chief sees the men exit the general's office, and he knows they are coming for him, for the Inabular Device. If they get their hands on the device, it is game over for him, the general and the Clio Project. He shouts to everyone in the room, telling them that they are about to be attacked and points to the door. Before anyone can secure it, the MISS and OSI agents burst into the room.

The agents stop, searching for the chief. Finally spotting the big NCO, they descend upon him. The military personnel in the room understand what is happening and try to stop the agents, but are pistol whipped or knocked down by martial arts moves or buttstrokes.

The chief knows time has run out for him and makes the only move he can. Reaching down he grasps the Inabular Device, twists and pulls while pressing a button on the device that activates a fail-safe self-destruct sequence. The entire time machine disengages in an instant and the fail-safe destruct sequence begins. The chief implanted a destructive mechanism that fries every computer component if the Inabular Device is removed before the time-transfer sequence is complete with the activation button depressed. They only way to disable it is to reinsert the device and type in a code within a certain amount of time.

Not hesitating, he grasps Nora's wrist and pulls her, yelling to the women, "Come on!" and moves towards the back of the control room. He opens a door and hustles the women inside, shutting and locking it from the inside.

The walls contain several fake computer banks that he shoves aside, revealing a lighted corridor. He pushes the women in and follows, pulling the fake computer door shut behind him.

He explains to the women that the men are now in limbo, somewhere he can't explain, not in 1862 nor in 1980, just stuck somewhere between the time periods. He can't bring them back until he can get back to Clio. He doesn't know it, but it will be another 38 years before he can accomplish this task.

***

Minten's men don't break into the room and find the hidden door until long after the chief and the women have made their escape. The Clio Project time machine destroys itself in front of everyone. Nothing is going as Minten had planned. The senator is furious and threatens the general with demotion for a failed project and the chief with arrest for desertion and destruction of Air Force property. He uses the excuse that his insertion into the facility was an Inspector General exercise to see if there were any flaws in security. Using this ploy, he believes his ass is covered and the general looks like a failure.

Later, a secret Senate investigation looks into the project's failure. Since Minten was on the Bank Council and had oversight of the project, he was deemed responsible for the failure of the Clio Project and disgracefully removed from office. Six months later he was found dead of an apparent suicide, or as so the press was led to believe.

Chapter 36

1862

Rees falls onto his back when he rematerializes. "Dammit!" he curses as his head strikes the ground. He lays that way for a few minutes, taking deep breaths and staring at the sky through the trees, listening to the rustling of branches as the wind blows through them. He is amazed he didn't hallucinate as he usually does during transport.

Groaning, he rolls onto his side and sees his horse staggering and wide eyed.

"Guess they should have given you more sedative," he tells the animal, then forces himself to his feet. He walks over to the horse, talking softly. "You hear any Bob Seger?" he asks, then takes the animal's reins. He gives it a cube of sugar and rubs its nose until it calms.

"It's okay, boy," he keeps saying to the horse. "It's OK. Now, to figure out where we are," he says out loud, still talking to the horse.

Rees looks around to find his bearing, hoping to see something he can use as a landmark. He climbs into the saddle and pulls out his compass. He takes a reading and decides to head southeast, hoping to run across a river or railroad tracks.

Rees scans the area, watching the swaying trees and scurrying animals. This makes him think of his time with Nora. This is a mistake on his part, letting his mind wander.

"Halt!" he hears in a definite Southern drawl.

Shit! he thinks, scolding himself for being so inattentive, again, in enemy territory. *When am I going to learn?*

He turns the horse away from the voice, hoping to make a run for it, but several Rebel soldiers move into view from different angles, surrounding him and making escape impossible. He knows his uniform will keep him safe, but the men are standing so close they could shoot his horse, or worse, his face.

"Hi guys," he says in his friendliest manner.

"Hands where we can see them, Yank, and get off the horse," a sergeant orders.

Rees climbs down and is mildly amused when the Rebel sergeant salutes him. Rees hesitates, then returns the salute.

"Sir, I will need your pistol and sword please," the NCO asks politely.

Rees reaches down to unbuckle his belt and sees the soldiers tense slightly. He removes the belt and hands it to the sergeant. The sergeant nods to one of his troopers, who moves and takes it from Rees.

"Sir, if you would be so kind as to place your hands in front of you," the NCO asks, again politely, and Rees complies. Another soldier comes forward and ties a rope around his wrists.

"You are now my prisoner, sir," the sergeant drawls and turns to another soldier. "Search him."

The soldier does as he is ordered and completes a shoddy pat down, finding Rees' watch and compass. Satisfied he isn't carrying anything of importance and is secure, the soldier nods at the Rebel NCO. "He ain't got nuttin' on him, sarge, 'cept this here watch and compass."

The sergeant takes the items and pockets them. Rees makes sure he sees where the man puts the items. The compass he doesn't really care about, but the watch is another matter.

"That watch is a family heirloom, sergeant. I would appreciate it back."

"You will get it back if'n my commander says you can. All right Yank, start walking," the sergeant orders.

"Okay, which way?" Rees asks.

One of the soldiers slams the butt of his rifle into the kidney area of Rees' back. The uniforms are bullet resistant, and the strike doesn't hurt as much as it should if he was wearing an ordinary uniform, but still. He grunts anyway and staggers forward, a little dramatically.

"Damn boy, I just asked which way."

The sergeant moves to the young soldier and gets in his face, "That's a damn officer, son. I don't care whose side he is on. Do something like that again and there will be hell to pay," he snarls. He looks at Rees and points in the direction he wants him to go. Rees walks a few hundred yards and can hear the soldiers behind him talking amongst themselves as they rifle through his belongings. Rees smiles slightly. *It's a good thing I don't have any of Capt. Epstein's hard tack or it would be gone, again,* he thinks.

"Something funny, Yank?" the sergeant asks.

"Yes, actually there is; something personal, you wouldn't understand," Rees answers.

The sergeant gives Rees the stink eye then moves forward a bit. "Move it y'all. I want to get back before dark."

"Where we going?" Rees asks casually.

The sergeant slows so Rees can catch up. "Taking you to a railroad depot where we keep prisoners. When we get enough of 'em, we transport 'em to Salisbury."

"Ah, good old Salisbury. Not Andersonville, huh? Always wanted to see that place."

The sergeant looks at Rees as if he was crazy.

"Are any of you guys over five-foot-eight?" Rees asks, looking around at each soldier. "Asking for a friend," he adds, laughing at his own joke, but still amazed that everyone is so short in this time period.

"Why don't ya shut your mouth, Yank, or I will have you gagged - officer or not," the sergeant says vehemently.

"Sorry, just making small talk. Get it, small talk," Rees replies then stares straight ahead, keeping track of his surroundings.

"Sergeant?" a soldier calls out, running up to him. "We found this letter in one of the bags. I can't read it all, but I can read that one name at the bottom."

The sergeant takes the paper from the soldier and begins reading, his eyes squinting as he realizes what he has. He drops the paper to his side and looks at Rees. "So, you're an important man with the Federals, huh. If'n you weren't in uniform, I would say you was a spy. The major will like this," he finishes, still holding the fake letter from President Lincoln. He pushes Rees forward to continue their trek.

They walk for almost two hours until Rees hears commotion in the distance. It's the sound of horses whinnying, men yelling, and equipment moving. A few minutes more and he can see fires and lanterns burning. They finally come out of the woods to an open area teeming with soldiers, horses, wagons, boxes of equipment, and the smallest train depot Rees has ever seen, either in person or in pictures.

"Wait here," the NCO says and walks toward the train depot. A few minutes pass before a major exits the shack, followed by the NCO, who is now carrying a lantern.

The major strolls up to Rees, the letter in his grasp. The NCO lifts the lantern so the major can see Rees' face. "Captain...?"

"Capt. Rees, sir. I would salute, but ...," he says, holding out his bound hands for emphasis. He smiles.

The major looks unmoved by the comment or the smile. "I'm Maj. Carter, commandant of this here depot. What outfit you with?"

"I'm with a special unit out of Washington, sir; no designation."

The major stares at Rees, thinking it odd the man has no unit insignia and claims no designation. "Okay, what are you doing here?"

"Sir, to be honest, I really don't know. I was on my way to meet up with a unit and receive my orders. Along the way, I became disoriented and got lost. I must have blacked out because when I came to, I was on my back, lying in the woods. I don't remember much else," Rees lies.

The major glares at Rees. "That dog don't hunt, captain," the major says, holding the letter up in front of Rees. "I think you are a scout or spy for that battalion coming here. Otherwise, why would you be carrying such a letter? We already caught one spy earlier tonight."

This intrigues Rees, but he remains poker-faced. "I wouldn't know about that, sir."

"Well, be that as it may, our little prisoner pen is being put to good use. One pen, no special treatment for officers. We will let you get acquainted with the others there as we are fix'n to send you up to Salisbury. I will be informing headquarters about this," he says, again holding up the letter. "They may just want to have a word with you."

The major turns to the NCO. "Good job, sergeant. Please escort the captain to the prisoner pen," he orders, then turns back to Rees. "Good to have met you, Capt. Rees. Please enjoy your stay," he says snidely, then heads back to his little depot.

The soldiers grab Rees by the arms and usher him over to a darkened area where a wrought-iron fence, interlaced with barbed wire, comes into view. As they get closer, he can see it's a good-sized pen, enough to hold about fifty men, but currently containing only two, who stand and look in Rees' direction. The soldiers remove Rees' bindings and push him into the pen, securing the gate behind him.

Rees turns back to the Rebel NCO. "What about my watch?" he asks.

The NCO stops and looks at Rees for a few seconds. He reaches into his pocket, retrieves the watch and stares at it. He bounces it in his hand, sighs, then walks over to Rees, the watch dangling from his fingers. "Sir, as much as I would love to keep this here watch, I could not in my good Christian conscience steal this, as that is what it would be in the eyes of the Lord," he says and hands the watch back to Rees.

Rees takes the watch and looks at the NCO. "Thank you, sergeant. I don't fault you for anything; it's war and war is hell. Good luck." He salutes the NCO.

The sergeant looks dumbfounded, then halfheartedly returns the salute, still thinking this Yank officer is crazy.

"Sgt. Rees?" Rees hears his name and turns to see Nionee and ... O'Toole?

Rees is surprised.

"Holy shit, Scott. It is you! Oh, hell, we thought we had lost you," Nionee says and moves closer.

Rees smiles and reaches out his hand. Nionee grabs it and pulls Rees into a bear hug. Rees returns the hug then pushes Nionee away. O'Toole stands there, silently taking it all in.

"What is going on, Ray? Why are you here?" Rees asks.

"Ah, got caught doing a recon on the Jeep over there."

"What Jeep?" Rees asks.

"The one that got destroyed. We were given a mission to bring it back, then to come find you. I guess that's two for me: found the Jeep and now I found you."

"Who all came?"

"Capt. Farnsworth, I mean Gen. Farnsworth," he corrects himself and sees the quizzical look on Rees' face. "Capt. Bouvier, Lt. Kriger, and Sgt. Tosseti, if you can believe it, along with Sgt. McGregor and ...," Nionee hesitates and looks at O'Toole. "Our mission is to get the Jeep, find you and go home," Nionee says, realizing he almost mentioned Emma.

"Ah, sir, can I talk to you privately?" Ray asks and, again, looks at O'Toole.

Rees realizes that O'Toole doesn't recognize him. And why should he; they haven't met yet. He motions for Nionee to follow him, and they walk a short distance away.

"What is going on?" he asks when out of earshot. "How did you get here?"

"We came to get you, well you and the Jeep that got blown up the last time we were here," Nionee explains and Rees arches an eyebrow.

"Listen, we can get to that later. First, we brought Miss Kelly back as well. We were planning on returning her to her home after we get the Jeep and found you," he says, glancing back at O'Toole, who is watching them. "O'Toole doesn't know. I wasn't sure if it was a good idea to let him know."

Rees nods. "Good call. We'll keep it that way for now. Once we get out of here, we can figure something out."

Ray continues. "Also, the Bank should know we are here," Nionee says, pointing to his camouflaged camera. "I would assume they have notified the others by now. That reminds me. When we do escape, which I assume we will, I also need to get my watch. Capt. Epstein gave us custom-made watches that allow the Bank to give us written messages."

Rees taps his buttons. "My camera got demolished after transport to 1980."

"Yeah, we saw the video."

Rees smiles. "He didn't happen to give you any hard tack, did he?" he asks chuckling.

"As a matter of fact," Ray replies and looks at Rees.

Rees look expectantly and Nionee shakes his head. "Ah, it's in my saddle bag, which is still on my horse, which I hope Kriger took back to camp."

"Oh well, had to ask," Rees jokingly says then looks at the far end of their cage and points to the darkest area of the fence. "That looks like a good spot to break out."

The two men move to the area and Rees grabs ahold of one of the iron bars. "Please tell me you have something for this. I'm all out of any material that can cut through this."

Nionee grins. "You ain't going to believe this," he says and opens the heel of one of his boots. Out drops a silver metal cylinder. He opens the other boot, and another cylinder falls out, this one gold.

"This is something Capt. Epstein made for us. I just happened to take these as my secret stash. Just like TV, I took the right tool for an unforeseen occasion and got it correct," he says with a smirk.

"Okay, what is it?" Rees asks.

"Corrosives, or explosives, depending on how you mix them. You take this one chemical," he says, holding up the silver cylinder, "and mix it full strength with this one," he holds up the gold cylinder, "and you can make a good-sized explosive."

"It takes a few minutes to react, but when it does, *Boom!*" he says smiling. "But, if you use a little of this chemical," he says, again holding the silver cylinder, "on the bars, then add a drop of this one," he adds, showing the other, "they will melt solid steel, or iron in this case. No explosions, just a wisp of chemical smoke and ta-da," he says with a little flare, "I wouldn't breathe it if I was you, but there shouldn't be much of a scent to tip off the guards."

"May the force be with you," Rees says with a smile.

"007 just wishes he were us," Nionee adds and both men share a laugh.

"It's good to see you, unalii."

Nionee smiles back, recognizing the Cherokee word for friend. "Good to see you, too, brother."

O'Toole sits back, still listening to the men's conversation, wondering what they are talking about and what kind of language they are speaking, thinking they are two of the strangest Cavalrymen he has ever met.

Chapter 37

1862

Kriger gallops back to the camp as fast and as safely as possible in the dark. *Damn, wish we had night vision,* he thinks, *Have to bring that up to Capt. Epstein.* When he believes he is close enough, he begins whispering into his built-in mic, calling for the others as he nears camp. Finally, Farnsworth answers him.

"We read you. How'd it go?"

"Not good, Nionee got caught. I'm coming in," Kriger replies and moves a little faster. He makes camp a minute later and jumps off his horse, releasing the reins of Nionee's horse at the same time.

"What happened?" Farnsworth asks, as he and the others approach. Kriger explains what transpired at the train depot.

"Dammit, I told you two to just conduct a recon and get back here," Farnsworth grumbles. "Now we have to go get him as well as get the Jeep, then go look for Rees."

"Sorry, sir. The only way we could verify_if it was the Jeep was to have one of us lift the tarp and see," Kriger says apologetically.

Farnsworth places his hands on his hip, looks down, then slowly releases a breath. "It's all right, sergeant. I know you men had to make a judgement call. I would've done the same, I'm sure. We've been in worse spots, and Nionee can handle himself."

"We're not going to leave him there, are we?" Bouvier asks.

Farnsworth looks sidelong at the man. "No, of course not. But we have to be smart about this and we still have a train to take care of tomorrow."

"Okay then, what youse want us to do?" Tosseti asks, wanting in on the conversation.

Farnsworth looks at Kriger. Then everyone else looks at Kriger. Kriger moves his head back and forth, watching them watch him.

"What?" he asks nervously.

Farnworth moves to the man. "You're going to go back and get yourself captured."

"What?!" Kriger cries, horrified.

"Hear me out. Not a big deal. Rees and I escaped easily. You have the equipment and hidden weapons. You get captured and, when they throw you in with Nionee, tell him the plan is still on and then you two make your escape. Nothing to it. It's not that far of a walk. And when you get within voice range, let us know. We will pick you up and continue on. Capture the Jeep, find Rees, and take the lady home."

Kriger shakes his head. "Why me? Why can't Tosseti go? He's dressed as an NCO; I'm an officer. What if they throw me into a different jail?"

"Not likely. They usually don't care until you get to either Andersonville or Salisbury prison, then they separate non-coms from officers. They don't have the manpower to watch over two prisoner pens. Don't worry," Farnsworth reassures him.

"Besides numb nuts," Bouvier chimes in, "You lost him; you go get him back."

Kriger is about to say something rude when he notices Emma watching him. Biting back the remark, he instead points his finger at Bouvier. "I'll get payback, Jack. Just wait." He looks at Farnsworth. "Let me get something to eat, then I'll head out, sir. But I still don't like it."

He moves to the fire and, not picky, scoops some of whatever is cooking onto a plate.

Bouvier moves over to Farnsworth. "Sir, you really think this is a good idea?"

Farnsworth smiles. "He'll be fine. I trust him. I know it can be dangerous, but these soldiers, most of them at least, have a code of honor. Some can be a bag of dicks, but from what I've seen so far, the older soldiers, NCOs and officers, treat prisoners well, unless they take him to Salisbury. Then he's screwed."

Bouvier's eyes widen, suddenly worried. Farnsworth smiles little more broadly, "Jack, lighten up. I'm kidding. He'll be fine," adding, "as long as they escape and don't get sent to Salisbury."

***

Kriger ensures he has everything he needs to get out of the prisoner pen, then he and Tosseti ride out of the camp. Once they are as close as they deem safe without being seen, Kriger dismounts and says good-bye to Tosseti. "Better youse than me, Dave," Tosseti says. "I would put a world of hurt on them Rebs. I ain't got youse patience. Have fun and tell Ray I said hello."

Kriger rolls his eyes and turns away, giving a half wave as he sets off walking to the train depot.

It doesn't take long before Kriger can hear the commotion of the railyard. He stops and watches it for a few minutes, takes a deep breath and continues walking. He doesn't get ten feet before he is challenged. Freezing in his track, he raises his arms in surrender.

A few seconds later, a gray-uniformed soldier carrying a long musket appears out of the shadows. He squints as he tries to see who he has stopped, then widens them when he realizes it's a Union officer.

"Stop right there," he orders.

"I am stopped, as you can plainly see," Kriger tells him, frustrated with the charade.

"Don't get smart with me Yank, or you'll be regretting it."

"Oh, I already am regretting it."

"I said shut your smart mouth, Yank. You are now my prisoner."

"I gather that, and it's sir. I am still an officer in the U.S. military," he replies, pointing to his rank, then adds, "private."

The young soldier presses his lips together, then shakes his weapon in the direction of the railroad. "Get moving, sir," he utters, disdain in his voice.

"Prisoner coming in!" the soldier shouts as they make their way to the depot and a well-lit area.

A couple of other soldiers join them as the major comes out to see what the noise is about. He watches as Kriger marches up to the small shack, the guard prodding him from behind.

"Stop right there, Yank," the guard orders.

Kriger looks up at the major, who is looking down at him from the platform, hands on his hips. Kriger keeps his hands at his sides.

"I would salute you, sir, but I do not wish to get shot."

The major chuckles. "I understand your predicament and I would do the same if I was in your shoes. I can overlook it, of course."

Maj. Carter jumps down to look Kriger in the eyes. "Well, well, well ... another Yankee officer. A lieutenant this time. First a corporal, then a sergeant, then a captain, now a lieutenant," he says with a grin and looks around. "Hell, boys. The way our night is going, we might just wind up winning this war with all the Yankees getting captured." He finishes to sounds of laughter from the Rebel soldiers standing around them.

"Search him," he orders, and the soldier who captured him does so, reporting that Kriger has nothing on him.

"Where is your equipment? Weapons?" Maj. Carter asks.

Kriger tells him the pre-planned story. "I became separated from my unit a few days ago, been trying to find them, or anyone. My horse spooked a few miles back and threw me and I lost my pistol. I became disoriented and ended up here."

Carter nods as he listens. "Okay lieutenant. You are now a prisoner of the Confederate Army. You will be placed in the pen with the others and then you will be sent to Salisbury as soon as possible," he informs Kriger, then looks at the guard who captured him. "Take the lieutenant to the pen, then return to picket duty."

He looks back at Kriger. "Make yourself at home," he says then turns to leave.

Kriger smiles, straightens, and salutes the major. The major stops, sighs and returns the salute.

The guard doesn't speak as he escorts Kriger to the pen. Once there, the guard on duty opens the gate.

"Dagnabit Frank, we done got us another mudsill," the guard says. "Four in one day. Not bad."

"Yup, caught him wandering around in the woods, lost. C'mon, get on in there, Yank, I mean *sir*," he says sarcastically. "I gotta get back to picket duty." He shoves Kriger into the pen unceremoniously, officer or not.

Kriger stumbles a few feet and turns back to face the guards. "Ya'll have a nice day now, ya hear?" he replies in a mocking southern accent.

"I remember saying almost the same thing the first time I was captured," a familiar voice says. Kriger whirls around to see Rees standing in front of him, hands on his hips, grinning broadly, with Nionee and O'Toole standing behind him.

"Scott!" Kriger shouts and moves to the man, grabbing his hand and pulling him into a hug. "Holy cow. I mean HOLY COW! Where the hell have you been? How did you get here?" As he blurts out questions, he glances at Nionee and O'Toole. "Hey Ray, hey Andy."

He returns his attention to Rees. "Damn, we thought we lost you forever," he says then stops. O'Toole is standing there, looking dumb struck.

Kriger's mouth drops open, and he looks back at Rees, who is holding his finger to his lips, indicating quiet.

O'Toole moves forward. "You know me as well?"

Kriger just stares. "Ah, no," he says, looking at Rees who is subtly shaking his head.

"Not our Andy, Dave," he whispers, shaking his head. "Long story."

"Oh, of that I have no doubt, Scott."

"Well, sir, how did you know my name, if I may ask?"

"You look like someone I know named Andy. I thought maybe you were him for a second. Now that I look at you, nope, not him."

O'Toole stares at Kriger, then slowly nods and walks away, shaking his head.

Rees begins to fill Kriger in on their plan. Kriger opens his belt buckle and removes a .22-caliber pistol.

"What do you have Rees?" he asks.

"Not much. I used my plastic explosive when Farnsworth and I were captured the first time. Still have my buttons, of course, and my knife. Most of my stuff is on my horse and my weapons are in the depot, I think. The Rebs took my belt and pistol and I saw them being handed to the major."

Rees looks at Nionee, who is also retrieving his pistol, then turns to O'Toole.

"Corp. O'Toole, are you with us on this?"

"Sir, I do not have any idea what you three are going to do. I know

I'm just a pie eater, but I do not know what you are jawing about.

"Corporal, we are a special unit out of Washington D.C. We were tasked to recapture a secret project that is due to leave this train depot. We are going to escape, then finish our mission, okay?"

O'Toole nods, unconvinced.

"Good. Now get what things you have; we're out of here in a few minutes," he orders, turning back to Nionee and Kriger, smiling.

"I think that will get him motivated. I might get used to this officer stuff."

The other men sigh and roll their eyes.

Rees keeps smiling. "Okay, here's the plan," he says, laying it out for them.

***

The four men wait until most of the railyard personnel are asleep and the area is quiet, except for the sounds of nocturnal animals scurrying about, the occasional snort of a horse, or the crunch of gravel as a soldier walks his post or heads for the woods to relieve himself.

The guard on duty at the gate is half asleep, so they deem it time to take advantage of the situation. Nionee pours the two chemicals onto the wrought-iron bars, and they watch as the fumes begin to drift away and the corrosive compound eats into the metal.

O'Toole is fascinated but knows not to say anything. He is impressed by these strange men from Washington D.C.

Once the iron is eroded, Nionee and Kriger each grab a bar and slowly begin twisting until they break free. Rees and O'Toole watch for anyone approaching and the guard. So far, so good.

Once enough bars are removed, the men make their way out of the pen. Kriger and O'Toole quietly move to where the horses are kept while Rees and Nionee walk through the woods to where they can see the depot.

Kriger's and O'Toole's assignment is to get to the horses, saddle four and head out of camp, undetected. Once safely away from the railroad station, they are to make as much noise as possible as a distraction, so Rees and Nionee can sneak into the depot and retrieve Rees' gear. Then Rees and Nionee will run into the woods and hide. When the dust settles, they will call Kriger with their location for a rendezvous. Easy as pie.

Kriger and O'Toole make it to the horses and are only able to saddle three of them. While Kriger is grabbing a saddle for the fourth animal, a groggy Rebel walks past, pulling his suspenders up over his shoulder as he makes his way back to his tent after relieving himself. He hears the two men among the horses and walks over.

"Hey, whatcha all doing there?" he asks, moving toward them.

Kriger stops trying to lift the saddle and looks at the half-asleep soldier.

"Ah, the major wants the horses ready to go first thing in the morning. I thought I would get a head start."

"What?" the soldier asks. As he gets closer, he sees that Kriger is wearing the blue uniform of a U.S. Cavalryman.

Kriger realizes this when he sees the man's eyes grow wide and begins to back away. "Yankees! Yankees escaping!" he starts shouting and running to the tents where a couple of Rebels emerge.

"Andy, we gotta go!" Kriger shouts, dropping the saddle and throwing himself onto one of the other horses. Andy does the same, grabbing the reins of the third horse, and both men whoop and shout to scatter the other horses. The startled animals begin running in every direction.

A gunshot rings out and Kriger swears a bullet whizzed by his head. He instinctively ducks and yells for Andy to get moving. Another musket is fired, then another. One round finds its mark, striking Kriger in the small of his back. Kriger winces, reaching around to rub the area of his back and cursing whoever shot him. He continues, but not before turning around and seeing the soldiers pouring out of their tents and giving chase.

Kriger reaches down and removes a button, turns the small bevel, and throws it hard over his shoulder in the direction of the Rebels. He turns his horse and chases after O'Toole.

The explosion and extremely bright flash blind all the soldiers running after them. Kriger closes his eyes to protect them from the illumination and gallops past the depot and into the woods. Once he is a good distance away, he throws another flash grenade button at the tracks and moves further into the woods, then back around to a safe area. The second button detonates with a loud blast, giving off another brilliant flash of blinding light.

Most of the soldiers are running in the direction they last saw Kriger and O'Toole ride off. Others are trying to round up horses so they can saddle them for the chase. No one is paying any attention to the two blue-clad individuals walking briskly to the train depot shack. The confusion Kriger caused makes it easy for Rees and Nionee to gain entry unnoticed.

Nionee keeps watch as Rees rummages through the small shack, looking for his belt. It takes less than a minute for him to locate his missing items. He hurriedly dons the belt, ensuring his weapon is still in the holster. He finds two watches and three compasses, gathering everything then tapping Nionee on the back before making his way out of the door.

The two walk toward the wooded area. Before they reach the safety of the woods, they hear the sound of a locomotive. Both men stop and turn, looking up the tracks to see the front light of the iron beast moving in their direction.

"We need to get back. That train's here for the Jeep," Nionee says.

Once in the woods, they run parallel with the tracks, going south a few hundred feet, then crossing over and making their way east.

"Kriger, you read me?" Nionee asks when they think they are safe. He calls a couple of times before Kriger answers.

"Yes, I can hear you. Where the hell are you?"

Nionee gives him an estimated position, and Kriger says they are on the way. Rees and Nionee keep hidden until they hear movement about fifty feet away.

"We hear movement. If that's you, stop."

"Roger, I'm stopped," Kriger answers.

"Stand by, we'll be there in a minute," he tells Kriger and nods at Rees. Both men stand and begin running.

When they find Kriger, there is no O'Toole.

"Where's O'Toole?" Rees asks.

"I have no idea. I thought he was behind me."

"Shit," Rees swears. "Okay, that's fine. I don't assume he was part of the plan anyway. He's probably heading back to his unit."

"What if he is, then finishes out the war and returns home? That's gonna cause some heart attacks," Nionee adds.

"Can't worry about that. Besides, if you remember, he wasn't in the history book," Rees says.

"As far as we know. Things change. Besides, not everyone was in the history books and not everyone was accounted for either."

Rees shakes his head. "Like I said, Ray, we can't worry about it. Oh, before I forget," Rees says, pulling out the compasses and watches. As he hands them out, both Kriger's and Nionee's begin vibrating. The men open them and read the message scrolling through it. Both chuckle. Kriger looks at Rees.

"Col. Black says he's glad you made it back, but your ass is his when you return."

"And," Nionee adds, "he says that you better make it back this time."

Rees smiles and nods, looking at Nionee's camera button. He salutes. "Yes, sir," and laughs.

"Okay, let's get going," Rees orders.

Kriger looks at the second horse, then Nionee. "I guess one of us rides bitch," he says and points at the lieutenant bar on his shoulder. Nionee shakes his head. Kriger reaches down and helps Nionee onto the back of the horse.

"You do realize that I'm a better horseman than you," Nionee says as he adjusts his weight to get comfortable.

"Oh, why is that? Because you're an Indian?" Kriger replies.

"That's Native American, and no. You, Tosseti and Rees are the worst horse riders I have ever seen. I'm just better."

Rees looks at Nionee. "I'm a great horseman."

Nionee snorts. "How many times you fall on your ass, sir."

Rees glares at the man. "Let's ride. We got a train to stop."

Once everyone is ready, they turn east and travel in a semi-circle back toward the temporary camp. They slowly make their way through the forest, not wanting to hit a low-hanging tree branch or have a horse stumble. They watch the rosy hue of the sky as the sun begins its ascent, bringing another cloudless day that will make their travels easier.

It doesn't take the three men long until they are within earshot of the camp. Kriger announces their return and informs Farnsworth that they have a guest with them. They make their way into the camp and are met by the rest of the team.

"Holy shit!" Tosseti swears when he sees Rees. "How the hell did you find us?"

Rees climbs off his horse and is greeted with handshakes, back slaps and smiles all around.

Farnsworth nods and looks at Rees. "Good to see you. What's the situation?"

"I went back to 1980."

"Yeah, we know that. Saw the video," he says, then points at Rees' head. "I see you got rid of the beard and hair."

Rees self-consciously rubs his scalp.

"Yeah, the general didn't like my SpecOps look."

The small gathering chuckles at the quip, then Farnsworth becomes serious again. "What happened while you were there?"

"Well, I'm not quite sure what is going on now ... I mean since I left ... but things changed because of my return, to what extent I have no idea. When I left the Bank, our former selves were not in the exact same situation as before. I knew you would be sent here because the chief knew when to send you."

"Yes, he explained that to us. Funny keeping a secret all these years," Bouvier interjects.

"Well, we will get the full story later. It's just good to have you back," Farnsworth says.

"Hey, what about us?" Kriger asks. "We were almost killed, and we don't get any love."

The others stare at Kriger, who looks incredulous.

"Hey, just asking."

"Welcome back Kriger, Nionee," Farnsworth finally says to the two men.

Rees moves closer to Farnsworth. "We need to move. The train just made it to the depot, so I'm sure they have the Jeep loaded by now."

"Yeah, thought I heard the whistle," Farnsworth says and tells everyone to break camp and get ready to move out. He turns back to Rees and goes over the plan with him. By the time he finishes, the squad is ready to depart. Everyone mounts up and they move northeast.

They arrive at the designated location to board the train, but before they can get to the crest of a hill that will lead them to the rail line, they hear an awful commotion on the other side. They hurry to the top of the hill overlooking the train tracks and watch as their plans are destroyed.

***

After the escape and during the confusion, O'Toole decides he doesn't want anything to do with these strange horsemen who say they are from a special unit. As he is fleeing the depot, following the one called Lt. Kriger, he turns his horse in a different direction to search for his own regiment.

Chapter 38

Sgt. Baine stands by the wagon with several others, guarding the precious cargo. There are men running all around, searching for the four escaped Yankee prisoners. Baine doesn't really care about the escapees; he just wants to get the captured item out of here and into Richmond's hands. Baines' thoughts are interrupted by a locomotive whistle sounding from down the tracks. A few minutes later, there is the hissing sound of air blowing as an engine comes slowly to a stop in front of him.

He turns toward the shack just in time to see the major emerge, walking briskly to the train. Baine can't hear what he says to the engineer, but he sees the major point to the flatcar. Baine approaches just as the major turns away from the engineer.

"Ah, sergeant. As you can see the train is here, finally. I ordered the engineer to get the train turned around and explained that he will be taking a very valuable piece of hardware to Richmond. Additionally, sergeant, I believe you and your men should go along."

Baine shakes his head. "I cannot do that, sir. I am sure Capt. Absher will be needing me with him."

"That's been taking care of, sergeant. I sent a message to the good captain explaining that I feel it best if you and your men guard this, whatever it is, until it arrives in Richmond. Besides, you can explain what this is better than some other sergeant or corporal who doesn't know what they have."

"Sir, I do not know what we have!"

"Be that as it may, sergeant, you have seen what it can do. I mean, you said you saw it working until y'all decided to blow it up," the major says with a wry smile. "Now get your men ready, get resupplied and I'll let the engineer know you'll be tagging along and that you are in charge of this contraption until you release it to officials in Richmond."

Baine bites his lower lip and looks at the flatcar, then back at the major.

"Yes, sir," he says, resigned to the situation. He salutes and goes to prepare his men.

It doesn't take long for the train to turn around, take on some wood and water, and connect to the flatcar. Once complete, Baine and his men load their horses onto one of the equestrian cars, then make their way to the flatcar carrying the horseless wagon. Baine has six extra men for the trip and tells them to go to the passenger car.

After he ensures the horseless wagon is secure, Baine joins his men in the passenger car. They are the only soldiers on the train. The train is light, as the only cars attached are the one with the mysterious cargo, the box car containing the horses, another flatcar with some old equipment going back for repair, and a caboose.

The engineer told Baine it will take more than a day to get to Richmond. They can't travel faster than fifteen miles per hour due to the older type of track. This section of the rail line has not received the new solid-steel tracks. These outdated tracks are made of wood and covered with a strip of metal. Baine isn't happy, but there's nothing he can do.

The train moves out slowly, gaining speed until it hits fifteen to sixteen miles per hour. Baine curses. "I can walk faster than this."

He settles into his seat, watching the scenery slowly creeping by, lulling him into a hypnotic state. They are about twenty miles into the trip when, without warning, the train begins braking hard. The sudden jolt brings him and the others out of their trances. Baine springs to his feet, ordering the others to get off their asses and get ready for trouble. He makes his way to the end of the car. Opening the door, he steps out onto the balcony and leans over the railing, looking toward the locomotive.

The engine is idling, steam spewing from underneath and the smokestack throwing small puffs of smoke into the still air. Baine jumps off the car and makes his way forward, his head on a swivel, looking for signs of trouble. Before he can get to the engine, one of the engineers climbs down, staring toward the front of the engine. He turns when he hears Baines footsteps crunching on the gravel behind him.

"What's the problem?" Blaine asks.

"See for yourself," the engineer replies, pointing at the missing section of track.

"Damn!" is all Blaine can say as his heart speeds up, knowing they are in for an attack. He begins backing up, looking into the woods, waiting for soldiers to come barreling out.

"Get back in there," he says to the engineer, "and get this thing moving backwards. We're about to be attacked, now move," he orders, pushing the man toward the locomotive.

Baine walks alongside the train as it begins reversing course. Still watching the woods, he jumps onto the steps leading to the engine compartment and joins the engineer and fireman.

"Move this thing faster!" he shouts.

"We can't. These tracks will only allow us to go about fifteen miles per hour," the engineer tells Baine, knowing this is something he already mentioned.

"I don't give damn! Get this thing moving or we are all dead. Now do it!" he orders, staring hard at the concerned engineer.

The engineer nods to the fireman, who dutifully begins adding more wood to the firebox. The engineer pushes on the throttle and the train begins to pick up speed. Twenty ... twenty-five ... thirty ... the speed increases.

Baine looks back up the tracks to see Union cavalry ride out of the woods, stop alongside the tracks and watch the train. He frowns. The cavalry then begins following them. The horsemen don't seem to be in a hurry and follow at a moderate gait. He turns his gaze in the opposite direction, looking back down the tracks.

He notices the guards on the flatcar are leaning out, looking in his direction, shouting and waving their arms. Suddenly he sees what they are getting excited about ... a section of the tracks that they were just on is now missing. He turns toward the engineer, eyes wide, shouting, "Stop the train! Stop the train!"

The engineer doesn't flinch as he reaches for the brakes. He has just enough time to place his hand on them before the caboose, now leading the train, leaves the tracks and pulls the first car, followed by the second, along with it. The caboose careens down the embankment, then strikes a boulder, causing it to cave in on itself, immediately killing the flagman riding inside.

The second car disengages from the caboose and speeds past it, only to dig into the ground and roll onto its side. The horses in the enclosed car begin screaming from fright and pain as the wooden sides begin breaking apart, the sliding door flying off. The car continues to slide, panels of wood breaking off until one side opens, spewing horses, both alive and dead, into the open.

The flatbed carrying the horseless wagon is next and, as it comes down the embankment, it slams into the car carrying the horses, causing even more damage and death. One guard tries to jump, but slips and falls underneath the car and is instantly crushed. A second guard leaps into the air and lands heavily on the ground, but he is crushed as the horseless wagon comes unstrapped and rolls a few times, with one roll landing right on top of the downed soldier.

The passenger car fares no better and follows suit with the others. It is pushed by the wood car and locomotive. Slowing, but unable to come to a complete stop, the locomotive continues to push the cars. The men inside are thrown about and either die or are severely injured as their bodies slam into each other. Windows, walls, seats and other flying objects become lethal weapons. The passenger car slides off the tracks and rolls once, then slides to a stop as the wood car crashes into it. The logs hurl into the air, becoming deadly projectiles. Many of those chunks of wood crash through the side of the passenger car, adding to the death toll.

Sgt. Baine jumps from the locomotive. Luckily for him, he strikes the embankment at an angle and is rewarded with only a broken arm and a twisted ankle. He bounces once and lands in a large puddle of stagnant water in a ditch at the bottom of the embankment. This cushions his tumble and prevents him from further injury.

The fireman and engineer stay with the locomotive as it is the last to leave the tracks, but on the opposite side. The initial jolt of the car leaving the track jostles the engineer, causing him to release the brake handle. The locomotive begins moving again, and the churning wheels grab the dirt, propelling the massive iron beast further down the embankment at a precarious angle. The engine leans and continues moving, but at a much slower pace. The engineer is bashed against the back of the cab, his skull caving from the impact. The fireman hangs on and is able to keep from being flung from the cab. The engine finally topples, and the water-filled steam tank breaks free from its mounts and releases massive amounts of steam that explodes directly into the cab. The fireman screams as the boiling air covers him, cooking him alive.

The Union soldiers arrive shortly after, all the men staring in awe at the spectacular crash they just witnessed. They stop their horses, but no one gets out of their saddle. Each man just gawks at the carnage.

Finally, the lieutenant unsaddles and orders his men to do the same. He tells them to search for anything useful and check for any survivors. The men run in all directions, moving broken boards and looking inside at what's left of the rail cars, some taking a quick glimpse at the grey-clad bodies spread around the area.

The box car was busted open, having spilled horses across the ground, most dead, others whinnying in pain, very few able to run away in fright. Gunshots ring out as the men mercifully shoot the injured horses, then continue their mission.

It doesn't take long for them to find the prize. The horseless wagon is lying upside down, several feet from the rest of the wreckage. The soldier who finds it yells, and the others join him. The men stare at the busted-up Jeep, not knowing what they were seeing. One by one the soldiers circle the mysterious contraption and began touching it, running their hands along the dark-green metal.

The lieutenant joins the gathering, stopping short as he stares.

"What is it, sir?" a trooper asks.

The lieutenant walks around the Jeep, brow furrowed in bewilderment. "I have no idea, but if the Rebs have it on a train, more than likely heading for Richmond, then it must be of some importance, otherwise we would not have been sent here to retrieve it," he answers, still examining the vehicle.

"All right, men. Quit your gawking," he orders, grabbing one soldier by the arm. "Sgt. Finley, go find the wagoneer and tell them to get over here. Johnson, go with him and grab a pulley so we can lift this thing onto the wagon."

It takes longer than the lieutenant would like to get the wagon. When it does arrive, it takes even more time to get the vehicle on to it, but so far, no Rebels have shown up. Once the wagon has its cargo onboard, the soldiers turn back the way they came, and with their prize, make way for their lines.

While the soldiers were looking for survivors, they missed Sgt. Baine, who was still unconscious and partially hidden, covered in water and mud. A few hours pass before he regains consciousness and does so cursing in pain and spewing dirty water from his mouth. His arm is broken; his ribs feel like they may be broken as well. He tries to stand and is rewarded with a sharp pain from his swollen and sprained ankle. Steeling himself against the discomfort, he stands, grimacing from the sharp pain running up his leg, dirty water pouring off his clothes.

Limping out of the water, he takes in the destruction all around. He slowly climbs up the embankment to the tracks. Using parts of the train for support, he makes his way back to where the horseless wagon should be, checking on the dead soldiers along the way. It is slow going, but he looks everywhere but can't find the wagon. Finally, he sees an area that has been greatly disturbed. There are lots of boot prints and hoof prints. Searching further he discovers wagon tracks leading to, then away from the area. The tracks are deeper in one direction, so he knows the wagon was carrying something extremely heavy, and that something is his "gift" to Richmond. It is now in the hands of the enemy.

Baine walks over to the wreckage, sits on the ground and leans against a wheelset that was separated during the crash. He leans his head back and passes out. A couple of hours later, he is awakened by the sound of horses approaching. He starts, wincing in pain. He realizes he doesn't have his weapon and doesn't know what to do. Did the Yanks return? If so, why? They got what they wanted. His eyes are blurry from just waking up and the pain racking his body. Before he can move, he sees boots coming in his direction. Still groggy, he doesn't notice the grey-clad men reaching for him. They attempt to get him up, but he yelps in agony when his arm is moved.

"Stop what y'all are doing right now. Can't you see he is badly injured? Get out of my way," the southern-tinged voice yells.

Baine recognizes a Confederate artillery uniform moving toward him.

Thank goodness, he thinks as the man stops and squats, placing a gentle hand on Baine's good shoulder and removing a white straw hat.

"Sgt. Baine?"

Baine gives a weak smile. "Good to see you, sir. I apologize for the mess, but there has been a bit of a situation, as I am sure you can see."

The captain snorts. "Yes, sergeant. I can see that."

Baine looks at the captain. "Sir, why are you here, may I ask?"

"I sent word of our discovery to the commander. I immediately received a reply that I was to bring the captured item by wagon to Richmond and, by no means, use the railroad. They said the Yanks were on their way to Hendricks Hill and that the rail would be captured or destroyed. I spoke with Maj. Carter, and he told me you had left several hours ago, but the train was only traveling at fifteen miles per hour. Upon hearing this news, I had hopes of catching up to you and taking the item by wagon before the Yanks showed up," he says, looking around. "But it looks like we were too late."

"I am sorry, sir; I should have been more alert."

"No, sergeant, you did your duty. It's unfortunate, but we can't do anything about it now," the captain says, patting the sergeant gently on the shoulder so as not to cause him any more pain. "We'll just have to hope God interferes and somehow makes that contraption disappear before them blue bellies can get it to Washington." He pauses, lost in thought for a second, then looks back at Baine. "That is not your nor my concern anymore, sergeant. Right now, we need to get you back to see the ol' sawbones."

"Oh captain, sir. That is not even funny."

***

Off in the distance U.S. Cavalry soldiers and a lone woman stand in the shadows, holding the reins of their horses and watching the scene below. The man dressed as a general shakes his head and looks at the captain standing next to him. The captain turns, pulls the reins of his horse and makes his way down the backside of the hill. The general takes a final look and moves away as well. The rest follow, all making their way away from the train wreckage.

Chapter 39

"Well, what's plan B?" Bouvier asks, riding up alongside Rees and Farnsworth.

"We still need to get the Jeep," Kriger adds.

Bouvier turns in his saddle and stares at Kriger. "Thank you very much, Capt. Obvious!"

Kriger gives Bouvier a derisive look and points to his silver bar. "That's Lt. Obvious, Capt. Jack-Ass!"

"You two, knock it off," Rees says then points to an area where there are trees and a stream. He orders the squad to move there and dismount. Once they do, the team gathers around Rees and Farnsworth. Farnsworth begins rubbing his chin in thought.

"Actually, I have an idea," he says, looking at the squad members. "We have a letter from President Lincoln."

Rees pats his uniform. "Ah shit. That major took mine and I didn't get it back," he tells the group.

As soon as he says this, Bouvier, Kriger, Tosseti, Nionee and Farnsworth all remove a letter from their saddlebags or person and hold it out to Rees.

"Ha, very funny. Okay, go on. You were saying?"

"We catch up to the unit that took the Jeep and show them the letter. We can either explain that we need to escort them to their destination, or we order them to relinquish control of the Jeep to us."

"Why would we escort them? I say just take control of the thing," Tosseti adds.

Bouvier looks at Tosseti. "We could, but they may start asking questions. If we take control of the Jeep and shoo them off, they will more than likely go running to their commander, who might send someone after us."

"I meant just shoot them and take it."

Everyone looks at Tosseti.

"First off, Sgt. Tosseti," Farnsworth says turning to look at the man, "we are not murderers. Killing during war or for our protection is one thing, but just shooting someone for no good reason is not acceptable," Farnsworth sternly chides him.

Tosseti stares Farnsworth in the eyes, not backing down, then lets out a breath. "Yes, sir. You are right, sir. Sorry."

Farnsworth nods. "Nothing to apologize for, sergeant. You're just saying what you feel, I get that. We good?"

"Yes, sir. We're good," Tosseti responds sincerely.

Rees breaks the awkward silence that follows. "Okay, good point. If we tell them we are added security from Washington, show them the letter, we can tag the Jeep whenever we want. Once we get to D.C, we can just ride off to Mount Airy and the Jeep gets transported back to where it belongs. Plus, we get an armed escort. A win-win for us."

"My thoughts exactly. Besides, as an added bonus, we get to see the city as it was in 1862. No sense in coming back in time if we can't do some sightseeing," Farnsworth says.

Rees shakes his head. "I don't know. Seems like all we do is get shot at, bombed, shoot back, get captured, escape, run. Not much time to really sightsee unless you like looking at the same old woods all the time."

"That's why I said I would like to see DC. Something different," Farnsworth adds then moves to his horse.

Following the visible hoof prints and deep furrows left by the wagon, it doesn't take the team long to catch up to the cavalrymen transporting the Jeep.

Once they find the Union soldiers, Farnsworth and Rees ride up to the officer. The captain salutes and introduces himself as Lt. Corbett.

"Lt. Corbett, I am Gen. Farnsworth and this is Capt. Rees. We are a special unit working out of Washington D.C.," he says, reaching for the letter. "If you don't mind, would you be so kind as to read this letter," he asks and hands it to the young officer.

The lieutenant reads the letter, and his face makes just the slightest change as he realizes who signed it. He folds it and hands it back to Farnsworth.

"What can I do for you, sir?" he asks formally.

"Well, we know what you have in the wagon, and I say congratulations on a well-executed plan. We were watching from afar and were extremely impressed," Farnsworth expounds, hoping to inflate the man's pride.

"Why, thank you sir," the lieutenant says, smiling proudly.

"Yes, well the thing is, we were sent to retrieve it as well, but you beat us to the punch, so to speak. Anyway, we will be accompanying you to Washington, as I assume that is your destination, is it not?"

"Why, yes, sir, it is. And let me say, thank you. I will be more than happy for some extra eyes on this thing. I do not know what it is, but somebody must think it's important, so the more help we have, the better. I am sorry, sir, but I know that protocol requires I relinquish command to you, and under normal circumstance I would, but due to my strict orders, I must retain my command, sir."

"Oh, no. Relinquishing your command will not be necessary, lieutenant. It's yours and I completely understand. You carry on as you were. You have proven yourself competent and I would not dream of taking your command. We will fall in behind you as rear security. You need not worry about us."

"Yes, sir. Thank you, sir," the beaming lieutenant says, saluting and returning to his unit to update his men. Within a couple of minutes, the wagon again begins moving.

Once the team is far enough ahead, Rees starts laughing. "Good grief, you can pour on some bull crap. You need to run for office when you get out of the Air Force."

"What? I meant it. I don't want his command; I just want us near the Jeep until we decide to place a transponder on it. And as for his well-executed plan, I meant that, too. Saved us from having to work up a sweat getting the damn thing."

Rees ponders this. "You know, you're right. Who needs action and excitement? We don't, that's for sure. But now I'll probably never get to do a train heist."

Farnsworth turns his horse around and signals for the others to move forward. "Why not? We have a time machine. We could come back and join up with Jesse James or the Farrington brothers. Hell, we could go out West and hook up with Black Jack Ketchum."

Rees shakes his head. "Sorry, I only know Jesses James."

"What I'm saying is, we could go be in any part of history we want."

"Ah, I don't think the Bank is going to let us use the Clio Project as our own little amusement park or for our private vacation travels."

Farnsworth laughs as the others approach. They explain their discussion with the lieutenant, then move out to catch up to the Union troops guarding the Jeep.

Rees spends some more time talking with the lieutenant and discovers the young man is from New York City and currently with the 1st District of Columbia Cavalry Regiment. He said that the Pinkerton Agency received information from one of their spies of a horseless wagon the Rebels had in their possession, so his unit was dispatched to find and capture it.

Rees spends the next few hours talking shop, home life, anything to make the lieutenant feel they are becoming friends. The lieutenant explains that they intend to skirt past Rocky Mount, cross the Roanoke River into Virginia, zigzagging until they reach Washington, trying their best to avoid any of Lee's men along the way.

"Why not go to Pamlico River and have a ship take you north? I thought Burnside held the entranceway."

"Still too many Rebel boats patrolling the river. Burnside only has sections blocked off; the Rebs still own the rivers."

The lieutenant apologizes, but that is all he can say at this point. Rees nods his understanding and moves back to the rear of the column where Farnsworth and the others are waiting.

"Any word?" Farnsworth asks when Rees moves beside him.

Rees chuckles. "Almost the same route we took taking O'Toole back. Same principle at least. Move past larger towns until we hit the river, then cross over into Virginia and make our way the best we can. The man isn't looking for a fight and I can't blame him."

Farnsworth shakes his head. "We are too big of a group to be crashing through Rebel territory and I can't see them making it to Washington. We know the history of the area, or some of it at least. We were closer to the mountains when we took O'Toole home. Moving through Virginia, in the center of the state, is asking for trouble."

"I agree. I know the lieutenant is appreciative of the extra help, but I don't think he is going to allow us anywhere near the Jeep."

"No, he won't, but we just need to get near it and throw the transponder into the wagon. They can transport the whole thing then. I want to travel with them as long as we can. Safety in numbers and all that, until we get closer to DC, which takes us closer to Mount Airy. We can signal for the Jeep to be transported, then move on to our last objective."

Rees nods. "Okay by me."

Farnsworth laughs. "Why thank you, captain."

***

That night they set up camp and the officers in Rees' group meet with Lt. Corbett, who has a small fire burning outside his tent. Kriger breaks out some of their rations and Rees' eyes grow wide when he gets a tin of hard tack.

"Thought you might be missing these," Kriger teases when he gives the treats to Rees, who beams with delight.

Kriger also produces coffee grounds and shares it with Corbett.

"Tosseti and Nionee are sharing theirs with your troops, lieutenant, if that's okay with you," Kriger informs the officer.

Corbett is thrilled and thanks the officers for their generosity.

While pouring coffee, the lieutenant looks over to Farnsworth. "I'm sorry Gen. Farnsworth, but I've never heard of a special unit in Washington like yours and I've been there for quite some time now."

Farnsworth takes a sip of coffee and smiles. "You wouldn't, lieutenant. That's the point. Even the Pinkertons don't know about us. We were picked by the president, Sec. Stanton, and Gen. McClellan. I'm sure there are a few others, but we only work for them."

The lieutenant leans against his tent pole, watching the strange group of men.

"And your accent, sir. I hear a twinge of the South in there."

Rees snorts and spews some coffee. The others chuckle and look at Farnsworth.

"Damn, sir. He's done figured you out," Bouvier says.

Farnsworth grins, then looks up at the Union officer. "Yes lieutenant, you do. I was born in the South, but reared most of my life in the North. I get it all the time."

"Sorry, sir. I wasn't making an accusation."

"I am sure you weren't, Lt. Corbett. It's quite all right. Now why don't we talk about our travel plans while we enjoy our coffee," Farnsworth says, changing the subject. The lieutenant takes a seat next to Kriger and explains the morning route.

The next day everyone is up before dawn. The quiet night transitions into energetic noise with the sounds of men talking, scurrying around, fires being stoked, pots and plates banging, and tents being broken down. The typical sounds of a military unit making ready for another day of traveling.

There is the smell of food cooking, thanks to the provisions given to the real Union troops from the time travelers. They were eating real pork as well as drinking real coffee. Things their own Sanitary could not provide them.

"How do we transfer into your unit?" one of the troopers asks, laughing.

"Well, I could tell youse, but then I'd have to kill ya," Tosseti informs the stricken-looking trooper. Even when Tosseti winks and gives him a smile, the man is still uncertain about the large, gruff, red-haired sergeant with the heavy New England accent.

Just as the first light of day is streaking through the trees, cutting little beams of brilliance into the morning mist, the order is given to move out.

The entire trip Rees and Farnsworth are worried about being seen by locals or, worse, a Rebel patrol. Farnsworth tells his team to keep alert, as his Spidey senses are tingling.

When they are a few hundred yards from the river, they halt. Rees and Farnsworth ride up to see what is going on and are met by Lt. Corbett.

"There's a bridge along this river, but I'm not exactly sure where. It shouldn't be too far along the bank. I am going to send a couple of my men east to scout, and I could use some help from your men, sir."

Rees looks at Farnsworth. "I'll go and I'll take Jack with me."

Rees and Bouvier ride off to the west. It doesn't take long for them to locate the bridge. They stop short of it and watch for any signs of Rebel soldiers guarding it or, possibly, lying in wait. Confident the bridge is clear, they ride back to inform the others.

The unit makes it across the bridge with no problems, something Farnsworth is glad for, but he is still anxious.

The trek through Virginia is long and tedious. The unit moves slowly and stops often as the soldiers must scout ahead to ensure clear travel routes. The unit must avoid towns and farms, as well as any people who may be hunting in the forests. Crossing roads is a hazard, but it is the one area where it is acceptable to be seen by locals or patrols who also are using them.

"I don't remember it taking this long to get to Maryland," Rees tells Farnsworth as they listlessly move along behind the wagon.

"It didn't, but we were a three-man unit. We were more maneuverable than we are now. That and this officer is extremely efficient. He's not taking any chances on getting caught. I'm sure Washington wants this Jeep badly, and while I would like him to move faster, the good lieutenant is determined to see his mission through, damn the time restraints. I admire that," Farnsworth tells Rees.

"Oh, I'm with you on that sir," Rees says and looks back at the others. "We should be getting close to the James River, if I'm reading this map right," he adds, showing his map to Farnsworth.

Farnsworth studies the map and smiles. "You are correct," he says and stops as the unit in front stops.

Lt. Corbett rides back to the two men and salutes Farnsworth. "Sir, we have arrived at the James River. This is where it gets dodgy, sir. The Rebs have control of the bridges."

"I assume you have a plan in place for this, lieutenant?" Farnsworth asks, looking in the direction of the river.

"Yes, sir. The plan was to use a boat to get the wagon across. There is an inlet where boats are supposed to be waiting on us. I was told this section of the river is the shortest for crossing. The river is still deep so I have men swimming across. They will pull a rope over and secure it to the other side. We should be able to pull ourselves across. Won't be easy, but it's what we were given as a plan."

"You hope," Farnsworth says, knowing this river somewhat well having boated and kayaked on it a few times.

"Yes, sir. I hope," the lieutenant replies with a slight grin. "I will let you know when we are ready to move out, sir." He salutes, leaving the time travelers to themselves.

"Well, this ought to be interesting," Rees says and turns as Bouvier and Kriger ride up.

"What's up?" Bouvier asks.

"River crossing, by boat," Rees tells him.

"Oh, this isn't going to be fun at all," Kriger adds.

"If I'm correct, this is a pretty big river. Saw it once when I was in Richmond. Can't we use a bridge?" Bouvier asks.

By now, the rest of the group is moving up. Emma looks tired, and Farnsworth feels for her. It's not easy being a woman in this century, much less traipsing for days through the woods with a bunch of smelly men.

"How are you, Miss Kelly?" he asks when she rides up to him.

"I am fine, general, and I told you to call me Emma. All of you, please call me Emma. No sense being formal out here in the woods."

"Yes ma'am, Emma," Farnsworth says with a smile. "Okay, everyone. We are at the James River. The plan is to pull ourselves across in boats."

"Oh joy, now I'm in the Navy," Tosseti says. "And what do you mean by pull?"

Kriger looks at Tosseti. "You remember when we went to see *The Outlaw Jose Wales*?"

Tosseti thinks a minute, then nods. "Yeah. Yeah, cool movie."

"You remember the part when that slimy bastard was taking Josey across the river, then went back to get the Red Legs soldiers who were chasing him."

"Oh, yeah. You mean we're pulling ourselves across like that?" Tosseti, a bit stunned.

"So, it would seem," Kriger answers, looking to Farnsworth for confirmation.

Tosseti's face scrounges up. "Hey, wait a minute. Didn't Wales shoot the rope and the boat went floating off down the river?"

"That's in the movie, Tosseti. Nobody's shooting the rope. Relax,"

Bouvier tells the man.

Rees turns at the sound of an approaching horse and sees the lieutenant returning.

"Our guys are swimming across now. The boats are ready. We can begin loading," he informs the group and heads back to the front of the column. A few minutes pass, then the wagon begins to move.

It doesn't take long to reach the large, flat boats. Soldiers are sliding a thick rope through holes in metal poles attached to the boats. The boats resemble small barges more so than usual boats; more like a ferry. Another rope is attached to the bow of the lead craft with the intent of having the soldiers on the shore assist by pulling.

The wagon is brought aboard and, one by one, the soldiers and Emma bring themselves and their horses on as well. By the time everyone is loaded and the ropes secured, they are ready to make their way across the river.

Each person grabs a section of rope, including Farnsworth, much to the dismay of Lt. Corbett, and begins pulling. Going is easy at first, as they are in calm water along the inlet. That doesn't last long as the boats meet the flowing waters of the James River, and they begin fighting the current.

Everyone pulls with all their might as sweat forms on their faces, streaming down in small rivulets. The real soldiers have it the worst, wearing heavy dark wool uniforms, making the already sweltering heat even worse. Luckily for Rees and his team, the new synthetics with nano technology keep them relatively cool.

It all seems to be going smoothly until they hear gun fire from the banks on the far side, catching everyone's attention. They can see the flashes of weapons and hear the reports of shooting.

One of the soldiers in the front boat yells and topples over the side into the river, disappearing as the current instantly pulls his body under. Small splinters of wood from the boat start flying as bullets strike the boards. The soldiers in the front boat start pulling faster, but minie' balls begin wreaking havoc as they have no protection other than the wagon.

A resounding boom is heard and, a second later, a large plume of water erupts next to where Rees is standing, soaking the man and those around him. Everyone hears more cannon and rifle fire.

The teams of horses in the front boat jump and scream as they, too, are shot, falling into the dark waters or dropping onto the wood planks of the boat, thrashing wildly in pain as they bleed out.

Tosseti begins cursing and threatening those who are shooting at them. The first boat slows to a stop and the second bumps into it. Rees runs and jumps over to the first boat and discovers Lt. Corbett lying on his back, eyes open with a look of surprise, a hole in his forehead. The river water is splashing onto the dead man in a type of baptism, washing away the blood that is still seeping from the wound.

Rees looks around to find a soldier hiding behind the wagon. He has an idea and runs back to the second boat to tell Farnsworth of his plan. Farnsworth agrees, so Rees grabs Tosseti, Bouvier, Nionee and Kriger. McGregor makes as if to go as well, but Rees orders him to stay. He knows he and the men from the future can take a round, but McGregor can't. The men run to the first boat. Rees goes to the wagon and can't find the last soldier but spots a bloody kepi where he once stood.

Rees and the others hurry to the front of the wagon. Nionee, Tosseti and Kriger grab the tongue and lift it to push. Bouvier and Rees lean against the wagon itself and begin shoving as well. At first the wagon resists, then it slowly begins to roll.

Tosseti curses louder as a minie' ball strikes him in the upper shoulder. The new uniform takes most of the impact but causes enough pain to remind Tosseti he is alive.

Rounds strike all around them and, soon, every person pushing the wagon has been hit at least once. They keep pushing until the wagon stops where the wheel drops off the first boat onto the second. The weight of the wagon causes the two boats to separate.

Farnsworth sees what is happening and he yells for McGregor to help. Both men release their rope and run toward the wagon. They grab it and begin pulling as hard as they can, straining to keep the boats together. Slowly the wagon wheels make it onto the second boat and begin rolling.

To make matters worse, while all this is happening, a thunderstorm moves in and torrents of rain begin cascading down. The boat planks are already slippery and the rain makes them more so. The men pulling and pushing slip, fall, get back up and slip again. The only good thing is that the shooting has slackened to almost nothing. The downpour is obscuring the visibility of those on the shore. Only an occasional gun shot and a sporadic cannon shot can be heard, neither coming as close to the boats as before.

In what seems like hours to the men when the wagon finally bounces over the lips of the two boats and rolls onto the deck of the second boat. The wagon comes to a rest and Emma drops down and quickly wedges pieces of loose wood under the wheels to keep it from rolling.

The exhausted men collapse to the deck, taking in gulps of air, some coughing, others spitting phlegm. Slowly they recover and look at each other and begin to laugh. Each man stands. Suddenly they realize they are moving, but they aren't pulling the rope. Everyone looks to the bow as the boat is being pulled toward the shore.

"Oh shit! The Rebs have the rope!" A couple of the men move to the ropes to start pulling in the opposite direction. Try as they might, they cannot stop the forward motion; there are too many on shore trying to reel them in like a giant fish.

Rees stops pulling and shakes his head. He looks at Tosseti, who stares back questioningly. Water pouring off the brim of his dark hat, Rees grins and Tosseti's eyes grow wide, suddenly understanding. He opens his mouth to say something then shuts it.

Rees pulls out his saber and runs to the raft's bow with the others watching in confusion. Rees finds the rope, taut as whoever is on the shore pulls. Rees raises his saber and begins whacking at the rope. It doesn't take but a few swipes with his razor-sharp sword to cut through the rope. The boat jerks as the pressure is released. Satisfied with his handy work, he jumps back onto the second boat.

"Good thinking, Capt. Rees," McGregor says with a wide smile. The men grab the rope and begin hauling themselves back the way they came. They only go a couple hundred feet when the rope goes slack. The boat begins to turn and move sideways as the current takes ahold of its navigation.

"Those sons of bitches cut the rope!" Kriger shouts over the din of thunderous rain.

Everyone on board sways as the boat bobs in the slightly choppy waters. Emma yelps as she loses her balance and Farnsworth grabs her arm just in time to keep her from toppling into the river.

The boats separate and both begin moving faster as they flow with the current. Slowly the raft they are on begins to spin, as there are no rudders to help keep it moving straight. Each person grabs whatever they can to steady themselves as the choppy water makes it hard to stand.

"What do we do?!" Bouvier shouts.

Farnsworth shakes his head. "Just go with it for now!"

"Why would they cut the rope?"

"Probably hoping they can catch us further down the river once we get near one of their bridges," Farnsworth shouts, trying to be heard over the storm and the now-raging waters.

"Oh, that's just great!" Bouvier shouts again. "What happens if we hit a bridge!"

Farnsworth turns to looks at the man somberly. "Then we go swimming!"

Chapter 40

Corp. O'Toole rides as fast as he can, mainly to get away from the train depot but also to get closer to his outfit. He travels almost non-stop, all day and all night, and still hasn't found his unit. He also believes he may be lost. Not wishing to run into any graybacks, he has been in the woods, trying to use the sun as a navigational beacon and checking rocks for moss. He believes he is heading in the right direction, but still worries. He knows his battalion was on its way south, toward Hendrick Hill. He is hoping to catch up to them there; problem is, he has to find the town.

Luckily for him, the horse he stole was saddled with some provisions: food, water, and a Spencer carbine. He stops at a small brook that has water trickling though some rocks and climbs down from his mount. He leads the horse to the brook and the animal quickly begins drinking. Watching the horse makes O'Toole thirsty, so he takes a swig of water, stares at the bubbling brook, then curses himself, frustrated for possibly being lost.

After patiently waiting for his stead to finish, he mounts the animal and continues moving south, now hoping to find any Union outfit.

O'Toole travels about five miles when he hears the faint sounds of battle. Concentrating, he locates the area from where the sound is coming and makes his way toward it. He knows that if there is fighting, he should be able to find a Union unit who may be able to direct him to his battalion, or maybe it's his battalion he hears. He spurs his horse and begins galloping as fast as he can through the woods, pulling the reins to make the horse dodge around the trees and ducking to avoid the lower branches.

He doesn't want to charge right in on the battle, at least not from one direction; no sense taking a chance of riding up behind the Confederates. His plan is to skirt around the fighting and approach from a flank. Doing it this way, he should be able to see who is fighting, then make his way to the Union lines.

The woods are thinning as he gets closer to the battle, the sounds intensifying, and he can ride a little faster as a result. He is excited, as is always the case when a battle is occurring. Not that he enjoys the brutality of war, but when the fighting begins, his adrenaline kicks in and he feels alive.

His mind is racing with all these thoughts and of what he needs to do when he gets to his lines. Still deep in thought, he breaks from the tree line at an angle and finds himself in the middle of ... he doesn't know what.

He can't stop his horse as he and the animal ride among men dressed in dark green, with green metal pots on their heads. Some are sprawled out along the top of a hill crest, others mill around a metal beast that looks like a water tank on wheels, with a man sticking halfway out of the top. All the unknown men are holding or carrying what look like weapons of a sort he's never seen.

His mind reels as he takes in the sight, turning his stead one way then another, not sure what to do. Who are they? Rebel? Union? Or something else?

O'Toole pulls his saber as the men begin moving around him. They seem just as surprised by his appearance as he is by theirs.

Some of the men raise their weapons at him. He thinks he is about to die when he feels movement behind him and turns to see a large, red-faced man charging him on foot. O'Toole's instincts take over and he pulls his saber and slashes at the man, catching him along the side of the face and flaying open his cheek. The startled man grabs his face and bellows, cursing like O'Toole has never heard.

O'Toole stares at the man, frozen and horrified at what he just did. His inattention gives some of the others time to come at him from another direction. He turns his horse to flee back from where he came. He doesn't get far when a shot rings out and his horse stumbles, then falls, trapping O'Toole's leg underneath. *Not again,* he thinks as the animal's weight pins him.

O'Toole yells from the pain and he senses movement. He turns to see several of the green-clad men running toward him, weapons at the ready. He struggles to remove his leg from under the dead horse, but the animal weighs too much for him to budge. Finally, the green-clad men are upon him, so he gives up trying to escape and flops to the ground, raising his hands in surrender.

"Don't shoot me!" he yells as they run up to him.

"Nobody's going to shoot you," a voice says.

"Then, can you please help get this beast off me?" he asks.

One of them, wearing several stripes on his sleeve, stands over him. O'Toole can see he has a name on his shirt: BOUVIER. The man looks at O'Toole and shakes his head.

"Shit!" is all Bouvier says, then, "You are a Union cavalryman, I take it? Corporal, is it?"

"Yes, sir. Now please, can you help me?"

The man who seems in charge nods to the others and they gather around the horse, pushing and pulling. O'Toole grimaces from the pain as the dead animal is moved off him and the man in charge helps him up, at the same time relieving him of his pistol.

"Can you walk, soldier?" he asks of O'Toole.

O'Toole sighs, trying to walk but the pain is too much, and he shakes his head.

"Tucker, McGuire, take him to the Duck."

Both men come to O'Toole's aid, draping his arms around their shoulders as they help him to the Duck, where Kriger is working on Tosseti. He has placed multiple bandages on his open wound and given him a shot of morphine. Tosseti is now in la-la land, blood still seeping through the white gauze, turning it bright red, but not as badly as before.

When they arrive at the Duck, they place him in a sitting position and Kriger moves to check on his leg. "Who are you? Who are you with?" O'Toole finally asks, breathing heavily from the struggle, as well as fear, hoping they are on his side.

O'Toole studies Kriger and his eyes grow wide as he recognizes the man. Before he can say anything, Rees approaches. "First answer my question. Who are you?"

O'Toole wasn't paying attention upon Rees' arrival, too busy watching Kriger work on his leg and trying to understand why the man hasn't said anything to him and why he is in a different set of clothing.

"Corp. Andy O'Toole, 3rd Regiment Maryland Volunteer Cavalry, 1st Brigade," he answers, looking up at his inquisitor. "And who ..." he starts to ask, then looks at Rees, his eyes growing wide for a second time, then he looks again at Kriger, then back at Rees.

"Lord, blessed Jesus," he says with his heavy Irish accent, then rubs his eyes.

"This can't be."

"What is the problem, corporal?" Rees asks with a worried expression.

"Sir, Capt. Rees, I just left you back at the train depot, you and Lt. Kriger here," he says pointing to Kriger.

Kriger stops working on the leg and stands next to Rees.

"His leg is fine, some swelling, slight sprain. Now what is this about leaving me, I mean us, at the train station. What train station?"

O'Toole just stares, listening to the sound of battle in the background, a sound that is coming closer. Without an answer, they hear several shots fired from the men on the crest of the hill.

"Watch him," Rees tells Kriger as he runs over to plop down next to Harris and Parks.

"Sgt. Parks, I thought I told you to stay in the Duck."

Parks grins. "Sorry, Sgt. Rees; can't let you have all the fun. Don't worry. I'm fine lying down like this."

Rees shakes his head as he looks out over the open field in front of him.

There are several cavalrymen charging their position, firing pistols and Sharps rifles in their direction. Some of his men return fire and Rees watches as one cavalryman tumbles off the back of his horse to land on the ground, bouncing once before coming to a rest. He doesn't move. The others are charging hard, and the shooting intensifies.

The M-60 on the Duck begins chattering and Rees watches Montoya sweeping the barrel and dropping several of the soldiers on horseback.

The M-60 grows silent and, when Rees looks again, no one is in the turret. Montoya has taken a minie' ball to the head, caving in his helmet and knocking him unconscious.

Parks stands up and begins what looks like a painful hobble towards the Duck to take control of the M-60. Rees is about to shout at him when the man is struck with a bullet in his back that goes right through his body, blowing blood and gore out the front of his chest. Parks falls face forward and lands heavily on the inclined ground, sliding down a few feet before coming to a rest.

Kriger runs over to his fallen comrade just as Rees drops down next to the man. They both roll Parks over and see the large exit wound in his chest and lifeless eyes staring heavenward.

O'Toole is shocked as well, not understanding who these men are, but seeing they can die just like the greyback or Yanks. He decides it's time to leave. He stands slowly, intent on running.

Rees is about to say something when his body begins to feel like there are thousands of ants crawling all over him. Kriger has the same feeling and looks at Rees.

The sky begins to grow gray, hazy; the air becomes thicker, heavier like a higher humidity than what they are already feeling. The air pressure builds and the pain in the men's ears becomes unbearable as each one, in turn, cups their hands to their heads in a futile attempt to stave off the pain. Soon they begin to moan or scream. O'Toole is confused as he, too, begins screaming from the pain. The screams are cut short as the men and equipment disappear, leaving only the sounds of a battle.

***

The rain-soaked men and lone woman on the boats are clinging to the railings in an attempt to stay upright. The boat is bobbing and spinning, making it almost impossible to stand. The horses are faring no better than their human counterparts as they bang into each other, sliding on the wet decking, but miraculously remaining upright, their whinnies of fear and confusion audible over the raging storm.

Lightning flashes across the sky giving the impression that Zeus does exist, and his anger is apparent by the bolts of electricity being thrown across the heavens. The torrents of rain are relentless as swells of cold water continually pummel the travelers.

With each flash of lightning, Rees can see the shorelines on both sides. He makes his way to Farnsworth and points this out to him.

"I noticed that, too. We might be able to work our way over to the north shore if we can somehow get control of this boat!" Farnsworth screams. "Any ideas?"

Of all the people to come up with a solution, it is none other than Tosseti. The man rocks back and forth, maintaining his balance the best he can as he lurches over to Rees and Farnsworth.

"I's got an idea to try to get this thing under control," he shouts over the storm.

Rees and Farnsworth stare, waiting for him to continue.

"We need to dump the Jeep, then use the wagon. Gonna need the planks. Use them as oars and a rudder!"

Farnsworth looks to Rees, who shrugs.

"Okay Matt, you're the skipper right now. What do we do?" Farnsworth asks, barely audible in the vicious storm.

"Place a transponder on the Jeep, then dump it overboard," he says. "The Bank should be able to transport it from there."

"Damn, good thinking Matt. Go on," Rees says.

"Take the long boards and tongue off the wagon. Use the boards as oars and I can fashion a rudder with the tongue and some wood," Matt explains.

Rees raises his arm above his head and swirls his hand in a circle, indicating to the SPs that they should gather around him. The men and Emma move to their position where Rees explains Matt's plan.

"Why not just put the transponder on the Jeep and have the Bank take it now?" Kriger asks.

Rees leans in to Kriger and shouts, "Because they might take the wagon, too, or worse, part of the boat!"

Kriger nods and moves away.

Rees orders the squad to get started, and he and Farnsworth remove the tarp from the wagon, revealing the slick green-and-black scarred metal of the ruined M151 truck.

Farnsworth takes a transponder and slaps it against the cold metal. Once finished, everyone begins breaking the back section of the wagon off, opening a gap for the Jeep to slide out. Several of the men grab the wagon tongue and hang onto it while the others begin pushing the wagon toward the stern. Farnsworth emphasizes that the wagon will want to go into the river with the Jeep, but they must hold onto it as the truck is pushed off the back end.

Everyone nods their understanding and Rees counts down ... three, two, one, push. Everyone begins moving the wagon to the lip of the boat. The rear wagon wheels hang on the edge for a few seconds, then drop over. The sudden jerking of the wagon wanting to carry itself into the water startles some of the squad members and they barely maintain their grasp.

"Hang on!" Rees screams, straining to keep the heavy wagon from falling completely off the boat. With a jolt, the wagon bottom meets the wooden planks of the boat and stops moving. The motion of the flowing river pushing against the wheel, and the weight of the wagon and Jeep cause the men's footing to slip as the wagon comes alive, struggling to escape the boat.

Nionee and Rees run to the side of the wagon and grab panels of the Jeep and begin shoving. Tosseti climbs into the back of the wagon where he places his squat, massive legs against the metal of the Jeep and his back against the wagon. He grunts and growls as he pushes with all his might. After a couple of seconds, and with the help of the river's choppy water, the Jeep breaks free and begins moving toward the back of the wagon.

Tosseti curses loudly and demands his legs give one giant thrust. It works, and the Jeep's weight causes it to slide faster until it looks as if it is leaping out of the wagon, landing with a splash and instantly disappearing into the dark, churning waters.

Tosseti's grins for a split second, then his eyes grow wide in fear as he begins to slide toward the opening as if he is supposed to join the Jeep. With a panic he starts kicking his feet in an effort to stop himself, attempting to gain traction as his feet slide against the steeply angled wet wood. He briefly thinks of Quint, from the movie *Jaws*, when he did the same thing as he tried to keep from being eaten by the shark, and he loses.

Angrily Tosseti yelps and turns over, grabbing a piece of the wagon to stop his decent into the cold, fast-moving waters. His flailing halts as a hand grabs his jacket, preventing him from dropping out of the opening. He looks up to see a Nionee holding on to him. With a grunt, Tosseti uses his free hand to grasp the wagon railing and pulls himself up and over, only to awkwardly fall on his ass on the wet deck. Cursing, as usual, he clambers back up and assists the team in pulling the wagon back onto the boat as if it was an everyday occurrence.

Once the wagon is secured, some of the squad drop to the deck, while others hang on to the wagon for support, all of them breathing heavily, sucking in gulps of air. This lasts about ten seconds before Rees yells at them to get back to work and start tearing the wagon down with tools from their saddles bags or whatever they find in the wagon.

Tosseti locates a box containing tools and nails attached to the side of the raft. He discovers an axe and begins hacking out chunks of wood from the center of the stern. He does this until he creates a wedge-shaped indentation. While he is doing this, Rees nails a piece of board onto the wagon tongue.

Tosseti and Rees lay the tongue into the groove, securing it with another board and nailing it down over the tongue, fashioning a home-made rudder.

Tosseti grabs the end of the tongue and moves it around, and, once satisfied that it will work, he gives Rees a thumbs up.

Rees smiles, returns the gesture, and moves back to the wagon where Nionee hands him a large section of planking. All the others have similar pieces and are on their knees along both sides of the boat. Farnsworth, Emma, Nionee and McGregor are on the starboard side, so Rees joins Bouvier and Kriger on the port side. The two men are already paddling, so Rees jumps right in to assist.

They paddle with all their might and are finally able to maneuver the boat so it is no longer turning but turned in a more or less forward direction with the flow of the fast-moving waters. The storm has let up some, helping them to see a little better.

Ever so slowly the boat moves closer to the north shore and, after about thirty minutes of exhausting work, they spot the shoreline.

Now they must find a spot where they can land safely without crashing the boat into some rocks or a sunken tree stump.

"Over there!" McGregor shouts, pointing to a section of the bank along a curve in the river, which is flat, like a small beach.

The rain is subsiding even more and the winds have died down, giving the travelers a reprieve. They are able to turn the boat more easily as they move into calmer waters. A few minutes pass and the bow of the boat slides up onto the shoreline with the hissing sound of the wood rubbing against sand, bringing it to a halt.

McGregor and Nionee run to the bow and jump off the boat, grabbing the small piece of rope still attached to it and pulling the craft further onto the shore.

The others, though wet, thirsty, and exhausted, begin unloading the animals and what equipment and weapons they still have.

The horses are skittish coming off the boat but then seem to realize they are on safer ground and calm. They are led away and secured to trees further up on shore.

Rees looks at Tosseti. "You did good," he says, then turns to look at the others.

Everyone is breathing hard, but they do not have time to slow down.

"All right, Tosseti. No rest for the wicked. You, Nionee and Kriger, move up further and see what's in front of us, then spread out and secure the area until we can get organized," Rees orders.

The three men acknowledge the order, move into the tree line and are out of sight in just a few seconds, only the sound of them moving through the brush and trees is heard until that sound dissipates.

Rees, Farnsworth, and the others gather near the horses.

"Any idea where we are, general?" Emma asks, shivering, her hair a mess from the soaking she has received.

Farnsworth looks at her, then removes his jacket and wraps it around her. The nano technology makes the coat warm, and she is too thankful for the gesture to wonder about why.

"Sorry, I don't," he replies and looks at Rees.

Rees grins wearily. "Ask the Bank," he says.

Farnsworth chuckles. "Duh."

Rees asks Emma to turn toward him. Rees then looks at Farnsworth's jacket and raises his hands in a "well?" gesture and cocks his eyebrow. Soon Farnsworth's pocket watch vibrates. He takes it out, opens the cover and reads the message scrawling across the front. Farnsworth face turns bleak, and he hands the watch to Rees.

"That's not good news," Rees says, his expression dour. He looks up to see the others staring at him, waiting.

"They retrieved the transponder, but not the Jeep. It must have dislodged. Dammit!"

"It's not that bad," Bouvier says and the small group turns to look at him. "They know where we are, don't they?"

"Says we're just southeast of Scottsville," Rees answers.

"So, they can send out teams to find the Jeep in the river. Apparently, no one's ever found it, so it's still sitting on the bottom of the river. More than likely under several feet of silt and mud, happily rusting away and awaiting a rescue."

Farnsworth grins. "Shit, he's right," he says and looks at Bouvier's jacket. "You hear that?" he asks, looking into the camera. A few seconds later the watch in Rees' hand vibrates. Rees looks at it and reads, "Roger Wilco."

Looking up he winks at Emma and McGregor. "Good, that's settled."

The two people from the nineteenth century stare blankly at Rees and nod their understanding while, in reality, not understanding at all.

Farnsworth pulls out his map and lays it on the ground. The night is being chased away by the arrival of a new dawn. The sun is just beginning its ascent and the first rays of light are shining on the low-lying mist but not bringing enough illumination to see the map.

Bouvier produces a small flashlight with a red lens and shines it onto the map. Farnsworth thanks him, then they all begin studying the map, locating Scottsville.

"Don't want to go there. Rebel territory," Farnsworth announces.

Bouvier snorts. "Sorry to say, sir, but this whole state is Rebel territory."

Farnsworth agrees. "Touché, captain. We need to move toward the mountains, then travel north-northeast. We can bypass most of the smaller towns in the area and, hopefully, in a few days, make it to the Shenandoah River. Once there we follow it up to Harpers Ferry, cross the river into Maryland, then it should be smooth sailing from there on to Mount Airy."

"What are we looking at, time-wise I mean?" Bouvier asks.

Rees looks at Farnsworth. "What do you think, ten, eleven days?"

"Yeah, give or take. We can probably get twenty-five or thirty miles a day, with a few breaks and, Lord willing, no trouble."

"We did all right last time, except for those damned Black Hats."

"Those the guys we saved your asses from last time we were here?" Bouvier asks with a grin.

"We were doing just fine without you," Rees replies, sarcastically.

"They were a nasty lot, them boys were," McGregor adds. "Wanted you lads bad, they did."

Emma looks at the men, confused, but remains quiet.

"Capt. Bouvier, can you call the perimeter security in and we'll get moving."

Bouvier acknowledges the order and tells the three men on guard duty to report back. In less than a minute, they hear the rustling of brush as each man appears from the undergrowth.

Once everyone is accounted for, they mount up and begin their journey to Mount Airy. They bypass Scottsville without incident and go around any towns in that area until sunset. The next day they turn north toward the town of Stanardsville, again without incident, though they did spot Confederate cavalry a few times. Farnsworth explains that they are traveling through territory that is full of Rebel troops due to the second battle of Manassas, or Bull Run, depending on which side you are on.

Tosseti asked why the two names, and Farnsworth explains that the Federal Army used the nearest river to name battles whereas the South used the nearest town. Tosseti just grunts.

The squad continues their trek north, veering slightly west, moving between the larger city of Charlottesville and the smaller town of Crozet until they are just east of the Blue Ridge Mountains, an area that will one day become Shenandoah National Park.

Once they arrive, they keep the mountain range to their left, slowly traveling north. They cross several small rivers and creeks and avoid many of the small towns along the way. Even if spotted by town folk or farmers, they know that by the time someone reports them, they will be so far away the Rebels won't know where to look.

After a few days traveling, they finally pass Stanardsville. They camp each night in heavily wooded areas, which are abundant, though always diligent for Rebel patrols. In actuality, they don't want to run into any Union patrols either. The fewer questions they have asked of them, the better.

Their travels are long on horseback, but they muster through with Tosseti complaining the most. But, like the rest, he does his job.

Once they reach an area called Chester Gap, a break in the ridgeline, they become much more alert as they skirt along the ridge. They are very close to where Rebel forces led by Gen. James Longstreet and Col. J.E.B. Stuart traveled north, looking to move around the Union forces at Manassas.

The small unit continues north and are close to the town of Hume when they run into trouble.

Gen. Stuart fought a battle at the town of Front Royal. His forces killed and captured the Union forces and, apparently, left troops behind to secure the town. This spot is located in a gap in the mountain range and the river runs through it. Farnsworth originally wanted to get to the river in this area then move north along the bank until they reached Harpers Ferry. After reviewing the map, it was decided it would be more beneficial, as well as safer, to keep traveling along the eastern side of the ridge until they run into the river just east of Harpers Ferry. From there they can skirt along the north side of the ridge where the river bends, move back west and cross the bridge into Harpers Ferry.

They are just outside the town limit when they hear a gunshot. A second later, Kriger lets out a loud curse.

The others turn and look as he grabs his shoulder where a bullet struck.

"Move!" Rees yells and the squad turns their mounts away from where they heard the shot and gallop across the open fields toward a large patch of woods. They hear more gunfire behind them and a round strikes Nionee's horse. The animal screams and stumbles as it tries to carry its rider onward. It makes a few more steps then collapses, throwing Nionee forward to land heavily on his back, knocking the wind out of him. All except for Tosseti and Rees continue; they are the only ones to notice Nionee has fallen behind, so they stop.

Seeing he is down, both spur their horses to the man's aid. Rees pulls his rifle from the scabbard and takes aim in the direction of the gunfire. He can still hear shots and the occasional buzz of a bullet zipping past his head, too close for comfort. Finally, a band of Confederate cavalry comes charging out of the woods, crossing the open field, heading straight for them.

Nionee is winded but manages to stand, trying to catch his breath. Tosseti offers his hand, but Nionee ignores the help. Instead, he wobbles to his downed horse, who is breathing heavily, looking around wildly and attempting to rise.

Nionee pulls his own rifle from the saddle, swiftly chambers a round and places the muzzle to the horse's head and pulls the trigger, putting the gentle beast out of its misery. Walking to the saddle again, he grabs the saddle bags. Straining and grunting he is able to dislodge them from underneath the weight of the massive dead animal. Checking the immediate area and satisfied he has everything, he finally takes Tosseti's hand. Grasping each other's forearms, Tosseti easily lifts the large Native American onto the back of his horse.

"We gotta move guys!" Rees shouts and begins firing. Some of his rounds find home as two riders tumble from their mounts, landing on the grass-covered field.

With a shout, Tosseti spurs his horse into action and turns the animal in the direction of the woods where the others have already dismounted and are setting up firing positions.

After Tosseti and Nionee pass Rees, he takes one final shot and follows them into the woods.

As the men reach their destination, Farnsworth, Bouvier, Kriger and McGregor begin firing.

Rees, Tosseti and Nionee jump from their mounts and hurry to help their comrades in arms.

"Ray, you okay?" Kriger shouts over the sound of gunfire.

"Yeh, yeh, just got the wind knocked out of me. I'm good," he replies, raising his upgraded Sharps rifle to spew death at the incoming riders.

The large group of cavalrymen discontinue charging when they realize they are losing too many men. Their captain knows it's suicide to run into an entrenched group, so he shouts at his troops to fall back, and they turn and flee to the relative safety of the wooded area opposite of where Rees' team is dug in.

Without having to be told, each squad member ceases firing at the retreating Rebels.

"What now?" Kriger asks. "Think they're finished for the day?"

Farnsworth looks around, then at Rees. "They ain't done. Probably regroup, send for more support. At least that's what I would do."

"We can just mount up and head further into the woods, move east, then turn back up north," Rees suggests.

"If I remember correctly, we are smack dab in the middle of a heavy fighting areas. The river is our best bet to avoid trouble, plus it's a straight shot to Harpers Ferry."

"What makes you think we won't run into trouble there as well? I mean, the Confederates could be holding it," Bouvier asks,

"No, I don't think so," Farnsworth says, looking at Bouvier. "If I'm right, a Col. Miles of the Union Army is in control of the town. We should be okay for a short time. If I remember correctly, the Rebs take back control of the town and burn the bridges. I don't know the exact time, but it was around this time period, so I say we hurry up and get there ASAP. It's only another forty or so miles. Once we get over the bridge, we will be in friendly territory. Or at or at least less non-friendly territory. Remember there are some copperheads in Maryland, not all are Yankee friendly."

"Yeah, why do you think we didn't bring Shepard along," Tosseti adds with a wicked smile.

They ignore the remark.

"I got movement," Bouvier says, interrupting the others' thoughts.

"Where?" Rees whispers.

"Looks like they are splitting up. I got troops to the left and to the right. And if that isn't enough, we got a cannon moving up."

Rees, Farnsworth, and Kriger extract their eyepieces and scan the area.

"Looks like one Napoleon," Farnsworth says. "That a break at least."

"Some break," Nionee answers.

Farnsworth looks behind them. "Rees, I like some of what you said. Let's move back a bit, slowly, so as not to be noticed." Then he taps Nionee on the shoulder. "Ray, stay here as overwatch. We're going to move back some. When we are out of sight, I want you to make some noise, rattle some branches, anything to keep their attention and make them think we are still here. Do this for about ten minutes, then meet us in that direction," he says, pointing to the area they will be heading. "We'll be waiting on you."

"Got it." Then, with a smile, Nionee looks at the fake general. "Knew you had good instincts when it comes to stuff like this. Sure you don't have a little Cherokee in ya?" he says with a chuckle.

"Funny," Farnsworth answers, then turns to explain the plan to the others.

Rees listens, then tells Farnsworth he is staying with Nionee. The man should have someone covering his back, plus they can make it look more realistic with two people moving around. Farnsworth agrees. He and the others slowly move deeper into the woods until they believe they can't be seen, then move north about a quarter of a mile before stopping.

Once the team is at the rendezvous point, they set up a small security perimeter and wait.

Rees and Nionee begin moving around, making as much noise as possible: shaking tree limbs, rustling bushes, clanging metal objects together and even firing off a round at the cannoneers.

This seems to piss off the officer in charge, as the front of the cannon answers the shot with an eruption of fire, smoke and a resounding blast. A black iron ball flies toward Rees and Nionee's position, sailing over their heads and striking a tree somewhere a little deeper in the woods, not even close to them.

Both men start laughing.

"That's not funny," Rees says, still laughing. "That could have hurt somebody."

The men begin jeering the cannoneers and fire off a few more shots. As they are laughing, Rees happens to look to his left and spies movement coming toward their position.

"Ray, nine o'clock, we got company!" he shouts as a folly of gunfire erupts.

Both men fall flat on the ground and wait a few seconds before daring to look.

"Fuck this," Rees says, removing several buttons and stringing them on the tree line running along the direction in which the enemy is approaching. They hear cannon fire again and this time the round is a little lower, but still misses them and only damages another tree.

Rees turns and sees Nionee removing something from a bag and watches, amazed, as the man begins piecing together a compound bow.

"What the ... where did you get that?" he asks in disbelief.

Nionee grins but doesn't answer as he puts two sections of arrow together to make a single one, then pulls out a bowstring and attaches it as well. Reaching into the sack again, he drags out a can of condensed milk that he ties to an arrow.

"You're not serious," Rees says more than asks, then sits with his back to a tree and watches as the man turns the can's lid, notches an arrow to the bow and raises the bow skyward. Ray looks in the direction he's aiming, pulls back the bowstring, adjusts for wind and distance, then, without a word, releases the arrow, dropping back down behind cover.

Rees strains to look in the direction that Nionee shot the arrow, then hears a tremendous explosion. He stands to get a better view, his mouth opens wordlessly. The small group of cannoneer are not to be seen and the cannon is leaning, a wheel missing.

Rees turns to look at Nionee.

Nionee shrugs. "Hey, I bow hunt. Don't be getting all stereotypical on me now, sir," he says, grinning ear to ear.

Before Rees can say anything, they hear the ear-piercing scream of the Rebel yell. The men know the Rebels on their left are charging through the woods, so they gather their gear and make for the horses. While mounting their rides, they spot a cavalry unit emerging from the woods where the cannon is located.

"Let's go," Rees shouts as they spur their horses and begin galloping through the dense woods, moving left and right, dodging and ducking to miss low-hanging branches. Both Nionee and Rees begin dropping buttons as they flee the area.

Rees hears Nionee talking and can only think that he is talking with the squad. He hears the man repeating the same thing over and over until he hears him says, "*Roger,*" knowing he made contact. A few seconds later Nionee turns his horse slightly, so Rees follows.

Nionee slows and Rees can see Tosseti lying on the ground behind a log, motioning them on. They proceed into the perimeter and dismount.

They find Farnsworth and kneel beside him.

"We have ground troops coming from that direction," Rees says pointing, "and cavalry coming from there," he points in the other direction.

Just as he finishes, they all hear an explosion from where they had just come.

"We left a few surprises for them," Rees adds.

"What was that large explosion earlier?" Bouvier asks. "It wasn't the cannon firing. That's was a different sound?"

Rees looks at the smirk on Nionee's face. "I'll let Sgt. Nionee explain that later. Right now, we need to get ready for a fight."

They wait patiently, listening to the sound of more explosions and, soon, the screams of wounded men. Slowly the detonations become louder and the screams clearer as the Rebel soldiers move closer to their position.

The Rebel cavalry unit is firing into the woods as they charge in the direction of Rees' team. When they don't receive any return fire, they stop and begin moving cautiously forward. As they are scanning the woods, they continue to hear the blasts and the cries of men. This causes the captain concern, but he knows there is nothing he can do right now other than keep up his pursuit, knowing he must use caution.

Back at the rendezvous site, Rees realizes that the explosives will not slow the Rebels for long. He looks at Farnsworth. "What say we get the hell out of here?"

Chapter 41

2020 – O' Dark Thirty

The conference room is dark, as it is closed for the night along with most of the building. It is late and most of the Bank's personnel have gone home and are soundly sleeping. The building is being run by a skeleton crew, most of whom are in the control room, a few in the clinic and some maintaining security.

The only light in the room comes from corridor lighting peeking through the closed blind slats or sneaking under the doors.

There is a sudden movement in the room and a grunt of discomfort followed by a chair being knocked over, then a curse and a thump against a wall as a body falls and slides to the floor. The room is silent again with only the sound of heavy breathing. A few seconds pass and the breathing is accompanied by more movement and groaning.

"You okay?" a man's voice asks in a whisper.

"I'm fine. Lost my balance and fell against this wall," a female voice answers softly.

Both people listen for a few seconds before they begin to move again.

"Where are we?" the female voice asks in a whisper.

"I'm not sure, but I have a hand on a chair," comes the reply, followed by more movement. "And there is a large table next to it."

"My eyes are beginning to adjust, I can see faintly," the female says and there is the sound of feet shuffling along carpet and hands sliding against the wall as she moves towards the faint light. Then there is a bump and the female curses.

"I just ran into another table."

"I can see the light, stay there. I think we are in an office. I see the outline of a door and what looks like blinds." The female can hear the man moving and she sees a faint outline of his body as her vision begins to adjust to the darkness. She hears a click, the sound of a door handle being pushed, then more light as the door opens slightly.

They finally have enough light to see they are inside a large room containing a long table, multiple chairs and large window made dark with closed blinds. A conference room.

She looks down at what stopped her movement. Reaching her hand out, she feels the table she bumped into, located underneath the largest television she has ever seen. She turns her attention back to the man and silently watches as he peeks outside, looking one way then the other before bringing his head back in. He signals to the female.

As the woman moves closer to the man, she notices the grin on his face. He opens the door a little more, indicating she should take a look. She moves to the door and tentatively sticks her head outside, looking up one corridor then down the other. It takes her a couple of seconds, then her eyes grow wide with sudden understanding. She swiftly pulls her head back into the room and the man closes the door. Neither can see the other as the darkness erases their vision, but they grasp each other by the arms.

"Oh, my, God!" she says.

"I know."

"We're in the Bank."

"I know."

"But how? And what year is this?"

"That I don't know."

"Aeson, we are not in the nineties. I just saw a picture of an aircraft on the wall that we do not have in our timeline. I think we are somehow in the future. What decade, I have no idea."

"What type of aircraft?" he asks.

"Doesn't matter but ...," she starts to say, then puts her fingertips to her brother's mouth. "Shhh. I hear something," she whispers as she moves closer to him, then reaches for one of the slats on the blind. Moving the slat ever so slightly, she takes a peek and sees two security personnel walking by. She notices the uniforms, which confirms her earlier assessment that they are not in the 1990s anymore. The uniforms, as well as the weapons - a type of M-16, but shorter with a small scope hanging on a sling, as well as some type of vest containing magazines, which she assumes are for the rifles.

She releases the slat and moves closer to her brother.

"They look like Air Force police, but the uniforms and weapons are different," she says. "Shit!" she curses softly, not sure what to do.

Aeson snorts. "I've got an idea," he says and quickly informs her of his plan.

***

Helen Hellberg, the daughter of Sen. Minten, is at the far end of the conference table and starts making noise by moving the chairs and knocking them against the table. Aeson moves behind the door and removes a Stiletto knife from his boot. He presses a button and a sharp *click* indicates the blade ejected, as intended.

It doesn't take long before the door opens and a female security guard enters the room. She shines her flashlight around and quickly spots Helen at the end of the table.

"Ma'am, who are you and how did you get in here?" the young guard asks, holding the flashlight so as to blind Helen while moving further into the room. Helen raises her hands to ward off the light and sees the woman's hand resting not on the rifle, but on the butt of a pistol.

The door opens further and a larger man, a staff sergeant, follows the younger senior airman into the room. He reaches over and flips on a light switch, bathing the room instantly in light.

Before he can say anything, Aeson moves behind him and throws his left hand over the sergeant's mouth, pulling his head back forcefully. Using his right hand, he stabs the blade of the knife into the base of the man's neck. The blade enters easily and only meets slight resistance as it slides through the spinal column and into his brain. Aeson expertly moves the knife around to ensure the most damage. The staff sergeant lets out a muffled grunt that slows into a soft mewing sound as his life drains. Aeson kicks the door closed, causing the younger airman to turn and watch in horror as her partner's eyes grow wide in surprise, fear and pain, his life already fading.

The airman, in shock at what she is witnessing, is stunned into silence. Before she can regain her senses and pull her pistol or raise her rifle or even call on her radio, Helen quickly grabs the woman's ponytail. With all the strength she can muster, she forcefully pulls the back of the woman's head down, slamming it against the table with a loud *smack*. Stunned, the SP falls to the floor, eyes fluttering as she tries to get up.

Hellberg stands over the younger woman, breathing hard. Using her body weight and one knee, she drops onto the woman's neck, crushing her windpipe and cutting off the air she desperately needs to stay alive. The woman grabs for her throat in a vain attempt to breathe. Hellberg snarls as she looks at the female cop thrashing around on the floor. Her blood is up, adrenaline flowing, so she drops down a second time onto the woman's neck, causing further damage, only this time she stays there, pressing into her neck until the flailing falters, slows, then eventually stops.

Helen looks up at her brother, who is busy laying the body of the sergeant onto the carpeted floor. Only when he finishes and moves to the window does he glance at her. Focused on his task, he looks through a slit in the blinds, waiting. He does this for a full minute until he believes they are in the clear as far as this part of his plan is concerned.

He walks over to his sister and gives her a hand up. Helen looks at the body of the woman she just killed and shakes her head in disgust.

"Stupid girl. Why in the hell is she wearing her hair in a ponytail? That's about as dumb as wearing a regular tie instead of a clip on; gives a person something to grab during a fight. What idiot would let her do that?" she asks rhetorically.

Aeson looks at the dead sergeant, then begins stripping him of his weapons, Molle vest, boots and uniform. Helen watches for a minute, then begins doing the same with the female. In ten minutes, both Aeson and Helen are dressed as security-force members.

"That uniform does you no justice, brother. You are bigger than he was," she says with a grin.

"Hey, as long as it gets us where we need to be without being detected," he replies, moving his arms in an attempt to get the shirt to fit better, only causing it to rip under the armpits, much to the delight of his twin sister.

"Ha, ha," he smirks, then watches as Helen shows off by doing a turn like a model on a runway.

"Not fair," he exclaims, smiling. "At least her uniform fits you," then adds, "Hey, you remember how to use those?" pointing to the weapons.

She stops preening and gives him the side eye, then the middle finger. She expertly checks the weapons, ensuring rounds are in the chamber and ready to fire, then smirks at her brother. He grins as she walks up to him, giving him a soft love tap to the face. They then begin the task of hiding the bodies underneath the conference table. It isn't perfect, but it should do the job long enough for the twins to proceed with their plan. After they finish making the room look as normal as before, Aeson turns off the lights and opens the door. Aeson and Sen. Hellberg, adorned as local security-force members, move down the corridor like they belong in the big happy USAF family. They stride in the direction of where they hope they can find the Clio Project control room.

Chapter 42

1862

Farnsworth and Rees are sure the Rebs are moving toward their location and they want very much to be long gone before the grey coats arrive. Hopefully the explosions slow the Confederates and make them more cautious.

When everyone is situated, they begin moving swiftly north toward Harpers Ferry. The squad travels at a good pace for about five miles before they take a break. Without being told, several of the squad members move in different directions, taking up security positions and providing 360-degree security. Rees is proud of how his squad has been working together, and in a fashion that allows them to almost read each other's minds. Even McGregor seems to have adjusted to how the team works and is blending in well with them.

Rees, Farnsworth, Bouvier, Kriger and Emma stand together in a small group.

"I don't believe we should use the Shenandoah River as our guide to Harpers Ferry," Farnsworth says, unfolding a map and laying it on the ground. "We are about here," he says, pointing to an area. The others bend down to look. "We need to move along this ridgeline to our left. We should run into the Potomac River. We will need to skirt around the base of the ridge to get to Harpers Ferry. There should be a road we can use."

"Looks to be only about thirty miles from here, give or take. Should be able to make it in about eight hours," Rees adds.

Bouvier looks at his watch, then at the sky. "It'll be dark soon."

"Uh-huh. That's why we need to get moving, try to get some distance between us and the fighting in this area," Farnsworth explains. "But we still have to remain vigilant. There could be more soldiers, either side, patrolling this area. I don't really foresee it, but you never know."

He folds the map and returns it to the pouch. "And you know what happens every time we aren't vigilant."

The squad mounts their horses and moves out.

They travel about five miles, receiving a break by finding an abandoned trail, or maybe it's a deer trail, that allows them to pick up the pace. The sun begins its slow descent to the west, turning the sky a salmon, orange, then purple tint. The shadows from the trees press in on them, making it more difficult to see, so they all agree to stop for the night.

They set up camp for the evening, with a fire going, food cooking, coffee perking and security measures in place. The woods are quiet and, if not for the fact that there is a war going on, one could almost think they were just a group of friends out camping. Rees thinks of this for a few seconds before coming back to the realization that they have traveled back in time, to an era that presents danger at every corner.

Bouvier and Kriger walk up behind Rees, who is sipping coffee and staring into the star-filled night sky.

"I think he's wishing he was an astronaut the way he stares at the stars," Kriger says by way of announcing their presence.

Rees turns and smiles at his friend, then looks at the sky once again.

"Naw, never wanted to do that. Besides, you never know, we might have to go back in time and save NASA or something."

"Let's hope not. If we start doing stuff like that, I think we're in some sort of *Outer Limits* TV show, or worse, the *Time Tunnel*," Bouvier says with a shudder.

The three men are quiet until Farnsworth approaches.

"Am I interrupting?"

"No, sir, just passing the time and enjoying the night. Come on over," Rees replies.

"Everything good?"

"Yes, sir," all three men answer.

Farnsworth joins the group, and the four men sip coffee and quietly stare at the clear night sky, enjoying the sounds of the fire crackling behind them and the others softly talking amongst themselves. After about five minutes, one by one, the group disbands and returns to the camp to get some rest.

Twenty feet away from the closest security measure stands a man with a telescope, watching the encampment. Knowing nothing of the security devices or how close he came to setting it off, he moves away from the encampment.

***

Capt. Mulgrew, part of the 12th Virginia Regiment, is pacing impatiently in front of his mount. The animal, being held by a private, snorts, pawing its hoof into the ground as if in empathy with its owner. Sgt. Dunlop, standing silently in front of his own mount, observes his commander as he stalks back and forth, hands clasped behind his back, staring at the ground. Lt. Waterman stands off to one side, watching the captain.

Mulgrew stops as he hears a rustling in the woods, quickly turning his attention toward the tree line. Dunlop reaches for his pistol and moves in front of his commander, his attention focused into the woods, eyes scanning for movement, pistol at the ready.

In this case, there isn't any danger as Corp. Hollar comes bounding out of the underbrush, breathing heavily. He stops short of the captain, taking a couple of deep breaths as he salutes. He gives the scope out to his sergeant, then stands a little straighter as he catches his breath, the dirty tan shirt he is wearing soaked with sweat.

"What did you find corporal?" the captain asks anxiously.

In between breaths, the corporal explains that he found the Union soldiers they have been pursuing.

Mulgrew smiles. "How far away?"

"About two miles sir. Looks like they followed an animal trail for some time, then they stopped when it got dark. They must think they are safe 'cause they ain't even put out a picket."

Mulgrew blinks. "Damn fools."

Sgt. Dunlop moves up behind the captain. "You want me to get the men ready sir?"

Mulgrew doesn't answer, still focused on the corporal. "How far is this trail from here?

"A mile, a little more, maybe, sir."

Mulgrew turns to speak to his sergeant but is interrupted by the corporal.

"And sir," Mulgrew says, causing the captain and sergeant to face him. "Something else, too."

This has Mulgrew's attention. "What is it corporal?"

Having finally caught his breath, the corporal speaks a little clearer. "They are not a large unit: eight people, and one of them is a woman."

"A woman? Why in the bejeesus do they have a woman with them?" Mulgrew says aloud, then looks intently at the corporal. "Did she look under duress?"

"Sir?" Hollar asks, looking perplexed.

Mulgrew lets out an exasperated breath. "Duress ... did she look like she was in trouble, being held against her will? Duress!" he explains impatiently.

"Oh, no, sir. She was walking around freely and laughing and talking with the soldiers, which is another thing, sir."

"Go on."

"Well, sir. They have a general, two captains, one lieutenant, and three sergeants, and the woman, of course."

Capt. Mulgrew's eyes widen slightly. "Seven men and one woman did what they did to us? That is impossible. Corporal, you must be mistaken. That or they split up somehow."

Corp. Hollar shakes his head empathically. "No, sir. I have been watching the horse tracks since we began following; seven horse tracks, one horse carrying two people. I'm sure of it, sir."

Mulgrew stares at the corporal for a couple seconds, decides he is telling the truth, then turns back to Sgt. Dunlop. Dunlop watches his commander intently.

"What do you think, sir?"

"Why in the devil's name would there be four officers and three sergeants, and a woman riding out here alone?"

Dunlop looks at the lieutenant. Waterman moves forward.

"Sir, maybe she's the wife of one the officers. Or she could be a fancy girl."

Mulgrew looks at the lieutenant and sergeant, snorts, then shakes his head. "I guess we will find out when we capture them damned Yanks now, won't we Dunlop?"

Lt. Waterman takes another step closer to the captain.

"Sir, if I may?" he asks in a whisper.

Capt. Mulgrew nods.

"Sir, we have lost too many men as it is chasing these soldiers. Our orders were to protect the gap from enemy infiltration until recalled for the attack on Harpers Ferry. We have been gone from our post for some time now and the attack has already begun."

Mulgrew looks at Waterman.

"Yes, yes, you are quite right," he replies, thinking. "Lieutenant, thank you for the advice. Now, here is what I propose. We will make one more attempt at capturing these blue bellies. If we do not succeed with this attack, we will make haste back to the gap."

Waterman looks at his commander and can only acknowledge the statement.

"Yes, sir. Your orders, sir?"

"We will ride the trail leading to their camp and stop short. Dismounting, we shall move with quiet determination and surround the Yanks and surprise them. Should be an easy task since they don't have any pickets on patrol," he explains to them, motioning for Dunlop to come to him.

"Sgt. Dunlop, Lt. Waterman will explain what we will be doing. Give the men half an hour to rest, eat, and be ready to move out."

Dunlop acknowledges the order and salutes the captain before he turns and walks away.

***

Bouvier rolls onto his side and curses quietly to himself. He has only managed a couple of hours sleep, his mind working overtime. For some reason he can't shut off his brain, thinking about nothing in particular, and everything in the world that really doesn't matter. That, plus he needs to relieve himself.

"Ah, fuck it," he whispers, throwing off his bed roll and moving away from the rest of the sleeping group as silently as he can.

"Can't sleep?"

Bouvier jumps at the voice and turns to face a grinning Kriger.

"What the hell, Dave. Scared the crap out of me. If I had a knife, I could have stuck you. And not by accident."

Kriger, still grinning, places his finger to his lips and cocks his head toward the sleeping camp.

Bouvier presses his lips together, glaring at Kriger. He shakes his index finger at the smaller man, then turns away, still having to pee.

Kriger follows and, when they are out of earshot of the camp, Bouvier stops and grabs Kriger by the arm, leaning in so he can see Kriger's face and speaks in an angry, hushed tone.

"Why are you following me? You gonna hold my pecker for me while I piss?"

Kriger, non-plussed, looks at the other man and shakes his head. "Oh, hell no. That's an airman's job and, besides, my hands aren't that small." He shakes free of Bouvier's grip, moving past him and further into the woods, also having to drain the weasel.

The two men find a spot to quietly take care of business. When finished they button up and begin to walk back to the campsite. After a few steps, Kriger stops and cocks his head like a dog. Bouvier walks about five more paces before he notices he is alone. He stops, turns to look at Kriger, exhales a frustrated breath, then walks back to stand next to him. Bouvier opens his mouth to ask what he is doing, but Kriger looks at him, finger to his lips for silence. Bouvier closes his mouth then watches as Kriger points at his own ear, then at the woods.

Bouvier slowly takes a step closer and turns his attention to where Kriger is pointing. He doesn't see or hear anything, so he leans into Kriger and whispers.

"What is it?"

"Shh, listen."

Bouvier straightens and turns an ear in the direction that Kriger is concentrating on.

Then he hears it. A jangling noise, faint and far away. Then they hear a cough. Both men look at each other and Bouvier hand signals for them to quietly move back to camp. It doesn't take them long to arrive and the men move silently to where Rees and Farnsworth are sleeping, only the two men are not asleep. At Bouvier's and Kriger's approach, both Rees and Farnsworth sit up and look at them.

"What's up?" Rees asks, as he throws off his blanket.

Crouching, the two men explain what they heard.

Farnsworth is already putting on his boots and standing.

"Show me," he orders.

The four men begin walking through the camp as calmly as they can, but some of the others are now stirring and silently watching as they walk away from the camp.

Bouvier and Kriger lead the small group deeper into the woods, then stop. All four stand still and begin listening. For several minutes there is nothing but the sound of the forest at night, then they hear a man-made sound: the clank of metal against metal.

Farnsworth taps the others on the shoulders and motions for them to move back to camp. Once there, other are already up and waiting.

"What's going on?" Tosseti asks in a hushed tone.

"I think we are about to have company. We can hear noise in that direction," Farnsworth says, pointing.

"That's the trail we took," Nionee says.

Farnsworth nods. "Yes, and if we have been followed, it will lead them straight to us. They aren't too close, maybe a half-mile away, give or take."

"Using your SpecOps Spidey sense, sir?" Kriger asks.

Farnsworth ignores the quip and looks at Rees. Rees tells the others to break camp and prepare to move out. Each man breaks from the group to gather their things. Farnsworth moves to where Emma is sleeping, but sees she is up and getting prepared to leave as well.

"You don't miss a thing, do you?" he asks.

Emma smiles. "That I do not, good sir. I was already awake when you boys came traipsing back into the camp, making more noise than milking cows in the mornin'."

Farnsworth chuckles. "Is that so? Well, I'll be sure to keep it down in the future."

She stops what she's doing and looks at Farnsworth, a slight smile twitching at the corner of her mouth. "The future huh? I might hold you to that, Gen. Farnsworth." Then she goes back to packing.

Farnsworth is standing there, staring at her, pondering her intent when Rees approaches. He stops short and watches for a few seconds before realizing Farnsworth doesn't notice him. "Ahem."

Farnsworth starts and turns. Emma also looks in his direction.

"Sorry to interrupt."

"Not at all, Capt. Rees," Emma replies.

"Can I borrow the general for a minute?"

Emma smiles. "Why, of course. He should be doing general things and not standing here staring at me."

Farnsworth looks at her, then Rees and stutters. "No, I ... I wasn't staring ... just making sure you were getting everything you need." He moves quickly away and jerks his head at Rees, indicating he is to follow him.

"Damn, that's embarrassing," he mutters when out of earshot.

"What? That? Why? She's a very attractive woman."

"I know, but she had or has a beau. I shouldn't be doing that. Never mind. What do you need?"

Rees takes the hint and gets back to business.

"Listen. I look at our predicament in two ways. One, we can move out now and try to make it to Harpers Ferry, where we may, and I emphasize *may*, have support and safety, or two ...," he trails off and Farnsworth picks up.

"Or two, we stay and fight. Set up an ambush."

Rees nods. "We would have to haul ass to get to Harpers Ferry. We still have, what, eighteen, twenty miles to go. Plus, we are down one horse."

Farnsworth is silent, thinking, then shakes his head. "We don't know the size of the force. I don't like it."

"Yeah, but we have the element of surprise, plus superior firepower. We know they are going to come down that trail. We can slow them down by setting up some mines, blow a few of them off and they will use more caution coming after us. It won't be light for a couple of hours. We can get a few miles between us before they even have a chance to catch us."

"That hasn't stopped them so far. We must have already killed or wounded a dozen or so, but here they are."

"I know, but that was just a few explosives, I'm talking about a real ambush. We unload on them with our weapons along with more explosives, I think we will either wipe them out or send them skedaddling."

Farnsworth snorts. "Skedaddling, huh?"

Rees smiles. "Yeah."

Farnsworth nods. "Okay, I agree. Let's send them back to tomorrow so we can be on our way."

A female voice breaks into their conversation.

"Excuse me?"

Both men turn to see Emma standing a few feet away.

"I am sorry. I do not mean to eavesdrop on your conversation, but I was thinking about the two men riding together on one horse. I just thought, if I may, I think I should ride with the general from here on. I am lighter, which will be easier on the horse than having two larger men on one. Plus, you need those soldiers alert and able to move freely if a problem should arise."

The men look at each other and Farnsworth cocks his head at Rees in a warning gesture.

"I think that to be a wonderful idea, Miss Kelly," Rees says, still eye to eye with Farnsworth, "don't you, general?"

Farnsworth's eyes narrow at Rees, then he turns to Emma, all smiles. "Of course, Miss Kelly. That is an excellent idea."

"Good. Then it is settled. Now Sgts. Nionee and Tosseti can have their own horses," she says, then turns and walks away.

Farnsworth leans into Rees. "Not one word, Scott. I'm warning you. Not one word."

***

Rees gathers the men and Emma and explains the plan. They will saddle the horses and move them away so they aren't in harm's way. The camp will remain the same, with some stuffing under the bed rolls, making it look as if everyone is asleep. They will plant booby traps in the surrounding area, then move to the other side of the trail and wait for the Rebels to enter the camp. When they trip the first explosive, everyone will open fire. The plan is to scare the Rebels enough so they leave for good.

When Rees finishes the briefing, the squad breaks and they begin setting up the bed rolls and planting the explosives. Once Rees and Farnsworth are satisfied the trap is set, the team walks to the far side of the trail to set up the ambush. Once in position they become quiet and wait.

***

Capt. Mulgrew turns in his saddle to look at the men behind him. It is dark and he can only make out the lieutenant and the shadowy figure of the sergeant following the lieutenant.

Satisfied that everyone is in position, he raises his arm and drops it down, an indication for the troops to move out. He knows his horse will move about four miles an hour, even with the thick foliage. He has estimated that they will be there in plenty of time for a surprise attack.

About forty minutes later, he sees the flickering glow of campfires. He stops his horse and looks back at his men, then waves for Lt. Waterman and Sgt. Dunlop to come to him. They move alongside the captain.

"Your orders, sir?"

"Sergeant, have the men dismount. Lieutenant, take twenty men and move into the encampment. Be as quiet as you can. I don't see any movement so the damn fools must still be asleep. This is going to be easier than I thought. Now go and, whatever you do, make sure that the general is captured alive. If you capture the other officers, that is a bonus, but if they get in the way, kill them all if need be."

"What about the woman?" Waterman inquires.

Mulgrew thinks for a couple of seconds." Try to capture her as well, but as with the others, if she gets in the way, do what you think best."

Both men salute and Dunlop backs his horse up until he is beside the next trooper in line. He explains the orders and that man relays the information to the next, and on down the line. As each soldier receives the order, they begin dismounting, then moving to where the captain and lieutenant are waiting. No one says a word as they meet and slowly move out toward where the federal soldiers are sleeping.

Waterman and Dunlop have their pistols drawn. Using hands signals, Waterman divides his men into two lines. He keeps one group with him, and points at an area to the right where he wants the second group to move. He instructs the corporal of the second group to move into the camp when he sees Dunlop's men move. They want to get into camp using a pincher move.

Once the corporal is in position, everyone begins walking toward the camp, amazed there is no movement. Moving closer, Waterman is confused. Why are they able to get in so close and no one in the camp has stirred? He stops walking when suddenly realizes that they are about to be ambushed. Before he can stop his soldiers, they have already moved into the kill zone.

Waterman jumps at the sound of the first explosion, which removes the feet of two soldiers. The men are flung up and away, screaming as they are lifted into the air by the force, landing unceremoniously together in a bloody mess.

The second explosion comes from a device placed on a tree about head high. The unlucky lad who triggers it never knew what happened as the force of the explosive turns his head into a red, misty pulp, his brains, bones, and blood spraying the few others near him. The man next to him is peppered with wood splinters that embed into his face, piecing an eye. The soldier screams and raises his hand to his face and begins flailing around, moving further into the camp only to step onto another button bomb, sealing his fate. This bomb removes his entire leg, and he is flung forward, dead before he hits the ground.

The scene is replicated a few times before Waterman can yell for the men to halt. This is unnecessary as those who are lucky enough to have escaped the explosives have done so on their own, some even taking steps backwards.

Before the Rebels can react, gunfire erupts from the west side of the wooded area. Several more men fall as round after round finds its mark with deadly accuracy. Lt. Waterman is one of the first to be hit. A 5.56 bullet strikes him in the left eye and exits out the back of his head, spraying brain matter, bits of skull and blood all over a tree where the bullet embeds itself. At first the gray-clad men are not sure where the bullets are coming from. Men turn left and right, some turn to leave as others seek cover and concealment, still others run directly into the gunfire.

Sgt. Dunlop keeps his cool as he searches the area for the enemy and, after a few seconds, sees the muzzle flash of the Yankees' weapons in the bushes and trees across the road. He begins barking orders for the soldiers to regroup and prepare to charge the enemy. The thunderous sound of weapons fire, the scream of the wounded and dying, the shouts of men overlapping others drown out most of what Dunlop is yelling.

A few of the men hear him and attempt to form up, but the barrage of fire is unrelenting and the soldiers fall one right after another. The woods echo with the sound of gunfire, the ground shakes and rumbles as the small mines continue to explode, shredding the men to pieces. Twenty men walk into the camp, and in only a few minutes, all are dead, dying or severely wounded ... all except for one.

Dunlop screams at what he is seeing. It's not that he has not seen the horrors of the war, but he has never witnessed this type of devastation in such a short amount of time. He has been spared, the only lucky one to have been behind a large pine tree that shielded him.

The shooting doesn't cease, it only turns its fury in a different direction. Dunlop realizes the battle has shifted from his men inside the encampment to the rest of the soldiers standing with Capt. Mulgrew. He realizes that the Yanks aren't quite finished. He screams again, only this time as a warning to his commander as he dashes back to where the officer is waiting. His efforts are for naught as he watches, in horror, as several rounds strike his commander in the legs, body, and head. The captain is dead before he even falls out of his saddle, landing with an audible thump on the ground in a bloody heap. The captain's horse flees, trailing blood from wounds it received only to pause and fall a few feet from its rider.

Dunlop runs toward the fallen man, all the while watching as other soldiers are struck by bullets as well. What's left of the company tries to rally. Some men return fire in a futile effort as their muzzleloaders are no match for the twenty-first-century semiautomatic rifles.

Dunlop reaches the bloodied body of his commander and realizes there is nothing he can do to help as lifeless eyes stare into nothingness. He looks at the remaining force and knows this battle is lost. Some of the men are already backing up, leap frogging behind trees to avoid the deadly hail of bullets that never seems to let up.

Sgt. Dunlop yells for a retreat and hears the bugle sound the call. *How the hell did the bugler survive?* he thinks. He turns to run and finds the color-bearer dead, still clutching the battle flag. He scoops it up and watches the handful of his men - yes, now his men - attempt to flee the onslaught brought on by these demon Yankees.

"Enough of this shit," he mutters. "Time to return to command."

Dunlop hands the colors off to a young Rebel and, when he is sure the last soldier has left the area, he turns and follows the others deeper into the woods, back toward Fort Royal.

Chapter 43

Helen Hellberg and Aeson Minten walk purposely down the corridors of the underground complex, both dressed as security force members and acting as if they both belong there.

"Charlie One, this is control," squawks over the radios they carry on their belts.

Both stop and look at each other.

"You think we're Charlie One?" Helen asks.

Minten shrugs. "I guess we will find out in a minute," he says, removing the radio from its carrier. Before he can answer, the radio calls for Charlie One again.

"Charlie One. You find anything in the room?"

Helen looks up at her brother. "I guess that answers that question."

"Charlie One here, negative," Minten answers.

"Roger that. We saw you walking down the hall but didn't get an all-clear on your big investigation."

Minten smirks and Helen shakes her head.

"Yeah, Roger. Just forgot to clear."

"We copy. You okay? You sound a little different."

"I am fine. I think I'm starting to catch a cold."

"Roger that. Control out."

Minten places the radio back into the carrier slot and shakes his head. Helen breathes a sigh of relief, and they continue along the passageway. It doesn't take them long to reach a bank of elevators. They look at a schematic of the floors located in front of the lifts and see they are one floor below where the Clio Project is located. Pressing a button, the doors open, and both enter. They know there are cameras watching and, most likely, someone is listening, so they remain silent, heads down, until they exit the car and wait for the doors to shut behind them.

"What are we going to do once we get there?" Sen. Hellberg asks her twin.

"I don't know about you, but I say we take over the Clio control room," he says. "Once we do that, we can activate Clio and send ourselves back to where we belong. Sorry sis, but we are in a precarious situation being here. We don't know anyone – well, anyone still young anyway – and even if we did, they are probably no longer in a position to help. That, and we would have to get out of here, find a way off base, then locate someone we may know who may or may not be alive, then what? We would be on the Most-Wanted list after offing two Air Force cops? No, we need to get back to our time and rethink our strategy. We know what has happened and can probably make corrections before we jump again."

Helen looks at her brother, trying to think of an alternate solution but ultimately ends up agreeing. "Okay, let's do it your way. Now, how are we going to do that?" she asks as he walks toward the control room.

"The old-fashioned way. We kick their asses and take it."

***

Col. Black and Chief Black are monitoring the progress of Sgt. Rees' team. Both men try to plan their time away for rest and food at the same time the team is resting themselves.

Coffee mug in hand, the chief takes a sip and stares at the monitor that shows the horsemen trotting along through the thick trees in an attempt to get away from the confederate soldiers.

"You know we could have just pulled them out, regrouped and then sent Miss Kelly and Sgt. McGregor back on their own," Col. Black says, moving next to his son.

The chief snorts. "Where's the adventure in that? Besides, secretly, I think the boys are enjoying themselves."

"You would think that."

"Plus, they have the means to get back on their own. That and they could ask for help at any time. So far, they haven't."

"Yeah, I see your point."

The phone buzzes on the colonel's desk and he steps over to answer it, at the same time looking down into the control room. He sees Sgts. Shepard and Montoya standing next to Maj. Washington, who is holding a receiver to his ear. All three are looking in his direction. Col. Black presses the speaker button. "Yes, Maj. Washington. What is it?"

"Sir, the sergeant found something that you might find important. Permission to send them to your office?"

Black glances at the chief, then turns his attention back to the control room.

"Permission granted," he replies. A short time passes before the two men enter the colonel's office. Both men salute and the colonel orders them at ease.

"What have you got for us?"

Both men exchange looks, and TJ nods for Montoya to speak.

"Sir, today is September 12."

"Yes, so what?"

"Well, sir. Around this time in 1862, Gen. Stewart starts his attack on Harpers Ferry. The Rebel forces took back the town after about four days of fighting. Stewart's troops surround the town and blast it with artillery, then attack."

"Sir, if I can bring up a map on your screen?" he asks, pointing to the large screen on the wall.

Col. Black nods and points to his computer. Montoya leans over the keyboard and begins typing. A map appears on the screen with red and blue lines running across three states, converging on Harpers Ferry.

TJ walks to the map and points to Frederick, Maryland. "Sir, confederate troops have already begun amassing here," he points to areas around the town, "and Gen. Stewart has already placed artillery on the ridgelines of Loudoun Heights and Maryland Heights to start the bombardment. The bombardment has already begun."

"Well, shit," Col. Black fumes, then looks at the chief. "I say we bring them back right now."

Chief Black takes a deep breath and purses his lips, releasing the breath as he stares at his son.

"We should pass this information along to the team and let them make the decision. Capt. Farnsworth is probably aware of the significance of the date, but it may have slipped his mind. They are so close to getting Miss Kelly home. They make it through Harpers Ferry and across the bridge, they are practically home free in what, less than two days?"

The colonel stares at the chief. "At what price? Is this really worth it to get one person home? Does she have anything to do with history?"

The chief shakes his head. "Dad, I have no idea. Even if she has had no effect on history, does it matter? We are responsible for bringing her here; we should at least have the decency to get her home."

The colonel is quiet for a few seconds then turns to the NCOs.

"What do you two think? You've been there in this type of situation, and you know Sgt. Rees pretty well."

Again, both men look at each other before TJ answers. "Sir, I say let them make the decision. Rees knows what he's doing, and Capt. Farnsworth, too. Even though Sgt. Montoya and I haven't been on a time-travel trip since that first time, I would do it again. Danger and all. I'm sure Sgt. Rees would want to finish his mission. He's not a quitter, and I'm sure the captain isn't either. And I know that pig-headed Tosseti is having a hoot, even if he is bitchin' about it, pardon my French, sir."

"Your French is pardoned, sergeant. Good little speech, I might add. Sgt. Montoya, do you feel the same?"

"Yes, sir, I do."

The colonel smiles and nods. "Okay, sergeants, get back to work and let them know the situation."

Both men come to attention, salute, and leave the office. Once back at their workstations, TJ sends the information to Rees.

***

Rees is riding behind Sgt. McGregor, who insisted on taking the lead for a while. The pocket watch in Rees' vest vibrates. He reaches in and opens the cover, looking at the face.

September 12-15. Battle of Harpers Ferry. We can bring you back or you can continue. Col. Black is leaving it up to you.

Rees speaks into the watch, acknowledging the information.

"Sgt. McGregor?" he shouts, and McGregor turns to look at him. "Sir?"

Rees raises his hand. "Hang on," he says, then realizes his mistake,

"I mean stop."

McGregor does so and comes back toward Rees. "I kinda thought that's what ya might mean, sir."

Rees grins and looks back at the others. The rest of the team approach and stop.

"What's up?" Farnsworth asks when he and Emma are next to him.

"Just got a message from the Bank. Said something about a battle at Harpers Ferry."

Farnsworth's mouth opens slightly as if to say something, then he closes it. He shuts his eyes and throws his head back. "Ahhhh!" he moans, then opens his eyes and shakes his head. "Shit! I should have thought about that. Yes, yes! J.E.B. Stewart attacks Harpers Ferry from September 12th through the 15th. He is already massing troops in the area. In fact, he has artillery on this ridge now. We are basically being closed in on and could be trapped if we don't get a move on."

"What do we do?" Bouvier asks. "We still got a ways to go."

"Why not just go straight ahead to the river, work our way up until we can cross?" Nionee suggests.

"Can't. Listen," Farnsworth says and everyone becomes still. In the distance, and coming from the top of the mounts, they hear cannon fire. "Damn, I'm dumb for forgetting the dates," he says as he checks his watch.

"What's going on?" Kriger asks, staring in the direction where he hears the echoing thunder.

"The battle of Harpers Ferry has already begun. The Rebels are firing cannons from this ridge and the other mountain ridge from across the Potomac. Stuart will be closing in and the town will surrender either tomorrow or the next day, can't rightly remember."

While they are talking, Tosseti is staring at the ridge and slowly moving toward it. "Can we go over the ridge instead of around it? There's a saddle right there, lowest point I can see, and it's not too far."

Everyone turns their attention to Tosseti, then to the low ridge.

Farnsworth looks at Rees and shrugs. "I guess being an enlisted man doesn't make you a dumbass."

"Hey!" Tosseti barks.

"I meant that as a compliment, sergeant. Good thinking. If we can get over it, we may be able to get to the Union lines of Harpers Ferry before the Rebel forces can get in. If I am correct on the dates, we may have a way over the Potomac."

Rees points at McGregor, who nods and spurs his horse on toward the base of the ridge known as Loundon Heights.

The climb up the ridge is slow due to the thick foliage, rocks, and fallen trees, and it is time consuming. The Rebel artillery is relentless, and the cannon fire is continuous. The team moves around the obstacles, including granite boulders, eventually reaching the crest.

Once on top the team stops and waits as Farnsworth helps Emma off the horse, then he and Rees climb down and walk to the edge of the ridgeline. They only have to go a few feet before coming across a clearing that allows them a scenic view of the valley below with the town of Harpers Ferry down and to their right. Watching for a few minutes, they see an occasional cannon ball fly through the air and land amongst the buildings, some exploding, others bouncing and flying back into the air, and some just burying themselves in the dirt or falling short into the river.

"Look down there," Farnsworth says, pointing to a section of the Shenandoah River. "Looks like a spot shallow enough for us to cross. And they aren't shelling the area."

Rees turns his gaze to where Farnsworth is pointing, then raises his binoculars for a better view. A mill of some sort is just below where they need to cross.

"I see it," Rees replies, then turns his attention back up the river after noticing movement. "You might want to see this."

Farnsworth raises his eyeglass and spots troop movement off in the distance, heading to Harpers Ferry.

"Time to get a move on," Farnsworth says and the two men return to the team, explaining the situation while mounting their rides. Rees kicks his horse and begins traversing down the ridge toward the section of the river where they aim to cross.

The group slowly makes its way to the river and finds an area shallow enough to cross in relative safety and out of the way of cannon fire. Once across, they move cautiously toward the mill, located on the outskirts of the town, until they are challenged.

"Halt!"

The team stops and sees a lone Union soldier holding a musket. The young man suspiciously eyes the group until he sees the ranks on the officers. He hesitates when he sees Emma, smiling at him from behind Farnsworth's back, but quickly recovers, comes to attention and salutes. "My apologies, sir, but you shouldn't be here. We're being bombarded and the Rebs are moving in on us."

"Nothing to apologize for, son. You're just doing your job. We need to get to Col. Miles' headquarters. Can you point us in the right direction?"

"Yes, sir. It's up that road, last building on the right. The armorer's home, the three-story home just past the Provost Marshall office," the young man explains, pointing in the general direction.

Farnsworth thanks the guard, salutes and everyone speeds up to get behind some type of cover as quickly as possible. People are running to and fro, soldiers are hurriedly moving equipment, sergeants are yelling orders. All the while, cannons are smashing into buildings and exploding in the streets.

A few seconds later, they reach the stone building being used as Col. Miles' headquarters, located not far from the Shenandoah River. The team dismounts and Rees tells the others to take care of the horses and try to find one for Miss Kelly. Farnsworth and Rees head for the headquarters' front door and enter a cramped, smoke-filled room. The light from the windows shoots beams across the floor as it filters through the smoke from smoldering cigars and oil-burning lamps. The room is cramped from all the men crowded around and smells from unwashed uniforms and bodies.

Rees and Farnsworth push their way through until they find Col. Miles, who is instructing his officers where they need to be, preparing for the inevitable ground attack. The officers, as well as a white-bearded Miles, look up as Farnsworth clears his throat. The soldiers straighten upon recognizing the rank.

Miles watches Farnsworth through bloodshot eyes that dart from him to Rees. Farnsworth notices the red eyes and wonders if it's from the smoke-filled room, long hours with little sleep or too much alcohol consumption. Probably a combination of all three. Miles scratches his beard and is at a loss for words, not expecting to see a general at Harpers Ferry in the middle of a bombardment. Finally, he comes to his senses. "General," he says, more as a statement than a question.

"I'm sorry to intrude like this, colonel. I am Gen. Farnsworth and this is Capt. Rees."

The colonel stands a little straighter, looks at both men and nods.

"Are you here to take command, general?" Miles asks, with a hint of relief mixed with anxiety in his voice.

"No colonel, no. You are doing what you need. We are only passing through," Farnsworth explains and Rees hands the letter with Lincoln's signature over to the man.

Miles reads the letter and hands it back, his shoulders sagging slightly.

"General, we are surrounded by the confederates, under heavy bombardment and are extremely busy. I cannot guarantee you or your men's safety while here. I will do what I can to assist you, but I do need to get back to the defense of this town."

"I understand, colonel, all we ...," Farnsworth begins then stops when several explosions rattle the house, causing dust from the rafters to slowly fall into the room, making it even gloomier.

More rumbling and more explosions fill the air and shake the house again.

The men instinctively flinch but are professional enough to know that if their time is up, there is little they can do about it, so they carry on.

Miles stares out the window, then lets out a breath. He turns back to Farnsworth. "Sir, what exactly can I do for you? As you can see, we are in the middle of a battle."

"Nothing, colonel. We just wanted to let you know we were passing through. We are looking for Col. Davis."

"Col. Davis?"

"Yes. I understand he has a plan to cross over the Potomac tonight."

Miles shakes his head disapprovingly. "A foolhardy plan, I might add. You are not thinking of going along with him, are you?" he asks, wondering how the general knew about Davis's plan.

"Yes, colonel, we are. Not to worry; we will locate him. Not too many places he can go. I just wanted to let you know we are here and will not be interfering," Farnsworth says, eyeing the colonel and knowing the man only has a short time to live. A shot from one of the cannons will strike the building and explode, sending a piece of shrapnel into the colonel's leg. He dies in the home they are in. Farnsworth nods, says his goodbyes to the group, and he and Rees head back to the door.

"What the hell?" Rees exclaims as a shell explodes in the road right outside the door as they exit, peppering them with bits of gravel and dirt.

"Let's go find the guys and Emma and see if we can get out of here."

The two men run to a barn, where they locate the rest of the squad.

When they find the team, they also find Kriger and Bouvier in a heated argument with a Union major.

"What is going on here?" Farnsworth demands, approaching the three men, who turn to face him.

"This dickweed wants us to give up our horses!" Kriger answers angrily.

Farnsworth looks at the major. "Major, you want to explain yourself?"

The major stares Farnsworth in the eyes and doesn't budge. "I am sorry, sir, but I have orders from Col. Miles to locate and confiscate all horses to be used in the defense of the town."

Just then another cannon ball lands and explodes across the road in front of the barn, making everyone jump.

Farnsworth returns his attention to the major. "I'm sorry, major, but we need our horses, and we are not attached to this unit. We are passing through on our way back to Washington. I must apologize for this, but not only are you not taking our horses, I am going to take one of yours, seeing as we are one short."

Another explosion erupts just outside the barn door, causing them to jump again.

"We need to find better shelter," Bouvier says.

"No, we need to get the hell out of here," Nionee says.

"Aye!" McGregor chimes in. "And right now, if I may add."

Farnsworth speaks up. "We wait until night, then we will escape along with Col. Davis and his troops," he tells the group, scanning the surrounding area, "who I need to find, by the way."

"Who?" Rees asks.

"Col. Davis is going to sneak across the Potomac tonight and I plan for us to tag along. Long story, but for now I think we should just lay low until I can find him and make plans to join up. You all take Miss Kelly and the horses up the street to the high point of that hill," he says, pointing up Washington Street, "then radio and let us know where you are. Once we have coordinated our escape with Davis, we'll rendezvous. Right now, Rees and I will go find the man while the rest of you get to safety."

Everyone acknowledges. Rees and Farnsworth leave the barn, staying close to the building, wishing to avoid a direct blast. In between the shelling and explosions, the two men have to ask frightened soldiers where they can locate Col. Davis. One soldier tells them he is located further up Potomac Street.

Maneuvering slowly down the street, Farnsworth spies soldiers throwing dirt onto a pontoon bridge spanning the Potomac River. When they finally reach the edge of the cannon ball's range, they relax some and continue on.

"Col. Davis," Farnsworth says by way of announcement upon approaching the man.

A soldier was speaking with the colonel when Farnsworth called his name. The soldier and Davis stop their conversation and turn to see who has spoken. He does not recognize the man, but he does recognize the rank. Standing straighter he comes to attention as Farnsworth raises his hand.

"None of that in a battle zone, colonel," Farnsworth says, waving his hand in a dismissive manner. "Sorry to intrude. I am Gen. Farnsworth, and this is Capt. Rees. We are a special unit out of Washington and could use your help," he explains as he hands the letter to Davis.

"Good to meet you, sir," Davis answers in a strong southern drawl and takes the letter, reading it over twice before handing it back, one eyebrow.

"We would like to join your unit when you make your way over the bridge tonight."

The look on Davis's face changes from questioning to surprise. "I am sorry, general, but I did not see you at the briefing when I spoke with Col. Miles. How do you know of this, if I may be so bold to ask?"

"No, colonel, it's quite all. We were making our way to Washington with some vital information when we were attacked by a Rebel company. We fled in this direction hoping to cross the Potomac. When we arrived and spoke with Col. Miles, he was kind enough to inform us of your plan, which, by the way, is brilliant. So, we would like to join you."

Col. Davis stares at the two men, then breaks into a smile. "Why of course, general. Glad to have you along. I must warn you - it will be dangerous, and we must maintain silence when crossing the bridge. The graybacks are watching us and I am quite sure they are wondering why we are laying so much dirt on the pontoon bridge."

Farnsworth nods. "Thank you, colonel. We appreciate this," he says, then smiles. "Alabama?" he asks.

Davis's smile widens. "Why yes, sir. How did you know?"

"Being a southern man myself, I am acquainted with the accent. But enough chatter. I know you have much to do. I assure you we will be as quiet as church mice, colonel. And as I said, wonderful plan."

Davis continues to smile. "I am glad you think so, general. Col. Miles was not as forthright. Now, if you and your aide ..."

Farnsworth cuts him off. "Uh, colonel, Capt. Rees is not my aide; he is part of my unit, as well as several others who are gathering supplies. Also, we have a female civilian with us. This is why we must get across the river and get her to safety and to those who need the information she possesses to help the cause."

Davis's eyes widen then he slowly begins to nod. "Ah, special unit, a letter signed by the president and secretary of war, and a civilian woman being escorted by a general officer. All right, sir. Please be ready to leave by eight o'clock, if you will."

They trade military pleasantries, and Farnsworth and Rees head back into the town as the iron balls of destruction continue to rain down.

Chapter 44

2020

Helen Hellberg and Aeson Minten calmly walk through the corridors leading to the Clio Project control room. As they pass the door to the colonel's office, Helen stops and places her hand on the handle. Aeson continues further to the control room. When he reaches it, he removes the identification card attached to his shirt pocket and places it on the security panel. When he hears the beep, he smiles at Helen and they both open the doors and step inside.

Helen rushes up the stairs two at a time and opens a second door, this one giving her entrance into Samantha Johnson's office. Hellberg already has her pistol out, opting to use it instead of the M4, and points it in Sam's direction as she enters. Sam begins to reach for her own weapon but stops when Helen moves closer, now aiming the weapon at her head.

"Ah, no. I wouldn't do that. Let me see those hands and stand up slowly. I have no problem shooting you," she says. "Now let us go visit the good colonel, shall we?" She waves the gun barrel toward the colonel's office door. Sam doesn't move, giving Helen a hard, hate-filled glare.

"Now, now sweetie, no need to get your panties in a bunch. Just do as I say, and we will get along just fine. I will be out of y'all's hair soon enough. Now move and open that door and get inside. Do something stupid and I will kill you. Go!"

Sam moves to the door, watchful of the gun barrel in her face. She reaches behind her and fumbles for the door handle, not taking her eyes off Helen. She finally grasps the handle and opens the door, stepping inside. Helen moves quickly and pushes Sam further into the room as she enters herself. Shuffling over to a corner, Helen now has a position to cover the entire room.

The colonel and chief are staring down into the control room, watching as an SF member enters with a raised M4. The man begins yelling as Helen and Sam come crashing into their office. They turn as one and stare in disbelief at Helen, at the same time trying to understand what the SF member is doing screaming and waving a rifle around in the control room.

"What the hell?!" Col. Black demands.

"Surprise!" Helen answers. "Now colonel, chief, please move over to where your assistant is standing, and place your hand in your pants pockets. I know about you, chief, and I'm not taking chances. Better yet ...," she says, reaching into a pouch for a set of handcuffs, "handcuff yourself," she instructs, throwing the cuffs to the colonel, "to the chief."

Helen walks to the window and glances into the control room, where her brother is taking charge.

Aeson Minten trains his weapon on those closest to him. "Everyone, listen the hell up!" he says loudly.

Only those closest to the door stop what they are doing and look in his direction. Not getting their attention, he fires off a three-round burst into the floor. The room grows silent except for the few asking what is happening. Some gasp and others murmur in confusion. Now he has their attention.

"I said listen up!" he shouts, and this time the room is quiet. He looks into the observation room and sees his sister looking at him. He gives her a thumbs up and her face disappears from the window as she moves back into the office.

Moving to the door, she holds it open and indicates the trio should move out of the office.

"We're going to the control room. I'm sure you know the way. Let's go, come on," she says waving the pistol like a directional wand.

Aeson's attention is distracted for just a second as he watches the observation room window. TJ is seated about fifteen feet from the intruder, so he reaches for his own sidearm. Montoya sees what he is doing, but can't tell him not to without alerting Aeson. TJ slowly stands, pulling his pistol out of the holster just as Aeson returns his attention to those in the control room. Before TJ can aim his pistol, three shots ring out. Aeson is quicker than TJ and sees what the cop is doing. One round strikes TJ in his artificial leg, another clips his hip, and the third, by sheer luck, strikes the gun in TJ's hand. The bullet shatters, sending fragments flying in different directions with one-piece striking TJ in the face, producing a large gash. TJ shouts, drops his weapon and dramatically falls to the floor, feigning unconsciousness as blood flows from the wounds.

Montoya moves to help, but Aeson shifts the barrel of the weapon in his direction. Montoya gets the message and stops.

"You fucking cops are alike, wanting to be heroes," he says and grabs the blue beret he is wearing, removing it and throwing it at Montoya. "You're lucky I didn't put those rounds through his head. Now that you know I mean business, I want you all to listen up. Everybody needs to go into that conference room over there," he says, cocking his head toward the room at the back of the control room. "But first, I want you," he says, looking at Montoya, "to remove your gun belt. Throw it over here to me."

Montoya slowly removes his belt and tosses it, with the gun still in its holster, in Aeson's general direction but just short of the man's reach. Aeson sighs and cocks his head, staring at Montoya and then slowly shakes it.

"I guess you think you're being funny, or you have some stupid plan in mind. Forget it. Now get on over there with the rest of them and into the conference room."

While he is talking, the control room door opens revealing the colonel, chief, Sam and Helen.

"You know security is probably already on their way here, right?" Helen inquires.

"Of course they are, sis. Shut the door," he tells her and she does. "Cover this group," he says and walks over to a control panel then points at Montoya.

"You, come here." Montoya moves to the control panel and Aeson instructs him to secure the doors and the control room windows.

"I don't have access to that," Montoya tries to explain.

Aeson, snorts, smiles, then smashes the butt of his weapon into Montoya's stomach, causing a rush of air to expel from the man and making him double over. Aeson lets out a breath. "Ouch, that looks like it hurt," then walks over to Samantha. "Come here!" he grumbles as he reaches up and grabs her by the hair. Sam cries from the pain and reaches up, grabbing his hand and twisting it back.

Aeson yelps, not expecting a woman to be able to put such a move on him. He grins like the Tasmanian devil and looks at Sam with hungry eyes. "Oh, so we have a trained secretary, do we," he says and, as quick as a rattlesnake, he snatches her hair again and slams her against the wall, stunning her. Aeson jerks her hair again, this time making her yelp. With a snarl, he drags the groggy, but still fighting Samantha over to Montoya, then places the barrel of the weapon under her chin.

"I like this one, but make no mistake, I will blow her brains out. Now stop fucking around, boy. I am better at this than you are, and I don't mind killing someone to get what I want, so, lock down this room. NOW!"

Trying to catch his breath, Montoya nods, slowly straightens then enters the code to secure the Clio Project control room. Aeson smiles his approval as he hears the door locks engage and turns to see the shutters sliding down over the glass of the colonel's office and the observation room.

"Now that we have that taken care of, you may join your friends," he says, shoving Samantha into Montoya, who grabs her to keep her from falling. Aeson points to the conference room and the two walk toward it.

Col. Black and the chief, who are handcuffed together, move to Aeson.

"Just what do you think you and your sister are going to accomplish here? This facility is now in lockdown; you have nowhere to go," the colonel says.

"Oh, you know us? Wow, I am impressed. I guess we're famous after all," he says and looks at Helen. "You hear that, sis? We are known entities within these hallowed walls."

He turns back to the colonel. "Now that the celebrity worship is over and, to answer your question, yes, we are quite aware of that, colonel. What we are going to accomplish is to get back to our timeline, then correct the mistakes that allowed you and that abomination you call the council to be in control of the Clio Project. You must know the story behind my father's downfall, I'm sure. Well, we intend to create a different outcome."

"Now, as much as I would love to get to know you better, we have a few things to get to, so if you please, join everyone in the conference room."

Col. Black squints at Aeson, then moves toward the conference room, stopping to look at TJ.

"What about him?"

Aeson looks down at TJ and shrugs. "Nothing. Once we are gone and, if you can get out of the room in time, maybe you can save him before he bleeds out. Now quit stalling and move," he finishes and points his weapon at the officer. Col. Black does as he is told, pulling the chief along with him.

"Chief, so glad to meet you. You look much older than I thought you would," Aeson says with a smirk, not getting any reaction from the chief.

Helen and Aeson follow the group to the conference room door and make sure everyone is inside. Aeson looks in the room and decides that all the furniture needs to be removed and orders it done. He disables the phones, computers, television, and cameras. Once he is satisfied the room is secure, he shuts the door and, using the code he watched Montoya type in, locks the door. With the butt of the weapon, he smashes the control panel, then turns and grins at his sister.

"Ready to go home?"

"Oh, you know it. I'll shut down this program and begin the restart sequence."

Before they can begin the procedure, they hear a loud banging from the main control room doors.

"Sounds like someone wants in pretty badly," Aeson says. "Hold on a second," he continues as he removes the radio from its carrier. He raises it to his mouth. "This is Aeson Minten. We have several hostages in the control room. Cease your attempts to gain entry or we will begin killing them. If you think I am bluffing, go check on your comrades in the conference room below."

A full minute passes, then the noise stops.

"I'm glad you heeded my warning. Stand by, be calm and we will be gone shortly," he finishes, throwing the radio away and nodding at Helen.

Helen hurriedly but meticulously moves from one computer to another, reprogramming each as they shut down and reboot. It takes her a few minutes, but when she is finished, the system is ready to be reactivated.

"Okay, you can insert the Inabular Device and I've set us a time delay for it to initiate. Gives us a little time to get to the sendoff room and get settled. In just a few minutes, we will be back to our timeline and get this shit corrected."

Aeson smiles broadly and inserts the device. Clio comes alive and the twins grin and walk into the disembarkation room. The air fills with static electricity and the computer monitors flash as numbers scroll along the screens. Aeson and Helen squat on the floor, awaiting the unpleasant feeling that comes with being disassembled into millions of atoms and then thrown through time to be reassembled. A humming sound pulses in their heads and they smile at each other in anticipation.

On the control room floor, Sgt. Shepard moans, rolls over and sits up, wincing as he reaches for the wound on his hip. He removes his hand to see it covered in blood. He snorts. "Just great, asshole. Got shot again."

Then, groaning from the pain from his hip and face, he pulls himself up so he is leaning on his computer console. He looks around and sees that Clio is ramping up, almost ready to time jump Helen and Aeson. Searching, he sees the one computer console he wants. Unsteadily, he makes his way to the computer and plops into the chair. He begins typing until the date 1982 appears. Pressing a key on the board he watches as the dates begins to change, first from 1982 to 1981 then 1980. Holding the key down, the dates begin to rapidly decrease.

He turns and watches Aeson and Helen in the room. Both siblings stare back. Aeson stands and moves to the window, wondering what the sergeant is doing. The man can't stop the sequence once it's started unless he removes the Inabular Device, and he is nowhere near it.

Helen moves beside him, also watching, the same thoughts were going through her head. Then realization dawns on him. Aeson opens his mouth to protest, to yell, but doesn't get a chance as Clio has reached her climax and both Aeson and Helen disappear in the blink of an eye.

TJ searches the empty room, then slowly, painfully stands and hobbles to the security console. He looks for his ID card and can't find it, so he manually types in the correct code. Immediately the door slams open as several security personnel rush inside, weapons drawn. TJ weakens, leans against the wall, and slides down, exhausted and in increasing pain. Someone yells and, in a few seconds, two med techs and a doctor come to his aid.

A security team makes their way to the conference room and realizes the security panel is disabled. The SF captain in charge calls for equipment to force the door. It only takes a few minutes for the equipment to arrive and even less time to break down door.

Col. Black and the chief had been released from their restraints by Montoya, who still had his handcuff keys. The men rush out to see what had transpired.

The room comes alive with activity as the officers, enlisted and civilian personnel hurriedly exit the conference room and head toward their stations. The colonel, chief and Sam scan the room until they spot Sgt. Shepard sitting on the floor being examined.

The trio rush over, reaching him as he is being placed on a stretcher. He is given a sedative and, as they wheel him away, the chief notices a satisfied grin on TJ's face.

"Col. Black, you may want to see this," a first lieutenant shouts from one of the computer terminals.

The colonel and chief walk over to where the lieutenant is staring at a monitor.

"What is it?" Col. Black asks as he approaches. The lieutenant steps back and allows the two men to see the monitor. The chief frowns as the colonel shakes his head.

"Seems like the good sergeant threw a monkey wrench into their plans," Col. Black says, looking up from the monitor screen displaying a readout with the date 1930.

Chief Black looks at his father. "This could spell trouble."

Chapter 45

1862

Rees, Farnsworth and the rest are on their horses at the rear of a long line of mounted infantry waiting to cross the river. The colonel wanted them to ride in the front of the column, but Farnsworth explained that Davis was in charge and they were just tagging along. Also, they were turning east once they were across.

Davis scoffed at the idea. "General, sir, I don't mean to criticize, but there are a lot of Rebel troops scattered along that route. You would do best to travel with us to Sharpsburg."

Farnsworth assured the man they would be perfectly fine and not to worry. Farnsworth thanks him in advance and adds, "Colonel, good luck and take care of those prisoners."

Col. Davis stares, bemused by the general's comment. "Prisoners?" he mutters to himself, watching the general and his team move to the rear of the column.

"What was that about?" Bouvier asks.

Farnsworth grins. "What, the prisoners?"

Bouvier nods as the rest watch Farnsworth.

"They will run into a Confederate wagon train during the pre-dawn. Col. Davis, who you know has a thick southern accent, so he passes his unit off as a Rebel cavalry unit and explains there are Union troops just ahead. He offers to protect the wagon train, to which they agree. Davis's men surround the wagon train and slowly turn it north toward

Pennsylvania. It isn't until the sun rises that the Rebels realize they are surrounded by Union cavalry, all pointing guns at them."

The men chuckle at the story.

"How many wagons?" Rees inquires.

"Close to one hundred, I believe, and a few hundred soldiers as well as several hundred horses. The wagons all contained ordnance and munitions belonging to Gen. Longstreet, whom I assumed found no humor in it."

Again, everyone chuckles at the story.

When they reach the back of the procession, it is almost 2100, or 9:00 p.m., and it is plenty dark. Slowly and as quietly as possible, the long line of soldiers begins to move across the bridge.

Rees stares down the river at the Bollman Bridge pylon ruins. The railroad tracks and the bridge that supported them had been destroyed, leaving only the pylons. Staring at the ruined structures makes him think of the dark maw of a giant's mouth, opening to reveal decayed and missing teeth. "Now that's a cheery thought," he mutters. *Hope it's not an omen of what's to come*, he thinks.

It takes them quite some time to cross the wobbly pontoon bridge, but they finally make it. When they do, Rees and Farnsworth turn onto the railroad tracks that will lead them along the river. Rees looks back to see the rest of the team following and watches the last of Davis's men move away in the opposite direction, fading into the darkness. Satisfied that everyone is accounted for, he returns his attention forward.

Farnsworth hopes they can sneak past any guards along the way. He's not too worried about the tracks being guarded this far down since the bridges leading into Harpers Ferry have all been destroyed.

They only travel about three miles when they reach the town of Sandy Hook. Being as cautious and quiet as they can, and watching for signs of trouble, they pass by the town. No one bothers them. They continue.

"When do you think we should turn north?" Rees asks. "Not that I'm worried about, you know, getting captured or shot or chased or any of that stuff because, you know, it seems that's all we've been doing."

Farnsworth snorts a laugh. "I get your point. Just up ahead, before Brunswick, we'll turn north. Should be in Mount Airy before morning light."

"Stop right there!" a voice commands from out of the darkness.

"Shit!" Rees says. "Every time I get distracted … I have got to stop that."

"You and me both, brother."

Rees and Farnsworth raise their hands, and Rees hopes the rest of the team are doing the same.

Farnsworth tries a tactic from Col. Davis's playbook.

"Gen. Farnsworth out of North Carolina. We got turned around when we ran into a Union cavalry outfit a ways back," he says, pouring on his already slight southern accent.

"That is a load of bull and we both know it, Yank. It's not so dark as I can't see the yellow stripes on those dark pants. You ain't Carolina cavalry, that's for damned sure. Now all y'all, just unbuckle them there pistol belts and drop 'em on the ground," the voice orders.

"Fuck youse!" Tosseti shouts and, before Rees or anyone else can stop him, he begins firing his pistol in the direction of the voice. Tosseti is rewarded with a shout of pain, but then is knocked off his horse when a shotgun blast strikes him full on in the chest. He grunts from the impact and is unceremoniously thrown from his saddle, landing with a hard *thump* on the rocky, dusty trail.

"Ahhhhhh!" he moans as the wind is knocked out of him. He rolls on the ground and grabs his left hand, where one of the pellets struck him, the rest of the rounds thankfully deflected by his uniform.

Flashes of light from musket muzzles begin lighting up the night like angry fireflies.

Farnsworth turns his horse around and looks back to Emma. She has no protection, so he intends to place himself between her and the gunfire. As he makes his way toward her, he can see Bouvier has already moved his steed up, using his horse and himself as her shield. He is grateful for that.

Minie' balls begin striking the airmen and horses. Before Farnsworth can get to Emma, Bouvier's horse is shot several times. The animal lurches sideways, slamming into Emma and her horse. Bouvier's horse goes down, the momentum causing Emma's horse to slide down the embankment toward the river. Right before it slips into the water, it rears and flips over into the rapidly moving waterway, carrying Emma along with it.

Emma screams as she is thrown from the animal and splashes into the cold water, where she goes under. The horse thrashes about in an attempt to gain footing, making it difficult for Farnsworth to see Emma.

"Dammit!" he screams in frustration, anger and worry.

Farnsworth spurs his horse down the river, and McGregor, who witnessed the entire scene, follows him. The men begin looking for Emma, yelling her name just before spotting her as her head pops up further down river. She is gasping for air and flailing her arms to swim, or at least to not go under again. Both men ignore the bullets whizzing by them as they spur their animals into a gallop along the track's edge. Emma is already a quarter-mile ahead of them, thanks to the rapid current.

They are finally able to catch up to her, then pass her. Once in front of Emma by several yards, they stop. The men try to make it as close as they can to where she will pass. The darkness makes it hard to see very far.

"There!" McGregor shouts when he spies Emma's head above water, bobbing in the current.

Farnsworth grabs his rope and runs into the water. He throws it toward the woman who is frantically trying to stay afloat. As he throws, Emma is caught in a whirlpool that sends her around a boulder. The rope lands on the boulder and slides off.

"The hell with this!" Farnsworth yells as he jumps into the river.

"General, wait," McGregor shouts, but to no avail. McGregor jumps off his mount and runs to the river's edge, watching Farnsworth splash in the water. "Bloody hell," he shouts in frustration before returning to the horses. He grabs the reins of Farnsworth's mount, then climbs back onto his own. With a swift kick and a yell, he encourages the horses into a gallop. He travels further up the river, hoping he can find both Emma and Farnsworth.

Meanwhile, Farnsworth battles the current for a few minutes before he realizes he is too heavy and is sinking. Flowing with the current, he sinks into the water so he can remove his gun belt, boots and jacket before the weight can pull him under for good. Farnsworth curses himself for not doing this before jumping into the water! Time is being wasted.

Emma is being pulled further away from him with each passing second.

He can't see her but that doesn't discourage him. Relieved of the added weight, he begins swimming in the direction he believes, he hopes, she is headed.

***

Rees and the rest of the team have their own hands full with the Rebels. They can't see the enemy and they have to rely on spotting the muzzle flashes and gunfire aimed in their direction. They hear curses and grunts as musket balls find their marks.

Damn, there must be a hundred of these guys, Rees thinks.

But the thought of the Rebels seeing bullets striking Rees and his men, but not causing any damage, must be confounding. Witchery! Or was it sorcery he heard it called during a previous battle? The thought came and went just as quickly as he returns his attention to the fighting.

Tosseti sits up and watches his horse run off. "Coward!" he screams, then realizes he is in the open as bullets whiz by, striking the ground around him. Seeing the river, he drops and crawls to the embankment, roughly sliding down it, gravel crunching under his weight that, in turn, raises a small dust cloud. Just before his head drops below the embankment, he hears a *buzzzit* sound in his right ear. His first instinct is to slap at it, thinking it's a bug, then he realizes it is a Minie' ball that, if an inch more to the left, would have blown his brains out.

As he slides to a halt, he grabs a handkerchief from a pocket. Hurriedly, he wraps it around his wounded hand, tightening it with his teeth. Cursing up a storm, he locates his pistol, reloads it and begins firing, muttering unflattering remarks against his horse as well as the Rebels.

Meanwhile, Bouvier jumps just before his mortally wounded horse tumbles over. He lands awkwardly on a large rock and screams in pain when his ankle turns at an angle it wasn't made to go.

"Arrrgh! Son of a bitch!" he shouts, sitting up and grabbing his ankle. As he sits, a round hits him square in the back. He curses again realizing he is out in the open being so close to the road, so he flops on his side and rolls down the embankment. He moves over to his dead horse and fumbles with the saddle, retrieving his rifle and joining the fight.

Rees is returning fire, his frightened horse moving one way then the other. He tries to avoid being hit - not that it would matter; unless a round finds his unprotected face, he will be fine, but the shots still sting and makes it hard to get off any shot of his own with accuracy. He is vaguely aware that Farnsworth, McGregor and Emma are not with them, and he wonders what happened, having not seen Emma go into the river.

Enough of this shit, he thinks and starts to pull a couple of his grenade buttons off his jacket when he hears Nionee yell, "Frag out!" Within three seconds a fiery flash of light brightens the night sky accompanied by a loud explosion, then followed by screams as the shrapnel tears through human flesh. Rees turns to see Nionee arming another grenade can and, at the same time, watches Kriger throw a can.

"Smoke out!" he shouts. Rees can barely see the can as it arches through the air then hits the ground, sparking and emitting plumes of smoke.

Rees reaches into his own saddle bag and feels around until he touches the double-notched can. He retrieves the smoke grenade, arms it and throws. He turns his attention to the remaining men, not waiting to see the results.

"Kriger, go get Bouvier. Nionee, get Tosseti. Then let's get out of here," he orders, turning back toward the attackers. He continues shooting while grabbing for a fragmentation grenade.

"Yes, sir," Kriger shouts. He fires his weapon once more before riding to Bouvier's position. He finds him lying on his back, reloading his rifle.

"Resting, are we?" Kriger shouts over the din of the battle.

"Fuck you," Bouvier snaps, keeping his attention on his weapon.

Kriger jumps off his horse. "You, okay?"

"Oh, I'm peachy. Twisted my ankle, got shot in the back, horse is dead. How are you doing?"

Kriger snorts. "Hey, leave the smart-ass comebacks to me, will ya?"

"Yeah, yeah. Help me up."

Kriger reaches down to give the wounded man a hand up. Bouvier leans on the smaller man as they shuffle to his dead horse. He removes the saddle bags and throws them over his shoulder.

They return to Kriger's horse, draping the saddlebags over the neck of the animal. Kriger climbs into the saddle, then helps Bouvier mount.

Bouvier wraps one arm around Kriger to steady himself.

"Damn Dave, didn't know you cared."

"Like I said before, fuck you and the horse you rode in on," Bouvier answers, "Now, can we get out of here?"

Nionee rides to Tosseti, who quickly stands and rushes over to Nionee, cursing the entire time. Not thinking, Tosseti reaches up with his left hand. When Nionee grips it, Tosseti grunts in pain, but works through it to climb onto the back of Nionee's steed.

When Nionee releases his grip, he looks at his own blood-covered hand. "What the hell, Tosseti?" he asks as he wipes his hand on his pants leg.

"I got shot. Anything else you need to know?"

"Yeah, where's your horse?" he asks, looking over his shoulder at Tosseti.

Tosseti points down the river where his horse is calmly drinking, oblivious to the battle.

"Over there," he shouts. Nionee spots the animal. Kicking his own horse's flanks, they gallop to Tosseti's steed who stops drinking and raises its head to watch. Once they reach it, Tosseti slides off Nionee's mount and stands, glaring at his horse.

"Get your sorry ass over here," he orders in his gruff voice. The animal stares for a couple of seconds then, slowly, makes his way to Tosseti.

Nionee raises his eyebrows in surprise.

"Well, that's something I didn't think I'd see. Now, get on your horse and let's beat feet."

Tosseti mumbles a few quiet curses, climbs onto his horse, and they make their way back to the others.

The Rebel gunfire has slowed as Nionee and Tosseti approach. "Let's go, sarge," Nionee hollers as he passes Rees.

Rees looks at them and yells, "Where in the hell are the others?"

"Emma went into the drink when her horse fell down the embankment. Farnsworth and McGregor went after her," Kriger shouts back.

"Where?"

Kriger looks down the river and shakes his head. "I guess, that way," he says jutting his chin in the direction of the flowing river.

"Great. Just fucking great," he mutters and turns his horse to follow the others.

***

The river is swift, the current strong, and the water cold as it pulls at Farnsworth. The man is a strong swimmer and swims with the current, using it to his advantage. He focuses on catching up to Emma and getting her out of the water.

If she is still alive, he thinks. *Oh, God, please let her be okay.* He forces himself through the waves. It is pitch black and he can't see much, but he pushes on. He has already gone a long distance and, as each second passes, he begins to fear the worst. Not one to give up, he continues until he hears the sound of a woman's voice, a voice in distress. It's Emma. He can't see her, but he knows it's her.

Farnsworth begins fighting against the current by swimming sideways toward the sound of the voice. As he nears, he can make out a shape. It's the shape of a person hanging onto a tree that has toppled into the river with the roots still attached to the riverbank.

He swims harder and finally grabs a tree branch several feet from Emma. He can see she is shaking, either from the cold, fear or the strain of trying to hang onto the tree, most likely all the above. She is struggling and the current is trying to dislodge her, reclaiming her for itself.

She doesn't notice him as he moves up behind her. She is concentrating on trying to stay alive.

Farnsworth moves to the section of the tree that Emma is holding and she gives a small squeak of fright.

"You startled me," she gasps.

"Not my intention," he says, moving closer to help.

"No, I'm sure it wasn't. I seem to have gotten myself into a predicament, thanks to those unruly soldiers back there. And they caused me to lose another horse."

"Sorry, but never mind that right now," he says calmly. "Let's get out of this river and try to get you dry somehow. Grab ahold of my shoulders and I'll pull us along until we get to shore."

He turns his back to her, but when she doesn't grab him, he looks back and notices the fear in her eyes. He smiles reassuringly. "Hey, it's all right. Trust me."

Emma nods. She tentatively releases her hold on the tree and hurriedly wraps her arms around Farnsworth's neck.

"Hey, young lady. Please, not so tight. Still gotta breathe," he jokes, trying to calm her.

"Oh, sorry." She loosens her grip slightly.

"That's better. Now hold on," he says and begins moving along the tree to the shoreline.

It takes but a few minutes. When they reach shore, both crawl further onto the land and collapse to the ground, rolling onto their backs and breathing heavily.

"Well, that's my cardio for the day."

Emma doesn't get the joke, so she doesn't answer. After a few minutes of rest, she sits up and touches her messy, damp hair.

"I must look a sight," she says, patting her water-soaked hair, then looking at her wet, dirty clothes.

Farnsworth sits up and looks at her. "Hey," he says, but she ignores him.

Reaching over, he gently touches her shoulder. "Hey, look at me."

Emma raises her green eyes and stares into his blue ones.

"You are beautiful to me no matter what."

She blushes, places a hand over his, then leans over and kisses him on the lips. Not a passionate kiss, just a kiss of gratitude. Well, maybe a little more than that.

She leans back from the kiss and smiles warmly at Farnsworth, who is a little flustered. A warm feeling begins to grow inside him. They are so busy looking at each other that they don't notice the Rebel patrol standing several feet away.

"Sorry to have to break up this here touching moment with you two love birds, but I am afraid that you are now my prisoners."

Both Farnsworth and Emma are startled and jump upon hearing the man's voice. There are the dark shapes of several men standing around them.

"If you would be so kind as to stand up," the silhouette of a man asks as he walks toward them.

"Now just who might'n you be, good sir? A deserter?" the shadowy form inquires and moves closer, revealing himself to be a Rebel sergeant.

"No, not a deserter. I was assigned to escort this young lady back to her home," Farnsworth answers. "She is the daughter of a prominent farmer in Mount Airy, and my commander thought it best if she was escorted."

"Sure looks like you're doing a fine job at it, from what I could see," the soldier scoffs, followed by a few chuckles from the shadowy figures around them. "Now, I ask you again. Who are you?"

Farnsworth realizes he doesn't have his jacket, belt, hat or anything that can identify him as an officer and decides to use that to his advantage ... he hopes.

"Sgt. Farnsworth, First Maryland Infantry."

Emma looks at him, but maintains her composure.

"Those yellow stripes on your legs say otherwise, Yank."

Farnsworth doesn't flinch at the reveal. "Lost my unit during battle, and I was the lone survivor. No cavalry units to join up with, so I was integrated. You know what integrated is, don't you?" he asks the leader.

The man's face reddens, but he makes no move toward Farnsworth.

"Anyway," Farnsworth continues, "I was added to the First Maryland and, since I was not part of their regulars, I was assigned this task."

The leader stares at Farnsworth, wondering whether he should believe him or not, then decides it really doesn't matter.

"Ah, well I'm Sgt. Peavy. Don't mind my regiment," the sergeant says by way of introduction. "You know, it is too bad you're only a sergeant. I was hoping you would be an officer. Seems like they would have entrusted an officer with such a fine detail, but I reckon you all are runnin' out of them by now, what with us kicking y'alls tail end every which way," he says, all the while leering at Emma. "Capturing a Yank officer sure would make me look better to the captain. No matter, we still have a Yankee prisoner and his fancy girl here."

Farnsworth becomes angry at the blatant remark and makes a furtive move toward Peavy, who - impressively - doesn't flinch. Farnsworth stops when he feels sharp pressure against his abdomen. Looking down he sees the point of a knife poking his stomach. Farnsworth now understands why.

Peavy tilts his head and gives Farnsworth a lopsided grin. "Now if'n you don't want this here Arkansas toothpick shoved into your bread-basket, I think you might want to take a step back, Yank."

Farnsworth stares at the knife for a couple of seconds before moving back a few steps. He doesn't have his bullet-resistant jacket on, and a knife wound would most definitely ruin his day.

"She is not a harlot, sergeant. I told you. I am just escorting her home."

Peavy shakes his head. "Be that as it may, she is still in the company of a blue belly, so that might even make her a spy. But these things are not for me to worry about. I will be taking both of you to my commander as prisoners. He will know what to do with you.

"Now if you please, place your hands together so my men can truss you up."

Farnsworth and Emma comply and silently watch as two grey-clad men tie ropes around their wrists.

Once secured Sgt. Peavy extends his arm in an *after you* gesture. Both Farnsworth and Emma, still soaking wet and shoeless, move in the direction indicated.

"All right everyone. Move out," Peavy orders and the soldiers and two prisoners begin walking north toward the Rebel encampment.

***

Sgt. McGregor can't find Farnsworth or Emma anywhere and becomes both frustrated and worried. He is in enemy territory, riding around blind in the middle of the night with no idea where to go. He stops moving and listens for the sound of someone in the river, but the noise of the water overrides any possibility of that. He nudges his horse and begins a slow walk, continuing down the river with Farnsworth's horse in tow.

McGregor continues searching until he spots a group of what can only be Rebel soldiers up the road. He becomes still, hoping they haven't spotted him.

"Shite," he whispers to himself and slowly backs the horses up. When he thinks he is far enough away, he turns around and heads back down the road, hoping to find Rees.

Meanwhile Rees and the others have galloped up the road far enough to believe they are out of danger. They slow to a trot and continue for a short time before stopping to allow Kriger to treat Tosseti's gunshot wound and wrap Bouvier's ankle. Once done, they continue. Nionee is in the lead, followed by Tosseti, then Kriger and Bouvier, with Rees bringing up the rear. They haven't travelled far when Nionee raises his fist, a silent command to stop. Rees rides up to him. Without saying a word, Nionee points up the road. Rees looks and observes a lone rider.

They all remain still, watching the rider as he approaches. Rees rests his hand to his pistol and narrows his eye to see better. Finally, the rider sees them and waves.

"It's McGregor," Rees whispers, relieved.

When the sergeant reaches them, he does not look pleased.

"Sgt. McGregor, where are Gen. Farnsworth and Emma?" Rees asks, glancing at Farnsworth's horse.

"I donna know sir," McGregor says forlornly, explaining what transpired after Emma went into the river.

"Well, that's just great. We got, what thirty miles or less to go and we lose two people," Kriger moans.

Rees looks at Kriger. "That's not helping, Dave," he admonishes, turning back to McGregor.

"I am sorry, sir. I tried to look for them but there was no way around that Rebel patrol, so I thought it best I try to find you."

"No, sergeant. You were right to find us. No sense us losing you as well. Damn!" Rees says, then looks at Kriger.

"Try contacting him."

"These intercom devices only go about a hundred yards, Scott."

"I know; try anyway."

Kriger shrugs then calls Farnsworth a couple of times but receives no answer. He shakes his head.

"Kriger, give me your pocket watch. I need to contact the Bank."

Kriger hands over his watch.

"Control, we have lost contact with Farnworth and Emma. They were last seen in the Potomac River. Can you get a location on them?"

The reply is almost immediate. *We were watching the situation. From what we saw on his bodycam, he removed his jacket, and, we assume, his boots. We are receiving multiple device locations along the river, including from his watch.*

Rees reads the message then places his hand over his face, rubbing it and pinching the bridge of his nose. Taking a deep breath, he releases it then brings the watch close to his mouth.

"Bank, copy that. We are close to Mount Airy, as you can see. We can't risk going further along the river, too many Rebel patrols. Suggestions?"

Several minutes pass and they don't receive an answer. Rees positions the watch close to his mouth. "Bank, do you have any suggestions?"

Two more minutes pass. No reply. Rees looks at Bouvier. "Try yours."

Bouvier and Nionee pull their watches out. First Bouvier calls in, but receives no answer, so Nionee tries as well. Same results.

"For crying out loud. Doesn't anything work?" Rees says exasperated.

"It was working fine a couple of minutes ago," Kriger says, puzzled.

Bouvier stares at him. "No shit, Sherlock. We all know that."

"Maybe we just hit a dead spot, or they blew a fuse or something. I'm sure we can get in touch with them later," Nionee says.

Rees stares at the ground in thought for a few seconds, then looks at each man.

"Farnsworth said you all have the capability to self-travel back to the Bank."

The four security forces members all acknowledge they do.

"Here is what we are going to do. I will take one of those devices. You four will go back to the Bank. Sgt. McGregor and I will go on to Mount Airy and wait. Maybe Farnsworth and Emma will show up. If they do, then mission accomplished, and we will return as well. If Farnsworth doesn't show, then I will come back by myself."

The four men stare at Rees then look at each other, mouths open, eyebrows raised in disbelief.

"Fuck that, Scott," Bouvier blurts. "We all go forward, or we all go home. You know better than that, for crying out loud."

The others all join in, each one talking over the others.

Rees raises his hands to quiet them.

"That is an order, not a suggestion."

"Like hell it is!" Kriger shouts angrily. "You don't get to do that. We haven't busted our asses to get this far only to let you decide you're going to be the big, selfish hero and go it alone. That's bullshit and you know it."

"There ain't no self-pitying, self-sacrificing individualism here. We're a team. Been a team since we were all together for that first time-traveling debacle and have been training together ever since. And may I remind you that you already went off on your own once and that is one of the reasons we are now here, looking for your sorry ass. So, get off that high horse of yours, no pun intended, and let's move our collective rears to Mount Airy and finish this mission so we all can go home."

Kriger glares at Rees, who just stares back. "Wow, Dave, tell me how you really feel," he replies, a grin forming on his lips.

The tension breaks and the men begin to laugh. Bouvier punches Kriger in the arm. "Great speech, Dave. Didn't know you had it in you."

The others make comments about Kriger's speech and he good naturedly takes the compliments and jeering with embarrassment and uncharacteristic humility.

"All right, Dave. You made your point. We continue on, together," Rees says and the others agree. "I still think you two should go back though," he says, looking at Bouvier and Tosseti.

"No way in hell, sarge. Kriger is as good a doctor as any real doctor I know. I'll stick it out," Tosseti answers and Bouvier agrees.

"I gave them both a localized pain killer. It doesn't mess with their mental capacity, just numbs the pain in the area of the injuries, sort of like Novocain. And I loaded Tosseti up with antibiotics. They both should be good until we get them back to the Bank to be seen by a doctor," Kriger tells Rees, then looks at Tosseti and Bouvier. "But thanks for that vote of confidence, guys."

"All right, stay alert, and that goes for me as well as the rest of you. I've been letting my mind wander and that has gotten me into trouble more than once," he tells the men. "Let's get to Mount Airy."

They turn their mounts and begin heading northeast to what they hope is their final destination.

***

The soldiers push and prod Farnsworth and Emma to keep moving. Their bare feet are sore from walking on gravel, grass and weeds. If they slow, a rifle butt or barrel poked into their backs quickly makes them move faster. Luckily, they don't have to go far before they are led into a Rebel camp and to a large tent bathed in a yellowish glow. They see shadows of people moving inside.

"Wait here," Peavy orders, then approaches one of the men on picket duty. He says a few words and the guard sticks his head inside the tent, then motions for Peavy to enter.

It only takes a few seconds before Peavy emerges and waves for Farnsworth and Emma to come to him. The soldiers release them, shoving them in the direction of the tent. Farnsworth turns, smirking at the soldier who pushed him. He raises his tied hands and points both his index fingers at him, dropping his thumbs in the classic pistol-shooting gesture while making a *phew, phew* sound like a blaster. The soldiers stare, puzzled.

When they enter the tent, they are greeted with stale, smoke-filled air, both from the oil-burning lanterns and the smoldering cigar the captain is holding between his fingers. The man is young, maybe 23, though he looks much older, and is sporting a couple days growth of beard. He is standing behind a table littered with papers, maps, and glasses filled with an amber liquid as well as steaming tin cups of coffee or tea. The captain is framed by two 1st lieutenants and a sergeant.

Sgt. Peavy points to the table and tells the two prisoners to stand in front of it. Farnsworth studies each man in the tent. Emma seems to be doing the same.

The captain, lieutenants and sergeant stand straight and focus their attention on the two arrivals. The captain begins.

"So, this is what you brought me today, Sgt. Peavy?"

"Yes, sir," Peavy replies.

"Pickin's getting low out there?" the captain asks with a slight smile, looking from Farnsworth to Emma, his gaze lingering a little longer on Emma.

"Sorry, sir. We didn't patrol as far as we were intending before we came upon these two along the shoreline."

The captain waves him off. "Just havin' a bit of fun with you, sergeant. No, this is good work," he says, turning his attention back to Farnsworth and Emma. "My name is Frank Duval, Capt. Duval," he says as introduction and turns to the two officers at his side. "This is Lt. Capshaw and Lt. Fletcher," he says, introducing the officers then glancing over his shoulder at the gruff looking NCO. "And of course Sgt. Maj. O'Hara."

O'Hara stares stoned-faced as the lieutenants nod to Emma.

When he finishes, Duval stares at Farnsworth, waiting for him to say who he is.

"I am Sgt. Farnsworth, 1st Maryland Infantry, and this is Miss Emma Kelly of Mount Airy, Maryland."

The captain nods his head. "Yes, good, good. Now why would you happen to be on the shores of the Potomac, soaking wet and shoeless I might add?" Duval asks looking at their feet.

"Accident, sir. I was assigned to escort Miss Kelly back to her home. As we attempted to traverse along the river, her horse became skittish and threw her into the waterway. I jumped in to help her. We both got carried down the river until we were able to make it to shore."

The captain stares, watching Farnsworth for any tell of a lie. Farnsworth knows what the man is doing, but he only slightly varied the story that was almost true. "Is that a Southern accent I detect, sergeant?" Duval asks Farnsworth with a sidelong glance.

"Yes, sir, it is. I am originally from Georgia."

Shaking his head, Duval looks down at the table. "Ah, a traitor as well as a deserter," Duval says as a comment rather than a question, watching for a reaction from Farnsworth.

"Neither sir. I was raised in the North and, as I said, I was ordered to escort this young woman home. I lost my orders when I removed my jacket before jumping in the water after Miss Emma."

"Of course, sergeant. How convenient," Duval says. Then, as if he is already tired of this conversation, turns his gaze down to his map. "And just where did this accident take place?" he asks as he turns the map so it is facing Farnsworth.

Farnsworth points to an area on the Virginia side of the river. "Right about here, sir."

"I see. Now is that where your unit is located? The 1st Maryland Infantry, you said?" Duval asks, his finger on the map where Farnsworth pointed while looking at Farnsworth.

Farnworth smiles but says nothing. The captain straightens and places his hands on his hips. "All right, sergeant. I understand. Well, be that as it may, you are now a prisoner of the Confederate army and will be taken to a way station and turned over to the sergeant-at-arms. From there you will take a train ride down to your home state of Georgia, where you will be held in the stockades of Andersonville until such time as you are either traded for one of our boys or the end of the war or, God forbid, death takes you."

"What about, Miss Kelly?" Farnsworth asks, getting a little nervous now, unsure if Rees can find him in time, if at all.

"Oh, we will take good care of her. I just have a few questions for her first. Not that we don't trust her, but you know that both of our sides have been using our women to spy for us. I just need to make sure she is who she says she is."

Farnsworth doesn't like the way the men are eyeing her and begins to breathe a little heavier.

"I told you who she was. Why don't you just let her go?" he asks a little forcibly.

"I am sorry, sergeant, but you are in no position to ask anything of us. And as far as Miss Kelly is concerned, well, it is out of your hands now, is it not?" he says and waves his hand dismissively. Lt. Fletcher moves around the table and takes Emma by the arm, a smile on his face. Emma is scared and looks pleadingly at Farnsworth. That is all it takes for him to lose control.

Seeing Farnsworth tense, Sgt. Peavy moves up and grasps Farnsworth's upper arms. Farnsworth lunges backwards, snapping his head back and into Peavy's face. Peavy screams as blood fountains from a busted nose. Farnsworth rushes toward the table, kicking the edge and causing it to slam into the captain and Lt. Capshaw before flipping over, spilling drinks, papers, and maps. Both men give a cry of alarm as they are knocked backwards, flailing their arms in an attempt to remain upright. Farnsworth then turns toward Lt. Fletcher, raising his tied hands and interlocking his finger to make a double fist. He swings them at the officer's head, but before he can strike, a gunshot explodes in the small confines of the tent. Farnsworth grunts as a bullet strikes him in the leg. The bullet-resistant material stops the round, but the impact is enough to stagger him.

With a savage grunt he straightens and moves back to where Emma is still being held. A second shot is fired. This round strikes Farnsworth in the shoulder, spinning him around and causing him to drop onto one knee. Sgt. O'Hara is also on one knee, holding his pistol at waist level, the barrel still smoking from the two rounds just fired. Farnsworth breathes hard for a few seconds then stands, turning to face O'Hara, who still has his weapon trained on him. Farnsworth bellows and charges. A third shot from the pistol hits Farnsworth in the chest, this time throwing him onto his back.

Emma screams and wrenches her arm out of Fletcher's grip. Fletcher is stunned by the commotion and lets her go. She rushes to Farnsworth's side. Dropping to her knees, she leans over the fallen and badly wounded man. She frantically runs her hands over his bleeding body, not sure what to do, her mind racing. *There is so much blood, so much blood!* she thinks while trying to staunch it with her hands.

"No, no, no, no, no," she keeps repeating as tears run down her dirty face, causing tiny streaks to form. "What have you done? What have you done!" she screams, still looking at Farnsworth's immobile form.

The tent becomes alive with activity as soldiers race inside, weapons at the ready. Lt. Capshaw helps Capt. Duval to his feet. Peavy is still in a sitting position, his hand over his bloody nose, staring at Emma and Farnsworth. Sgt. O'Hara screams at the soldiers to "Get that woman out of here."

Two of the young men look around in confusion, not sure what to do until they see Emma on the ground next to Farnsworth. They scurry over, grabbing her by both arms and lifting. Emma begins shouting louder, kicking, attempting to bite one of them.

Sgt. O'Hara curses. "A fuck'n nuff of this shite!" he grumbles as he strides to where the two soldiers are struggling with Emma. Shaking his head, he backhands Emma across the face. She goes limp in the soldier's hands. The two soldiers stare at O'Hara who leans toward them when he sees they aren't moving. "What are you waiting for? Get her out of here!" he orders, and the two soldiers drag a semi-conscious Emma from the tent.

"Thank you, sergeant," Capt. Duval says, brushing himself off as he tries to regain his dignity.

"Yes, sir. You are welcome, sir," O'Hara says and looks at Sgt. Peavy, who is still sitting, looking dumfounded, his hand covering his bleeding nose. "Ya, might want to get back to your men there, Isaac. You're not looking so well," he says with a smirk. He then looks at Farnsworth. "What about him sir?"

Capt. Duval snorts. "Get him the hell out of here and throw him into the river. I don't want my men to waste any time or energy digging a grave."

When O'Hara opens the tent flap, he looks at the horizon. The sky is a salmon-orange color, with a tint of dark blue as the sun begins its journey into a new day. He turns his attention back to the task at hand and points to four of Peavy's men unlucky enough to be standing around the tent, being nosey.

"You four there, get in here," he orders and the four men run to do his bidding.

Two men grab Farnsworth's legs and, the other two, his arms. "What are we doin' with him, sergeant?" one of the men asks as they carry him out of the tent.

"Throw his traitorous blue-belly arse into the river, boy. That's what. Now hurry it up."

The four men carry Farnsworth several feet when one of the soldiers tells the others to drop him and wait. The soldier scurries off and returns a few seconds later with an unsaddled horse.

"Sarge didn't say anything about taking a horse," one of the soldiers protests.

"He didn't say not to either, ya idjit. You want to carry his body all the way to the river?" he whispers back. The first soldier looks resigned and shakes his head.

"I didn't think so," the soldier says and looks at the other two, who nod in agreement. They throw Farnsworth over the horse, secure him, then make their way to the river, discussing the events of the night.

When they reach the Potomac, they free the bonds securing Farnsworth to the horse, as well as the ropes securing his hands. "No sense wasting good rope," one of the men says as he unties his hands and slips the ropes around his waist.

After they drag Farnsworth off the horse and place him on the ground, they hear a noise. The four men stop and look at Farnsworth. One of them leans over and places his ear close to Farnsworth's mouth and hears in a barely audible whisper.

"Emma."

The soldier jumps up, shaken. "My Lord, he's still alive."

"He can't be. Look at all that blood," another says.

"I'm telling ya, he is still alive. Look, he is breathing."

"Oh heck, what do we do now?" the third soldier asks.

Farnsworth's eyes open slightly, and his lips are still moving so the soldier bends over him again.

"Emma. Tell her I love her. And tell Rees to live long and prosper," he says, making a feeble attempt at a Vulcan hand sign, then closes his eyes.

The soldier stands and looks to the others.

"What'd he say?" asks one of the soldiers.

"Said to tell Emma he loves her then something strange."

"What?"

" 'Tell Rees to live long and prosper' and then made some strange hand gesture," he says, shrugging his shoulders and making the sign.

"What does that mean?"

"Who cares," says the one soldier who had the idea of using the horse as he looks at the river. "We have our orders."

"What? Throw a wounded man into the river?" one soldier asks.

"Ain't right. Do ya think they know he wasn't dead?" ask another.

"What's with all the questions? All I know is we were told to throw this man into the river. I didn't hear anything about if'n he was dead or not. You want to take him back to the sergeant and say what? Huh? 'Hey sarge, we weren't clear on your orders to throw this man into the river. Did you say only do it if he was dead?' Huh? You going to tell him that?"

Sheepishly the other three soldiers shake their heads.

"I didn't think you would. Can we just get this over with and get back for some vittles? I'm starved."

And with that, the four men take Farnsworth to the bank of the Potomac and toss him into the current. They watch for a few minutes as his body floats along the waters, moving up and down with the churning waves, then disappears. When he is out of sight, the soldiers return to camp.

***

Emma wakes and, groggily, reaches up to rub her sore jaw. *What happened to me,* she thinks touching the spot where the sergeant struck her. "Ouch," she exclaims.

"Sorry I had to do that to ya missy, but you were carrying on some'n fierce you were," a gruff voice says from behind her.

Emma starts and swiftly turns to see who spoke. Still rubbing her jaw, she gives the man sitting on a stool the stink eye. "I have you to thank for this, as well as killing Gen. Farnsworth?" she angrily retorts, not realizing she mentioned his rank.

"Don't ya mean Sgt. Farnsworth, missy," O'Hara asks.

Realizing her mistake, she nods. "Yes, I meant Sgt. Farnsworth. But that is not the issue here. I was in love with that man, and you took him away from me. I hate you. How can an Irishman do something like that to an Irish girl?"

O'Hara stands and looks down at Emma. "Missy, there ain't no difference in who we are in this here war. Killin' is killin' and that's what we are here for. That man was the enemy, and the enemy attacked my commander. That be just cause for a killin'. Now you just wait here for a spell. The captain is wanting to have a word with ya."

O'Hara opens the tent flap and steps out. Before he is completely out of the tent, he stops and looks back at Emma for a second, then drops the tent flap as he exits.

***

"No sir, I am sure, she called him Gen. Farnsworth," O'Hara tells Duval, who is shaking his head.

"If that is true, we just lost out on a great opportunity, sergeant."

"I agree, sir."

Duval paces a few more times then asks O'Hara to bring Emma back. After a few minutes, the tent flap opens and Emma walks in followed by O'Hara.

"Ah, Miss Kelly. Please have a seat," Duval says with a smile, sitting behind the now-righted table.

Stoned faced, Emma stands defiantly. "I'll stand."

"Have it your way," Duval says, standing and placing his hands behind his back as he looks at Emma. "Miss Kelly, I am sorry about this incident, but you know that in time of war, people die. I am so sorry that we had to kill the general," he says watching Emma, who falls for the bait as her eyes flicker for an instant. She tries to recover but the captain catches the furtive movement.

"You mean Sgt. Farnsworth, do you not. captain?" she says.

"Oh, no, Miss Kelly. I mean Gen. Farnsworth," Duval says and raises his hand to stop her from arguing. "Please, you and I both know he was a general. When Sgt. O'Hara told me what you said, it made sense. That man's mannerism, his bearing were more in tune to an officer than an enlisted man. No, Miss Kelly, he was a general. I am just sorry we killed him."

Emma looks at her hands as she twists them, unsure what to say. Does it really matter? Farnsworth is dead. She has now lost two men she has loved.

"Captain, what difference does it make if he was one or the other? The fact is, I was in love with that man and he with me. Now he is gone."

Duval studies her for a few seconds, then looks at O'Hara. O'Hara gives a small shrug. Duval leans back in his chair, rubs his hand over his face, then abruptly stands.

"Miss Kelly?"

Before he can continue, he hears a ruckus outside his tent and looks at Sgt. O'Hara. O'Hara moves to the tent opening and steps out.

"What in blazes is going on? The captain is trying to work in here."

The four soldiers who took Farnsworth to the river are standing a few feet away with Peavy arguing with them.

"Sgt. Peavy," O'Hara barks.

"Sorry, Sgt. O'Hara. I didn't mean to be bothering ya, but these men came back with some story about the Yank sergeant being alive and saying some nonsense to them."

"What??" O'Hara bellows, stomping toward the young soldiers, whose eyes grow wide with fear. "What?" he yells again. "The man was alive?"

Three of the soldiers stare at the one soldier who thought he was in charge of their small group. They slowly move away from him. O'Hara notices and turns his scowl onto him. Leaning into the man's personal space, he raises his eyebrows. "Well?"

"Ah, yes, sergeant, we ah, we..."

"Spit it out you Nob, or you'll be wearing my boot in your arse."

One of the other soldiers moves forward. "Sergeant major, we thought the man was dead up until he wasn't."

O'Hara, to the relief of the blowhard soldier, turns his attention to the new spokesman.

"What do you mean soldier, 'until he wasn't'?"

"We were readying him for the river when he made noises."

"Noises? Noises you say? And pray tell, just what were these noises?" he asks, his hands on his hips, glaring at the soldier.

"A rasping sound," he says, hurriedly continuing so as not to keep the sergeant major waiting. "I bent down and put my ear near his mouth, and he spoke, well whispered," he says, looking at the others for a second, then back at O'Hara.

O'Hara glares. "Well?"

"He said to tell Emma he loves her, then just some nonsense, just gibberish really, probably his last words I'm sure," he stammers, then tells him the rest.

O'Hara stares for a few seconds then looks around the encampment, seemingly searching for something.

"Okay, where is he?" he asked, returning his gaze to the four soldiers.

None of them answer, but the fear on their faces is all the sergeant major needs. He straightens, his face going flush, his mouth opening in bewilderment. He sighs heavily, shaking his head.

Inside the tent, Capt. Duval and Emma cannot hear the entire conversation, just O'Hara's loud voice. There is a muttering of conversation then O'Hara screaming profanities and something about someone's mother, death, dismemberment and several additional profanities.

After several long seconds of this profanity, it suddenly becomes silent. O'Hara throws open the tent flap and strides back in, coming to a stop in front of the captain.

"Sorry, sir. This is not my finest day."

"What is it, sergeant?"

"Well, sir. It seems that Sgt. or Gen. Farnsworth was not dead when the men took him to the river."

"What?" the captain bellows.

"My apologies, sir. I take full responsibility for this. I did not check the man before turning him over to those ... soldiers," O'Hara stammers through gritted teeth.

"What happened? Did they bring him back?"

Taking a breath and letting it out, O'Hara shakes his head. "No, sir. They say he muttered something to them just before they tossed him into the river."

"Alive?!" Duval shouts.

"It seems so, sir."

Emma clasps her hands to her mouth in shock.

"They threw him into the river alive?" she asks, horrified.

O'Hara looks at her. "I am afraid so, missy."

Duval rubs his face, shaking his head in disbelief.

"Yes, sergeant major, not *our* finest moment. I am just as responsible as anyone," he says, then asks, "What did he say to the men?"

The sergeant looks at Emma. "He said to tell you that he loved you."

Emma's eyes water as the tears begin to flow, her lower jaw quivers as she fights to maintain her composure. She fails and breaks down sobbing.

The sergeant watches her for a few seconds, then looks at the captain.

The captain shakes his head. "Thank you, sergeant," he says and moves from behind his table to stand in front of Emma. "I am sorry, Miss Kelly, but what is done is done. We still have the matter of what is to be done with you."

Emma looks at the man with red-rimmed eyes full of hate. The captain pretends not to notice.

"I like to think of myself as a Southern gentleman," he continues. "In a prior life, I was a lawyer. I do not wish for this war. I abhor the killin', the mutilation of men and animals, and, of course, women as well. I have a job to do, and I have my orders. We are moving out and I do not see the need for us to take you with us. Therefore, I am releasing you. You will be given a few provisions that I hope will last for your trip to, where is it?"

"Mount Airy," Emma answers, barely audible.

"Yes, Mount Airy. Not too far from here. I do hope you make it home safely," he says and turns his attention to papers on his table. "Sergeant, would you be so good as to see to her needs and report back to me?"

"Sir, before I go. I wasn't sure if this mattered, the men told me he also said something that made no sense."

Duval looks at the sergeant, exasperated. "Go on."

"The men said he muttered 'Tell Rees to live long and prosper' while making some hand gesture." He makes the gesture he was shown by the troops.

"You are right. It makes no sense. The delusional banter of a dying man. Either that or the men are mistaken."

"Yes, sir," O'Hara responds. "My thoughts as well." He then takes Emma by the elbow, helping her stand, and leads her from the tent, a small sad smile on her face.

Chapter 46

Rees and the remainder of the squad slowly make their way north-east toward Mount Airy. They remain quiet, each man lost in his own thoughts. There is an occasional cough or a quiet whisper as Kriger checks the status of Tosseti and Bouvier.

Rees is thinking about Farnsworth and Emma. He desperately hopes they are okay and will meet them at the farm. He thinks of the farm, wondering what it will look like when they arrive. The battle they fought before is, of course, over. He feels like a criminal returning to the scene of a crime, but he is not gloating. They killed a lot of men, and of course, there was the loss of O'Toole.

His mind continues to wander as the horses plod along. *What is going on with the Bank?* he ponders. This is very worrisome. They have never lost contact like this. What could have happened? He took Kriger's watch and has been attempting contact with the Bank since they left the river and still no word.

Lost in thought, time slips by and only when Nionee rides up along-side him does he realize they are almost at their destination.

"You okay, Rees?" Nionee asks in a low voice.

"Yeah, yeah, I'm fine. Just a lot on my mind."

"Capt. Farnworth and Emma?" Nionee asks.

"That and not being able to contact the Bank."

"Yes, that has been on my mind as well."

"Well, let's hope they only had a minor glitch or something," Rees says.

Nionee nods and they continue in silence until they crest the hill where Cpl. O'Toole died.

The cerulean sky announces the beginning of a new day as they travel down the dirt road toward the farmhouse, or what is left of the home. As the first rays of dawn peek over the horizon, the men can see the smoking rubble of the barn and the smoldering ruins of the home. They stop and stare at the destruction.

"Honey, we're home," Kriger says in a monotone, moving alongside Rees and Nionee, with Tosseti and McGregor right behind them.

There is movement on the grounds, and they can see the faint outline of people. There also appears to be campfires burning.

"Seems the cleanup crew has arrived," Bouvier says, looking over Kriger's shoulder.

The area has been almost cleared of the bodies that were strewn about after the battle and just before the team transported out.

"Well, at least they cleaned up the mess for us," Tosseti quips.

Rees looks at the men. "Shall we?" and they move toward the ruins. When they approach the row of tents set up on the property, they hear someone yell, "Maj. Smathers!" They continue through the make-shift camp, seeing a soldier standing off to one side near a row of tents and pulling open a flap. A few seconds later a major comes out. Rees turns his horse to greet the officer. Before reaching the man, he stops and climbs off his horse, handing the reins to Nionee. Rees walks up to the major and salutes. The major returns his salute.

"Good morning, sir."

"Good morning to you as well, captain..."

"Rees, sir. Capt. Scott Rees out of Washington D.C.," he answers, reaching into his jacket and removing the worn letter that he hands to the major. Smathers takes the letter and reads it, his eyebrows lifting in surprise. He looks at Rees, folds the letter and hands it back.

"Is Washington interested in what going on here, captain?" Smathers asks in a friendly way.

"Yes and no, sir. Washington is, of course, concerned about what transpired here, disrupting the schedule of the trains, but we weren't sent here for that. We are here, hoping to meet Gen. Farnsworth and a Miss Emma Kelly."

At the mention of Emma's name, Maj. Smathers perks up.

It's Rees' turn to look surprised. "You know her, sir?"

"No, just the name. Her family has been hounding us about her. They said she was here when, well, when whatever happened, happened here. So, do you know where she is?"

"No, sir, I don't. As I said we were hoping she arrived with the general. It's a long story, but we would be grateful for any help you might give us. I would like to go to the Kelly family and ask a few questions and I would be more than happy to intercede on your behalf."

The major's grin tells Rees all he needs to know.

"Of course, captain. That will be much appreciated. They live just up that road a fair piece, if you are so inclined to visit. Is there anything we can do for you?"

Rees looks over his shoulder at the team still on horseback. "We could use a place to set up, away from you and your men, if you don't mind. I have two wounded men with me; one was shot, the other has a sprained ankle."

"Of course. I can get a doctor," Smathers says.

"No need, sir. We have a doctor with us," he says, pointing at Kriger. We just need a place for them to rest and to allow Lt. Kriger to work on them."

Smathers nods, then calls for some of his men. When they approach, he orders them to set up tents for Rees and his men. The soldiers dutifully scamper off to accomplish the task.

"If you don't mind, sir. What happened here? Looks like a war was waged," Rees asks, hoping to hear that Smathers and his men haven't a clue, for which he is rewarded.

"Captain, we don't have the foggiest idea. We got word of a major battle occurring in this area and, at first, we thought that Johnny Reb had snuck his way this far north to ambush the trains or sabotage the tracks or even take over the station. When we arrived, there were a few of the locals milling around the area, the Kellys being one of them, looking for Emma. They were in the company of a couple of young girls and told us the girls belonged to the family that lived here, the O'Tooles. No idea where their mother and father are. They told me that Timothy Walsh, the son of the man who owns, or I should say owned, the railroad here in Mount Airy, had been courting their daughter. Her old beau, Andy

O'Toole, returned from the war quite unexpectedly because they had been informed he was dead. When he showed up, he was accompanied by several Union cavalry soldiers led by a colonel. Seems there was a heated exchange between O'Toole and Walsh over Miss Kelly. Later Cpl. O'Toole was shot and killed out there," Smathers says, pointing back from where Rees and his team came, "while fence mending."

"That's all I know for now except that the bodies of both Timothy and Joshua Walsh were identified by the Kellys. They both had apparently been killed during whatever battle occurred here. No Rebel bodies around, just civilians. Some of these civilians we know from wanted posters, so we assume that Walsh hired a group of thugs or mercenaries to attack this place. The only other bodies we found were the unidentifiable remains of Federal troops in the burned-out barn. The only reason we know they were Union are the accoutrements we found."

Rees takes this all in solemnly and nods. "Did you find anything useful in the ruins?"

"No, captain. We haven't done a thorough search. Not much more we can do. We have the remains of our boys from the barn, a few bodies in and around the house, nothing as far as anything useful, so we will be packing up soon and leaving."

"Do you mind if we look around? The unit we belong to does investigative work from time to time. In fact, all of us were prior police."

Smathers looks surprised. "Well, no. We can use all the help we can get. You are quite the fellow, Capt. Rees, and you arrived just in time. Maybe we can hold off a day or two to see if you find anything we may have missed."

"Thank you, sir. I will let you know if we discover anything worthwhile."

"And for that, I will be most grateful," he says, turning to check the status of the tents. He sees the soldiers are almost finished. "Ah, there you go. You and your men can use those tents over there," he says, pointing. "I hope that is satisfactory, captain."

Rees smiles and salutes. "That will do nicely, Maj. Smathers."

Smathers returns the salute and walks back to his own tent. Rees watches for a couple more seconds, then walks back to his men to explain the situation. Nionee and Kriger help Bouvier off the horse and into the tent. Tosseti climbs down, favoring his wounded hand and, begrudgingly, goes into the tent as well. Kriger grabs some medical supplies and follows the two wounded time travelers. Rees, Nionee and McGregor stand just outside the tent, watching Kriger work on the men.

"Listen up guys. I'm going to take McGregor and Nionee with me and ride on up to the Kelly place. Looks like they were here earlier with the O'Toole girls looking for Emma and the girls' parents."

Kriger looks up from where he is working on Tosseti's hand.

"What about us?"

Rees grins. "You're not going to like it. Well, I know you won't, Dave."

Kriger opens his mouth to say something, then closes it.

"I need you to comb through the barn over there and look for the 'Gaitlin gun'," he says, making air quotes with his fingers.

Bouvier and Tosseti smirk and Kriger groans. "Ah, come on, Scott. You know I hate getting dirty."

Rees gives him an unsympathetic stare. "You're already filthy, Dave; don't make no difference now."

Tosseti stands. "I'll help ya out, Dave,"

Kriger shakes his head. "No, Matt, you won't. I don't want you taking a chance of doing further damage to your hand, least of all, getting it infected. I've only a limited amount of amoxicillin with me."

"I can help without using my hand. I still have two good eyes, you know."

"Dave, let the man help," Rees says, then looks pointedly at Tosseti. "But you just search with your eyes, no grabbing crap and moving it around."

Tosseti raises his good hand and waves at Rees. "I gotcha, sarge, I mean captain, sir."

Rees grins. "Okay, we'll be back as soon as we can. Jack, keep trying to contact the Bank. And one more thing guys," Rees says, getting their attention again. "No one knows we're the cause of this mess, so I'd like to keep it that way. The Kellys know us, of course, as do the O'Tooles, but I will explain the situation to the Kellys while there. Good hunting, Dave," he says, turning to leave, motioning for Nionee and McGregor to follow.

Rees explains to Smathers what they are doing, and the three faux cavalrymen ride off.

The trip to the Kelly farm is uneventful and, when they ride onto the property, Mr. Kelly comes out of the door with a shotgun in his hand. He stares for a few seconds until Rees, removing his Kepi, approaches.

"Oh, Capt. Rees!" he says with surprise, then turns to call for his wife, but hears the door open and sees she is already coming outside.

"Capt. Rees!" she exclaims. "My goodness, it is good to see you," she says, rushing down the porch steps to greet him, followed by Mr. Kelly and the two girls who also have run out of the house.

"What happened? Where is Emma? The O'Tooles?" she asks, placing her hands on Rees' horse's snout and gently rubbing it.

Mr. Kelly walks up as well. "We thought you all were dead, what with the bodies they found in the barn."

"That's why we're here," Rees answers, dismounting his horse. Nionee and McGregor do as well.

"I am sorry to have scared you all," he said before being interrupted again, this time by the girls.

"Where are Ma and Pa?"

"Hang on, please. I mean, please give me time to explain," he says, realizing he hadn't thought of a story to tell.

"First, we all made it safely away after the battle. Your daughter is fine, as far as I know," he says, raising his hands toward the Kellys and girls in a 'wait a minute' gesture, knowing they are going to interrupt. "Before you start asking me questions, please let me finish.

"During the battle, we sent the O'Tooles away for their own protection. I do not know where they went or when they will return, but I am hoping they will be home soon. After the battle, we needed to return to our regiment to inform the commander of the situation here. Before we could get back, we were bushwhacked and, in the confusion, became separated. We are hoping some of the men made it back and that Gen. ... I mean Col. Farnsworth and Miss Kelly make it back here. She was riding with him because her horse was incapacitated. Before we became separated, he ordered us to make our way back here, to inform you of what had transpired as well as explain the situation to whomever may looking into what happened at the O'Toole farm. I also thought it meant he and Miss Kelly would meet us here."

Rees stares at each of them, anxiously rolling his cap in his hands.

Mrs. Kelly looks at her husband, then back at Rees. "My goodness, you poor men. We saw the bodies and feared the worst."

"Again, we are sorry to have worried you, Mrs. Kelly. We just wanted you to know we are back and will be searching for your daughter and the colonel, who I know will protect her with his life. I just wanted you to know that," he says, then looks at the girls. "When your folks return, we will bring them here."

"Of course you will, captain. They are our friends, and they will stay with us until we can help them rebuild," Mr. Kelly announces, then walks up to Rees and shakes his hand. "Thank you, son, and thank you for doing what you can to find our daughter. Now, before you leave," he says and looks at his wife, who understands.

"Yes, my manners, you must be hungry. Please come in and I'll fix you something to eat."

"There is one more thing I need to ask of you," Rees continues. "For reasons I cannot really go into, no one knows who we are except for you four, Emma and, of course, Mr. and Mrs. O'Toole. I would appreciate it if you would keep it under your hats."

"Why of course, Capt. Rees," Mr. Kelly replies. "We know you must have your reasons and we can appreciate that. Of course, this will be our little secret, right Ma, girls?"

"It goes without saying, captain," Mrs. Kelly says, and everyone looks at the two girls, who are smiling and nodding.

"Are you gonna find our parents, Capt. Rees?" one of the daughters, Kailee, asks.

Rees squats, looking at first Kailee then at the other girl, Ada. "You bet! I will do what I can to find them, young ladies."

Standing back up, Rees starts to decline the invitation for lunch when his stomach growls. He realizes he hasn't eaten anything in quite some time, so he changes his mind.

"That will be wonderful, ma'am. We thank you."

"Good. That's settled. Tie up your horse, then come into the house where you men can wash up," she says and turns on her heels, shooing the two girls and hurrying behind them into the house.

Rees looks at Nionee and McGregor and gestures toward the house.

The men get the signal, climb off their horses and follow everyone into the Kelly home.

***

Kriger and Tosseti are rummaging through the ruins of the barn. Tosseti is being unusually quiet, not having said one curse word, and keeping his wounded hand in a sling, being careful not to bump it or get the bandage soiled.

Kriger, on the other hand, fills each quiet moment with an occasional grumble and muttered curses.

"Why the hell did he pick us, huh? He mad at us or something?"

"Just you. I volunteered remember?" Tosseti responses with a grin.

"Ha, ha, funny man," Kriger sneers, then smacks his shin on something hard. "Dammit," he shouts, grabbing his sore shin. Looking down to see what caused his discomfort, he smiles. "Got it, you worthless piece of shit," he announces, then reaches down and tentatively touches the damaged weapon, checking for heat. The weapon is warm but can be handled.

Tosseti tiptoes around the debris until he is standing next to Kriger.

"Well, that wasn't so hard," he says, looking at the charred barrel of a gun. "You gonna pick it up or just stare at it?" he adds when Kriger doesn't move.

"Yeah, yeah, hold your horses," he replies, then sighs and grabs the barrel, shaking the weapon to loosen it from the charred wood covering it. Once free, he grasps the receiver group, lifts and gently blows off the soot and ash covering it.

"Capt. Epstein is going to be so happy about this," Kriger says as they both eye the once-useful weapon, "Not!" he adds, cradling the filthy weapon in his arm, cursing the thing for getting his uniform dirtier than it already is.

"Well, at least Rees will be happy," Tosseti says as they walk around the mound of rubble.

Emerging from the barn's ruins, Kriger puts the weapon on the ground and both men begin brushing themselves off. Kriger looks up when he hears a wagon approaching from the direction they had come. Tosseti stops as well, watching as the wagon closes the distance until they recognize the O'Tooles. Kriger hurriedly grabs the Gatling gun and makes his way to one of their tents, throwing the remains inside and closing the tent flap. He makes his way back to where the O'Tooles have stopped their wagon beside Tosseti.

Tosseti is helping Mrs. O'Toole down by holding one of her hands with his good one. She smiles sheepishly, thanking him for the assistance. Mr. O'Toole is staring at what remains of his property as he walks around the front of the horses.

"My Lord, what have they done?" he asks no one in particular.

"Now father, don't take the Lord's name in vain," Mrs. O'Toole gently scolds.

"Sorry, sorry. It's just ... oh my. There is nothing left."

Tosseti looks at Kriger. Bouvier, using a crutch, is making his way to them as well. Mrs. O'Toole notices Bouvier.

"Oh, my! Are you boys all right?" she asks with concern.

Tosseti raises his bandaged hand. "It's nothing, ma'am. Just a scratch."

Kriger shakes Mr. O'Toole's hand, as does Bouvier.

"We are glad to see you made it back," Bouvier says.

"We are glad to be back. But to what, I do not know. The house is gone. The barn is gone," Mr. O'Toole says, still assessing the damage.

Mrs. O'Toole looks around. "Where are the girls?" she asks in a mild panic.

"I believe they are still with the Kelly family, ma'am. In fact, Capt. Rees and a couple of the men just traveled there."

"What went on here after we left?" Mr. O'Toole asks, satisfied that the girls were safe.

Not sure how to answer, Kriger looks at Bouvier who tells the O'Tooles that they should wait for Rees to return and he will explain it all.

"What about Col. Farnsworth?" Mr. O'Toole asks.

"Well, sir, again, I would ask that you wait for Capt. Rees. I don't want to say something different from him. There was a lot of confusion during the fighting, as you know."

Bouvier hears a noise, turns and sees Maj. Smathers walking toward them. He turns back to the O'Tooles.

"Ah, Mr. and Mrs. O'Toole, the major doesn't know we were involved in the fighting here," he explains in a low voice. "Capt. Rees asks that it remain that way. We would appreciate it if you could act like you don't know us, that you have just met us. You do know Col. Farnsworth though. Again, Capt. Rees will explain later."

Mr. O'Toole hesitates for a second, then nods. The group turns to meet Maj. Smathers. After introductions are made, the major asks the O'Tooles to join him in his tent for refreshments, which they happily accept. He tells a corporal to escort them to his tent and assures them he will join shortly. He says he needs to speak with Kriger, Bouvier and Tosseti.

"Have you found anything useful in your investigation?"

"Not too much, sir. We have determined the barn was set ablaze by dynamite explosions," Kriger says. "From the way some of the charred boards are lying, it indicates the walls were blasted. Since bales of hay are usually stored in a barn, a few sticks of dynamite will cause them to ignite and burn hot and fast."

The major listens intently. "Okay, that's a little more than I knew before. I do not know if that helps me, but still good to know. Thank you," he says, returns their salutes and walks away.

When out of earshot, Bouvier turns to Kriger.

"What? Are you a freaking fire marshal now?"

"Hey, you were here. You know that's how it went down. I just told him something we already knew. I thought it would appease him; show him we are doing something."

"Man's right, Jack," Tosseti adds.

"Yeah, I guess," Bouvier concedes.

They hear the sound of hooves and look toward the front of the farm to see Rees and the others galloping down the road. They stop in front of the men and dismount.

"What's the good word?" Rees asks.

"Found the SAW, or Gatling gun I should say," Kriger says, smiling.

"Good work."

"And the O'Tooles are back," Tosseti adds.

"Really? Where are they?" Rees asks turning around, not seeing the couple.

"They are in Maj. Smathers' tent, having refreshments," Tosseti explains.

"We asked them to act like they didn't know us," Bouvier adds.

Rees, nods. "Good. Thanks," he says, then heads to the major's tent. He taps on the post and opens the flap, sticking his head in. "Permission to enter," he says, smiling at the O'Tooles.

"Of course, captain," Smathers answers, instructing Rees to come inside. Rees does so and walks over to Mr. O'Toole with an outstretched hand. "Mr. O'Toole, I take it, and Mrs. O'Toole," he says, nodding to her. Mr. O'Toole stands to shake Rees' hand.

Rees quickly tells the O'Tooles that his group is here, hoping to find Gen. Farnsworth and Emma Kelly. Mr. and Mrs. O'Toole glance at each other, confused, but they recover quickly.

Rees continues. "Your daughters are safe and doing fine. The Kellys are looking forward to having you as their guest until such time as you can rebuild."

Mrs. O'Toole smiles at Rees. "That is wonderful news, captain. We are very grateful for that information and the help," she says, then looks at her husband. "I would very much like to see the children, Pa."

The O'Tooles look at Maj. Smathers, who nods, and thank him for his hospitality. Mr. O'Toole informs him that he and his men may remain on the property for as long as they need. They say their goodbyes and exit the tent, making their way back to the wagon. A few minutes later, Rees hears the rattle of the wagon bouncing along the road as it leaves.

Once they are gone, Smathers asks Rees to stay for a minute.

"Capt. Rees, I'm somewhat confused."

"About what, sir?"

"Your Gen. Farnsworth. The O'Tooles were under the impression he was a colonel, if it is the same man, of course."

Rees keeps his poker face, thinking quickly.

"Ah, yes, sir. I can see why you would be. From what I understand, Gen. Farnsworth was wearing the rank of colonel when here. He had been promoted to general but did not have the insignia to place on his uniform. He just kept his colonel rank to avoid any confusion among the local residents as well as the soldiers assigned here who did not know him."

Smathers nods. "Yes, of course. That makes sense."

Rees tells the major about the visit to the Kelly farm. The major thanks Rees for his help. They make small talk for a few minutes before Rees excuses himself, saying he wants to check on his men.

Outside their tents, Rees' men are standing around, talking.

"Any word from the Bank?" he asks as he walks up to them.

"No," Bouvier answers. "While Kriger and Tosseti were playing in the soot, I kept calling. No response."

"Damn. What the hell is going on?"

Knowing the question was rhetorical, no one answers.

Rees sighs. "I guess we just wait to see if Farnsworth and Emma show up."

"How long?" Kriger asks.

"Play it by ear. Now, how about we settle in and start acting like we're doing some investigative work?"

Rees and the squad members begin going through the motions of looking for clues. Rees wants to get Smathers out of the picture as soon as possible. He even sends Nionee and Kriger into town to question the sheriff, town folk and some of the soldiers guarding the train depot. While the fake in-depth investigative work is progressing, Rees and Bouvier begin writing a report.

Chapter 47

Later that evening, Rees makes his way back to the major's tent. Knocking on the post, he hears, "Come in," and does so.

"Good evening, sir. I have a report for you," Rees says, handing a few sheets of paper to the surprised major. Bouvier did the writing since he has the best penmanship and a better grasp of the English language.

The major reads the report, then rereads it. Placing the papers on his table, he looks at Rees.

"Damn fine work, Capt. Rees. Please, have a seat."

Rees pulls a small chair up to the table. "Glad you approve, sir. I hope this helps you."

The report states almost everything that happened on the property since the previous Farnsworth and Rees had been there. Rees, of course, left out that he and his men had any involvement.

"So, this wasn't just over a woman?" Smathers asks with a grin. "Sounds better that way though. Makes a great novel for some aspiring writer. Love, death, drama, set in the background of a war."

Rees chuckles. "Yes, sir. It would at that. But in the end, we believe it was just an excuse to allow the Walshes to take over the O'Toole property. As it states in the report, Mr. Walsh had been bragging about taking over this property to anyone who would listen. I am no lawyer, sir, but it would seem to me that the railroad is partially responsible for this tragedy and should be held accountable. That, and maybe restitution to the O'Tooles for the loss of their son, as well as property damage."

Smathers scans the report and smiles. "Well, as it so happens, captain, I am a lawyer and if what you have discovered is true, and I have no doubt it is, then I will do what I can to see that justice is served, and hopefully help these good people. I understand they had two other sons in the rebellion, fighting for the Confederacy."

"I did not know that, sir," Rees says, feigning ignorance.

"Yes, too bad for the family. All three sons killed in this God-awful war. Too many so far, on both sides. What a waste," Smathers says forlornly. Then he snaps out of it, returning to a cheerful expression. "Well, I guess that does it for now, captain. I cannot thank you enough for your help."

He stands and shakes Rees' hand while simultaneously pulling out his pocket watch to check the time.

"Corporal!" Smathers shouts and a young corporal sticks his head inside.

"Sir?"

"Find the sergeant and inform him that we will be leaving tomorrow and to pass the word."

"Yes, sir," the corporal replies and disappears.

"Again Capt. Rees, I thank you for this," he says holding the papers. "If there is anything I can ever do for you, please let me know. Hopefully our paths shall cross again someday."

Rees grins. "You never know sir. You just never know."

***

The next morning, Smathers' unit wakes up, rekindles their fires, makes breakfast and coffee, and prepares to leave. Rees and his men are up as well, sipping a better cup of coffee than their fellow soldiers as they watch Smathers' men break camp.

"Well, that was fun. What's next?" Bouvier asks.

Rees looks at McGregor. "Sgt. McGregor."

"Sir?"

"You are free to go. You have served us well and I am sorry you got caught up in this mess. I think it's time for you to return to your regiment."

McGregor looks stunned. "Ah, no, sir."

Rees raises his eyebrows questioningly.

"What I mean to says is, if'n it's all the same to you, I would like to stay, sir. If'n you will be havin' me, that is."

The men stare at McGregor.

"You remember that we are from the future."

"Aye, sir. Who would be forgettin' that?" he beams.

"And we will be going back to our time."

"Of course, sir. I would like to be joining ya. Kriger and I have a shite load of whisky to drink, and that hootch you have in your time is some mighty fine taste'n stuff."

Everyone looks to Rees. Rees looks back at the men. "Jack?" he asks.

"Ah, not sure yet."

Kriger jumps in. "Oh, hell yeah! Let the man come back with us."

Tosseti says, "I'm for it."

"Can't wait to see the colonel's face," Nionee says, which gets Bouvier's attention.

Bouvier pulls Rees aside. "I don't know about this. You think it's a good idea? What will the colonel say? What about the timeline? There's a lot to consider, Scott."

"We won't know until we get back. Come on, Jack. Who is it going to hurt? You never know; maybe it's supposed to happen this way. Bringing a man from the past to the future, a man who wants to come to the future, can't be all bad. Better than someone like us staying here and possibly manipulating the future on purpose. Come on, lighten up."

Bouvier sighs. "Yeah, okay," he says looking at McGregor, "besides, he is a hoot to have around."

Rees looks at McGregor as well. "Welcome to the squad, sergeant."

This causes the men to cheer as they push and pull McGregor, slapping him on the back and welcoming him in.

Maj. Smathers notices the cheering and ambles over to Rees and his men.

"Good morning," Smathers says, walking up to Rees, who salutes. "You all are in a good mood this morning," he says, eying each man and smiling.

"Yes, sir. We were just glad to help you out and, hopefully, we can find the good general and Miss Kelly today," Rees says. "We were just having some fun with Sgt. McGregor, sir. Anything we can do for you? Need a hand breaking camp?"

Smathers shakes his head and sips his coffee. "No, not necessary, captain. You have done enough for us. Your quick work in figuring out what happened here allows us to get back to the regiment early. You gentlemen, have a great day," Smathers says, raising his coffee cup in salute and walking off.

***

Emma Kelly is given a horse and some provisions. She is quite surprised about the horse, previously believing they were in short supply. *Maybe the Rebs are better off than the Yanks think,* she muses to herself as she is led to the edge of the Rebel encampment and released.

Emma is heartbroken at the loss of Farnsworth. Her first true love, Andy O'Toole, was killed by that awful Tommy Walsh and now, just as she was starting to have feelings for Farnsworth, he is snatched away as well. "Am I cursed?' she asks herself aloud as her horse trots through the woods.

The Rebels didn't let her go until late in the afternoon. Duval had sent scouts along the river in hopes of finding Farnsworth, so he allowed Emma to stay in camp to await their return. Several hours later, the soldiers reported back empty handed.

The sun begins to sink behind the mountains and the light dims. Shadows form around her as the trees take on darker shapes. When the darkness makes it impossible for her to travel any further safely, she decides to find a place to camp for the night.

She climbs off her horse and walks a little further until she locates an area she likes. Tying the horse to a tree, she retrieves some oats and pours it on the ground for the animal to eat. She pulls out some hard tack and venison jerky for herself.

Grabbing a blanket roll, she spreads it out and sits, leaning against a tree, the rough bark feeling good as she uses it to scratch her back. Chewing on the jerky and hard tack, she begins to drift off with a funny feeling that she is being watched. Sleep overcomes her before she can dwell on the thought further.

A lone Rebel soldier is standing out of sight, observing Emma. When she falls asleep, he leaves his position and quietly makes his way back to Capt. Duval and Sgt. Maj. O'Hara.

Duval, O'Hara and a column of soldiers have been following Emma since she departed camp. Duval was suspicious from the start, thinking

Emma to be a Yankee spy. He hopes she is on her way to meet a contact so he can capture her as well as her contact.

The young man makes it back to the company and reports.

"She is done for the night, it would seem," he tells them. "Fed her horse and herself, then fell asleep against a tree."

"Okay. O'Hara, have the men set up a cold camp, no fires, be quiet as you can. I want your best man keeping an eye on her. If she wakes and looks to be leaving, I want to know. We need to be ready to follow her within a moment's notice."

"Yes, sir," O'Hara says and quietly moves down the column, explaining the plan.

Nothing happens during the night and, before sun up, Emma stirs. The soldier watching her tenses but remains still. Emma stretches and looks around, confused for a few seconds, then remembers where she is. She shivers from the chill of the morning air, then stands, again stretching. She re-rolls the blanket and places it back on the saddle, securing it with a thin leather strap. Arching her back, she yawns and walks a few paces, squatting beside a tree to relieve herself. The guard smiles to himself, then slowly backs away, returning to report to the sergeant and captain.

Emma looks up through the trees and gets her bearing. Climbing onto her horse, she grabs more jerky and slowly chews on a piece. She glances over her shoulder, the feeling of being watched returning. She scans the trees, looking for anything out of place, then she shakes it off. Is melancholy getting the best of her? Taking one more glance around, she concentrates on returning home.

Emma sets a steady pace with the horse, weaving around trees, brush and bushes that seem to cover the landscape. The sun brings much-needed light to help her see where she is going. She keeps moving until she is finally rewarded with the familiar O'Toole property fence, located several miles in the back of the property. The sensation of being watched is gone now that she is almost home, but she glances over her shoulder anyway, just to be sure.

Nothing.

With a renewed sense of purpose, she kicks the flanks of the horse and begins galloping towards the farm. She wants to head for her own homestead, but she believes Rees and the other men will be at the O'Toole farm, hopefully waiting for her. She has a pang of remorse as she passes the spot where Andy O'Toole was gunned down, and then another pang as she knows she also is returning without Farnsworth. The men will be devastated to learn of his fate.

She slows her horse to a fast trot as she nears the remains of the farm house and barn. She sees soldiers milling around the burned-down barn and another group breaking camp. As she nears, she hears a shout and someone call for Rees. Emma recognizes several of the men and smiles as the group spots her and gathers to greet her.

"Emma!" Rees shouts.

"Capt. Rees! Oh, it's so good to see you. Good to see all of you," she exclaims while dismounting her horse.

Rees looks up the road from where she came, searching. "Where is Farnsworth?"

Emma's eyes begin to water. Everyone looks shocked, realizing she is about to deliver bad news. Emma sniffles and holds back the tears, staring at Rees.

"He was shot, and those bastards threw him in the river."

The squad begins asking questions of her all at once. Rees orders them to stop and they do.

"Okay, tell us what happened."

Emma relays the series of events from where she fell into the river to her being released.

While she is telling her story, Maj. Smathers approaches. Emma stops talking and the men turn to him.

"I take it this must be Miss Kelly?" he asks, smiling.

"Yes, sir. Emma Kelly, this is Maj. Smathers. He and his company arrived after the battle."

Smathers touches the brim of his hat. "Ma'am," he says politely, then looks at Rees. "And what of Gen. Farnsworth?"

"Seems he was shot and dumped into the Potomac River, sir."

Smathers shakes his head. "I am so sorry to hear that. I take it then that your mission is also finished?"

Rees nods. "Yes, sir. We will escort Miss Kelly back to her home, then be on our way back to Washington."

"I just want to thank you again for your help and wish you luck. We are ready to be on our way. Sorry about your general," he says, tipping his hat again to Emma, then returning the men's salute.

"Good luck to you as well, major," Rees says, but to the man's back as he is already walking away. When Smathers is out of ear shot, Rees turns back to the group.

"Emma, any chance Farnsworth could still be alive?"

She shakes her head. "I have no idea, Capt. Rees. The sad thing about this is he was alive when they dragged him to the river. The soldiers that threw him in said he was alive. Oh, yes, I almost forgot. He told one of the soldiers something strange. He said, 'Tell Rees to live long and prosper,' or something like that," and she made an approximation of the Vulcan hand gesture.

The men look at Rees, who doesn't know what to make of it. Was it a hint? A message? Or was it just Farnsworth being Farnsworth. No time to dwell on it right now. He looks at the men and shrugs. "I have no idea. We can worry about that later. Right now, I want the horses saddled up so we can escort Miss Kelly home and let the O'Tooles know the other soldiers are leaving."

The men break away to do as ordered. Rees saddles his own mount, still wondering about Farnsworth. He also still hasn't made contact with the Bank. He is sure if he can contact them, they will be able to locate and retrieve Farnsworth.

***

A short distance away, two Rebel soldiers watch the troops. One soldier is wearing the stripes of a sergeant major, the other is a private. The sergeant studies the two different groups of soldiers. The six Union cavalrymen are all talking with the Kelly girl. The company-sized group of regulars are walking around, though it does seem they are breaking camp. To O'Hara, it looks like two different outfits, cavalry and infantry operating separately. Why they are even here he hasn't a clue. *Looks like someone came through here like wildfire,* he thinks as he scans the rubble of the home, barn and scorched landscape.

He watches a Union major approach the cavalrymen. It looks like introductions are made with the Kelly girl. He talks for a few minutes, then departs.

The cavalrymen then proceed to different horses and begin saddling them. The sergeant hopes they are not all leaving together. He watches as the company of regular army continue to break down the encampment. He returns his attention to the cavalrymen and the woman; no, the cavalrymen are going to leave before the infantrymen.

"So, she is a spy after all," O'Hara says and looks at the private. "Stay here. Watch what they do. If they leave, don't follow, just observe which direction they travel." He grumbles and walks down the hill to where the horses are tied out of sight. A few seconds later, the private hears the sergeant riding off.

Once back with the others, he gives Capt. Duval a report on what he saw.

"It sounds like we must make haste so as not to lose them," Duval muses.

"Yes, sir. As I reported, sir, they look like they are about to leave."

"Okay sergeant. Get the men ready to march. Hopefully we can catch up to," he says, looking at Lt. Fletcher as O'Hara salutes and begins barking orders. "Concerns, lieutenant?"

Fletcher looks up the road. "My only concern, sir, is being this far north with just a company of men. I just hope we don't run into a larger force of blue-bellies."

Duval snorts. "I don't think we have to worry about that, lieutenant. Most of the Yanks are stationed at the rail depot, Sgt. O'Hara reports a company of them are breaking camp, and I will take a chance in saying I believe they are going to go back east when they do. Also, with the battles engaged in Virginia, with us pushing toward Washington, I do not think that tyrant Lincoln is going to be having troops running around out here in this farm community. We need to either kill or capture that woman and, of course, those Union boys she is with. There is no telling what information she is passing along to them, but we must ensure it does not get back to anyone who can use it against us.

"Us against six cavalrymen and one woman. I do not think there is a need to worry, Lt. Fletcher. I foresee us triumphing over our enemies and striking a blow against them for the cause."

Flecther, still looking concerned, just nods his consent.

In less than a minute, the men are in files of two, ready to move out.

Capt. Duval, Lt. Fletcher, and Sgt. O'Hara, along with a couple of others, are in their saddles awaiting Duval's signal to move out.

They reach the hilltop where the lone soldier is still watching the farm. He turns when he hears riders coming up behind him. Duval, Fletcher and O'Hara gallop up to him and stop.

Duval scans the area, not seeing anything of importance. He looks at the corporal.

"Where in blazes are they?" he asks.

"They rode out about five or six minutes ago, sir," the corporal responds. "Took a left at the gate over there," he points, "then began making their way along the road. I lost sight of them when they reached that there yonder hill."

Duval looks at the farm and the company-sized unit that is still there. "Damn, I was hoping they would not be gone before we got here," he says, looking around. "Didn't we pass a hole cut in that fence line back there?" he asks, pointing back down the road from where they had just come.

Fletcher and O'Hara nod. "Yes, sir," Fletcher's responds.

"Okay, we go back that way, cut through the opening and travel northwest," he says.

They make their way back to the open fence and move through it. Once on the other side, Duval looks at O'Hara. "Sergeant major, take the corporal and these two men," he says, pointing to two soldiers on horseback, "and ride ahead. Try to find those Yanks and report back to me. They have the advantage of knowing this area. Being on horseback, they may be able to outpace us before we can find them. Send a runner back with updates. Now go! God's speed," he barks, returning the salute as the four horsemen gallop off.

Duval turns to the remaining soldiers and orders them to quick march, and he speeds up his steed following O'Hara and his men.

***

Rees and the others are moving at a steady trot and should make the Kelly farm in an hour or so. Everyone is in a good mood, despite what happened to Farnsworth and their continued inability to contact the Bank.

They reach the farm without incident. The Kellys and the O'Tooles are outside doing chores when the cavalrymen and Emma arrive. Rees shouts as they move off the road and onto the property.

The young girls, who are hanging clothes, shriek with excitement when they see the soldiers and Emma.

"They're here, they're here! Emma's here!" they giddily shout as they run toward the squad. The Kellys come around the house just as Emma jumps down from her horse. She runs to her parents, hugging the girls and patting their heads as she passes them. Both the Kellys rush to their daughter, grabbing and hugging her until she can't breathe.

"Whoa, Ma, Pa! Let me breathe, please."

The parents back away, still holding onto their girl, refusing to break contact.

"My poor child, you look a sight. What has been done to you?" Mrs. Kelly asks Emma while looking at the state of her clothes and hair.

"I am fine, mother. It's been a long trip. I will tell you all about it later. Right now, I would just like to get cleaned up and change clothes," she says wearily, but with a smile of relief.

By now Mr. and Mrs. O'Toole have arrived and also are pleased to see Emma. Rees and the others climb off their horses and shake hands with the families, making small talk, answering questions as best they can, and happily enjoying the reunion.

"Yes, Emma Kelly, you certainly go get yourself cleaned up," Mrs. Kelly says, "while the girls and I ..." she starts to say.

"And I," Mrs. O'Toole interrupts.

"While we get some coffee started and some food prepared for you and these young men."

The women go into the house as the men take care of their horses and speak with Mr. Kelly and Mr. O'Toole, filling them in on what has happened since the battle at the O'Tooles' farm.

It's not too long before Ava comes skipping out of the house, announcing that the food and coffee are ready. The men make their way into the home. Emma has cleaned up and is in a fresh dress, the one given to her by Col. Thompson, her hair still wet from her bath. The men drink full cups of steaming coffee and eat plates of chicken, corn bread, green beans, and apple pie for dessert.

As they did with the O'Tooles when they first met, the time travelers bring out some condiments for the Kelly family, much to their delight. The men make their way out to the front porch and yard.

"I'll take the horses to the barn, sir," Tosseti says. He, Nionee and McGregor, knowing they will be leaving soon, lead the horses inside the barn so they can be unsaddled and fed and watered. The animals will remain behind; a gift for the two families.

Tosseti clumsily, one-handed climbs up into the loft to throw down some hay. He casually glances out the barn opening that faces the southern fields of the farm. He spies movement as he throws the hay down. He moves closer to the opening, squinting to see better.

"Hey Ray," he calls out to Nionee, "throw me them binoculars of Rees'."

"What's up?" Nionee asks, reaching into Rees' saddlebag.

"I think we've got company. Get up here, will ya."

Nionee grabs the binoculars and, with McGregor following, he climbs the ladder. Reaching the loft, he hands them to Tosseti, who raises them to his eyes so he can get a better look.

"Ah shit," he says and hands the binoculars to Nionee, who takes a gander himself.

"Ah shit, is right."

"What in tarnation are you two yammering about?" McGregor asks, to which Nionee hands him the field glasses.

"Ah, shite! Damn grey backs all the way up here? How? And why?"

"Doesn't matter," Nionee says. "Matt, go let Rees know, but throw me my bag. The one with the bow."

Tosseti and McGregor fly quickly down the ladder and, after Tosseti throws Nionee his bag, the men rush out of the barn, yelling for Rees.

Rees, Bouvier and Kriger are standing in the yard in front of the house with Mr. O'Toole and Mr. Kelly.

"We got company!" Tosseti yells.

The five men turn to watch the soldiers running toward them, yelling over each other. The only words that catch Rees' attention are "Rebel soldiers."

"What?" he asks, then takes off in a run to the barn, with Kriger and a limping Bouvier following. Mr. O'Toole and Mr. Kelly head back to the house to get their guns. They run straight into the women, who were on their way out to see what all the fuss is. Pushing the confused women aside, they explain what they know and tell them to stay inside.

Rees and the others make it to the barn and run around the back. None of them can see anything but open fields. Rees looks up to see Nionee watching the area with binoculars.

"What have we got here, Ray?"

"Looks like a company-sized Rebel army heading this way. They are led by what looks like a captain and a few others on horseback. Not regular cavalry."

Kriger and Bouvier look at each other.

"Why in the hell does this keep happening to us?" Kriger moans.

"Why are they even here?" Bouvier asks. "They got some balls; I'll give them that. One company this far north?"

Rees shakes his head. "I would say now is a good time to zip back to the Bank, but we can't leave these folks alone."

"Maybe they're deserters," Tosseti suggests.

The others all look at him.

"What?"

"No, they're either here for us - why, I wouldn't know - or they followed Emma, thinking she's a spy," Rees says. "What we got here is another one of those glory seekers. I bet ten to one he thinks Emma is a spy and she has some great secret and we are her escort back to D.C. This jack-off wants to capture or kill her, and us as well, all for the greater good." He looks at his men. "Just saying."

Bouvier nods, smiling. "You do have a conspirator's mind, don't ya?"

Rees looks back up at Nionee. "What are they doing, Ray?"

"I think we are going dancing, Scott. They are forming a line, looking like something out of the *Gettysburg* movie, only smaller."

"Okay, keep me informed," Rees says and walks back around the barn, where he sees the O'Tooles and Kellys walking hurriedly toward them.

"Shit," he says and goes to meet them.

"What is going on here, captain?" Mr. Kelly asks, shotgun in hand.

"We have a company-sized group of Rebel soldiers over that hillcrest. It looks like they intend to come this way."

Mr. Kelly becomes angry. "I might be a copperhead, captain, but I will not allow any army to come onto my land and threaten my family, be it North or South."

Rees stares at the man, then glances at the rest of the family members. "Listen folks. Let us handle this, please."

"You can't take on a company of soldiers alone," Mr. Kelly says. "We will help."

"No!" Rees says, too forcefully, then he apologizes. "You all go back to the house. Protect it. We are the soldiers here and, not trying to be disrespectful, you will be in our way. Protect your family first. We will handle the other soldiers," he explains and looks at Emma. "Emma, tell them, please."

"Pa, he is right. I have seen them outnumbered by the Rebs five to one and still whip the tar out of them. Capt. Rees will not disappoint us."

Rees is flattered and smiles his thanks at Emma. Slowly the women move back toward the house. The two men stand their ground for a few more seconds until the women yell at them to get their tails back into the house. Reluctantly, and shaking their heads, they comply.

"Hey Rees, you got a plan? 'Cause they look like they are about to attack, weapons at the ready," Nionee shouts.

"Saddle the horses. Hurry!" Rees shouts, and the men scramble to make it happen.

"What are we doing, Rees?" Bouvier asks, cinching his saddle tight.

"Ray, how long we got?" Rees yells.

"If they start walking, maybe ten minutes before they get here."

"Come on down," Rees says, then looks around. "Get me some hay, some sticks or two by twos, anything like that," he orders. "I'll be right back."

Rees runs toward the house. He returns in two minutes with a grin on his face, throwing some items on the ground and looking at his men. Kriger and Nionee understand and smile, while the others look dumbfounded.

"Well, get to it," Rees says, grabbing a couple of the long sticks piled in front of him.

***

Sgt. O'Hara and his soldiers spot the farm after about a ten-mile ride. He sends one of his runners back to inform the captain and pulls his eyeglasses out for a better look. He grins when he sees seven horses tied in front of the home, six of them being Union cavalry and the other is the mare the captain gave to the woman.

Looky here, me pretty, he muses to himself.

An hour later, Capt. Duval rides up and stops beside the sergeant.

"What have you found?"

"They are there, I'm sure, sir," he answers and hands the eyeglass to Duval. He points out the horses and Duval smiles. Just before Duval gives the eyeglasses back to O'Hara, he spies movement in front of the home. Returning the glasses to his eyes, he sees three soldiers take the horses by the reins and walk toward the barn.

"This should be easy pickin's, sergeant. Easy pickin's. Have the men form up. We are going to march on that barn first, then the home."

***

Rees and his men mount up and move out of the barn. They form up, side by side, weapons out, and begin moving toward the southern soldiers at a trot.

The Confederate captain, the lieutenant and the sergeant are in front of their men when they spot the Union cavalrymen riding toward them, along with a woman.

Duval is startled, not sure what he is seeing, but they are actually charging. Suddenly two of the cavalrymen and the woman turn and flee in a different direction, toward a tree line a mile away.

Duval is confused, but only for a second. He orders Lt. Fletcher and half of his mounted infantry and half of his foot soldiers to give chase.

He looks back at the four horsemen still riding straight for them. *What is wrong with these men? Don't they know they are outnumbered?* he thinks. The cavalrymen stop, dismount and take aim. Duval's eyes widen as the four men fire ... once, twice, three times ... all without reloading. *Impossible,* he thinks just before he hears the scream of the men behind him. Turning his steed, he sees five men lying on the ground, wounded or dead.

"Fire!" he screams, and several of his men stop, raise their muskets and let loose with a volley of their own. Flames spew from the barrels as the black gunpowder ignites, filling their immediate area with smoke.

Duval turns back to see what damage was inflicted on the Yanks. He moves his head in an effort to see through the smoke. When it begins to clear, his heart races, realizing he can't see the Union soldiers and assuming they are dead. Before he can issue new orders, he is surprised when the Yanks stand up and begin firing at them again. More screams fill the air as 5.56 mm bullets rip into clothing and flesh, sending geysers of blood, brain matter and gore from backs, bodies and skulls.

Duval becomes angry. "Charge!" he yells and spurs his horse toward the enemy. Sgt. O'Hara yells at the men to move their asses and places himself among them, yelling encouragement. It does them no good as one by one, men fall faster than O'Hara has ever seen. The Yankees have a new weapon. They don't even stop to reload.

O'Hara looks forward and sees the captain getting too far in front of his men. "Capt. Duval! Capt. Duval! Stop!" he screams, but Duval doesn't hear him over the roar of musket fire. To his horror he watches several bullets strike the captain in the chest, arm and neck. Blood flies into the air as his jugular is severed.

"Dammit!" O'Hara yells. "Retreat!" he orders the remaining men as he watches his commander tumble from his horse, landing in a bloodied heap on the ground. Those soldiers who hear the command do so, and those unlucky enough not to hear it or see the retreat, meet death in the form of bullets from the future.

Rees orders his men to cease fire when he sees the soldiers backing up, then turning to flee. Rees looks at Tosseti, McGregor and Bouvier, who are also watching the retreat. They all are grateful, but sad. Bouvier hobbles a second then plops down, rubbing his ankle and looking at Rees. "I think we need to go home, Scott."

"Not yet, Jack. You stay here and take care of your ankle. Sgt. McGregor, Matt, let's go help the others," he says, mounting his horse. Cursing under his breath, Bouvier stands and mounts his horse as well.

***

Lt. Fletcher and four mounted infantries give chase to Nionee, Kriger, and a third horseman whom they think is Emma. Rees borrowed the clothes Emma was wearing earlier and the men made a dummy out of the sticks, stuffing the clothes, gloves and a using a flour sack filled with hay for a head, adding a hat and ... instant Emma. They attached the dummy to a horse and admired their craftsmanship.

"Looks like a dummy," Nionee says.

"I dunno. Bend it over a bit like it's urging the horse on, and from a distance, I don't think the Reb will be able to tell the difference," Rees says beaming.

***

Nionee, Kriger and the dummy make it to the woods and quickly dismount. Nionee sets up his bow and takes aim at the soldiers bearing down on them.

"Really, Ray?" Kriger says.

Nionee notches an arrow, draws back the bowstring, aims and releases. The men watch as one of the soldiers flips backward off his mount, landing with a bounce on the ground before rolling to a stop, an arrow shaft sticking out of his chest.

Without a word, Nionee notches another arrow so fast Kriger is astounded.

"Show off," Kriger says, then fires three quick shots, knocking two more men off their horses.

"Not bad, not bad," Nionee says, then releases another arrow, which finds its mark in Lt. Fletcher's shoulder. Fletcher was lucky as he turned his horse at the last second to yell at his men. Otherwise, the arrow hit its target, his chest. Nionee can see the shaft sticking through Fletcher's shoulder, the arrowhead protruding out his back. Fletcher bends forward in obvious pain as his horse continues galloping. He tries to maintain his balance, but loses the fight and slowly slides out of the saddle, landing hard on the ground.

"Ouch!" Kriger exclaims and watches as the infantry keeps coming, leveling muskets and firing a volley at the two men. One round knocks Kriger onto his back.

"Owwwww!" he yells and sits back up. "I hate that!" he screams, aiming his weapon. "Fuck youse, as Matt says." He fires several times, causing men to tumble and fall. Both men hear gunshots from behind the advancing soldiers. The lone remaining Rebel horse rider turns his steed around and rides back through the foot soldiers, intent on charging whoever is shooting from behind them. His efforts only lead to him being flung off his horse by an unseen object.

Continuing to watch, they see four blue-clad horse soldiers charge headlong into the group of Rebel infantry, causing confusion that leads to panic. The men have no leadership and know they are losing this battle. They shoot at the new threat, some finding their marks and hear the yells of men in pain, but none of them die or even fall off their horses.

One by one the grey-clad soldiers drop their weapons and raise their hands in surrender. Rees and his three men cover the soldiers until Nionee and Kriger join them, pulling the horse with the dummy behind them.

Rees climbs off his horse. The Rebel soldiers stare at him with a mixture of hate, awe, confusion, and indifference.

"You men." Rees shouts, "Your commander is dead. This is over, finished, you understand me?" he instructs them in a stern voice. Some men bow their heads, others stare and a few glare, but eventually they all nod their understanding.

Rees watches. Once satisfied they get his meaning, he tells them, "You are free to go. You will leave your weapons where they are and make your way to wherever it is you want to go, so long as you head back south. Grab your wounded and get out of here. What is left of your company, including a sergeant major, is riding home now. Hurry and you may catch up to them."

The men stare, and Rees shakes his head. "We are not going to shoot you in the back. We aren't that way and besides, there has been enough killing for today, wouldn't you agree?" he asks, looking one man straight in the eyes. The young man shakes his head and moves around Rees, making his way to Lt. Fletcher, as the others check on the rest of their comrades.

Kriger reaches into his saddlebag and pulls out gauze and morphine, holding them up. Rees thinks about it, then nods. Kriger and Nionee jump down and begin administering first aid to the wounded.

They patch wounded the best they can, including Lt. Fletcher. Fletcher groggily asks about the dead. Rees assures him they will be given proper burials. Rees and his men also give them some rations and water before sending them on their way. One of the corporals, the one who was staring Rees down earlier, salutes then walks out of sight with the others.

Kriger stands beside Rees. "Did you just give them your hardtack?"

"Yup. Don't think I'll be needing it," Rees replies. "Okay, let's get back to the farm, tell the good folks what happened, say our goodbyes and be on our way."

The men disperse and mount up. They ride in a line, talking on the way back.

"What about Farnsworth?" Bouvier asks.

"Nothing we can do right now. When we get back to the Bank we can hopefully figure something out."

"If he's not dead," Tosseti adds solemnly.

No one replies.

As they approach the farmhouse, both families are standing outside. They heard the battle but refrained from running out to the field to witness it. Rees and the others explain what transpired and assure them that was more than likely the end of it. They ask if the families could bury the dead and all agree it is the Christian thing to do.

"We are leaving now, but we want you to have these horses."

"What are you talking about, captain? You'll need them to get back to wherever you are going." Mr. Kelly says.

Rees shakes his head. "No, we have transportation ready for us," he says, looking at Emma, who gives a knowing smile.

The men shake hands, give hugs and grab what material things they need from the saddle bags and begin walking back toward the area of the battle. Rees stays behind for a minute to talk with Emma.

"I am sorry for your loss of Andy, Emma. I am also sorry for our mutual loss of Farnsworth. I know he was fond of you, and I really respected and liked the man. I do wish you and your family, as well as the O'Tooles, the best in your lives. You never know; we all may meet again."

Emma's green eyes shine with unshed tears. "Thank you, captain, or is it sergeant?" she says laughing. "Hard to keep it right with you men. Thank you for your help, and yes, it would be good see you all again one day. I would just ask that it not be during this cursed war. I have had enough of the running and fighting, and, of course, swimming."

Rees chuckles, then touches the tip of his Kepi to the others standing on the porch and walks away.

***

Rees catches up to his men and, together, they walk to where the battle was fought. When they stop, Kriger hands out the pills to help with the time-jump sickness.

After searching the area to ensure there are no prying eyes, Bouvier sits on the ground, favoring his twisted ankle. The others kneel around him. Each man clasping the arm of the one next to him, gear and weapons placed among them. Bouvier pulls out his pocket watch, activates the arming mechanism and touches the switch.

As with previous time jumps, the air sizzles with static electricity. The surrounding area becomes alive, moving, shifting. The day becomes hazy, darker, like being surrounded by a fog bank that doesn't reach you. Some of the men close their eyes in pain, forcing themselves to keep holding onto the man next to him. All six fight the pain and the urge to clasp their hands over their ears as a piercing sound wails and the pressure bears down on them.

Then they are gone with an almost soundless pop and the air rushes to fill the void left when they disappeared.

Chapter 48

2025

Col. Black and his father are standing in the colonel's office, watching the Clio control room activity. They were just informed that a return activation had been initiated. Control room personnel are manning their stations and waiting eagerly for the transference.

The room is quiet except for the murmur of those in the room speculating, whispering into headsets as they read their computer screens. As everyone waits and watches, the transportation room starts to shudder, then, in a split second, the room is filled with six additional men, all wearing Civil War-era uniforms.

The room erupts into cheers of joy, with some back slapping, fist bumps and high fives being thrown in for good measure.

Chief Black smiles and looks at his son. The colonel nods his approval and motions for the two of them to go greet the time travelers.

SMS Scott Rees, MSgt. Jack Bouvier, TSgts. Dave Kriger, Ray Nionee, Matt Tosseti and Union soldier Sgt. Ian McGregor all appear out of thin air inside the deportation room. The men release each other's arms and shoulders and begin the process of adapting to a new century.

Each man recovers from the jaunt in his own way, either gagging, falling to the floor breathing heavily, almost puking and, of course, the loud Scottish-accented voice yelling curse words, louder and more colorful than Tosseti.

Rees is thankful for the pills Kriger gave them. Though they don't ease the motion sickness completely, the effects of time travel do not linger as long and he hasn't been visited by Bob Seger since taking them. Rees leans against the wall for support and takes a couple of deep breaths. Slowly feeling better, he straightens and looks around the control room.

He sees the familiar faces of the Bank crew, including Col. Black and Chief Black, but something seems off.

The door opens and medical personnel enter. They begin examining the men. Rees pushes past them and exits the room, looking around the familiar, yet unfamiliar control room.

Col. Black and the chief make their way to Rees.

"Welcome back, Sgt. Rees. We lost contact with you a couple of days ago. Are you and the others okay?" Col. Black asks, concerned. "Where is Capt. Farnsworth?"

Rees looks around the control room, suddenly realizing they arrived at Janus, not Clio. Rees looks back at Col. Black, then Chief Black. "We lost him, sir."

"What happened, sergeant?" the colonel asks firmly.

Still looking around the room, Rees says, "He went into the Potomac after Emma fell in, then was captured. Emma was released and found us and told us he had been shot and dumped into the river, sir."

"Did you verify that Capt. Farnsworth was dead, Sgt. Rees?" the colonel asks, this time even more sternly.

Rees looks at the man. Something has changed in him since he last saw him. He is sterner, still a professional, but more - what is the word he is looking for? Hard.

"No, sir, we did not," Rees says, then gives a *Reader's Digest* version of what happened.

The other men make their way from the disembarkation room, looking around as well. They are met by the other squad members: Shepard, Montoya, Tucker, Sgt. Sean McQuire, Harris and Green.

The newly arrived time travelers gather around Rees, who turns to look at them, his eyes questioning. He can see the confusion on the faces of the men, except McGregor, who seems to think everything is normal. Well, it is for him anyway.

The members of the squad who were left behind start to realize something is amiss with their friends. Col. Black exchanges a look with his father, his expression quizzical.

"Sgt. Rees, are you okay?" Chief Black asks as Rees looks back at him, wondering why the chief is in uniform. *He's retired*, he thinks. *And what type of uniform is he wearing? They couldn't have changed uniform styles in the short time he was away, could they?*

Rees takes a breath and shakes his head. "I am not entirely sure, sir," he says and looks around again. "Why are we at Janus, sir? Did something happen to Clio?"

Those who hear the question look perplexed.

"What are you talking about, sergeant? This is Clio," Col. Black says, his hands on his hip, head cocked, staring hard at Rees. "Are you sure you men are all right?"

Rees ignores the question. "Sir, the uniforms?"

Col. Black looks down at his uniform.

"Something is different, sir. We don't have that type of uniform, nor those patches, and this is Janus, the backup time machine located in the desert."

"Sgt. Rees, I am ordering you and your men to the infirmary for a complete checkup. If there is something wrong, it is with you. Maybe time traveling has finally done something to your minds."

Rees opens his mouth to protest, looks at his men, thinks better of it and walks out of the control room.

After they leave, the colonel and chief exchange worried looks then head back to the colonel's office. They pass Sam, who glances at them, then continues her work.

"What do you think, dad?" Col. Black asks, sitting behind his desk.

"I am not sure what to make of it. Could be like you said, time travel messed with their heads. We really don't have much data to go on about the physical and psychological effects of time travel," he says, then thinks aloud. "Or could it be something else?"

"What else could it be, dad?"

"I'm not sure, yet. But what is this Janus he was talking about, and what is wrong with our uniforms?"

Col. Black cocks his head and spreads his hands in an *I don't know* gesture.

***

Rees and the others receive physical exams personally by Col. Thompson and psychological tests by Capt. Lockhart (much to Bouvier's delight) and Capt. Wells (much to Rees' displeasure). Rees is surprised to find Wells is in very good spirits and quite helpful. Not the overbearing *I'm in charge and I know better than you* doctor he knows. Though it's refreshing, he also finds it disturbing.

After all the testing, probing and questioning, the men seem fine, and each is given a uniform, unfamiliar to them but said to have been retrieved from their rooms. They dress. All are dehydrated, have minor cuts and scrapes, and, of course, bruising. Bouvier and Tosseti receive extra care because of their more serious wounds.

Rees is glad that McGregor is cooperative. He was afraid the rough Scotsman would go off about needles and being seen naked by women, but it appears that he is genuinely liking it, smiling at the female doctors, nurses, technician, and airmen.

The men dress in the uniforms, which – to their surprise - have the correct names and ranks. McGregor is given a plain uniform. They are told they are free to leave, except Bouvier and Tosseti, who are remanded to the infirmary for further care. This did not sit well with Tosseti, but Bouvier was very content to stay, especially since he asked to have Capt. Lockhart check in on him - for mental health benefits, of course.

Chief Black meets Rees, Kriger, Nionee and McGregor in the hallway outside the infirmary just as they are leaving.

"Doctor said y'all are fit for duty, can't find anything physically or mentally wrong. But we need to talk before you leave. Col. Black is waiting for us in the conference room. There will be food for you when we arrive."

"Sir?" McGregor asks, and Chief Black and the others look at him. "Will there be any of that bourbon?" He grins; Kriger rolls his eyes.

"Sorry, chief. I think I've created a monster," Kriger says.

The chief sniffs and continues along the corridor. When they reach the conference room, each man files in. Col. Black is seated at the head of the conference table. Chief Black, Rees and Nionee take chairs to the right of the colonel, with Kriger and McGregor taking chairs on his left.

The colonel looks at each man then points at a table in the back of the room loaded with sandwiches, chips, pickles, fruit, and a few other items.

"Go ahead, men. You have got to be hungry," he says and the men go over to the table and load up. McGregor leans over to Kriger. "Where is the bloomin' bourbon?"

"Not now!" Kriger says, giving the man the stink eye. McGregor feigns being hurt. "I was just curious, lad."

The men return and eat as the colonel and chief silently watch, knowing they won't have the men's full attention until they are satiated. Once finished, they push their plates aside and turn to Col. Black.

"Something is wrong, and we need to find out what it is. But first I want a full report on what happened after the Bank lost contact with you."

Rees explains the incident at the Potomac River and when communication with the Bank stopped. "Sir, we tried to contact you constantly for the last couple of days we were there until we finally jumped."

Col. Black nods. "Okay, fine. Now let's talk about why it is you think we are not at the Bank."

Everyone looks to Rees. "Sir, I believe this is the Bank, just not Clio."

"Explain yourself, sergeant," Col. Black says.

"Yes, sir. You see, this is Janus," Rees says. "It was built by Sen. Helen Hellberg to reset the timeline; to correct the perceived wrongdoings she accused Chief Black and your predecessor, Gen. Lucas, of doing to her and her family, namely her father Sen. Dick Minten. When we left, Sen. Hellberg and her brother, Aeson Minten, thought that their father, a senator in the 1980s, was slandered after his attempt to forcibly take over the Clio Project failed. He was removed from office and, allegedly, committed suicide. She and her brother then decided to build Janus. The project was completed in the 1990s. Our intelligence community discovered the project and captured it, but not before Hellberg and her brother time jumped."

"Time jumped? To where?"

"I have no idea, colonel."

Col. Black leans back in his chair, eying Rees, then nods. "Go on."

"We were sent back to 1862 to return Andy O'Toole to his time. After the mission, we transported back, except I was sent to 1980 to try to stop the first experiment from happening. That's when Capt. Farnsworth, these men, Tosseti, Bouvier, and Miss Kelly, were sent back to find me."

Rees watches the colonel, wondering why he hasn't stopped him from repeating what he should already know.

He continues. "Well, sir you know the rest. Now we are back in 2022," Rees says, but the colonel raises his hands. "You mean 2025, don't you?"

The room is silent.

"Sir?" Rees asks.

"The year, it's 2025, not 2022."

"Uh," Rees begins, looking at the other men and seeing the confused looks, then returning his attention to the colonel, "I don't know what to say, sir."

"Well, that might be the reason for your confusion. But let's be clear. This has always been the Bank, home base for the Clio Project. After the war and the loss of Washington, D.C., and the eastern seaboard," he begins but stops when he sees more confusion in addition to disbelief and shock on the men's faces.

The colonel leans forward. "Okay, by the look on all of your faces, I can tell that you have no clue as to what I am talking about," he says and looks at his father. "Chief Black?" he asks formally, in a tone expressing his wish for the older man to speak. The formality causes Rees to think Chief Black is still enlisted.

"Yes, sir," he says and looks around the table. "What do you know of World War II?" he asks.

The men look at each other and Rees speaks. "Well, chief, I wish Bouvier was here. He knows more about it than any of us, but from what I remember, we went to war with Germany. We tried to stay out of it, but Winston Churchill ..." he says, but is interrupted by Col. Black. "Who?"

Rees blinks. "Ah, Winston Churchill, the Prime Minister of England at that time. He talked us into joining the war," Rees explains. The colonel again looks at the chief, who shrugs.

"Go on, sergeant," Col. Black says.

"Yes, sir. Well, while we were fighting in Europe, Japan attacked us at Pearl Harbor," he explains and notices yet another look pass between the chief and the colonel, but continues talking. "The United States and our allies, including Britain, Canada, and several European countries, finally beat Hitler and won the war in 1945. Those are the basics that I know."

"Don't forget Russia," Kriger adds.

"Oh, yes. Russia was involved, too. Against Germany, not us. They won and became our reluctant ally. The old 'the enemy of my enemy' thing," Rees says.

Col. Black leans back in his chair, crosses his arms, then raises his right hand to his mouth, rubbing it. He looks at each man, seeing the questions on their faces. He scoots up in the chair and says, "Men, Europe lost the war against Germany in 1945. Hitler discovered the atomic bomb at the same time as we did, neither of us knowing the other had it. We planned on announcing it to the world, but before we could, Hitler destroyed a few European cities, as well as Moscow. Europe and Russia surrendered immediately. We were not involved in the war, other than sending supplies to the Europeans at the beginning. Hitler thought this was just as bad as sending soldiers, so he declared war on us. Before we could show him that we had the bomb, he used his V-5 rockets to launch atomic bombs against us, destroying Washington, D.C., New York City, and Boston. They also hit our sub-bases in Connecticut. Luckily the one sent to knock out the Virginia Naval Yards fell short, but he threw a couple more at New Jersey and Philadelphia. This all happened before we could retaliate.

"Hitler thought it would be enough to force us to come to the table for a complete, unconditional surrender. We did surrender, but Hitler was in for a surprise. After the surrender, Hitler sent his troops to the southern regions to round up all those he thought not to be of pure Aryan race, you might say. Well, before he could do that, we evacuated the rest of the East Coast states, Virginia, North and South Carolina, Georgia, Florida and some of the eastern regions of Tennessee, Alabama, Kentucky and West Virginia.

"Believe you me, that was a massive undertaking, and, unfortunately, it was not completely successful; we lost thousands in the race to evacuate." Col. Black stops, shaking his head before continuing. "Anyway, when his troops hit the coastline, they were surprised to find that almost everyone was gone. I say almost because there are always those holdouts who don't want to listen. We allowed him to send in hundreds of thousands of troops, equipment, weapons, whatever he wanted. When our intelligence community thought it best, we detonated several of our own atomic weapons, destroying more than half of his army as well a large portion of his navy. Let's just say he wasn't happy about it and I'm sure he wanted to retaliate. Luckily, one of his top aides had had enough of the man's insanity and shot Hitler in the head. The traitor was, of course, executed by Himmler, who took control, but he had a cooler head, if one is to believe it. He conceded to just running Europe and Russia and leaving us alone. The man was not as greedy as Hitler, it seemed. Still fanatical, but the devil you know, as they say. So that's where we stand. Most of the East Coast was unlivable for years. It's just within the last few decades that any rebuilding has begun."

The room is silent as each man takes in the story. Kriger lets out a low *humph* and shakes his head. "That's some *Man in the High Castle* shit right there."

The colonel looks at Kriger but ignores the remark, not knowing what he is talking about anyway. He clears his throat. "Now, about Clio. Just where do you think Clio is supposed to be?"

Rees looks at the man. "Fort Bragg, North Carolina. The chief and Gen. Lucas built it in North Carolina. In 1980, the Bank Council used it to send me and the entire squad back to the Civil War, without our consent I might add, and that's how this all got started."

"Well, of course, Fort Bragg is abandoned, as are all the bases in North Carolina," Chief Black explains. "When we created Clio, the government decided on this area to set up and we have been here since before 1980."

Col. Black interjects. "And as far as you and the team go, you all were volunteers for the project. Each of you was vetted, good at your jobs, all of you single. No family ties. This was a prerequisite in case something happened, like if you didn't return, which, of course, you did," the colonel says then stops. "I'm sorry, I meant to say, most of you did," he corrects, looking apologetic.

"You accidentally brought back a Cpl. O'Toole, so you were sent back a second time to return him. You came back that time with Emma Kelly and Sgt. McGregor there," he says pointing to the Scotsman. "So, you were sent back again with express orders not to bring home any more 'pets,' which is why I am wondering why Sgt. McGregor is still here," he finishes with his eyebrows raised, looking at Rees for an answer.

"Sir, he asked to come back with us. Wants to stay with the squad."

The colonel lets out an exasperated sigh and rolls his eyes. The chief stifles a laugh.

Col. Black gets back to business. "Okay, okay, that's fine for now," he says, waving his hand dismissively. "We need to concentrate on how you came to be here. Something has gone wrong, and we need to figure out what."

Rees speaks. "I don't understand something, sir. Churchill got us involved in the war. We didn't detonate the bomb until after we defeated Germany. We used it twice, but it was on two cities in Japan, not here, never on our own soil."

Chief Black clears his throat, and the men look at him. "I might have an answer to why this has happened. You mentioned the senator and her brother used the time machine before your men could stop them, and no one knows where they went," he says and looks at Rees, who nods. "So, what if they went back somewhere before World War II and messed with the timeline?"

Rees thinks about it and begins nodding some more. "Of course. They must have done something to stop Churchill from becoming prime minister and, even worse than that, they somehow made it possible for Hitler to get the bomb. From what I remember, uranium-235 was needed to build the bomb and it was a long process to make just a small amount."

The chief nods. "Yes, but we knew Germany was looking to build a bomb in the 1930s. We received that information from German scientists who defected to the U.S. Once we learned about it, we began assisting more scientists in defecting. It only took a couple of years to accomplish this, but we had plenty of resources to build secret sites throughout the country to separate the uranium. The war broke out and, in 1944, we tested the first bomb. It was successful, so we began producing as many as we could. But, as the colonel explained, Hitler used his before we could demonstrate ours."

"Chief, I agree. Hellberg and Minten must have gone back and screwed up the timeline. I think what we need to do next is find out why Winston Churchill wasn't prime minister."

"That's easy to resolve. We have all the history of the world at our fingertips. Stuff even Wikipedia will never know," Col. Black says and turns on the large monitor at his back and begins typing on a computer.

The men all watch the monitor, reading current historical facts until they find what they are looking for.

The colonel shuts down the monitor and looks at the men. He stands and begins pacing. No one bothers him. "I should run this up the chain to the council," the colonel says, facing away from the men at the table. He turns around, places his hand on the chief's shoulder. "Dad?" he asks.

The chief looks at him. "No. You know as well as I do that they will drag this out, trying to make a decision until hell freezes over. We are allowed some autonomy, so I say we make the decision ourselves. If what these men are saying is true, then this is a wrong timeline. I say we let them go."

The colonel looks at each man. "You all realize that if I do allow you to go on another mission to correct what you say never happened in your timeline, it will erase ours."

"Not necessarily," Rees interrupts. "From what Chief Black told me once, there may be multiple timelines in the universe, all running simultaneously. I am beginning to see his logic. The last mission these men were on occurred while our second mission was being conducted, so, there were two of the same people walking around at the same time. That means, to me, that there are two different timelines running right now. Timelines that didn't exist before, so your timeline may stay the same, while we can hopefully correct ours so when we return, everything will be as it should."

The colonel looks for the chief's reaction. The chief smiles. "We'll if I said it, it must be true."

The men chuckle.

"All right then. I've made my decision, and the hell with the council. You have another mission to prepare for," the colonel announces, to the relief of the others.

The meeting ends and Rees and the men make their way back to the infirmary to update Bouvier and Tosseti. Once they arrive, they find the men gone. They are told that both were released, declared fit for duty in twenty-four hours, and are probably in the dining facility.

After getting directions to the chow hall (Rees still can't call it a dining facility), they arrive to find both missing squad members sitting at a long table talking with TJ, Green, McQuire, and the rest of the original squad.

"Well, lookey here," Kriger says. "I didn't think you would leave the infirmary as long as Dr. Lockhart was treating you for your mental illness ... oops, I mean mental health."

Bouvier looks up, smiles, and gives Kriger a crotch salute, which Kriger returns.

TJ stands and walks over to Rees, holding out his hand. Rees shakes it, noticing the man is not limping.

"How's the leg," Rees asks.

TJ looks confused. "Why, it's fine as frog hair, sarge. But why are you asking? You like my legs or sumpin'?" he asks with a grin.

Rees bends over and slaps what should be an artificial leg replacing the one TJ lost.

"Holy shit!" he exclaims. "You still have your leg."

The rest of the squad is confused now.

"Ah, you all right there, sarge? Of course, I got my leg," TJ says.

"Uh, sorry, it's just ... never mind."

TJ laughs and slaps Rees on the back. "Naw, sarge, it's all good. Tosseti and Sgt. Bouvier done filled us in on y'all's adventures and how we ain't in the same time zone as you fellas and 'bout my leg and all."

Tosseti shakes his head. "This here fuck'n redneck can't speak no gooder English here as the one from where we come from, Rees."

The men all laugh, enjoying the camaraderie they haven't had in a while.

Rees and the others join the table and Rees looks at Matt and Jack. "Nurse said you two are good to go in twenty-four hours. What's up with that?"

Tosseti raises his hand and flexes his fingers. Bouvier stands and places weight on his foot.

"You wouldn't believe the medicines they got here, Scott. Some type of Nanobot shit that can patch a person up in no time," Bouvier says.

Kriger stands up and heads for the exit.

"Just where are you going?" Rees demands.

"To see the colonel; be right back," he says over his shoulder, not stopping.

Rees returns his attention to the men at the table and explains the situation. Once finished, Rees walks over to get some more coffee. A young airman approaches and explains that Col. Black would like the men to go to Capt. Epstein's office and that Sgt. Kriger will meet them there.

As Rees and the others approach the entrance of the lab, Kriger is standing by the doorway. "Oh, boy, more toys from the mad laboratory of the good 'Kapiton'," Kriger says as the small group reaches him.

"Just where the hell did you run off to?" Bouvier asks of him.

"Just had to ask the colonel for a favor. He's looking into it," Kriger says. Seeing the looks his team is giving him, he continues. "All will be revealed, my children. All in good time." He opens the door for the others.

They enter an outer office and are met by a senior airman, who instructs them to go on in the lab; they are expected. They pass through another door only to see Capt. Epstein busy working on something. None of them would know what it is, they are sure.

"Capt. Epstein?" Rees calls out and Epstein turns and looks at them with no emotion. In fact, he seems peeved that he was interrupted.

"It's about time you showed up. My time is precious, and I hate wasting it on people who do not appreciate what it takes for me to create the instruments that I am *told* you so desperately need only to have you destroy my work or lose it. Come on now, follow me. I have lots to show you and so little time," the man says and bustles off into another room.

The six men stare in confusion as Epstein walks away.

"What the hell?" Rees says, then follows the captain.

They find him in a type of dressing room, similar to the one in Epstein's lab from their time period.

"These clothes are for each of you. Period pieces, of course, but they have the same qualities as the uniform I have made for you in the past:

bullet resistant, exploding buttons, hidden knives, hidden compart-
ments, blah, blah, blah. Please take the appropriate items and we will
continue," Epstein says without the usual excitement. The confused
men grab their garments and follow him to another room.

"These are your weapons, Colt model in looks only. This has an
extended magazine capacity, and you have a choice of bullet - hollow
point, of course, plus exploding rounds. You may pick the weapons up
before you leave on whatever mission you are going on," he snips, then
turns away from the men. "Come on," he says and walks to yet another
room where they see stacks of money and what looks like gold coins.

Epstein stops in front of the table and points to the money stack.

"This money is for you. It's from the time period you are going. It is
more than you will make in your time in the U.S. Air Force," he says
sarcastically.

Rees thinks, *Sorry captain, but you don't have a clue what we make
and I'm sure you would be pissed if you found out.*

Epstein continues. "The gold can be turned into the banks for cash
if you run low, but unless you are planning a trip to the French Riviera
and blowing it in a casino, you probably won't need it. If not used, we
do expect it back. Just fair warning, the money will simply dissolve in a
few months' time, so no use trying to keep it. You may sign for the gold
pieces, as well as the guns and clothes on your way out. Do have a good
day, gentleman," Epstein says, walking away without another word.

"What was that?" Nionee asks.

"Not our Epstein, that's for sure," Kriger says. "More like 'A' than a
'Q'."

"Okay, I'll bite. What's the 'A' stand for?" Bouvier asks.

Kriger smiles. "Why asshole, of course."

The men call the colonel's office and are told they are released for
the remainder of the day but to report at 0600 in the morning, ready
to depart. Rees informs the team, and they head for their rooms to get
some rest.

Rees finally has time to think. His mind wanders to Nora, wondering
if he ever met her or if she is even alive. Then his mind drifts to Sam. Is
she here? Looking at the clock, he sees it's too late to go to the colonel's
office to look for her. Of course, even if she is there, is their relationship

even the same? Neither the colonel nor the chief mentioned her. He lies in the bed, his mind slowly shutting down until he finally drifts off to sleep.

***

The next day the men gather in the chow hall for an early breakfast. They are met by the entire squad, as well as the colonel and chief - no Sam. Rees wants to ask about her, but thinks better of it. After all, he won't be coming back here. At least he hopes he won't.

The squad make their *ohhs* and *ahhs* about the six members' 1939 period clothing. Tosseti proudly shows off his outfit and turns his flat cap at a jaunty angle, making him look like the toughest paperboy on the block. The others are also dressed in '30s-era clothing, some in suits, others in plain clothes, all with varying colors from blue to beige, cream and grey. Some wear the fedora-style hats common during that period. Bouvier has a bowler hat, and Tosseti, a flat cap.

"Looks better than those Civil War getups," Montoya says.

"I think Tosseti should go as the world's oldest paperboy, the way he looks in that getup," TJ laughs.

"Blow me, you half-witted pecker-head," Tosseti responds.

"Naw, I'll leave that up to your sister," TJ replies.

Middle finger.

"As I have to say all the time, you two, knock it off," Rees tells them.

Col. Black stands, announcing it is time to go. Everyone follows him out of the chow hall and into the Clio control room.

The men shake hands, say their goodbyes and wish everyone good luck, then the six-member team makes its way into the disembarkation room and the door closes behind them.

Rees and the others look out of the window, into the control room. They see the chief, colonel and Sam observing from the colonel's office window. Sam waves and Rees smiles.

"Good luck, men, and God's speed," the colonel tells the men through a hidden speaker.

The team watches as a technician begins the equipment's start-up sequencing and they see a lieutenant placing the Inabular Device into its slot. The room becomes still and quiet with only the faint sound of breathing. Slowly, static electricity causes the hairs on each man to rise.

Pressure builds and the men wince, their ears pop and begin to ache. The window looks to be moving in and out, like a plate-glass window during an earthquake. The pressure increases and each man covers his ears and opens his mouths in silent screams as the discomfort almost overwhelms them.

An instant later, they disappear.

Chapter 49

1931

The middle-aged Englishman arrives at the New York Passenger Ship Terminal on a cool day in December 1931. He deftly strides down the gang plank and is met by cheery American businessmen and politicians who welcome him to their country. The Englishman shakes hands all around, introduces his wife, and is led to a waiting automobile that will take him to his destination.

They drive through the busy Manhattan streets and arrive at the Waldorf Astoria in a short time. The Englishman exits the vehicle, where he and his wife are ushered inside the warm, welcoming building and led straight to their room. He thanks his hosts and closes the door so he and his wife may relax and freshen up before dinner. The nobleman takes a copy of the lecture he is going to give in Brooklyn the next day and begins to read it.

A few hours pass before he hears a knock on the door. One of his hosts is there to escort them to the restaurant for dinner. He and his wife follow the host to the elevator and take it down the twenty-nine floors to the lobby. They are met, yet again, by others who walk with them into the bar where they enjoy a few choice libations and, then, on to the restaurant where they are treated to fine cuisine.

After the meal, the men indulge in after-dinner drinks and cigars. Finally, the Englishman excuses himself and his wife so they may retire for the evening; he does have a lecture in Brooklyn the next day, after all. They thank their hosts and say their good evenings to everyone, then return to their room.

The couple climb into bed, where the Englishman begins reading his lecture again. Around 9 p.m., the room telephone rings and the Englishman answers. He is glad to hear from an old friend who lives on Fifth Avenue. His friend insists that he come over for a few drinks and to meet some very important businessmen who are eager to speak with him.

The Englishman enthusiastically agrees and says he will be there shortly, as it's only a ten-minute trip by taxi. After explaining to his wife who called, he climbs out of bed and dresses for the cool evening. He calls down to the lobby and requests that a taxi be available for him. He kisses his wife before departing.

The Englishman, again, takes the twenty-nine-story trip to the lobby and thanks the doorman, who opens the hotel door for him, and again, as he holds open the taxi door.

Wonderful people here, these American cousins, he thinks as the taxi door is closed. He leans toward the taxi driver to give him the address and suddenly remembers he has forgotten the house number of his friend's residence. He knows he lives on Fifth Avenue, and it's somewhere around the 1100 block, but can't remember the exact number. He has only been there once, and it was during the daytime a few years ago. He recalls the apartment is nestled between two like buildings, smaller than those around them. He believes he will recognize it. The taxi driver has a phone book with him and attempts to find the address, but only comes up with a business address for the Englishman's friend.

The two men drive up Fifth Avenue and the Englishman stares out the window, intently searching the buildings as they pass. He spots a building he believes is the one he seeks and asks the taxi driver to stop. The Englishman exits the taxi and approaches the doorman. They converse and the Englishman discovers that he is at the wrong building. The doorman offers to look his friend's name up in the Yellow Pages, but the Englishman explains that he has already tried, to no avail. He gives his thanks and re-enters the taxi.

The taxi moves slowly along Fifth Avenue until the Englishman asks him to turn around and go back. The driver does so and travels along the avenue using the inside lane. The Englishman, again, stares intently out the window, trying desperately to locate his friend's building. It's been almost an hour and he begins to worry that his friend and his guests will begin to think something happened to him.

Suddenly the Englishman believes he has found the building and, again, asks the taxi driver to stop the car. The driver pulls the vehicle to the curb and stops. The Englishman pays the fare and exits the vehicle. Forgetting that the traffic pattern is the opposite in America than in the United Kingdom, the man looks to his right for traffic and begins to step into the roadway.

The 1930s dark-red, Chevrolet four-door sits idling down the street. The two people sitting in the front seat look more like Bonnie and Clyde than they do brother and sister.

"Stop your pouting, sis; it's very unbecoming of you," Aeson says, staring up the road, waiting.

"I'm not pouting. I do not pout. I just accept what is and wait for my revenge. This was my idea, so I thought I should be the one to pull it off," Helen tells her twin brother.

Aeson chuckles. "Maybe next time. You know I am better trained at doing this sort of wet work," he says and turns to see a taxi carrying the Englishman for whom they are waiting. "Show time," he states as he releases the parking brake and lightly places his foot on the accelerator, slightly releasing the clutch with his other foot. They watch as the taxi pulls over and stops. After a few seconds of waiting, they see the rear passenger door open and the man they are here to kill steps out of the vehicle, looking the wrong way for traffic.

Aeson smirks. *Dumb ass,* he thinks and presses hard on the gas pedal, the engine revving as Aeson holds the clutch in until the engine is almost screaming, then he releases the clutch. The car lunges forward and quickly picks up speed.

Helen's eyes grow wide, not in fear, but from the adrenaline rush she is experiencing, giddy inside as she anticipates running down a human being.

Aeson steers the automobile directly at the unsuspecting man standing in the street, shifting gears. He lets out a snort then, just as he is about to strike, the man is yanked out of the way. Aeson is surprised and turns the steering wheel toward the man, only to succeed in sideswiping the taxi, startling the taxi driver, who throws himself sideways onto the bench seat with a yelp.

The car careens off the side of the taxi and continues on.

Helen shouts and turns in her seat to see behind them.

"What the hell was that?" she screams.

"I don't know!" Aeson shouts, as he looks into the rearview mirror. They both watch as two men run into the street, pistols raised. "Gun!" he yells, but nothing happens as they drive further away from the scene and out of sight.

***

The Englishman exits the taxi and looks to his right for oncoming traffic, having forgotten that the Americans drive on the opposite side of the road than they do in England. He is so lost in thought about being late to the meeting that he doesn't hear the roar of the car engine, nor does he see the monstrous front end of the Chevrolet bearing down on him.

Without a word, hands grab him from behind and roughly pull him away from the road and back behind the taxi. He loses his balance as he trips over the curb and sprawls onto the sidewalk. He is aware enough to hear an engine, then crashing and metal scraping against metal. He rolls over and sees three men standing near him. The Englishman does not comprehend what is happening. *Am I being mugged?* he thinks.

Rees, Nionee and Tosseti are on the sidewalk where the taxi is supposed to stop to let the Englishman out. The taxi passes them, and they hurriedly walk toward it. When the taxi finally stops, and they see the Englishman's head emerge from the passenger side door, they break into a run. Just as the Englishman is about to walk across the street, they reach him. With arms outstretched, two sets of hands clasp the man, pulling him back toward the sidewalk to land roughly onto the concrete just as a dark-red vehicle passes where the man was just standing, slamming into the side of the taxi and continuing down the road.

Tosseti has his gun drawn. Nionee pulls his gun as well and leans around the taxi, taking aim at the fleeing automobile. Both are about to shoot when Rees yells at them.

"No, don't fire. Too many people watching. Let's just get out of here. There, across the street, into that building," he shouts, pointing. He looks around until he sees Kriger, Bouvier and McGregor watching from across the street. He gets their attention and points to the building; they all nod their understanding.

"Go!" he shouts, "get to the restaurant; wait for me." He hurries back to the man, who is attempting to stand. He grasps the man's elbow and helping him rise. The man, startled by the touch, and still reeling from the excitement, jerks his elbow from the stranger's grasp.

"Bloody hell!" he exclaims, looking at Rees.

"Are you all right, Mr. Churchill?" Rees asks.

Now the man looks bewildered. "You know me?"

Rees smiles. "Indeed, I do, sir. I am terribly sorry for the rough treatment, but you were looking the wrong way for traffic when that car almost struck you. If we hadn't been here, there's no telling what may have happened."

Winston Churchill winces from his mild injuries: a few scratches and a little pain, and he is sure there will be bruising.

"Yes, quite right, of course. Damn silly thing, forgetting something like that. Quite a fright you gave me there. Thought I was at the hands of American hooligans, but I see I really had no concern at all; just the opposite, you might say. I do want to thank you, mister ...?"

"Rees," Scott answers.

"Rees. Rees?" Churchill mutters to himself, then he snaps his gloves on his hands and points at Rees. "Welsh!" he exclaims, with a smug smile.

Rees nods. "Very perceptive, sir."

"No, no, nothing at all, I have always had a good memory, especially about names and origins," he says and looks Rees in the eye. "May I offer you a libation to repay my gratitude?"

Rees shakes his head and turns to see a small crowd gathering across the street, looking their way.

"Mr. Churchill," Rees says, turning back to the man, "I am very sorry, sir. As much I would like to, I have a prior engagement. Might I suggest you make your way to the hospital to get checked out? You might have injuries you can't feel or see right now. Better safe than sorry."

Churchill nods. "Very well. I just want to thank you again, good sir," he says as he moves to the side of the taxi away from the road and opens the passenger side door. As he places a hand on the roof to assist himself inside, he peers over the top to look at Rees. "Good luck with your future travels," he finishes and disappears into the vehicle.

Rees tilts his head, considering what Winston said about future travels. He wonders what the diplomat meant, then dismisses it as overthinking everything he hears with a connection to time travel. He looks across the street to see most of the onlookers are gone. He eyes the restaurant entrance and makes his way there.

Once inside he likes the way it looks, very upscale New York workmanship. A maître d' approaches and asks if he can help. Rees tells the man he is looking for five other men.

"Ah, you must be Mr. Rees. We have been expecting you. Please, this way," he says and leads Rees further into the restaurant. The place is large, very large, swank comes to mind. The maître d' escorts Rees to a section of the room that sits apart from the rest of the restaurant. Now Rees is confused.

Winston Churchill did not do this, and the guys wouldn't go to this extreme, and on such short notice. This place only takes reservations, Rees thinks as he makes his way to the table where the others are already seated, full drinks in front of them, but no one moving.

The men look at Rees while they all talk to each other. Rees pulls out a chair and watches the men.

"What gives? What's going on?" he asks no one in particular.

"We were asked to wait on you first," Kriger tells him.

"What are you talking about?" Rees inquires, looking from one man to the next for an answer. "Who asked you to wait?"

Bouvier leans forward. "No idea, Scott. Really! The maître d' greeted us at the door as if he had been waiting for us. Then he herded us here and told us that our host asked us to do nothing until you arrived. Now here we are."

Service staff arrive with plates heaping with food and begin placing succulent dish after dish in front of the men. The maître d' walks in as soon as the staff departs. "Gentlemen, please enjoy your meal and if you need ..." the man starts to say before Rees interrupts.

"Yes, there is. Just what in the hell is going on? Who set this up?" Rees asks.

The maître d' smiles. "To answer your question, Mr. Rees. I was told that if you asked, I was to inform you that all your questions will be answered very soon. Your host said that you all of you are Bank employees and should be well treated."

With that, the maître d' turns and walks out of the dining room.

Rees' face is a mask of confusion as he stares at the man's back, watching him leave. "I don't like this; something isn't right and I think we should leave."

Bouvier agrees. "You heard the man. We're leaving," he says and the men begin to rise but stop when they hear a familiar voice.

"Scott Rees, Have you lived long and prospered?"

The six men look at each other, then search the room for the face behind the voice. A curtain opens next to the table and two partially obscured figures move into view.

Tosseti snorts. "Well, fuck me."

Kriger and Bouvier both exhale in a huff of a laugh.

McGregor just stares.

Rees knows who the voice belongs to and turns with a smile to greet Farnsworth and Emma Kelly. Rees' smile wavers as he looks at the two new arrivals. Farnsworth grins at the perplexed look on Rees' face.

"Not what you were expecting, Scott?" Farnsworth asks.

Rees is at a loss for words. He is glad to see them both, and not surprised that Farnsworth beat death. Just how, he doesn't know but is sure that he will be filled in later. But something else overshadows that train of thought. Farnsworth should be in his 90s and Emma in her 80s. Rees is looking at a 25-year-old Farnsworth and an 18-year-old Emma Kelly. Neither has aged a day since Rees last saw them in 1862.

Rees smiles warmly at the two of them and thinks to himself, *Well this opens a new can of worms.*